"Thank you for my scarf," Emmy said to the professor. "I've never had anything cashmere before."

Ruerd didn't say anything, but wrapped his great arms around her and kissed her.

She was so taken by surprise that she didn't do anything for a moment. She had no breath anyway. The kiss hadn't been a social peck; it had lingered far too long. And besides, she had the odd feeling that something was alight inside her, giving her the pleasant feeling that she could float in the air if she wished. If that was what a kiss did to one, she thought hazily, then one must avoid being kissed again.

She disentangled herself. "You shouldn't..." she began. "What I mean is, you mustn't kiss me. Anneliese wouldn't like it...."

He was staring down at her, an odd look on his face. "But you did, Em

BETTY NEELS

A Christmas to Remember

HQN™

ISBN 0-373-77013-8

A CHRISTMAS TO REMEMBER

Copyright © 2004 by Harlequin Books S.A.

The publisher acknowledges the copyright holder
of the individual titles as follows:

THE MISTLETOE KISS
Copyright © 1997 by Betty Neels

ROSES FOR CHRISTMAS
Copyright © 1976 by Betty Neels

www.HQNBooks.com

Printed in U.S.A.

CONTENTS

THE MISTLETOE KISS

CHAPTER ONE

IT WAS a blustery October evening, and the mean little wind was blowing old newspapers, tin cans and empty wrapping papers to and fro along the narrow, shabby streets of London's East End. It had blown these through the wide entrance to the massive old hospital towering over the rows of houses and shops around it, but its doors were shut against them, and inside the building it was quiet, very clean and tidy. In place of the wind there was warm air, carrying with it a whiff of disinfectant tinged with floor polish and the patients' suppers, something not experienced by those attending the splendid new hospitals now replacing the old ones. There they were welcomed by flowers, a café, signposts even the most foolish could read and follow...

St Luke's had none of these—two hundred years old and condemned to be closed, there was no point in wasting money. Besides, the people who frequented its dim corridors weren't there to look at flowers, they followed the painted pointed finger on its walls telling them to go to Casualty, X-Ray, the wards or Out Patients, and, when they got there, settled onto the wooden benches in the waiting rooms and had a good gossip with whoever was next to them. It was their hospital, they felt at home in it; its

9

lengthy corridors held no worries for them, nor did the elderly lifts and endless staircases.

They held no worries for Ermentrude Foster, skimming up to the top floor of the hospital, intent on delivering the message which had been entrusted to her as quickly as possible before joining the throng of people queuing for buses on their way home. The message had nothing to do with her, actually; Professor ter Mennolt's secretary had come out of her office as Ermentrude had been getting into her outdoor things, her hours of duty at the hospital telephone switchboard finished for the day, and had asked her to run up to his office with some papers he needed.

'I'm late,' said the secretary urgently. 'And my boyfriend's waiting for me. We're going to see that new film...'

Ermentrude, with no prospect of a boyfriend or a film, obliged.

Professor ter Mennolt, spectacles perched on his magnificent nose, was immersed in the papers before him on his desk. A neurologist of some renown, he was at St Luke's by invitation, reading a paper on muscular dystrophies, lecturing students, lending his knowledge on the treatment of those patients suffering from diseases of the nervous system. Deep in the study of a case of myasthenia gravis, his, 'Come,' was absent-minded in answer to a knock on the door, and he didn't look up for a few moments.

Ermentrude, uncertain whether to go in or not, had

poked her head round the door, and he studied it for a moment. A pleasant enough face, not pretty, but the nose was slightly tip-tilted, the eyes large and the wide mouth was smiling.

Ermentrude bore his scrutiny with composure, opened the door and crossed the room to his desk.

'Miss Crowther asked me to bring you this,' she told him cheerfully. 'She had a date and wanted to get home…'

The professor eyed her small, slightly plump person and looked again at her face, wondering what colour her hair was; a scarf covered the whole of it, and since she was wearing a plastic mac he deduced that it was raining.

'And you, Miss…?' He paused, his eyebrows raised.

'Foster, Ermentrude Foster.' She smiled at him. 'Almost as bad as yours, isn't it?' Undeterred by the cold blue eyes staring at her, she explained, 'Our names,' just in case he hadn't understood. 'Awkward, aren't they?'

He had put down his pen. 'You work here in the hospital?'

'Me? Yes, I'm a telephonist. Are you going to be here for a long time?'

'I can hardly see why the length of my stay should interest you, Miss Foster.'

'Well, no, it doesn't, really.' She gave him a kind smile. 'I thought you might be a bit lonely up here all by yourself. Besides I rather wanted to see you— I'd heard about you, of course.'

'Should I feel gratified at your interest?' he asked coldly.

'No, no, of course not. But they all said how handsome you were, and not a bit like a Dutchman.' She paused then, because his eyes weren't cold any more, they were like blue ice.

He said levelly, 'Miss Foster, I think it might be a good idea if you were to leave this room. I have work to do, and interruptions, especially such as yours, can be annoying. Be good enough to tell Miss Crowther on no account to send you here again.'

He bent over his work and didn't watch her go.

Ermentrude went slowly back through the hospital and out into the wet October evening to join the queue at the nearest bus stop, thinking about the professor. A handsome man, she conceded; fair hair going grey, a splendid nose, heavy-lidded eyes and a firm mouth—which was a bit thin, perhaps. Even sitting at his desk it was easy to see that he was a very large man. Still quite young, too. The hospital grapevine knew very little about him, though.

She glanced back over her shoulder; there were still lighted windows on the top floor of the hospital; one of them would be his. She sighed. He hadn't liked her and, of course, that was to be understood. She had been ticked off on several occasions for not being respectful enough with those senior to her—and they were many—but that hadn't cured her from wanting to be friends with everyone.

Born and brought up in a rural part of Somerset, where everyone knew everyone else, she had never quite got used to the Londoners' disregard for those around them. Oblivious of the impatient prod from the woman behind her, she thought of the professor sitting up there, so far from anyone... And he was a foreigner, too.

Professor ter Mennolt, unaware of her concern, adjusted his spectacles on his nose and addressed himself to the pile of work on his desk, perfectly content with his lot, careless of the fact that he was alone and a foreigner. He had quite forgotten Ermentrude.

The bus, by the time Ermentrude got onto it, was packed, and, since it was raining, the smell of wet raincoats was overpowering. She twitched her small nose and wondered what was for supper, and, after a ten-minute ride squashed between two stout women, got off with relief.

Five minutes' walk brought her to her home, midway down a terrace of small, neat houses in a vaguely shabby street, their front doors opening onto the pavement. She unlocked the door, calling, 'It's me,' as she did so, and opened a door in the narrow hallway. Her mother was there, sitting at a small table, knitting. Still knitting, she looked up and smiled.

'Emmy—hello, love. Supper's in the oven, but would you like a cup of tea first?'

'I'll make it, Mother. Was there a letter from Father?'

'Yes, dear, it's on the mantelpiece. Have you had a busy day?'

'So-so. I'll get the tea.'

Emmy took off her raincoat and scarf, hung them on a peg in the hall and went into the kitchen, a small, old-fashioned place with cheerful, cheap curtains and some rather nice china on the dresser shelves. About all there was left of her old home, thought Emmy, gathering cups and saucers and opening the cake tin.

Her father had taught at a large school in Somerset, and they had lived in a nearby village in a nice old house with a large garden and heavenly views. But he had been made redundant and been unable to find another post! Since an elderly aunt had recently died and left him this small house, and a colleague had told him of a post in London, they had come here to live. The post wasn't as well paid, and Mrs Foster found that living in London was quite a different matter from living in a small village with a garden which supplied her with vegetables all the year round and hens who laid fresh eggs each day.

Emmy, watching her mother coping with household bills, had given up her hopes of doing something artistic. She drew and painted and embroidered exquisitely, and had set her sights on attending a school of needlework and then starting up on her own—she wasn't sure as what. There had been an advertisement in the paper for a switchboard operator at St Luke's, and she had gone along and got the job.

She had no experience of course, but she had a pleasant voice, a nice manner and she'd been keen to have work. She'd been given a week's training, a month's trial and then had been taken on permanently. It wasn't what she wanted to do, but the money was a great help, and one day her father would find a better post. Indeed, he was already well thought of and there was a chance of promotion.

She made the tea, offered a saucer of milk to Snoodles the cat, handed a biscuit to George the elderly dachshund, and carried the tray into the sitting room.

Over tea she read her father's letter. He had been standing in for a school inspector, and had been away from home for a week. He would be coming home for the weekend, he wrote, but he had been asked to continue covering for his colleague for the next month or so. If he accepted, then it would be possible for Mrs Foster to be with him when it was necessary for him to go further afield.

'Mother, that's wonderful—Father hates being away from home, but if you're with him he won't mind as much, and if they're pleased with him he'll get a better job.'

'I can't leave you here on your own.'

'Of course you can, Mother. I've Snoodles and George for company, and we know the neighbours well enough if I should need anything. I can come home for my lunch hour and take George for a quick walk. I'm sure Father will agree to that. Besides, Father gets moved from one school to the other, doesn't he? When he is nearer home you can be here.'

'I'm sure I don't know, love. The idea of you being on your own...'

Emmy refilled their cups. 'If I had a job in another

town, I'd be on my own in some bedsitter, wouldn't I? But I'm at home. And I'm twenty-three...'

'Well, I know your father would like me to be with him. We'll talk about it at the weekend.'

By breakfast time the next morning Mrs Foster was ready to concede that there was really no reason why she shouldn't join her husband, at least for short periods. 'For you're home by six o'clock most evenings, when it's still quite light, and I dare say we'll be home most weekends.'

Emmy agreed cheerfully. She was due to go on night duty in a week's time, but there was no need to remind her mother of that. She went off to catch a bus to the hospital, glad that the rain had ceased and it was a nice autumn day.

The switchboard was busy; it always was on Fridays. Last-minute plans for the weekend, she supposed, on the part of the hospital medical staff—people phoning home, making appointments to play golf, arranging to meet to discuss some case or other—and all these over and above the outside calls, anxious family wanting news of a patient, doctors' wives with urgent messages, other hospitals wanting to contact one or other of the consulting staff. It was almost time for her midday dinner when a woman's voice, speaking English with a strong accent, asked to speak to Professor ter Mennolt.

'Hold the line while I get him for you,' said Emmy. His wife, she supposed, and decided that she didn't much like the voice—very haughty. The voice became a person in her mind's eye, tall and slim and beautiful—because the professor wouldn't look at anything less—and well used to having her own way.

He wasn't in his room, and he wasn't on any of the wards she rang. She paused in her search to reassure the voice that she was still trying, and was rewarded by being told to be quick. He wasn't in Theatre, but he was in the Pathology Lab.

'There you are,' said Emmy, quite forgetting to add 'sir'. 'I've a call for you; will you take it there?'

'Only if it's urgent; I'm occupied at the moment.'

'It's a lady,' Emmy told him. 'She told me to hurry. She speaks English with an accent.'

'Put the call through here.' He sounded impatient.

It wouldn't hurt him to say thank you, reflected Emmy as she assured his caller that she was being put through at once. She got no thanks from her either. 'They must suit each other admirably,' said Emmy under her breath, aware that the bossy woman who went around with a clipboard was coming towards her. As usual she was full of questions—had there been delayed calls? Had Ermentrude connected callers immediately? Had she noted the times?

Emmy said yes to everything. She was a conscientious worker, and although it wasn't a job she would have chosen she realised that she was lucky to have it, and it wasn't boring. She was relieved for her dinner hour presently, and went along to the canteen to eat it in the company of the ward clerks and typists. She got on well with them, and they for their part liked her, though considering her hopelessly out of date, and pitying her in a friendly way because she had been born and brought up in the country and had lacked the pleasures of London. She lacked boyfriends, too, despite their efforts to get her to join them for a visit to a cinema or a pub.

They didn't hold it against her; she was always good-natured, ready to help, willing to cover a relief telephonist if she had a date, listening to emotional outbursts about boyfriends with a sympathetic ear. They agreed among themselves that she was all right—never mind the posh voice; she couldn't help that, could she, with a father who was a schoolmaster? Besides, it sounded OK on the phone, and that was what her job was all about, wasn't it?

Home for the weekend, Mr Foster agreed with Emmy that there was no reason why she shouldn't be at home on her own for a while.

'I'll be at Coventry for a week or ten days, and then several schools in and around London. You don't mind, Emmy?'

She saw her mother and father off on Sunday evening, took George for a walk and went to bed. She wasn't a nervous girl and there were reassuringly familiar noises all around her: Mr Grant next door practising the flute, the teenager across the street playing his stereo, old Mrs Grimes, her other neighbour, shouting at her husband who was deaf. She slept soundly.

She was to go on night duty the next day, which meant that she would be relieved at dinner time and go back to work at eight o'clock that evening. Which gave her time in the afternoon to do some shopping at the row of small shops at the end of the street, take George for a good walk and sit down to a leisurely meal.

There was no phone in the house, so she didn't have to worry about her mother ringing up later in the evening. She cut sandwiches, put *Sense and Sensibility* and a much thumbed *Anthology of English Verse* in her shoulder bag with the sandwiches, and presently went back through the dark evening to catch her bus.

When she reached the hospital the noise and bustle of the day had subsided into subdued footsteps, the distant clang of the lifts and the occasional squeak of a trolley's wheels. The relief telephonist was waiting for her, an elderly woman who manned the switchboard between night and day duties.

'Nice and quiet so far,' she told Emmy. 'Hope you have a quiet night.'

Emmy settled herself in her chair, made sure that everything was as it should be and got out the knitting she had pushed in with the books at the last minute. She would knit until one of the night porters brought her coffee.

There were a number of calls: enquiries about patients, anxious voices asking advice as to whether they should bring a sick child to the hospital, calls to the medical staff on duty.

Later, when she had drunk her cooling coffee and picked up her neglected knitting once again, Professor ter Mennolt, on his way home, presumably, paused by her.

He eyed the knitting. 'A pleasant change from the daytime rush,' he remarked. 'And an opportunity to indulge your womanly skills.'

'Well, I don't know about that,' said Emmy sensibly. 'It keeps me awake in between calls! It's very late; oughtn't you to be in your bed?'

'My dear young lady, surely that is no concern of yours?'

'Oh, I'm not being nosy,' she assured him. 'But everyone needs a good night's sleep, especially people like you—people who use their brains a lot.'

'That is your opinion, Ermentrude? It is Ermentrude, isn't it?'

'Yes, and yes. At least, it's my father's opinion.'

'Your father is a medical man, perhaps?' he asked smoothly.

'No, a schoolmaster.'

'Indeed? Then why are you not following in his footsteps?'

'I'm not clever. Besides, I like sewing and embroidery.'

'And you are a switchboard operator.' His tone was dry.

'It's a nice, steady job,' said Emmy, and picked up her knitting. 'Goodnight, Professor ter Mennolt.'

'Goodnight, Ermentrude.' He had gone several paces when he turned on his heel. 'You have an old-fashioned name. I am put in mind of a demure young lady with ringlets and a crinoline, downcast eyes and a soft and gentle voice.'

She looked at him, her mouth half-open.

'You have a charming voice, but I do not consider you demure, nor do you cast down your eyes—indeed their gaze is excessively lively.'

He went away then, leaving her wondering what on earth he had been talking about.

'Of course, he's foreign,' reflected Emmy out loud. 'And besides that he's one of those clever people whose feet aren't quite on the ground, always bothering about people's insides.'

A muddled statement which nonetheless satisfied her.

Audrey, relieving her at eight o'clock the next morning, yawned widely and offered the information that she hated day duty, hated the hospital, hated having to work. 'Lucky you,' she observed. 'All day to do nothing…'

'I shall go to bed,' said Emmy mildly, and took herself off home.

It was a slow business, with the buses crammed with people going to work, and then she had to stop at the shops at the end of the street and buy bread, eggs, bacon, food for Snoodles and more food for George. Once home, with the door firmly shut behind her, she put on the kettle, fed the animals and let George into the garden. Snoodles tailed him, warned not to go far.

She had her breakfast, tidied up, undressed and had

a shower and, with George and Snoodles safely indoors, went to her bed. The teenager across the street hadn't made a sound so far; hopefully he had a job or had gone off with his pals. If Mr Grant and Mrs Grimes kept quiet, she would have a good sleep... She had barely had time to form the thought before her eyes shut.

It was two o'clock when she was woken by a hideous mixture of sound: Mr Grant's flute—played, from the sound of it, at an open window—Mrs Grimes bellowing at her husband in the background and, almost drowning these, the teenager enjoying a musical session.

Emmy turned over and buried her head in the pillow, but it was no use; she was wide awake now and likely to stay so. She got up and showered and dressed, had a cup of tea and a sandwich, made sure that Snoodles was asleep, put a lead on George's collar and left the house.

She had several hours of leisure still; she boarded an almost empty bus and sat with George on her lap as it bore them away from Stepney, along Holborn and into the Marylebone Road. She got off here and crossed the street to Regent's Park.

It was pleasant here, green and open with the strong scent of autumn in the air. Emmy walked briskly, with George trotting beside her.

'We'll come out each day,' she promised him. 'A pity the parks are all so far away, but a bus ride's nice enough, isn't it? And you shall have a good tea when we get home.'

The afternoon was sliding into dusk as they went back home. George gobbled his tea and curled up on his chair in the kitchen while Snoodles went out. Mrs Grimes had stopped shouting, but Mr Grant was still playing the flute, rivalling the din from across the street. Emmy ate her tea, stuffed things into her bag and went to work.

Audrey had had a busy day and was peevish. 'I spent the whole of my two hours off looking for some decent tights—the shops around here are useless.'

'There's that shop in Commercial Road...' began Emmy.

'There?' Audrey was scornful. 'I wouldn't be seen dead in anything from there.' She took a last look at her face, added more lipstick and patted her blonde head. 'I'm going out this evening. So long.'

Until almost midnight Emmy was kept busy. From time to time someone passing through from the entrance hall stopped for a word, and one of the porters brought her coffee around eleven o'clock with the news that there had been a pile-up down at the docks and the accident room was up to its eyes.

'They phoned,' said Emmy, 'but didn't say how bad it was—not to me, that is. I switched them straight through. I hope they're not too bad.'

'Couple of boys, an old lady, the drivers—one of them's had a stroke.'

Soon she was busy again, with families phoning with anxious enquiries. She was eating her sandwiches in the early hours of the morning when

Professor ter Mennolt's voice, close to her ear, made her jump.

'I am relieved to see that you are awake and alert, Ermentrude.'

She said, round the sandwich. 'Well, of course I am. That's not a nice thing to say, sir.'

'What were you doing in a bus on the Marylebone Road when you should have been in bed asleep, recruiting strength for the night's work?'

'I was going to Regent's Park with George. He had a good walk.' She added crossly, 'And *you* should try to sleep with someone playing the flute on one side of the house, Mrs Grimes shouting on the other and that wretched boy with his stereo across the street.'

The professor was leaning against the wall, his hands in the pockets of his beautifully tailored jacket. 'I have misjudged you, Ermentrude. I am sorry. Ear plugs, perhaps?' And, when she shook her head, 'Could you not beg a bed from a friend? Or your mother have a word with the neighbours?'

'Mother's with Father,' said Emmy, and took a bite of sandwich. 'I can't leave the house because of George and Snoodles.'

'George?'

'Our dog, and Snoodles is the cat.'

'So you are alone in the house?' He stared down at her. 'You are not nervous?'

'No, sir.'

'You live close by?'

What a man for asking questions, thought Emmy, and wished he didn't stare so. She stared back and said 'Yes,' and wished that he would go away; she found him unsettling. She remembered something. 'I didn't see you on the bus…'

He smiled. 'I was in the car, waiting for the traffic lights.'

She turned to the switchboard, then, and put through two calls, and he watched her. She had pretty hands, nicely well-cared for, and though her hair was mouse-brown there seemed to be a great deal of it, piled neatly in a coil at the back of her head. Not in the least pretty, but with eyes like hers that didn't matter.

He bade her goodnight, and went out to his car and forgot her, driving to his charming little house in Chelsea where Beaker, who ran it for him, would have left coffee and sandwiches for him in his study, his desk light on and a discreet lamp burning in the hall.

Although it was almost two o'clock he sat down to go through his letters and messages while he drank the coffee, hot and fragrant in the Thermos. There was a note, too, written in Beaker's spidery hand: Juffrouw Anneliese van Moule had phoned at eight o'clock and again at ten. The professor frowned and glanced over to the answering machine. It showed the red light, and he went and switched it on.

In a moment a petulant voice, speaking in Dutch, wanted to know where he was. 'Surely you should be home by ten o'clock in the evening. I asked you specially to be home, did I not? Well, I suppose I must forgive you and give you good news. I am coming to London in three days' time—Friday. I shall stay at Brown's Hotel, since you are unlikely to be home for most of the day, but I expect to be taken out in the evenings—and there will be time for us to discuss the future.

'I wish to see your house; I think it will not do for us when we are married, for I shall live with you in London when you are working there, but I hope you will give up your work in England and live at Huis ter Mennolt—'

The professor switched off. Anneliese's voice had sounded loud as well as peevish, and she was reiterating an argument they had had on several occasions. He had no intention of leaving his house; it was large enough. He had some friends to dine, but his entertaining was for those whom he knew well. Anneliese would wish to entertain on a grand scale, fill the house with acquaintances; he would return home each evening to a drawing room full of people he neither knew nor wished to know.

He reminded himself that she would be a most suitable wife; in Holland they had a similar circle of friends and acquaintances, and they liked the same things—the theatre, concerts, art exhibitions—and she was ambitious.

At first he had been amused and rather touched by that, until he had realised that her ambition wasn't for his success in his profession but for a place in London society. She already had that in Holland, and she had been careful never to admit to him that that was her goal... He reminded himself that she was the woman he had chosen to marry and once she had understood that he had no intention of altering his way of life when they were married she would understand how he felt.

After all, when they were in Holland she could have all the social life she wanted; Huis ter Mennolt was vast, and there were servants enough and lovely gardens. While he was working she could entertain as many of her friends as she liked—give dinner parties if she wished, since the house was large enough to do that with ease. Here at the Chelsea house, though, with only Beaker and a daily woman to run the place, entertaining on such a scale would be out of the question. The house, roomy though it was, was too small.

He went to bed then, and, since he had a list the following day, he had no time to think about anything but his work.

He left the hospital soon after ten o'clock the next evening. Ermentrude was at her switchboard, her back towards him. He gave her a brief glance as he passed.

Anneliese had phoned again, Beaker informed him, but would leave no message. 'And, since I needed some groceries, I switched on the answering machine, sir,' he said, 'since Mrs Thrupp, splendid cleaner though she is, is hardly up to answering the telephone.'

The professor went to his study and switched on the machine, and stood listening to Anneliese. Her voice was no longer petulant, but it was still loud. 'My plane gets in at half past ten on Friday—Heathrow,' she told him. 'I'll look out for you. Don't keep me waiting, will you, Ruerd? Shall we dine at Brown's? I shall be too tired to talk much, and I'll stay for several days, anyway.'

He went to look at his appointments book on his desk. He would be free to meet her, although he would have to go back to his consulting rooms for a couple of hours before joining her at Brown's Hotel.

He sat down at his desk, took his glasses from his breast pocket, put them on and picked up the pile of letters before him. He was aware that there was a lack of lover-like anticipation at the thought of seeing Anneliese. Probably because he hadn't seen her for some weeks. Moreover, he had been absorbed in his patients. In about a month's time he would be going back to Holland for a month or more; he would make a point of seeing as much of Anneliese as possible.

He ate his solitary dinner, and went back to his study to write a paper on spina bifida, an exercise which kept him engrossed until well after midnight.

Past the middle of the week already, thought Emmy with satisfaction, getting ready for bed the next morning—three more nights and she would have two days off. Her mother would be home too, until she rejoined her father later in the week, and then he would be working in and around London. Emmy heaved a tired, satisfied sigh and went to sleep until, inevitably, the strains of the flute woke her. It was no use lying there and hoping they would stop; she got up, had a cup of tea and took George for a walk.

It was raining when she went to work that evening, and she had to wait for a long time for a bus. The elderly relief telephonist was off sick, and Audrey was waiting for her when she got there, already dressed to leave, tapping her feet with impatience.

'I thought you'd never get here...'

'It's still only two minutes to eight,' said Emmy mildly. 'Is there anything I should know?'

She was taking off her mac and headscarf as she spoke, and when Audrey said no, there wasn't, Emmy sat down before the switchboard, suddenly hating the sight of it. The night stretched ahead of her, endless hours of staying alert. The thought of the countless days and nights ahead in the years to come wasn't to be borne.

She adjusted her headpiece and arranged everything just so, promising herself that she would find another job, something where she could be out of doors for at least part of the day. And meet people...a man who would fall in love with her and want to marry her. A house in the country, mused Emmy, dogs and cats and chickens and children, of course...

She was roused from this pleasant dream by an outside call, followed by more of them; it was always at this time of the evening that people phoned to make enquiries.

She was kept busy throughout the night. By six o'clock she was tired, thankful that in another couple of hours she would be free. Only three more nights; she thought sleepily of what she would do. Window shopping with her mother? And if the weather was good enough they could take a bus to Hampstead Heath…

A great blast of sound sent her upright in her chair, followed almost at once by a call from the police—there had been a bomb close to Fenchurch Street Station. Too soon to know how many were injured, but they would be coming to St Luke's!

Emmy, very wide awake now, began notifying everyone—the accident room, the house doctors' rooms, the wards, X-Ray, the path lab. And within minutes she was kept busy, ringing the consultants on call, theatre staff, technicians, ward sisters on day duty. She had called the professor, but hadn't spared him a thought, nor had she seen him as he came to the hospital, for there was a great deal of orderly coming and going as the ambulances began to arrive.

She had been busy; now she was even more so. Anxious relatives were making frantic calls, wanting to know where the injured were and how they were doing. But it was too soon to know anything. The accident room was crowded; names were sent to her as they were given, but beyond letting callers know that they had that particular person in the hospital there was no more information to pass on.

Emmy went on answering yet more calls, putting through outside calls too—to other hospitals, the police, someone from a foreign embassy who had heard that one of the staff had been injured. She answered them all in her quiet voice, trying to ignore a threatening headache.

It seemed a very long time before order emerged

from the controlled chaos. There were no more ambulances now, and patients who needed admission were being taken to the wards. The accident room, still busy, was dealing with the lesser injured; the hospital was returning to its normal day's work.

It was now ten o'clock. Emmy, looking at her watch for the first time in hours, blinked. Where was Audrey? Most of the receptionists had come in, for they had rung to tell her so, but not Audrey. Emmy was aware that she was hungry, thirsty and very tired, and wondered what to do about it. She would have to let someone know…

Audrey tapped on her shoulder. She said airily, 'Sorry I'm late. I didn't fancy coming sooner; I bet the place was a shambles. I knew you wouldn't mind…'

'I do mind, though,' said Emmy. 'I mind very much. I've had a busy time, and I should have been off duty two hours ago.'

'Well, you were here, weren't you? Did you expect me to come tearing in in the middle of all the fuss just so's you could go off duty? Besides, you're not doing anything; you only go to bed…'

The professor, on his way home, paused to listen to this with interest. Ermentrude, he could see, was looking very much the worse for wear; she had undoubtedly had a busy time of it, and she had been up all night, whereas the rest of them had merely got out of their beds earlier than usual.

He said now pleasantly, 'Put on your coat, Ermentrude; I'll drive you home. We can take up the matter of the extra hours you have worked later on. Leave it to me.'

Emmy goggled at him, but he gave her no chance to speak. He said, still pleasantly, to Audrey, 'I'm sure you have a good reason for not coming on duty at the usual time.' He smiled thinly. 'It will have to be a good one, will it not?'

He swept Emmy along, away from a pale Audrey, out of the doors and into his Bentley. 'Tell me where you live,' he commanded.

'There is no need to take me home, I'm quite able—'

'Don't waste my time. We're both tired, and I for one am feeling short-tempered.'

'So am I,' snapped Emmy. 'I want a cup of tea, and I'm hungry.'

'That makes two of us. Now, where do you live, Ermentrude?'

CHAPTER TWO

EMMY told him her address in a cross voice, sitting silently until he stopped before her home. She said gruffly, 'Thank you, Professor. Good morning,' and made to open her door. He shook her hand and released it, and she put it in her lap. Then he got out, opened the door, crossed the pavement with her, took the key from her and opened the house door. George rushed to meet them while Snoodles, a cat not to be easily disturbed, sat on the bottom step of the stairs, watching.

Emmy stood awkwardly in the doorway with George, who was making much of her. She said again, 'Thank you, Professor,' and peered up at his face.

'The least you can do is offer me a cup of tea,' he told her, and came into the hall, taking her with him and closing the door. 'You get that coat off and do whatever you usually do while I put on the kettle.'

He studied her face. Really, the girl was very plain; for a moment he regretted the impulse which had urged him to bring her home. She had been quite capable of getting herself there; he had formed the opinion after their first meeting that she was more than capable of dealing with any situation—and with a sharp tongue, too. She looked at him then, though,

33

and he saw how tired she was. He said in a placid voice, 'I make a very good cup of tea.'

She smiled. 'Thank you. The kitchen's here.'

She opened a door and ushered him into the small room at the back of the house, which was, he saw, neat and very clean, with old-fashioned shelves and a small dresser. There was a gas stove against one wall—an elderly model, almost a museum piece, but still functioning, he was relieved to find.

Emmy went away and he found tea, milk and sugar while the kettle boiled, took mugs and a brown teapot from the dresser and set them on the table while Emmy fed Snoodles and George.

They drank their tea presently, sitting opposite each other saying little, and when the professor got to his feet Emmy made no effort to detain him. She thanked him again, saw him to the door and shut it the moment he had driven away, intent on getting to her bed as quickly as possible. She took a slice of bread and butter and a slab of cheese with her, and George and Snoodles, who had sidled upstairs with her, got onto the bed too—which was a comfort for she was feeling hard done by and put upon.

'It's all very well,' she told them peevishly. 'He'll go home to a doting wife—slippers in one hand and bacon and eggs in the other.'

She swallowed the last of the cheese and went to sleep, and not even the flute or Mrs Grimes' loud voice could wake her.

The professor got into his car, and as he drove away his bleep sounded. He was wanted back at St Luke's;

one of the injured had developed signs of a blood clot on the brain. So instead of going home he went back and spent the next few hours doing everything in his power to keep his patient alive—something which proved successful, so that in the early afternoon he was at last able to go home.

He let himself into his house, put his bag down and trod into the sitting room, to come to a halt just inside the door.

'Anneliese—I forgot...'

She was a beautiful girl with thick fair hair cut short by an expert hand, perfect features and big blue eyes, and she was exquisitely made-up. She was dressed in the height of fashion and very expensively, too. She made a charming picture, marred by the ill-temper on her face.

She spoke in Dutch, not attempting to hide her bad temper.

'Really, Ruerd, what am I to suppose you mean by that? That man of yours, Beaker—who, by the way, I shall discharge as soon as we are married—refused to phone the hospital—said you would be too busy to answer. Since when has a consultant not been free to answer the telephone when he wishes?'

He examined several answers to that and discarded them. 'I am sorry, my dear. There was a bomb; it exploded close to St Luke's early this morning. It was necessary for me to be there—there were casualties. Beaker was quite right; I shouldn't have answered the phone.'

He crossed the room and bent to kiss her cheek. 'He is an excellent servant; I have no intention of discharging him.' He spoke lightly, but she gave him a questioning look. They had been engaged for some months now, and she was still not sure that she knew him. She wasn't sure if she loved him either, but he could offer her everything she wanted in life; they knew the same people and came from similar backgrounds. Their marriage would be entirely suitable.

She decided to change her tactics. 'I'm sorry for being cross. But I was disappointed. Are you free for the rest of the day?'

'I shall have to go back to the hospital late this evening. Shall we dine somewhere? You're quite comfortable at Brown's?'

'Very comfortable. Could we dine at Claridge's? I've a dress I bought specially for you…'

'I'll see if I can get a table.' He turned round as Beaker came in.

'You had lunch, sir?' Beaker didn't look at Anneliese. When the professor said that, yes, he'd had something, Beaker went on, 'Then I shall bring tea here, sir. A little early, but you may be glad of it.'

'Splendid, Beaker. As soon as you like.' And, when Beaker had gone, the professor said, 'I'll go and phone now…'

He took his bag to his study and pressed the button on the answering machine. There were several calls from when Beaker had been out of the house; the rest he had noted down and put with the letters. The professor leafed through them, listened to the answering machine and booked a table for dinner. He would have liked to dine quietly at home.

They talked trivialities over tea—news from home and friends, places Anneliese had visited. She had no interest in his work save in his successes; his social advancement was all-important to her, although she was careful not to let him see that.

He drove her to Brown's presently, and went back to work at his desk until it was time to dress. Immaculate in black tie, he went to the garage at the end of the mews to get his car, and drove himself to the hotel.

Anneliese wasn't ready. He cooled his heels for fifteen minutes or so before she joined him.

'I've kept you waiting, Ruerd,' she said laughingly. 'But I hope you think it is worth it.'

He assured her that it was, and indeed she made a magnificent picture in a slim sheath of cerise silk, her hair piled high, sandals with four-inch heels and an arm loaded with gold bangles. His ring, a large diamond, glittered on her finger. A ring which she had chosen and which he disliked.

Certainly she was a woman any man would be proud to escort, he told himself. He supposed that he was tired; a good night's sleep was all that was needed. Anneliese looked lovely, and dinner at Claridge's was the very least he could offer her. Tomorrow, he reflected, he would somehow find time to take her out again—dancing, perhaps, at one of the nightclubs. And there was that exhibition of paintings at a gallery in Bond Street if he could manage to find time to take her.

He listened to her chatter as they drove to Claridge's and gave her his full attention. Dinner was entirely satisfactory: admiring looks followed Anneliese as they went to their table, the food was delicious and the surroundings luxurious. As he drove her back she put a hand on his arm.

'A lovely dinner, darling, thank you. I shall do some shopping tomorrow; can you meet me for lunch? And could we go dancing in the evening? We must talk; I've so many plans...'

At the hotel she offered a cheek for his kiss. 'I shall go straight to bed. See you tomorrow.'

The professor got back into his car and drove to the hospital. He wasn't entirely satisfied with the condition of the patient he had seen that afternoon, and he wanted to be sure...

Emmy, sitting before her switchboard, knitting, knew that the professor was there, standing behind her, although he had made no sound. Why is that? she wondered; why should I know that?

His, 'Good evening, Ermentrude,' was uttered quietly. 'You slept well?' he added.

He came to stand beside her now, strikingly handsome in black tie and quite unconscious of it.

'Good evening, sir. Yes, thank you. I hope you had time to rest.'

His mouth twitched. 'I have been dining out. Making conversation, talking of things which don't interest me. If I sound a bad-tempered man who doesn't know when he is lucky, then that is exactly what I am.'

'No, you're not,' said Emmy reasonably. 'You've had a busy day, much busier than anyone else because you've had to make important decisions about your patients. All that's the matter with you is that you are tired. You must go home and have a good night's sleep.'

She had quite forgotten to whom she was speaking. 'I suppose you've come to see that man with the blood clot on the brain?'

He asked with interest, 'Do you know about him?'

'Well, of course I do. I hear things, don't I? And I'm interested.'

She took an incoming telephone call and, when she had dealt with it the professor had gone.

He didn't stop on his way out, nor did he speak, but she was conscious of his passing. She found that disconcerting.

Audrey was punctual and in a peevish mood. 'I had a ticking off,' she told Emmy sourly. 'I don't know why they had to make such a fuss—after all, you were here. No one would have known if it hadn't been for that Professor ter Mennolt being here. Who does he think he is, anyway?'

'He's rather nice,' said Emmy mildly. 'He gave me a lift home.'

'In that great car of his? Filthy rich, so I've heard.

Going to marry some Dutch beauty—I was talking to his secretary...'

'I hope they'll be very happy,' said Emmy. A flicker of unhappiness made her frown. She knew very little about the professor and she found him disturbing; a difficult man, a man who went his own way. All the same, she would like him to live happily ever after...

If he came into the hospital during the last nights of her duty, she didn't see him. It wasn't until Sunday morning, when the relief had come to take over and she was free at last to enjoy her two days off, that she met him again as she stood for a moment outside the hospital entrance, taking blissful breaths of morning air, her eyes closed. She was imagining that she was back in the country, despite the petrol fumes.

She opened her eyes, feeling foolish, when the professor observed, 'I am surprised that you should linger, Ermentrude. Surely you must be hellbent on getting away from the hospital as quickly as possible?'

'Good morning, sir,' said Ermentrude politely. 'It's just nice to be outside.' She saw his sweater and casual trousers. 'Have you been here all night?'

'No, no—only for an hour or so.' He smiled down at her. She looked pale with tiredness. Her small nose shone, her hair had been ruthlessly pinned into a bun, very neat and totally without charm. She reminded him of a kitten who had been out all night in the rain. 'I'll drop you off on my way.'

'You're going past my home? Really? Thank you.'

He didn't find it necessary to answer her, but popped her into the car and drove through the almost empty streets. At her door, he said, 'No, don't get out. Give me your key.'

He went and opened the door, and then opened the car door, took her bag from her and followed her inside. George was delighted to see them, weaving round their feet, pushing Snoodles away, giving small, excited barks.

The professor went to open the kitchen door to let both animals out into the garden, and he put the kettle on. For all the world as though he lived here, thought Emmy, and if she hadn't been so tired she would have said so. Instead she stood in the kitchen and yawned.

The professor glanced at her. 'Breakfast,' he said briskly and unbuttoned his coat and threw it over a chair. 'If you'll feed the animals, I'll boil a couple of eggs.'

She did as she was told without demur; she couldn't be bothered to argue with him. She didn't remember asking him to stay for breakfast, but perhaps he was very hungry. She fed the animals and by then he had laid the table after a fashion, made toast and dished up the eggs.

They sat at the table eating their breakfast for all the world like an old married couple. The professor kept up a gentle meandering conversation which required little or no reply, and Emmy, gobbling toast, made very little effort to do so. She was still tired, but the tea and the food had revived her so that presently she said, 'It was very kind of you to get breakfast. I'm very grateful. I was a bit tired.'

'You had a busy week. Will your mother and father return soon?'

'Tomorrow morning.' She gave him an owl-like look. 'I expect you want to go home, sir...'

'Presently. Go upstairs, Ermentrude, take a shower and get into bed. I will tidy up here. When you are in bed I will go home.'

'You can't do the washing up.'

'Indeed I can.' Not quite a lie; he had very occasionally needed to rinse a cup or glass if Beaker hadn't been there.

He made a good job of it, attended to the animals, locked the kitchen door and hung the tea towel to dry, taking his time about it. It was quiet in the house, and presently he went upstairs. He got no answer from his quiet, 'Ermentrude?' but one of the doors on the landing was half-open.

The room was small, nicely furnished and very tidy. Emmy was asleep in her bed, her mouth slightly open, her hair all over the pillow. He thought that nothing short of a brass band giving a concert by her bedside would waken her. He went downstairs again and out of the house, shutting the door behind him.

Driving to Chelsea, he looked at his watch. It would be eleven o'clock before he was home. He was taking Anneliese to lunch with friends, and he suspected that when they returned she would want to make plans for their future. There had been no time so far, and he would be at the hospital for a great deal of the days ahead. He was tired now; Anneliese wasn't content to dine quietly and spend the evening at home and yesterday his day had been full. A day in the country would be delightful...

Beaker came to meet him as he opened his front door. His, 'Good morning, sir,' held faint reproach. 'You were detained at the hospital? I prepared breakfast at the usual time. I can have it on the table in ten minutes.'

'No need, Beaker, thanks. I've had breakfast. I'll have a shower and change, and then perhaps a cup of coffee before Juffrouw van Moule gets here.'

'You breakfasted at the hospital, sir?'

'No, no. I boiled an egg and made some toast and had a pot of strong tea. I took someone home. We were both hungry—it seemed a sensible thing to do.'

Beaker inclined his head gravely. A boiled egg, he reflected—no bacon, mushrooms, scrambled eggs, as only he, Beaker, could cook them—and strong tea... He suppressed a shudder. A small plate of his home-made savoury biscuits, he decided, and perhaps a sandwich with Gentlemen's Relish on the coffee tray.

It was gratifying to see the professor eating the lot when he came downstairs again. He looked as though he could do with a quiet day, reflected his faithful servant, instead of gallivanting off with that Juffrouw van Moule. Beaker hadn't taken to her—a haughty piece, and critical of him. He wished his master a pleasant day in a voice which hinted otherwise. He was informed that Juffrouw van Moule would be returning for tea, and would probably stay for dinner.

Beaker took himself to the kitchen where he unburdened himself to his cat, Humphrey, while he set about making the little queen cakes usually appreciated by the professor's lady visitors.

Anneliese looked ravishing, exquisitely made-up, not a hair of her head out of place and wearing a stone-coloured crêpe de chine outfit of deceptive simplicity which screamed money from every seam.

She greeted the professor with a charming smile, offered a cheek with the warning not to disarrange her hair and settled herself in the car.

'At last we have a day together,' she observed. 'I'll come back with you after lunch. That man of yours will give us a decent tea, I suppose. I might even stay for dinner.'

She glanced at his profile. 'We must discuss the future, Ruerd. Where we are to live—we shall have to engage more servants in a larger house, of course, and I suppose you can arrange to give up some of your consultant posts, concentrate on private patients. You have plenty of friends, haven't you? Influential people?'

He didn't look at her. 'I have a great many friends and even more acquaintances,' he told her. 'I have no intention of using them. Indeed, I have no need. Do not expect me to give up my hospital work, though, Anneliese.'

She put a hand on his knee. 'Of course not, Ruerd.

I promise I won't say any more about that. But please let us at least discuss finding a larger house where we can entertain. I shall have friends, I hope, and I shall need to return their hospitality.'

She was wise enough to stop then. 'These people we are lunching with—they are old friends?'

'Yes. I knew Guy Bowers-Bentinck before he married. We still see a good deal of each other; he has a charming little wife, Suzannah, and twins—five years old—and a baby on the way.'

'Does she live here, in this village—Great Chisbourne? Does she not find it full? I mean, does she not miss theatres and evenings out and meeting people?'

He said evenly, 'No. She has a husband who loves her, two beautiful children, a delightful home and countless friends. She is content.'

Something in his voice made Anneliese say quickly, 'She sounds delightful; I'm sure I shall like her.'

Which was unfortunately not true. Beneath their socially pleasant manner, they disliked each other heartily—Anneliese because she considered Suzannah to be not worth bothering about, Suzannah because she saw at once that Anneliese wouldn't do for Ruerd at all. She would make him unhappy; surely he could see that for himself?

Lunch was pleasant, Suzannah saw to that—making small talk while the two men discussed some knotty problem about their work. Anneliese showed signs of boredom after a time; she was used to being the centre of attention and she wasn't getting it. When the men did join in the talk it was about the children eating their meal with them, behaving beautifully.

'Do you have a nursery?' asked Anneliese.

'Oh, yes, and a marvellous old nanny. But the children eat with us unless we're entertaining in the evening. We enjoy their company, and they see more of their father.'

Suzannah smiled across the table at her husband, and Anneliese, looking at him, wondered how such a plain girl could inspire the devoted look he gave her.

She remarked upon it as they drove back to Chelsea. 'Quite charming,' she commented in a voice which lacked sincerity. 'Guy seems devoted to her.'

'Surely that is to be expected of a husband?' the professor observed quietly.

Anneliese gave a little trill of laughter. 'Oh, I suppose so. Not quite my idea of marriage, though. Children should be in the nursery until they go to school, don't you agree?'

He didn't answer that. 'They are delightful, aren't they? And so well behaved.' He sounded remote.

He was going fast on the motorway as the October day faded into dusk. In a few days it would be November, and at the end of that month he would go back to Holland for several weeks, where already a formidable list of consultations awaited him. He would see Anneliese again, of course; she would want to plan their wedding.

When they had first become engaged he had expressed a wish for a quiet wedding and she had agreed. But over the months she had hinted more and more strongly that a big wedding was absolutely necessary: so many friends and family, and she wanted bridesmaids. Besides, a quiet wedding would mean she couldn't wear the gorgeous wedding dress she fully intended to have.

Anneliese began to talk then; she could be very amusing and she was intelligent. Ruerd wasn't giving her his full attention, but she was confident that she could alter that. She embarked on a series of anecdotes about mutual friends in Holland, taking care not to be critical or spiteful, only amusing. She knew how to be a charming companion, and felt smug satisfaction when he responded, unaware that it was only good manners which prompted his replies.

He was tired, he told himself, and Anneliese's chatter jarred on his thoughts. To talk to her about his work would have been a relief, to tell her of his busy week at the hospital, the patients he had seen. But the cursory interest she had shown when they'd become engaged had evaporated. Not her fault, of course, but his. He had thought that her interest in his work was a wish to understand it, but it hadn't been that—her interest was a social one. To be married to a well-known medical man with boundless possibilities for advancement.

He slowed the car's speed as they were engulfed in London's suburbs. She would be a suitable wife—good looks, a charming manner, clever and always beautifully turned out.

On aiming back he said, 'We'll have tea round the

fire, shall we? Beaker will have it ready.' He glanced at his watch. 'Rather on the late side, but there's no hurry, is there?'

The sitting room looked warm and welcoming as they went indoors. Humphrey was sitting before the fire, a small furry statue, staring at the flames. Anneliese paused halfway across the room. 'Oh, Ruerd, please get that cat out of the room. I dislike them, you know—I'm sure they're not clean, and they shed hairs everywhere.'

The professor scooped Humphrey into his arms. 'He's a well-loved member of my household, Anneliese. He keeps himself cleaner than many humans, and he is brushed so regularly that I doubt if there is a single loose hair.'

He took the cat to the kitchen and sat him down in front of the Aga.

'Juffrouw van Moule doesn't like cats,' he told Beaker in an expressionless voice. 'He'd better stay here until she goes back to the hotel. Could you give us supper about half past eight? Something light; if we're going to have tea now we shan't have much appetite.'

When he went back to the sitting room Anneliese was sitting by the fire. She made a lovely picture in its light, and he paused to look at her as he went in. Any man would be proud to have her as his wife, he reflected, so why was it that he felt no quickening of his pulse at the sight of her?

He brushed the thought aside and sat down opposite her, and watched her pour their tea. She had beautiful hands, exquisitely cared for, and they showed to great advantage as she presided over the tea tray. She looked at him and smiled, aware of the charming picture she made, and presently, confident that she had his attention once more, she began to talk about their future.

'I know we shall see a good deal of each other when you come back to Holland in December,' she began. 'But at least we can make tentative plans.' She didn't wait for his comment but went on, 'I think a summer wedding, don't you? That gives you plenty of time to arrange a long holiday. We might go somewhere for a month or so before settling down.

'Can you arrange it so that you're working in Holland for a few months? You can always fly over here if you're wanted, and surely you can give up your consultancies here after awhile? Private patients, by all means, and, of course, we mustn't lose sight of your friends and colleagues.' She gave him a brilliant smile. 'You're famous here, are you not? It is so important to know all the right people...'

When he didn't reply, she added, 'I am going to be very unselfish and agree to using this house as a London base. Later on perhaps we can find something larger.'

He asked quietly, 'What kind of place had you in mind, Anneliese?'

'I looked in at an estate agent—somewhere near Harrods; I can't remember the name. There were some most suitable flats. Large enough for entertaining. We would need at least five bedrooms—guests, you know—and good servants' quarters.'

Her head on one side, she gave him another brilliant smile. 'Say yes, Ruerd.'

'I have commitments for the next four months here,' he told her, 'and they will be added to in the meantime. In March I've been asked to lecture at a seminar in Leiden, examine students at Groningen and read a paper in Vienna. I cannot give you a definite answer at the moment.'

She pouted. 'Oh, Ruerd, why must you work so hard? At least I shall see something of you when you come back to Holland. Shall you give a party at Christmas?'

'Yes, I believe so. We can talk about that later. Have your family any plans?'

She was still telling him about them when Beaker came to tell them that supper was ready.

Later that evening, as she prepared to go, Anneliese asked, 'Tomorrow, Ruerd? You will be free? We might go to an art exhibition...?'

He shook his head. 'I'm working all day. I doubt if I shall be free before the evening. I'll phone the hotel and leave a message. It will probably be too late for dinner, but we might have a drink.'

She had to be content with that. She would shop, she decided, and dine at the hotel. She was careful not to let him see how vexed she was.

The next morning as the professor made his way through the hospital he looked, as had become his habit, to where Ermentrude sat. She wasn't there, of course.

She was up and dressed, getting the house just so, ready for her mother and father. She had slept long and soundly, and had gone downstairs to find that the professor had left everything clean and tidy in the kitchen. He had left a tea tray ready, too; all she'd needed to do was put on the kettle and make toast.

'Very thoughtful of him,' said Emmy now, to George, who was hovering hopefully for a biscuit. 'You wouldn't think to look at him that he'd know one end of a tea towel from the other. He must have a helpless fiancée...'

She frowned. Even if his fiancée was helpless he could obviously afford to have a housekeeper or at least a daily woman. She fell to wondering about him. When would he be married, have children? Where did he live while he was working in London? And where was his home in Holland? Since neither George nor Snoodles could answer, she put these questions to the back of her mind and turned her thoughts to the shopping she must do before her parents came home.

They knew about the bomb, of course; it had been on TV and in the papers. But when Emmy had phoned her parents she had told them very little about it, and had remained guiltily silent when her mother had expressed her relief that Emmy had been on day duty and hadn't been there. Now that they were home, exchanging news over coffee and biscuits, the talk turned naturally enough to the bomb outrage. 'So fortunate that you weren't there,' said Mrs Foster.

'Well, as a matter of fact, I was,' said Emmy. 'But I was quite all right...' She found herself explaining about Professor ter Mennolt bringing her home and him making tea.

'We are in his debt,' observed her father. 'Although he did only what any decent-thinking person would have done.'

Her mother said artlessly, 'He sounds a very nice man. Is he elderly? I suppose so if he's a professor.'

'Not elderly—not even middle-aged,' said Emmy. 'They say at the hospital that he's going to marry soon. No one knows much about him, and one wouldn't dare ask him.'

She thought privately that one day, if the opportunity occurred, she might do just that. For some reason it was important to her that he should settle down and be happy. He didn't strike her as being happy enough. He ought to be; he was top of his profession, with a girl waiting for him, and presumably enough to live on in comfort.

Her two days went much too quickly. Never mind if it rained for almost all of the time. Her father was away in the day, and she and her mother spent a morning window shopping in Oxford Street, and long hours sitting by the fire—her mother knitting, Emmy busy with the delicate embroidery which she loved to do.

They talked—the chances of her father getting a teaching post near their old home were remote; all the same they discussed it unendingly. 'We don't need a big house,' said her mother. 'And you could come with us, of course, Emmy—there's bound to be some job for you. Or you might meet someone and marry.' She peered at her daughter. 'There isn't anyone here, is there, love?'

'No, Mother, and not likely to be. It would be lovely if Father could get a teaching post and we could sell this house.'

Her mother smiled. 'No neighbours, darling. Wouldn't it be heaven? No rows of little houses all exactly alike. Who knows what is round the corner?'

It was still raining when Emmy set off to work the following morning. The buses were packed and tempers were short. She got off before the hospital stop was reached, tired of being squeezed between wet raincoats and having her feet poked at with umbrellas. A few minutes' walk even on a London street was preferable to strap-hanging.

She was taking a short cut through a narrow lane where most of the houses were boarded up or just plain derelict, when she saw the kitten. It was very small and very wet, sitting by a boarded-up door, and when she went nearer she saw that it had been tied by a piece of string to the door handle. It looked at her and shivered, opened its tiny mouth and mewed almost without sound.

Emmy knelt down, picked it up carefully, held it close and rooted around in her shoulder bag for the scissors she always carried. It was the work of a moment to cut the string, tuck the kitten into her jacket and be on her way once more. She had no idea what she was going to do with the small creature, but to leave it there was unthinkable.

She was early at the hospital; there was time to beg a cardboard box from one of the porters, line it with yesterday's newspaper and her scarf and beg some milk from the head porter.

'You won't 'arf cop it,' he told her, offering a mugful. 'I wouldn't do it for anyone else, Emmy, and mum's the word.' He nodded and winked. She was a nice young lady, he considered, always willing to listen to him telling her about his wife's diabetes.

Emmy tucked the box away at her feet, dried the small creature with her handkerchief, offered it milk and saw with satisfaction that it fell instantly into a refreshing sleep. It woke briefly from time to time, scoffed more milk and dropped off again. Very much to her relief, Emmy got to the end of her shift with the kitten undetected.

She was waiting for her relief when the supervisor bore down upon her, intent on checking and finding fault if she could. It was just bad luck that the kitten should wake at that moment, and, since it was feeling better, it mewed quite loudly.

Meeting the lady's outraged gaze, Emmy said, 'I found him tied to a doorway. In the rain. I'm going to take him home…'

'He has been here all day?' The supervisor's bosom swelled to alarming proportions. 'No animal is allowed inside the hospital. You are aware of that, are you not, Miss Foster? I shall report this, and in the meantime the animal can be taken away by one of the porters.'

'Don't you dare,' said Emmy fiercely. 'I'll not allow it. You are—'

It was unfortunate that she was interrupted before she could finish.

'Ah,' said Professor ter Mennolt, looming behind the supervisor. 'My kitten. Good of you to look after it for me, Ermentrude.' He gave the supervisor a bland smile. 'I am breaking the rules, am I not? But this seemed the best place for it to be until I could come and collect it.'

'Miss Foster has just told me…' began the woman.

'Out of the kindness of her heart,' said the professor outrageously. 'She had no wish to get me into trouble. Isn't that correct, Ermentrude?'

She nodded, and watched while he soothed the supervisor's feelings with a bedside manner which she couldn't have faulted.

'I will overlook your rudeness, Miss Foster,' she said finally, and sailed away.

'Where on earth did you find it?' asked the professor with interest.

She told him, then went on, 'I'll take him home. He'll be nice company for Snoodles and George.'

'An excellent idea. Here is your relief. I shall be outside when you are ready.'

'Why?' asked Emmy.

'You sometimes ask silly questions, Ermentrude. To take you both home.'

Emmy made short work of handing over, got into her mac, picked up the box and went to the entrance. The Bentley was outside, and the professor bundled her and her box into it and drove away in the streaming rain.

The kitten sat up on wobbly legs and mewed. It was bedraggled and thin, and Emmy said anxiously, 'I do hope he'll be all right.'

'Probably a she. I'll look the beast over.'

'Would you? Thank you. Then if it's necessary I'll take him—her—to the vet.' She added uncertainly, 'That's if it's not interfering with whatever you're doing?'

'I can spare half an hour.' He sounded impatient.

She unlocked the door and ushered him into the hall, where he took up so much room she had to sidle past him to open the sitting-room door.

'You're so large,' she told him, and ushered him into the room.

Mrs Foster was sitting reading with Snoodles on her lap. She looked up as they went in and got to her feet.

'I'm sure you're the professor who was so kind to Emmy,' she said, and offered a hand. 'I'm her mother. Emmy, take off that wet mac and put the kettle on, please. What's in the box?'

'A kitten.'

Mrs Foster offered a chair. 'Just like Emmy—always finding birds with broken wings and stray animals.' She smiled from a plain face very like her daughter's, and he thought what a charming woman she was.

'I offered to look at the little beast,' he explained. 'It was tied to a door handle…'

'People are so cruel. But how kind of you. I'll get a clean towel so that we can put the little creature on it while you look. Have a cup of tea first, won't you?'

Emmy came in then, with the tea tray, and they drank their tea while the kitten, still in its box, was put before the fire to warm up. George sat beside it, prepared to be friendly. Snoodles had gone to sit on top of the bookcase, looking suspicious.

Presently, when the kitten had been carefully examined by the professor and pronounced as well as could be expected, he thanked Mrs Foster for his tea with charming good manners, smiled at Emmy and drove himself away.

'I like him,' observed Mrs Foster, shutting the front door.

Emmy, feeding the kitten bread and milk, didn't say anything.

CHAPTER THREE

ANNELIESE found Ruerd absent-minded when they met on the following day—something which secretly annoyed her. No man, she considered, should be that while he was in her company. He was taking her out to dinner, and she had gone to great pains to look her best. Indeed, heads turned as they entered the restaurant; they made a striking couple, and she was aware of that.

She realised very soon that he had no intention of talking about their future. She had a splendid conceit of herself—it never entered her head that the lack of interest could be anything else but a temporary worry about his work—but she had the sense to say no more about her plans for the future, and laid herself out to be an amusing companion.

She considered that she had succeeded too, for as he drove her back to the hotel she suggested that she might stay for several more days, adding prettily, 'I miss you, Ruerd.'

All he said was, 'Why not stay? Perhaps I can get tickets for that show you want to see. I'll do my best to keep my evenings free.'

He drew up before the hotel and turned to look at her. She looked lovely in the semi-shadows, and he bent to kiss her.

She put up a protesting hand. 'Oh, darling, not now. You always disarrange my hair.'

He got out, opened her door, went with her into the foyer, bade her goodnight with his beautiful manners and drove himself back home, reminding himself that Anneliese was the ideal wife for him. Her coolness was something he would overcome in time. She was beautiful, he told himself, and she knew how to dress, how to manage his large household in Holland, how to be an amusing and charming companion...

He let himself into his house and Beaker and Humphrey came into the hall.

'A pleasant evening, I trust, sir?' asked Beaker smoothly.

The professor nodded absently. Humphrey had reminded him about the kitten and Ermentrude. He frowned; the girl had a habit of popping into his thoughts for no reason. He must remember to ask about the kitten if he saw her in the morning.

Emmy, still refreshed by her days off, was a little early. She settled down before the switchboard, arranged everything just as she liked it and took out her knitting. She was halfway through the first row when she became aware that the professor was there. She turned to look at him and, since it was a crisp autumn morning and the sun was shining and she was pleased to see him, she smiled widely and wished him good morning.

His reply was cool. He took his spectacles out of his pocket, polished them and put them on his commanding nose in order to read the variety of notes left for him at the desk.

Emmy's smile dwindled. She turned back and picked up her knitting and wished that she were busy. Perhaps she shouldn't have spoken to him. She was only being civil.

'It's Friday morning,' she said in a reasonable voice, 'and the sun's shining.'

He took his specs off, the better to stare down at her.

'The kitten—is it thriving?'

'Yes. Oh, yes, and Snoodles and George are so kind to it. Snoodles washes it and it goes to sleep with them. It's a bit of a squash in their basket.' She beamed at him. 'How nice of you to ask, sir.'

He said testily, 'Nice, nice...a useless word. You would do well to enlarge your knowledge of the English language, Ermentrude.'

'That is very rude, Professor,' said Emmy coldly, and was glad that there was a call which kept her busy for a few moments. Presently she turned her head cautiously. The professor had gone.

I shall probably get the sack, she reflected. The idea hung like a shadow over her for the rest of the day. By the time she was relieved, Authority hadn't said anything, but probably in the morning there would be a letter waiting for her, giving her a month's notice.

She went slowly to the entrance, wondering if a written apology to the professor would be a good idea. She began to compose it in her head, pausing on her way to get the words right so that the professor had plenty of time to overtake her as she crossed the entrance hall. He came to a halt in front of her so that she bounced against his waistcoat. Emmy, being Emmy, said at once, 'I'm composing a letter of apology to you, sir, although I really don't see why I should.'

'I don't see why you should either,' he told her. 'What were you going to put in it?'

'Well—"Dear sir", of course, to start with, and then something about being sorry for my impertinence.'

'You consider that you were impertinent?' he wanted to know.

'Good heavens, no, but if I don't apologise I dare say I'll get the sack for being rude or familiar or something.'

She received an icy stare. 'You have a poor opinion of me, Ermentrude.'

She made haste to put things right. 'No, no, I think you are very nice...' She paused. 'Oh, dear, I'll have to think of another word, won't I?' She smiled at him, ignoring the cold eyes. 'But you are nice! I suppose I could call you handsome or sexy...'

He held up a large hand. 'Spare my blushes, Ermentrude. Let us agree, if possible, on nice. I can assure you, though, that you are in no danger of being dismissed.'

'Oh, good. The money's useful at home, you know.'

Which presumably was why she was dressed in less than eye-catching fashion.

'The matter being cleared up, I'll drive you home. It's on my way.'

'No, it's not. Thank you very much, though; I can catch a bus…'

The professor, not in the habit of being thwarted, took her arm and walked her through the door.

In the car he asked, 'What are you doing with your evening? Meeting the boyfriend, going to a cinema, having a meal?'

She glanced at him. He was looking ahead, not smiling.

'Me? Well, I haven't got a boyfriend, so I won't be going to the cinema or out for a meal. Mother and Father are home, so we'll have supper and take George for a walk and see to Snoodles and the kitten. And we'll talk…' She added, 'We like talking.'

When he didn't answer she asked, 'Are you going to have a pleasant evening, Professor?'

'I am taking my finacée to Covent Garden to the ballet, and afterwards we shall have supper somewhere. I do not care for the ballet.'

'Well, no, I dare say men don't. But supper will be fun—especially as it's with your fiancée. Somewhere nice—I mean, fashionable…'

'Indeed, yes.'

Something in his voice made her ask, 'Don't you like going out to supper, either?' She wanted to ask about his fiancée but she didn't dare—besides, the thought of him getting married made her feel vaguely unhappy.

'It depends where it is eaten and with whom. I

would enjoy taking a dog for a long walk in one of the parks and eating my supper...' He paused. 'Afterwards.' Which hadn't been what he had wanted to say.

'That's easy. Get a dog. You could both take it for a walk in the evenings and then go home and have a cosy supper together.'

The professor envisaged Anneliese tramping round Hyde Park and then returning to eat her supper in his company. No dressing up, no waiters, no other diners to admire her—his mind boggled.

He said slowly, 'I will get a dog. From Battersea Dogs Home. Will you come with me and help me choose him, Ermentrude?'

'Me? I'd love to, but what about your fiancée?'

'She returns to Holland in a few days.'

'Oh, well, all right. It'll be a lovely surprise for her when she comes back to see you again.'

'It will certainly be a surprise,' said the professor.

He dropped her off at her house with a casual nod and a goodnight, and began to drive to his own home. I must be out of my mind, he reflected. Anneliese will never agree to a dog, and certainly not to long walks with it. What is it about Ermentrude which makes me behave with such a lack of good sense? And why do I enjoy being with her when I have Anneliese?

Later that evening, after the ballet, while they were having supper, he deliberately talked about Ermentrude, telling Anneliese something of the bomb scare, mentioning the kitten.

Anneliese listened smilingly. 'Darling, how like you to bother about some little girl just because she got scared with that bomb. She sounds very dull. Is she pretty?'

'No.'

'I can just imagine her—plain and mousy and badly dressed. Am I right?'

'Yes. She has a pretty voice, though. A useful attribute in her particular job.'

'I hope she's grateful to you. I mean, for a girl like that it must be a great uplift to be spoken to by you.'

The professor said nothing to that. He thought it unlikely that Ermentrude had experienced any such feeling. Her conversation had been invariably matter-of-fact and full of advice. As far as she was concerned he was just another man.

He smiled at the thought, and Anneliese said, 'Shall we talk about something else? I find this girl a bit boring.'

Never that, thought the professor. Though unable to hold a candle to Anneliese's beauty. If circumstances had not thrown them together briefly, he would never have noticed her. All the same he smiled a little, and Anneliese, despite feeling quite confident of Ruerd's regard for her, decided there and then to do something about it.

Emmy told her mother and father about going to Battersea Dogs Home with the professor.

'When does the professor intend to marry?' asked her mother.

'I've no idea. He doesn't talk about it, and I couldn't ask him. We only talk about things which don't matter.' She sighed. 'I expect he'll tell me when he's got the time to choose a dog.'

But although he wished her good morning and good evening each day, that was all. He didn't ask after the kitten either.

It was towards the end of the next week when Emmy came back from her dinner break and found someone waiting for her. After one look she knew who it was: the professor's fiancée; she had to be. He would, she thought, decide for nothing less than this beautiful creature with the perfect hairdo and the kind of clothes any woman could see at a glance had cost a small fortune.

She said, 'Can I help? Do you want the professor?'

'You know who I am?'

Emmy said diffidently, 'Well, not exactly, but Professor ter Mennolt mentioned that his fiancée was staying in London and—and you're exactly how I imagined you would be.'

'And what was that?' Anneliese sounded amused.

'Quite beautiful and splendidly dressed.' Emmy smiled. 'I'll show you where you can wait while I try and get him for you.'

'Oh, I don't wish to see him. He was telling me about the bomb scare here and what an unpleasant experience it was for everyone. He told me about you, too.' She gave a little laugh. 'I would have known you anywhere from his description—plain and mousy and badly dressed. Oh, dear, I shouldn't have said that. Forgive me—my silly tongue.'

Emmy said quietly, 'Yes, that's a very good description of me, isn't it? Are you enjoying your visit? London in the autumn is rather special.'

'The shopping is good, and we enjoy going out in the evenings. Do you go out much?'

Her voice, too loud and with a strong accent, grated on Emmy's ears.

'Not very much. It's quite a long day here. When I do go home I walk our dog…'

'You have a dog? I do not like them, and certainly not in the house. I dislike cats also—their hairs…'

Emmy's relief telephonist was showing signs of impatience, which made it easy for her to say that she had to return to her switchboard.

'It's been nice meeting you,' said Emmy mendaciously. For once she agreed with the professor that 'nice' was a useless word and quite inappropriate. She hoped that she would never see the girl again.

'I won't keep you from your work. It was most satisfying to find that Ruerd's description of you was so accurate.'

Anneliese didn't offer a hand, nor did she say goodbye. Emmy and the relief watched her go.

'Who's she?'

'Professor ter Mennolt's fiancée.'

'The poor man. She'll lead him a dance; you see if she doesn't.'

'She's very beautiful,' said Emmy, in a voice which conveyed nothing of her feelings. Though her goodnight in reply to the professor's passing greeting was austere in the extreme.

The following evening, after a wakeful night, and a different day, it held all the hauteur of royalty in a rage.

Not that the professor appeared to notice. 'I'm free on Sunday. Will you help me choose a dog—some time in the morning—or afternoon if you prefer?'

He didn't sound friendly; he sounded like someone performing an obligation with reluctance. 'My fiancée has gone back to Holland this morning,' he added inconsequentially.

'No,' said Emmy coldly. 'I'm afraid I can't.'

He eyed her narrowly. 'Ah, of course—you consider it very incorrect of me to spend a few hours with someone other than Anneliese. The moment she sets foot in the plane, too.'

'No. At least partly.' She frowned. 'It was the bomb which…' she sought for the right words '…was the reason for you speaking to me. In such circumstances that was natural. There is no need—'

He said silkily, 'My dear Emmy, you do not for one moment imagine that you are a serious rival to Anneliese? For God's sake, all I have asked of you is to help me choose a dog.'

'What a silly thing to say,' said Emmy roundly. 'It is the last thing I would think. I am, as you so clearly described me, plain and mousy and badly dressed. Certainly no companion for you, even at a dogs' home!'

He said slowly, 'When did you meet Anneliese?'

'She came here to see me. She wanted to see if you had described me accurately.' Emmy added stonily, 'You had.'

The professor stood looking at her for a long minute. He said, 'I'm sorry, Ermentrude, it was unpardonable of me to discuss you with Anneliese and I had no idea that she had come here to see you.'

'Well,' said Emmy matter-of-factly, 'it's what any woman would do—you could have been lying about me.' She gave a rueful smile. 'I might have been a gorgeous blonde.'

'I do not lie, Ermentrude. I will not lie to you now and tell you that you are neither mousy nor plain nor badly dressed. You are a very nice—and I use the word in its correct sense—person, and I apologise for hurting you. One day someone—a man—will look at you and love you. He won't notice the clothes; he will see only your lovely eyes and the kindness in your face. He will find you beautiful and tell you so.'

Emmy said, 'Pigs might fly, but it's kind of you to say so. It doesn't matter, you know. I've known since I was a little girl that I had no looks to speak of. It's not as though I'm surprised.' She gave a very small sigh. 'Your Anneliese is very beautiful, and I hope you'll be very happy with her.'

The professor remained silent and she put through an outside call. He was still there when she had done it.

He was not a man in the habit of asking a favour twice, but he did so now.

'Will you help me choose a dog, Ermentrude?'

She turned to look at him. 'Very well, Professor. In the afternoon, if you don't mind. About two o'clock?'

'Thank you. I'll call for you then.'

He went away, and just for a while she was too busy to reflect over their conversation. Which was a good thing, she decided, for her bottled up feelings might spill over. She would go with him on Sunday, but after that good morning and good evening would be sufficient.

Later, when she considered she had cooled down enough to think about it, she thought that it wasn't that he had discussed her with Anneliese so much as the fact that he hadn't denied calling her plain which had made her angry. On the other hand, supposing he had denied it—and she'd known that he was lying? Would she have been just as angry? In all fairness to him she thought that she would. She liked him even if there was no reason to do so.

Her mother and father, when she told them on Sunday, answered exactly as she had known they would. Her mother said, 'Wear a warm coat, dear, it gets chilly in the afternoons.'

Her father said, 'Good idea—enjoy yourself, Emmy!'

Her parents were going to Coventry on the following day—the last week away from home, her mother assured her, for her father would be round and about London after that. 'You're sure you don't mind?' she asked anxiously. 'I know you're busy all day, but it's lonely for you, especially in the evenings.'

'Mother, I've heaps to do, honestly, and I'll get the garden tidied up for the winter.' Though the garden was a miserably small patch of grass surrounded by narrow flowerbeds which Emmy would hopefully plant.

The professor arrived punctually, exchanged suitable and civil remarks with her mother and father and ushered Emmy into the car. She had gone to great pains to improve her appearance. True, her jacket and skirt were off the peg, bought to last, and therefore a useful brown—a colour which didn't suit her. But the cream blouse under the jacket was crisp, and her gloves and shoulder bag were leather, elderly but well cared for. Since her brown shoes were well-worn loafers, she had borrowed a pair of her mother's. Court shoes with quite high heels. They pinched a bit, but they looked all right.

The professor, eyeing her unobtrusively, was surprised to find himself wishing that some fairy godmother would wave a wand over Emmy and transform the brown outfit into something pretty. He was surprised, too, that she wore her clothes with an air—when he had thought about it, and that hadn't been often, he had supposed that she had little interest in clothes. He saw now that he was wrong.

He made casual conversation as he drove, and Emmy replied cautiously, not at all at her ease, wishing she hadn't come. Once they had reached the dogs' home she forgot all about that. She had never seen so many dogs, nor heard such a concert of barking.

They went to and fro looking at doggy faces, some pressed up to the front of their shelters, eager for attention, others sitting indifferently at the back. 'They're pretending that they don't mind if no one wants them,' said Emmy. 'I wish we could have them all.'

The professor smiled down at her. Her face was alight with interest and compassion and, rather to his surprise, didn't look in the least plain.

'I'm afraid one is the best I can do. Have you seen a dog which you think might suit me? There are so many, I have no preference at the moment.'

They had stopped in front of a shelter to watch the antics of an overgrown puppy, chosen by a family of children and expressing his delight. There were a lot of dogs; Emmy looked at them all and caught the eye of a large woolly dog with the kindly face of a Labrador and a tremendous sweeping tail. He was sitting in the corner, and it was obvious to her that he was too proud to attract attention. Only his eyes begged her...

'That one,' said Emmy. 'There.'

The professor studied the dog. 'Yes,' he said. 'That's the one.'

The dog couldn't have heard them, but he came slowly to the front of the shelter and wagged his tail, staring up at them. When, after the necessary formalities had been gone through, the professor fastened a new collar round the dog's powerful neck, he gave a small, happy bark.

'You see?' said Emmy. 'He knew you'd have him. He's so lovely. Did they say what breed he was?'

'Well, no. There is some uncertainty. He was left to fend for himself until some kind soul brought him here. He's been here for some time. He's rather on the large side for the average household.'

They got into the car, and the dog settled warily on a blanket on the back seat.

'You do like him?' Emmy asked anxiously.

'Yes. An instant rapport. I can only hope that Beaker will feel the same way.'

'Beaker?'

'Yes, my man. He runs the house for me. Did I mention him when I told you about Humphrey? He's a splendid fellow.'

He drew up in front of his house and Emmy said, 'Oh, is this where you live? It's not like London at all, is it? Is there a garden?'

'Yes—come and see it?'

'I'd like to, but you'll have a lot to do with the dog, and you have a day off today, too, haven't you?'

He said gravely that, yes, he had, but he was doing nothing else with it. 'So please come in and meet Beaker and Humphrey and help me to get this beast settled in.'

Beaker, opening the door, did no more than lift a dignified eyebrow at the sight of the dog. He bowed gravely to Emmy and shook the hand she offered. 'A handsome beast,' he pronounced. 'Straight into the garden, sir?'

'Yes, Beaker. He's been at the home for a long time so he's a bit uncertain about everything. Ten minutes in the garden may help. Then tea, if you please.'

Beaker slid away and the professor led Emmy across the hall, into the sitting room and out of the French window into the garden. For London it was quite large, with a high brick wall and one or two trees—a mountain ash, a small silver birch, bare of leaves now, and a very old apple tree.

The dog needed no urging to explore, and Emmy said, 'Oh, how delightful. It must look lovely in the spring—lots of bulbs?'

When he nodded, watching her face, she added, 'And an apple tree. We used to have several...'

'You had a large garden?' he asked gently.

'Yes. A bit rambling, but everything grew. It was heaven to go out in the morning. And the air—there isn't much air here, is there? Well, not around St Luke's.' She turned away, annoyed with herself for saying so much, as though she had asked to be pitied. 'What will you call him?'

'I was hoping you would think of a name.'

'Something dignified and a bit regal to make up for his unhappy life.' She thought about it. 'No, it should be a name that sounds as though he's one of the family. Charlie—when I was a little girl I wanted a brother called Charlie.'

'Charlie it shall be.' The professor called the dog,

and he came at once, lolloping across the lawn, his tongue hanging out, his preposterous tail waving.

'You see?' said Emmy happily. 'He knows.'

The professor put a gentle hand on Charlie's woolly head. 'I think he has earned his tea, don't you? Let us go indoors; we've earned ours, too.'

'Oh, well,' said Emmy. 'I didn't mean to stay, only to see your garden.'

'Charlie and I will be deeply offended if you don't stay for tea. What is more, Beaker will think his efforts aren't sufficiently tempting.'

Not meaning to, she smiled at him. 'Tea would be very nice.'

They had it in the sitting room, sitting by the fire with Beaker's efforts on a low table between them. Tiny sandwiches, fairy cakes, a chocolate cake and miniature macaroons, flanked by a silver teapot and paper-thin china cups and saucers.

Charlie, mindful of his manners, sat himself carefully down before the fire, hopeful eyes on the cake. Presently Beaker opened the door and Humphrey came in, circled the room slowly and finally sat down beside Charlie. He ignored the dog and stared into the flames, and Emmy said anxiously, 'Will they get on, do you think?'

'Yes. Humphrey has no intention of losing face, though. Charlie will have to play second fiddle.'

'Oh, well, I don't suppose he'll mind now he has a family of his own. Will your fiancée like him?'

The professor bit into some cake. 'No. I'm afraid not.'

When Emmy looked concerned he added, 'I spend a good deal of the year in Holland and, of course, Charlie will stay here with Beaker.'

She poured second cups. 'Do you have a dog in Holland?'

'Two. A Jack Russell and an Irish wolfhound.'

She wanted to ask him about his home in Holland, but although he was friendly he was also aloof. Emmy, willing and eager to be friends with everyone, found that daunting. Besides, she wasn't sure what to make of him. In his company she was happy even when they weren't on the best of terms, but away from him, looking at him from a distance as it were, she told herself that there was no point in continuing their friendship—if it could be called that.

Tea finished, she said a little shyly, 'I think I had better go home, Professor. Mother and Father are going to Coventry in the morning. It will be Father's last job away from home.'

'He enjoys his work?' the professor asked idly.

'He'd rather be a schoolmaster, and not in London.'

'If he were to get a post in the country, you would go with your parents?'

'Yes, oh, yes. I expect I'd have to look for another kind of job. I like needlework and sewing. I expect I could find work in a shop or helping a dressmaker.' She added defiantly, 'I like clothes...'

He prudently kept silent about that. He had a brief memory of Anneliese, exquisitely turned out in clothes which must have cost what to Emmy would have been a small fortune. Emmy, he reflected, would look almost pretty if she were to dress in the same way as Anneliese dressed.

He didn't ask her to stay, but waited while she said goodbye to Charlie and Humphrey and thanked Beaker for her tea, and then went with her to the car.

The streets were almost empty on a late Sunday afternoon and the journey didn't take long. At the house he declined her hesitant offer to go in. He opened her door, thanked her for her help, still standing on the pavement in the dull little street, and waited while she opened the house door and went inside.

Driving back home, he reflected that he had enjoyed his afternoon with Emmy. She was a good companion; she didn't chat and she was a good listener, and when she did have something to say it was worth listening to. He must remember to let her know from time to time how Charlie progressed.

A pleasant afternoon, Emmy told her parents, and the dog, Charlie, was just what she would have chosen for herself. 'And I had a lovely tea,' she told them. 'The professor has a man who runs his home for him and makes the most delicious cakes.'

'A nice house?' asked her mother.

Emmy described it—what she had seen of it—and the garden as well.

'It's not like London,' she told them. 'In the garden you might be miles away in the country.'

'You miss our old home, don't you, Emmy?' her father asked.

'Yes, I do, but we're quite cosy here.' Empty words which neither of them believed.

'I dare say the professor will tell you how the dog settles down,' observed her mother.

'Perhaps.' Emmy sounded doubtful.

She didn't see him for several days, and when he at length stopped to speak to her on his way home one evening, it was only to tell her that Charlie was nicely settled in.

'A very biddable animal,' he told her. 'Goes everywhere with me.'

He bade her good evening in a frosty voice and went away, leaving her wondering why he was so aloof.

He's had a busy day, reflected Emmy, he'll be more friendly in the morning.

Only in the morning he wasn't there. Audrey, who always knew the latest gossip, told her as she took over that he had gone to Birmingham.

'Gets around, doesn't he? Going back to Holland for Christmas too. Shan't see much of him—not that he's exactly friendly. Well, what do you expect? He's a senior consultant and no end of a big noise.'

Which was, Emmy conceded, quite true. And a good reason for remembering that next time he might pause for a chat. He was beginning to loom rather large on the edge of her dull, humdrum life, which wouldn't do at all. Sitting there at her switchboard, she reminded herself that they had nothing in common— Well, Charlie perhaps, and being in the hospital when the bomb went off.

Besides, she reminded herself bitterly, he considered her plain and dowdy. If I could spend half as much on myself as that Anneliese of his, reflected Emmy waspishly, I'd show him that I'm not in the least dowdy, and a visit to a beauty salon would work wonders even with a face like mine.

Since neither of their wishes were likely to be fulfilled, she told herself to forget the professor; there were plenty of other things to think about.

It was a pity that she couldn't think of a single one of them—within minutes he was back in her thoughts, making havoc of her good resolutions.

She was in the professor's thoughts too, much to his annoyance. The tiresome girl, he reflected, and why do I have this urge to do something to improve her life? For all I know she is perfectly content with the way she lives. She is young; she could get a job wherever she wishes, buy herself some decent clothes, meet people, find a boyfriend. All of which was nonsense, and he knew it. She deserved better, he considered, a home and work away from London and that pokey little house.

But even if she had the chance to change he knew that she wouldn't leave her home. He had liked her parents; they had fallen on bad times through no fault of her father. Of course, if he could get a post as a schoolmaster again away from London that would solve the problem. Ermentrude could leave St Luke's and shake the dust of London from her well-polished but well-worn shoes.

The professor put down the notes he was studying, took off his spectacles, polished them and put them back onto his nose. He would miss her.

'This is ridiculous,' he said to himself. 'I don't even know the girl.'

He forbore from adding that he knew Ermentrude as if she were himself, had done since he had first seen her. He was going to marry Anneliese, he reminded himself, and Ermentrude had demonstrated often enough that she had no interest in him. He was too old for her, and she regarded him in a guarded manner which made it plain that in her eyes he was no more than someone she met occasionally at work…

The professor was an honourable man; he had asked Anneliese to marry him—not loving her but knowing that she would make a suitable wife—and there was no possible reason to break his word. Even if Ermentrude loved him, something which was so unlikely that it was laughable.

He gave his lectures, dealt with patients he had been asked to see, arranged appointments for the future and always at the back of his mind was Ermentrude. She would never be his wife but there was a good deal he could do to make her life happier, and, when he got back once more to Chelsea, he set about doing it.

CHAPTER FOUR

DESPITE her resolutions, Emmy missed the professor. She had looked forward to seeing him going to and fro at St Luke's, even if he took no notice of her. He was there, as it were, and she felt content just to know that he was. Of course, she thought about him. She thought about Anneliese too, doubtless getting ready for a grand wedding, spending money like water, secure in the knowledge that she was going to marry a man who could give her everything she could want.

'I only hope she deserves it,' said Emmy, talking to herself and surprising the porter who had brought her coffee.

'If it's women you're talking about, love, you can take it from me they don't deserve nothing. Take my word for it; I'm a married man.'

'Go on with you!' said Emmy. 'I've seen your wife, she's pretty, and you've got that darling baby.'

'I could have done worse.' He grinned at her. 'There's always an exception to every rule, so they say.'

'No sign of our handsome professor,' said Audrey when she came on duty. 'Having fun in Birmingham, I shouldn't wonder. Won't be able to do that once he's a married man, will he? Perhaps he's going straight over to Holland and not coming back here until after Christmas.'

'Christmas is still six weeks away.'

'Don't tell me that he can't do what he chooses when he wants to.'

'I think that if he has patients and work here he'll stay until he's no longer needed. I know you don't like him, but everyone else does.'

'Including you,' said Audrey with a snigger.

'Including me,' said Emmy soberly.

Emmy was on night duty again. Her mother was home and so was her father, now inspecting various schools in outer London and coming home tired each evening. He didn't complain, but the days were long and often unsatisfactory. He had been told that the man he had replaced would be returning to work within a week or ten days, which meant that he would be returning to his badly paid teaching post. Thank heaven, he thought, that Emmy had her job too. Somehow they would manage.

Emmy had dealt with the usual early enquiries, and except for internal calls the evening was quiet. She took out her knitting—a pullover for her father's Christmas present—and began the complicated business of picking up stitches around the neck. She was halfway round it when she became aware of the professor standing behind her. Her hand jerked and she dropped a clutch of stitches.

'There, look what you've made me do!' she said, and turned round to look at him.

'You knew that I was here?' He sounded amused. 'But I hadn't spoken...'

'No, well—I knew there was someone.' She was mumbling, not looking at him now, remembering all at once that what was fast becoming friendship must be nipped in the bud.

She began to pick up the dropped stitches, and wished that the silent switchboard would come alive. Since he just stood there, apparently content with the silence, she asked in a polite voice, 'I hope that Charlie is well, sir?'

The professor, equally polite, assured her that his dog was in excellent health, and registered the 'sir' with a rueful lift of the eyebrows.

'Your kitten?' he asked in his turn.

'Oh, he's splendid, and George and Snoodles take such care of him.'

The professor persevered. 'Has he a name?'

'Enoch. Mother had a cat when she was a little girl called Enoch, and now he's clean and brushed he's the same colour. Ginger with a white waistcoat.' She added, 'Sir.'

The professor saw that he was making no headway; Ermentrude was making it plain that she was being polite for politeness' sake. Apparently she had decided that their friendship, such as it was, was to go no further. Just as well, he reflected, I'm getting far too interested in the girl. He bade her a cool goodnight and went away, and Emmy picked up her knitting once more.

A most unsatisfactory meeting, she reflected. On

the other hand it had been satisfactory, hadn't it? She had let him see that their casual camaraderie had been just that—casual, engendered by circumstances. He was shortly going to be married, she reminded herself; he would become immersed in plans for his wedding with Anneliese.

She was mistaken in this. The professor was immersed in plans, but not to do with his future. The wish to transform Emmy's dull life into one with which she would be happy had driven him to do something about it.

He had friends everywhere; it wasn't too difficult to meet a man he had known at Cambridge and who was now headmaster of a boys' prep school in Dorset. The professor was lucky: a schoolmaster had been forced to leave owing to ill health and there was, he was told cautiously, a vacancy. 'But for the right man. I've only your word for it that this Foster's OK.'

The headmaster wrote in his notebook and tore out the page. 'He can give me a ring...'

The professor shook his head. 'That wouldn't do. If he or his daughter discovered that I was behind it, he'd refuse at once.'

'Got a daughter, has he? Thought you were getting married.'

The professor smiled. 'You can rule out any romantic thoughts, but I would like to help her get out of a life she isn't enjoying; away from London. To do that her father must get a post somewhere in the country, for that's where she belongs.'

His friend sighed. 'Tell you what I'll do. I'll con-
coct a tale, you know the kind of thing—I'd met
someone who knew someone who knew this Foster,
and as there was a vacancy et cetera… Will that do?
But remember, Ruerd, if I contract any one of these
horrible conditions you're so famous for treating, I
shall expect the very best treatment—free!'

'A promise I hope I shall never need to keep.' They
shook hands, and his friend went home and told his
wife that Ruerd ter Mennolt seemed to be putting
himself to a great deal of trouble for some girl or
other at St Luke's.

'I thought he was marrying that Anneliese of his?'

'And still is, it seems. He was always a man to
help lame dogs over stiles.'

'Anneliese doesn't like dogs,' said his wife.

It was the very next day when the letter arrived, inviting Mr Foster to present himself for an interview.
And it couldn't have come at a better time, for with
the same post came a notice making him redundant
from his teaching post on the first of December. They
sat over their supper, discussing this marvellous
stroke of luck.

'Though we mustn't count our chickens before they
are hatched,' said Mr Foster. 'How fortunate that I
have Thursday free; I'll have to go by train.'

Emmy went into the kitchen and took the biscuit
tin down from the dresser-shelf and counted the
money inside. It was money kept for emergencies,
and this was an emergency of the best kind.

'Will there be a house with the job?' she asked. 'Littleton Mangate—that's a small village, isn't it? Somewhere in the Blackmore Vale.' She smiled widely. 'Oh, Father, it's almost too good to be true…'

'So we mustn't bank on it until I've had my interview, Emmy. Once that's over and I've been appointed we can make plans.'

The next day, replying sedately to the professor's grave greeting, Emmy almost choked in her efforts not to tell him about the good news. Time enough, she told herself, when her father had got the job. Only then, too, if he asked her.

'Which he won't,' she told George as she brushed him before taking him on his evening trot.

The professor, it seemed, was reluctant as she was to resume their brief conversations. He never failed to greet her if he should pass the switchboard, but that was all. She felt bereft and vaguely resentful, which, seeing that she had wanted it that way, seemed rather hard on him. But at least it boosted her resolve to forget him. Something not easily done since she saw him willy-nilly on most days.

Her father, in his best suit, a neatly typed CV in his coat pocket, left on Thursday morning on an early train, leaving Emmy to fidget through her day's work, alternately positive that her father would get the post and then plunged into despair because he had been made redundant, and finding a job would be difficult, perhaps impossible. In a moment of rare self-pity she saw herself sitting in front of the switchboard for the rest of her working life.

The professor, catching sight of her dejected back view, was tempted to stop and speak to her, but he didn't. A helping hand was one thing, getting involved with her spelt danger. It was a good thing, he reflected, that he would be going over to Holland shortly. He must see as much of Anneliese as possible.

The bus ride home that evening took twice as long as usual, or so it seemed to Emmy. She burst into the house at length and rushed into the kitchen.

Her mother and father were there, turning to look at her with happy faces. 'You've got it,' said Emmy. 'I knew you would, Father. I can't believe it.'

She flung her coat onto a chair, poured herself a cup of tea from the pot and said, 'Tell me all about it. Is there a house? When do you start? Did you like the headmaster?'

'I've been accepted,' said Mr Foster. 'But my references still have to be checked. There's a house, a very nice one, a converted lodge in the school grounds. I am to take over as soon as possible as they are short of a form master. There are still three weeks or so of the term.'

'So you'll be going in a day or two? And Mother? Is the house furnished?'

'No. Curtains and carpets…'

Mr Foster added slowly, 'Your Mother and I have been talking it over. You will have to give a month's notice, will you not? Supposing we have as much furniture as possible sent to Dorset, would you stay on for the last month, Emmy? Could you bear to do that? We'll take George and Snoodles and Enoch with us. The house can be put up for sale at once. There's little chance of it selling quickly, but one never knows. Could you do that? In the meantime your mother will get the house at Littleton Mangate habitable. We can spend Christmas together...'

Emmy agreed at once. She didn't much like the idea of living alone in a half-empty house, but it would be for a few weeks, no more. The idea of leaving St Luke's gave her a lovely feeling of freedom.

'Money?' she asked.

'The bank will give me a loan against this house.' Her father frowned. 'This isn't an ideal arrangement, Emmy, but we really haven't much choice. If you give a month's notice you'll be free by Christmas, and in the meantime there is always the chance that the house will sell.'

'I think that's a splendid idea, Father. When do you start? Almost at once? Mother and I can start packing up and she can join you in a few days. I'll only need a bed and a table and chairs. There's that man—Mr Stokes—at the end of the street. He does removals.'

'I'm not sure that we should leave you,' said her mother worriedly. 'You're sure you don't mind? We can't think what else to do. There's so little time.'

'I'll be quite all right, Mother. It's for such a short time anyway. It's all so exciting...'

They spent the rest of the evening making lists,

deciding what to take and what to leave. Tired and excited by the time she got to her bed, Emmy's last waking thought was that once she had left St Luke's she would never see the professor again.

Going to work the next morning, she thought that perhaps she would tell him of the unexpected change in her life.

However, he didn't give her the chance. Beyond an austere good morning he had nothing to say to her, and later, when he left the hospital, he had a colleague with him.

Oh, well, said Emmy to herself, I can always tell him tomorrow.

Only he wasn't there in the morning; it wasn't until the day was half-done that she heard that he had gone to Holland.

She told herself that it didn't matter at all, that there was no reason to expect him to be interested in her future. She had already given in her notice and would not tell anyone about it.

Back home that evening, she found her mother already busy, turning out drawers and cupboards. 'Your father's arranged for Mr Stokes to collect the furniture in three days' time.' She beamed at Emmy. 'Oh, darling, it's all so wonderful. I don't believe it. Your father is so happy; so am I. It is a great pity that you can't come with us. I hate the idea of you being here on your own.'

Emmy, wrapping up the best china in newspaper and stowing it carefully in a tea chest, paused to say,

'Don't worry, Mother. I'll be working all day, and by the time I get back here and have a meal it'll be time to go to bed—the days will fly by. Won't it be lovely having Christmas away from here?'

Her mother paused in stacking books. 'You've hated it here, haven't you, darling? So have I—so has your father. But we can forget all this once we're at Littleton Mangate. Just think, too, when we've sold this house there'll be some money to spend. Enough for you to go to a school of embroidery or whatever else you want to do. You'll meet people of your own age, too.'

Emmy nodded and smiled and, much against her will, thought about the professor.

He, too, was thinking about her, not wishing to but unable to prevent his thoughts going their own way. It was easier to put her to the back of his head while he was at the various hospitals—Leiden, the Hague, Amsterdam, Rotterdam. There were patients for him in all of these, and he was able to dismiss any thoughts other than those to do with his work while he was in the hospitals consulting, examining, deciding on treatment, seeing, in some cases, anxious relations and reassuring patients.

His days were long and busy but when he drove himself home each evening he had time to think. Anneliese was in France, but she would be back soon and he would spend his leisure with her. But in the meantime his time was his own.

Each evening he turned into the drive leading to

his house and sighed with content at the sight of it. It was on the edge of a village, a stately old house behind the dunes, the North sea stretching away to the horizon, magnificent stretch of sand sweeping into the distance, north and south. The house had been built by his great-great-grandfather, and was a solid edifice, secure against the bitter winter winds, its rooms large, the windows tall and narrow, and the front door solid enough to withstand a siege.

Ruerd had been born there, and between schools, universities and hospital appointments went back to it as often as he could. His two sisters and younger brother—the former married, the latter still at medical school—were free to come and go as they wished, but the house was his now that his father, a retired surgeon, and his mother, lived in den Haag.

He had had a tiring day in Rotterdam, and the lighted windows welcomed him as he got out of the car. They were not the only welcome either—the door was opened and the dogs dashed out to greet him, the wolfhound and the Jack Russell pushing and jostling to get near their master. They all went into the house together, into the large square hall with its black and white marble floor, its plain plastered walls hung with paintings in ornate gilded frames.

They were halfway across it when they were joined by an elderly man, small and rotund, who trotted ahead of them to open double doors to one side of the hall.

The room the professor entered was large and high-ceilinged, with a great hooded fireplace on either side of which were vast sofas with a Regency mahogany centre table between them. There were two tub wing armchairs with a walnut card table between them, and a couple of Dutch mahogany and marquetry armchairs on either side of a Georgian breakfast table set between two of the long windows overlooking the grounds at the back of the house.

Against the walls there were walnut display cabinets, their shelves filled with silver and porcelain, reflecting the light from the cut-glass chandelier and the ormolu wall lights. It was a beautiful room, and magnificent; it was also lived in. There were bowls of flowers here and there, a pile of newspapers and magazines on one of the tables, a dog basket to the side of the fireplace.

The professor settled his vast frame in one of the armchairs, allowed the Jack Russell to scramble onto his knee and the wolfhound to drape himself over his feet, and poured himself a drink from the tray on the table beside him. A quiet evening, he thought with satisfaction, and, since he wasn't due anywhere until the following afternoon, a long walk with the dogs in the morning.

He was disturbed by his manservant, who came bearing letters on a salver, looking apologetic.

The professor picked them up idly. 'No phone calls, Cokker?'

'Juffrouw van Moule telephoned, to remind you that you will be dining with her family tomorrow evening.'

'Oh, Lord, I had forgotten…thank you, Cokker.'

'Anna wishes to know if half an hour is sufficient for you before dinner, *mijnheer*.'

'As soon as she likes, Cokker. It's good to be home...'

'And good to have you here,' said Cokker. They smiled at each other, for Cokker had been with the family when the professor had been born and now, a sprightly sixty-year-old, had become part and parcel of it.

The professor took the dogs for a walk after dinner, across several acres of his own grounds and into the country lane beyond. It was a chilly night, but there was a moon and stars and later there would be a frost.

He strolled along, thinking about Ermentrude. By now her father would know if he had the post he had collocated. No doubt Ermentrude would tell him all about it when he got back to St Luke's. She would give in her notice, of course, and go to Dorset with her parents and he wouldn't see her again. Which was just as well. It was, he told himself, merely a passing attraction—not even that. All he had done was to take the opportunity to improve her life.

'She will be quite happy in the country again,' he told Solly, the wolfhound. He stooped to pick up Tip, who was getting tired, and tucked the little dog under one arm. He turned for home, dismissed Ermentrude from his mind and steered his thoughts to his future bride.

Later, lying in his great four-poster bed, Ermentrude was there again, buried beneath his thoughts and contriving to upset them.

'The girl's a nuisance,' said the professor to the

empty room. 'I hope that by the time I get back to St Luke's she will be gone.'

His well-ordered life, he reflected, was being torn in shreds by a plain-faced girl who made no bones about letting him see that she had no interest in him. He slept badly and awoke in an ill humour which he had difficulty in shaking off during the day.

It was only that evening, sitting beside Anneliese at her parents' dining table, joining in the talk with the other guests, aware that Anneliese was looking particularly beautiful, that he managed to dismiss Ermentrude from his mind.

Anneliese was at her best. She knew that she looked delightful, and she exerted all her charm. She was intelligent, asking him all the right questions about his work at the hospitals he was visiting, talking knowledgeably about the health service in Holland, listening with apparent interest when he outlined the same service in England.

'Such a pity you have to go back there before Christmas. But of course you'll be back here then, won't you? Mother and I will come and stay for a while; we can discuss the wedding.'

She was clever enough not to say more than that, but went on lightly, 'Do you see any more of that funny little thing you befriended at St Luke's?'

Before he could answer, she said, 'Ruerd got involved in a bomb explosion in London.' She addressed the table at large. 'It must have been very exciting, and there was this girl who works there whom he took home—I suppose she was in shock. I saw her when I was staying in London. So plain, my dears, and all the wrong clothes. Not at all his type. Was she, Ruerd?' She turned to smile at him.

The professor had his anger nicely in check. 'Miss Foster is a brave young lady. I think perhaps none of us know enough of her to discuss her. It is quite difficult to keep calm and do whatever it is you have to do when there's an emergency, and to keep on doing it until you're fit to drop. In such circumstances, it hardly matters whether one is plain or pretty, old or young.'

Anneliese gave a little laugh. 'Oh, Ruerd, I didn't mean to be unkind. The poor girl. And we, all sitting here in comfort talking about something we know very little about.' She touched his arm. 'Forgive me and tell us what you think of the new hospital. You were there yesterday, weren't you?'

The rest of the evening passed off pleasantly enough, but, driving himself home, the professor reflected that he hadn't enjoyed it. He had never liked Anneliese's family and friends overmuch, supposing vaguely that once they were married she would welcome his more serious friends, live the quiet life he enjoyed. He tried to imagine them married and found it impossible.

She had seemed so suitable when he'd asked her to marry him—interested in his work, anxious to meet his friends, telling him how she loved to live in the country. 'With children, of course, and dogs and horses,' she had added, and he had believed her.

Yet that very evening he had stood by, while she

talked to some of her friends, and listened to her complaining sharply about the nuisance of having to visit a cousin with young children. 'They're such a bore,' she had said.

Her mother, a formidable matron who enjoyed dictating to everyone around her, had chimed in, saying, 'Children should stay in the nursery until they're fit to mix with their elders. I have always advised young girls of my acquaintance that that is the best for them. Besides, they can hamper one's life so. A good nanny is the answer.' She had smiled around at her listeners, saying, 'And I have given Anneliese the same advice, have I not, my dear?'

Her words, echoing in his head, filled him with disquiet.

Emmy meanwhile was busy. She was happy too. At least she told herself that she was several times a day. To live in the country again would be heaven—only would it be quite heaven if she was never to see the professor again? It wouldn't, but there was nothing to be done about that, and it was, after all, something she had wanted badly. Besides that, her mother and father were over the moon. She applied herself to the packing up with a cheerful energy which wasn't quite genuine, buoyed up by her mother's obvious delight.

Mr Stokes, with his rather decrepit van, and an old man and a young boy to help him, stowed the furniture tidily, leaving Emmy's bedroom intact, and a table and two chairs in the kitchen, as well as the bare necessities for living.

'It won't be for long,' said Emmy cheerfully. 'There are two lots of people coming to view the house tomorrow; I'm sure it will be sold by the time I leave.'

Her mother said anxiously, 'You will get a hot meal at the hospital, Emmy? And do keep the electric fire on while you are in the house. Empty houses are so cold.' She frowned. 'I do wonder if there might have been some other way...'

'Stop worrying, Mother. I only need a bed and somewhere to have breakfast.' She didn't mention the long evenings alone and the solitary suppers. After all, it was for such a short time.

She was on night duty again, so she was there to see her mother, sitting beside Mr Stokes, leave for their new home. After they had gone she went into the kitchen and made herself some coffee. The house looked shabbier than ever now that it was almost empty, and without the animals it was so quiet. She put everything ready for an evening meal and went to bed. She was already some days into her notice. It was a satisfying thought as she dropped off. Everything was going according to plan, she thought with satisfaction.

Only she was wrong. Audrey hardly gave her time to get her coat off the following evening before bursting into furious speech.

'The nerve,' she cried. 'And there's nothing to be done about it—or so I'm told. Reorganisation, indeed, necessary amalgamation to cut expenses...'

Emmy took the envelope Audrey was offering her. 'What's the matter? What are you talking about?'

'Read it for yourself. I'm going home—and don't expect to see me tomorrow.'

She stomped away and Emmy sat down and read the letter in the envelope.

There were to be changes, she read, and regretfully her services would no longer be required. With the opening of the new hospital across the river, St Luke's and Bennett's hospitals would amalgamate and the clerical staff from Bennett's would take over various functions, of which the switchboard was one. The letter pointed out that she would be given a reference, and the likelihood of her getting a new job was high. It ended with a mealy-mouthed paragraph thanking her for her loyal services which as she had already given notice, would terminate on Friday next.

She read it through again, carefully, in case she had missed something. But it was clear enough—in two days' time she would be jobless.

She could, of course, join her mother and father. On the other hand there was far more chance of the house being sold if there was someone there to keep the estate agents on their toes and show people around. By the end of the night she had decided to say nothing to her parents. She would be able to manage on her own and she would have a week's salary, and surely an extra month's money, since she had been given barely two days' notice.

It would have been nice to have had someone to

have talked things over with. The professor would have been ideal...

As it was, when the porter brought her coffee she forgot her own troubles when he told her that he was to go too. 'They've offered me a job in that new place across the river—less money, and takes me much longer to get to work. Haven't got much choice, though, have I? With a wife and baby to look after?' He glanced at her. 'What'll you do, Emmy?'

'Me? Oh, I'll be all right. Audrey was very angry...'

'You bet she was. Proper blew her top, she did. Didn't do no good. Wrongful dismissal, she said, but it seems it isn't. It's like when a firm goes bankrupt and everyone just goes home. If there's no money, see? What else is there to do?'

'Well, good luck with your job, anyway, and thanks for the coffee.'

Emmy hadn't believed Audrey when she had said that she wouldn't be there in the morning, but she had meant it. Emmy, going off duty late because a relief telephonist had had to be called in, was too tired to notice the icy rain and the leaden sky. Home, she thought, even if it is only my bedroom and a table and chairs.

Only they didn't look very welcoming when she let herself into the empty house. She boiled an egg, made toast and a pot of tea and took herself off to bed. When she had had a sleep she would mull over the turn of events and see how best to deal with it. One thing was certain: there was no way of changing it. And, being a sensible girl, she put her head on the pillow and slept.

She had time enough to think when she got up in the late afternoon. It was still raining and almost dark, and she was glad they had left the curtains hanging and some of the carpets. She showered, made tea and sat down in the kitchen to think. She would call into the estate agents on her way home in the morning and spur them on a bit. The market was slow, they had told her father, but the house was small, in fairly good order and soundly built, like all the other houses in the row. Its selling price was modest, well within the reach of anyone prudent enough to have saved a little capital and who could get a mortgage.

She allowed herself to dream a bit. There would be a little money—not much, but perhaps enough for all of them to have new clothes, perhaps have a holiday—although being in Dorset would be like a holiday itself. She would get a chance to go to a needlework school—night classes, perhaps? Start a small arts and crafts shop on her own? The possibilities were endless. She got her supper presently, and went to work for the last time.

It was a busy night, and when it was over she bade goodbye to those she had worked with and left the hospital for the last time. She had her pay packet in her purse, and an extra month in lieu of notice, and she handed over to her older colleague, who told her that she had been working for the NHS for more than twenty years.

'I don't know what I would have done if I had been made redundant,' she said. 'I've an elderly mother and father who live with me. We make ends meet, but only just—to be out of work would have been a catastrophe.'

It was heartening to find on her way home that there had been several enquiries about the house. The agent, a weasel-faced young man she didn't much like, had arranged for them to inspect the house at any time they wished.

'You'll be there,' he told her airily. 'So it really doesn't matter when they call, if they do.'

'I can't be there all day,' Emmy told him, and was silenced by him.

'You're not on the phone—stands to reason, doesn't it? Someone will have to be there.'

'Will you ask anyone who wants to look round the house to come after one o'clock? I will stay at home for the rest of the day.'

'Suit yourself, Miss Foster. The two parties interested said they'd call in some time today.'

To go to bed was impossible; one never knew, whoever was coming might decide to buy the house. Emmy had her breakfast, tidied away the dishes and sat down on the one comfortable chair in the kitchen. Of course she went to sleep almost at once, and woke to the sound of someone thumping the door knocker and ringing the bell.

The middle-aged couple she admitted looked sour.

'Took your time, didn't you?' observed the man grumpily, and pushed past her into the hall. He and his meek-looking wife spent the next ten minutes looking round and returned to Emmy, who was waiting in the kitchen after taking them on their first survey.

'Pokey, that's what it is,' declared the man. 'You'll be lucky to sell the place at half the asking price.'

He went away, taking his wife, who hadn't said a word, with him. Emmy hadn't said anything either. There seemed to be no point in annoying the man more than necessary. There would be several more like him, she guessed.

The second couple came late in the afternoon. They made a leisurely tour and Emmy began to feel hopeful, until the woman remarked, 'It's a lot better than some we've seen. Not that we can buy a house, but it gives us some idea of what we could get if we had the money.' She smiled at Emmy. 'Nice meeting you.'

Not a very promising start, decided Emmy, locking the door behind them. Better luck tomorrow. Though perhaps people didn't come on a Saturday.

She felt more hopeful after a good night's sleep. After all, it was early days; houses didn't sell all that fast. Only it would be splendid if someone decided to buy the place before she joined her parents.

No one came. Not the next day. She had gone for a walk in the morning and then spent the rest of the day in the kitchen, listening to her small radio and knitting. Monday, she felt sure, would bring more possible buyers.

No one came, nor did they come on Tuesday, Wednesday or Thursday. She wrote a cheerful letter to her parents on Friday, did her morning's shopping and spent the rest of the day waiting for the doorbell to ring. Only it didn't.

The professor, back in London, striding into St Luke's ready for a day's work, paused on his way. While not admitting it, he was looking forward to seeing Emmy again. He hoped that all had gone according to his plan and that her father had got the job the professor's friend had found for him. Emmy would have given her notice by now. He would miss her. And a good thing that she was going, he reminded himself.

He was brought up short by the sight of the older woman sitting in Emmy's chair. He wished her a civil good morning, and asked, 'Miss Foster? Is she ill?'

'Ill? No, sir. Left. Made redundant with several others. There's been a cutting down of staff.'

He thanked her and went on his way, not unduly worried. Ermentrude would have gone to Dorset with her father and mother. He must find time to phone his friend and make sure that all had gone according to plan. She would be happy there, he reflected. And she would forget him. Only he wouldn't forget her...

He left the hospital rather earlier than usual, and on a sudden impulse, instead of going home, drove through the crowded streets and turned into the street where Emmy lived. Outside the house he stopped the car. There was a FOR SALE board fastened to the wall by the door, and the downstairs curtains were drawn across. There was a glimmer of light showing, so he got out of the car and knocked on the door.

Emmy put down the can of beans she was opening. At last here was someone come to see the house. She turned on the light in the hall and went to open the door, and, being a prudent girl, left the safety chain on. Peering round it, recognising the vast expanse of waistcoat visible, her heart did a happy little somersault.

'It is I,' said the professor impatiently, and, when she had slid back the chain, came into the narrow hall, squashing her against a wall.

Emmy wormed her way into a more dignified stance. 'Hello, sir,' she said. 'Are you back in England?' She caught his eye. 'What I mean is, I'm surprised to see you. I didn't expect to…'

He had seen the empty room and the almost bare kitchen beyond. He took her arm and bustled her into the kitchen, sat her in a chair and said, 'Tell me why you are here alone in an empty house. Your parents?'

'Well, it's a long story…'

'I have plenty of time,' he told her. 'And I am listening.'

CHAPTER FIVE

EMMY told him without embellishments. 'So you see it's all turned out marvellously. We just have to sell this house—that's why I'm here. We thought I'd have to give a month's notice, and it seemed a splendid idea for me to stay on until I could leave and try and sell the house at the same time. Only being made redundant was a surprise. I've not told Father, of course.'

'You are here alone, with no furniture, no comforts?'

'Oh, I've got my bed upstairs, and a cupboard, and I don't need much. Of course, we thought I'd be at the hospital all day or all night. Actually,' she told him, wanting to put a good light on things, 'It's worked out very well, for I stay at home each day from one o'clock so that I can show people round...'

'You get many prospective buyers?'

'Well, not many, not every day. It isn't a very attractive house.'

The professor agreed silently to this. 'You will join your parents for Christmas? Have you a job in mind to go to?'

'Yes. Well, I've hardly had time, have I?' she asked reasonably. Then added, 'Perhaps I'll be able to take a course in embroidery and needlework...'

She didn't go on; he didn't want to know her plans. She asked instead, 'Did you have a pleasant time in Holland?'

'Yes. I'll wait here while you put a few things into a bag, Ermentrude. You will come back with me.'

'Indeed, I won't. Whatever next? I'm quite all right here, thank you. Besides, I must be here to show people round.' She added on a sudden thought, 'Whatever would your fiancée think? I mean, she's not to know that we don't like each other.' Emmy went bright pink. 'I haven't put that very well…'

'No, you haven't. You have, however, made it quite plain that you do not need my help.'

The professor got to his feet. He said coldly, 'Goodbye, Ermentrude.' And, while she was still searching for the right reply, let himself out of the house.

Emmy listened to the car going away down the street; she made almost no sound. She sat where she was for quite some time, doing her best not to cry.

Presently she got up and got her supper, and since there was nothing to do she went to bed.

She wasn't sure what woke her up. She sat up in bed, listening; the walls were thin, it could have been Mr Grant or Mrs Grimes·dropping something or banging a door. She lay down again and then shot up once more. The noise, a stealthy shuffling, was downstairs.

She didn't give herself time to feel frightened. She got out of bed quietly, put on her dressing gown and slippers and, seizing the only weapon handy—her father's umbrella which had somehow got left behind—she opened her door and peered out onto the landing. Someone was there, someone with a torch, and they had left the front door open too.

The nerve, reflected Emmy, in a rage, and swept downstairs, switching on the landing light as she did so. The man was in the empty sitting room, but he came out fast and reached the hall. He was young, his face half hidden by a scarf, a cap pulled down over his eyes and, after his first shock, he gave a nasty little laugh.

'Cor, lummy— An empty 'ouse an' a girl. Alone, are you? Well, let's 'ave yer purse, and make it quick.'

Emmy poked him with the umbrella. 'You get out of this house and you make it quick,' she told him. She gave him another prod. 'Go on...'

He made to take the umbrella from her, but this time she whacked him smartly over the head so that he howled with pain.

'Out,' said Emmy in a loud voice which she hoped hid her fright. She switched on the hall light now, hoping that someone, even at two o'clock in the morning, would see it. But the man, she was glad to see, had retreated to the door. She followed him, umbrella at the ready, and he walked backwards into the street.

Rather puffed up with her success at getting rid of him, she followed him, unaware that the man's mate was standing beside the door, out of sight. She heard him call out before something hard hit her on the head and she keeled over.

She didn't hear them running away since for the moment she had been knocked out. But Mr Grant, trotting to the window to see why there was a light shining into the street, saw them. Old though he was, he made his way downstairs and out of his house to where Emmy lay. Emmy didn't answer when he spoke to her, and she was very pale. He crossed the road and rang the bell of the house opposite. It sounded very loud at that time of the night. He rang again, and presently a window was opened and the teenager hung his head out.

'Come down, oh, do come down—Ermentrude has been hurt.'

The head disappeared and a moment later the boy, in his coat and boots, came out. 'Thieves? Take anything, did they? Not that there's anything to take.' He bent over Emmy. 'I'll get her inside and the door shut.'

He was a big lad, and strong; he picked Emmy up and carried her into the kitchen and set her in a chair. 'Put the kettle on,' he suggested. 'I'll be back in a tick; I'll get my phone.'

As he came back into the kitchen Emmy opened her eyes. She said crossly, 'I've got the most awful headache. Someone hit me.'

'You're right there. Who shall I ring? You'd better have a doctor—and the police.' He stood looking at her for a moment, and was joined by Mr Grant. 'You can't stay here, that's for certain. Got any friends? Someone to look after you?'

Mr Grant had brought her a wet towel, and she was holding it to her head. She felt sick and frightened and there was no one... Yes, there was. He might not like her, but he would help and she remembered his number; she had rung it time and again from the hospital.

She said muzzily, 'Yes, there's someone, if you'd tell him. Ask him if he would come.' She gave the boy the number and closed her eyes.

'He'll be along in fifteen minutes,' said the boy. 'Lucky the streets are empty at this time of night. Did they take anything?'

Emmy shook her head, and then wished she hadn't. 'No. There's nothing to take; my purse and bag are upstairs and they didn't get that far.' She said tiredly, 'Thank you both for coming to help me; I'm very grateful.'

As far as she was concerned, she thought, they can make all the noise they like and I'll never even think of complaining.

Mr Grant gave her a cup of tea and she tried to drink it, holding it with both shaky hands while the boy phoned the police. Then there was nothing to do but wait. The boy and Mr Grant stood drinking tea, looking rather helplessly at her.

'I'm going to be sick,' said Emmy suddenly, and lurched to the sink.

Which was how the professor found her a couple of minutes later.

The boy had let him in. 'You the bloke she told me to phone?' he asked suspiciously.

'Yes. I'm a doctor. Have you called the police?'

'Yes. She's in the kitchen being sick.'

Emmy was past caring about anyone or anything. When she felt the professor's large, cool hand on her wrist, she mumbled, 'I knew you'd come. I feel sick, and I've got a headache.'

He opened his bag. 'I'm not surprised; you have a bump the size of a hen's egg on your head.' His hands were very gentle. 'Keep still, Ermentrude, while I take a look.'

She hardly felt his hands after that, and while he dealt with the lump and the faint bleeding he asked what had happened.

Mr Grant and the boy both told him at once, talking together.

'The police?'

'They said they were on their way.'

The professor said gravely, 'It is largely due to the quick thinking and courage of both of you that Ermentrude isn't more severely injured. I'll get her to hospital just as soon as the police get here.'

They came a few minutes later, took statements from Mr Grant and the boy, agreed with the professor that Ermentrude wasn't in a fit state to say anything at the moment and agreed to interview her later. 'We will lock the door and keep the key at the station.' The officer swept his gaze round the bare room. 'No one lives here?'

'Yes, me,' said Ermentrude. 'Just for a few

weeks—until someone wants to buy it. Do you want me to explain?' She opened her eyes and closed them again.

'Wait until you know what you're talking about,' advised the professor bracingly. He spoke to one of the officers. 'Miss Foster is staying here for a short time; her parents have moved and she has stayed behind to settle things up.' He added, 'You will want to see her, of course. She will be staying at my house.' He gave the address, heedless of Emmy's mutterings.

'Now, if I might have a blanket in which to wrap her, I'll take her straight to St Luke's. I'm a consultant there. She needs to be X-rayed.'

Emmy heard this in a muzzy fashion. It wouldn't do at all; she must say something. She lifted her head too quickly, and then bent it over the sink just in time. The professor held her head in a matter-of-fact way while the others averted their gaze.

'The blanket?' asked the professor again, and the boy went upstairs and came back with her handbag and the quilt from Emmy's bed. The professor cleaned her up in a businesslike manner, wrapped her in the quilt and picked her up.

'If I'm not at my home I'll be at the hospital.' He thanked Mr Grant and the boy, bade the officers a civil goodnight, propped Emmy in the back of the car and, when she began to mumble a protest, told her to be quiet.

He said it in a very gentle voice, though. She closed

her eyes, lying back in the comfortable seat, and tried to forget her raging headache.

At the hospital she was whisked straight to X-Ray. She was vaguely aware of the radiographer complaining good-naturedly to the professor and of lying on a trolley for what seemed hours.

'No harm done,' said the professor quietly in her ear. 'I'm going to see to that lump, and then you can be put to bed and sleep.'

She was wheeled to Casualty then, and lay quietly while he bent over her, peering into her eyes, putting a dressing on her head. She was drowsy now, but his quiet voice mingling with Sister's brisk tone was soothing. She really didn't care what happened next.

When he lifted her into the car once more, she said, 'Not here...' But since the professor took no notice of her she closed her eyes again. She had been given a pill to swallow in Casualty; her headache was almost bearable and she felt nicely sleepy.

Beaker was waiting when the professor reached his house, carried Emmy indoors and asked, 'You got Mrs Burge to come round? I had no time to give you details. If I carry Miss Foster upstairs perhaps she will help her to bed.'

'She's upstairs waiting, sir. What a to-do. The poor young lady—knocked out, was she?'

'Yes. I'll tell you presently, Beaker. I could do with a drink, and I expect you could, too. Did Mrs Burge make any objections?'

'Not her! I fetched her like you told me to, and she'll stay as long as she's wanted.'

The professor was going upstairs with Emmy, fast asleep now, in his arms. 'Splendid.'

Mrs Burge met him on the small landing. 'In the small guest room, sir. Just you lay her down on the bed and I'll make her comfortable.'

She was a tall, bony woman with hair screwed into an old-fashioned bun and a sharp nose. A widow, she had been coming each day to help Beaker for some time now, having let it be known from the outset that through no fault of her own she had fallen on hard times and needed to earn her living.

Beaker got on well with her, and she had developed an admiration for the professor, so that being routed out of her bed in the early hours of the morning was something she bore with equanimity. She said now, 'Just you leave the young lady to me, sir, and go and have a nap—you'll be dead on your feet and a day's work ahead of you.'

The professor said, 'Yes, Mrs Burge,' in a meek voice, merely adding that he would be up presently just to make sure that Emmy's pulse was steady and that she slept still. 'I know I leave her in good hands,' he told Mrs Burge, and she bridled with pleasure.

For all her somewhat forbidding appearance she was a kind-hearted woman. She tucked Emmy, still sleeping, into bed, dimmed the bedside light and sat down in the comfortable armchair, keeping faithful watch.

'She's not moved,' she told the professor presently. 'Sleeping like a baby.'

He bent over the bed, took Emmy's pulse and felt her head.

'I'll leave these pills for her to take, Mrs Burge. See that she has plenty to drink, and if she wants to eat, so much the better. A couple of days in bed and she'll be quite herself. There's only the mildest of concussions, and the cut will heal quickly.

'I'm going to the hospital in an hour or so and shall be there all day. Ring me if you're worried. Beaker will give you all the assistance you require, and once Ermentrude is awake there is no reason why you shouldn't leave her from time to time. I'll be back presently when I've had breakfast so that you can have yours with Beaker.'

He went away to shower and dress and eat his breakfast and then returned, and Mrs Burge went downstairs to where Beaker was waiting with eggs and bacon.

Emmy hadn't stirred; the professor sat down in a chair, watching her. She suited the room, he decided—quite a small room, but charming with its white furniture, its walls covered with a delicate paper of pale pink roses and soft green leaves. The curtains were white, and the bedspread matched the wallpaper exactly. It was a room he had planned with the help of his younger sister, whose small daughter slept in it when they visited him.

'Though once you're married, Ruerd,' she had told him laughingly, 'you'll need it for your own daughter.'

Emmy, with her hair all over the pillow, looked

very young and not at all plain, he decided. When Mrs Burge came back he said a word or two to her, bent over the bed once more and stopped himself just in time from kissing Emmy.

It was late in the morning when Emmy woke, to stare up into Mrs Burge's face. She was on the point of asking 'Where am I?' and remembered that only heroines in books said that. Instead she said, 'I feel perfectly all right; I should like to get up.'

'Not just yet, love. I'm going to bring you a nice little pot of tea and something tasty to eat. You're to sit up a bit if you feel like it. I'll put another pillow behind you. There…'

'I don't remember very clearly,' began Emmy. 'I was taken to the hospital and I went to sleep.'

'Why, you're snug and safe here in Professor ter Mennolt's house, dearie, and me and Beaker are keeping an eye on you. He's gone to the hospital, but he'll be home this evening.'

Emmy sat up too suddenly and winced. 'I can't stay here. There's no one at the house—the estate agent won't know—someone might want to buy it…'

'Leave everything to the professor, ducks. You may be sure he'll have thought of what's to be done.'

Mrs Burge went away and came back presently with a tray daintily laid with fine china—a teapot, cup and saucer, milk and sugar. 'Drink this, there's a good girl,' she said. 'Beaker's getting you a nice little lunch and then you must have another nap.'

'I'm quite able to get up,' said Emmy, to Mrs Burge's departing back.

'You'll stay just where you are until I say you may get out of bed,' said the professor from the door. 'Feeling better?'

'Yes, thank you. I'm sorry I've given you all so much trouble. Couldn't I have stayed in hospital and then gone home?'

'No,' said the professor. 'You will stay here today and tomorrow, and then we will decide what is to be done. I have phoned the estate agent. He has a set of keys for your house and will deal with anyone who wishes to view it. The police will come some time this afternoon to ask you a few questions if you feel up to it.'

'You're very kind, sir, and I'm grateful. I'll be quite well by tomorrow, I can go...'

'Where?' He was leaning over the foot of the bed, watching her.

She took a sip of tea. 'I'm sure Mrs Grimes would put me up.'

'Mrs Grimes—the lady with the powerful voice? Don't talk nonsense, Ermentrude.' He glanced up as Mrs Burge came in with a tray. 'Here is your lunch; eat all of it and drink all the lemonade in that jug. I'll be back this evening.'

He went away and presently out of the house, for he had a clinic that early afternoon. He had missed lunch in order to see Ermentrude, and had only time to swallow a cup of coffee before his first patient arrived.

Emmy ate her lunch under Mrs Burge's watchful eye and, rather to her surprise, went to sleep again to wake and find another tray of tea, and Mrs Burge shaking out a gossamer-fine nightie.

'If you feel up to it, I'm to help you have a bath, love. You're to borrow one of the professor's sister's nighties. You'll feel a whole lot better.'

'Would someone be able to fetch my clothes so that I can go home tomorrow?' asked Emmy.

'Beaker will run me over this evening. You just tell me what you want and I'll pack it up for you. Professor ter Mennolt's got the keys.'

'Oh, thank you. You're very kind. Were you here when I came last night?'

'Yes—Beaker fetched me—three o'clock in the morning...'

'You must be so tired. I'm quite all right, Mrs Burge. Can't you go home and have a good sleep?'

'Bless you, ducks, I'm as right as a trivet; don't you worry your head about me. Now, how about a bath?'

Getting carefully out of bed, Emmy discovered that she still had a headache and for the moment wished very much to crawl back between the sheets. But the thought of being seen in her present neglected state got her onto her feet and into the adjoining bathroom, and once in the warm, scented water with Mrs Burge sponging her gently she began to feel better.

'I suppose I can't wash my hair?'

'Lawks, no, love. I'll give it a bit of a comb, but I

daren't go messing about with it until the professor says so.'

'It's only a small cut,' said Emmy, anxious to look her best.

'And a lump the size of an egg—that'll take a day or two. A proper crack on the head and no mistake. Lucky that neighbour saw the light and the men running away. It could have been a lot worse,' said Mrs Burge with a gloomy relish.

Emmy, dried, powdered and in the kind of night-gown she had often dreamed of possessing, sat carefully in a chair while Mrs Burge made her bed and shook up her pillows. Once more settled against them, Emmy sighed with relief. It was absurd that a bang on the head should make her feel so tired. She closed her eyes and went to sleep.

Which was how the professor found her when he got home. He stood looking down at her for a long minute, and in turn was watched by Mrs Burge.

They went out of the room together. 'Go home, Mrs Burge,' he told her. 'You've been more than kind. If you could come in tomorrow, I would be most grateful. I must contrive to get Ermentrude down to her parents—they are in Dorset and know nothing of this. They are moving house, and I don't wish to make things more difficult for them than I must. Another day of quiet rest here and I think I might drive her down on the following day...'

Mrs Burge crossed her arms across her thin chest.

'Begging your pardon, sir, but I'll be back here to sleep tonight.'

He didn't smile, but said gravely, 'That would be good of you, Mrs Burge, as long as you find that convenient.'

'It's convenient.' She nodded. 'And I'll make sure the young lady's all right tomorrow.'

'I'm in your debt, Mrs Burge. Come back when you like this evening. Is there a room ready for you?'

'Yes, sir, I saw to that myself.' She hesitated. 'Miss Ermentrude did ask if someone could fetch her clothes. I said I'd go this evening…'

'Tell me when you want to go; I'll drive you over. Perhaps you had better ask her if she needs anything else. Money or papers of any sort.'

Emmy woke presently and, feeling much better, made a list of what she needed and gave it to Mrs Burge.

'I'm off home for a bit,' said that lady. 'But I'll be back this evening. Beaker will bring you up some supper presently. You just lie there like a good girl.'

So Emmy lay back and, despite a slight headache, tried to make plans. Once she had been pronounced fit, she decided, she would go back to the house. She didn't much fancy being there alone, but reassured herself with the thought that lightning never struck twice in the same place… She would go to the estate agents again, too, and there was only another week or so until Christmas now.

Her thoughts were interrupted by the professor and her supper tray.

He greeted her with an impersonal hello. 'Beaker has done his best, so be sure and eat everything.'

He put the tray down, set the bed table across her knees and plumped up her pillows. 'I think you might get up tomorrow—potter round the house, go into the garden—well wrapped-up. I'll take you home the day after.'

'You're very kind, but I must go back to the house, just in case someone wants to buy it. I mean, I can't afford to miss a chance. It'll have to be left empty when I go home at Christmas, and you know how awful houses look when they're empty. So if you don't mind...'

'I do mind, Ermentrude, and you'll do as I say. I'll phone the estate agent if it will set your mind at rest and rearrange things. Do you want me to tell your parents what has happened?'

'Oh, no—they're getting the house straight, and Father's at the school all day so it's taking a bit of time. They've enough to worry about. They don't need to know anyway.'

'Just as you wish. Does Mrs Burge know what to fetch for you?'

'Yes, thank you. I gave her a list. I've only a few clothes there; Mother took the rest with her.'

'Then I'll say goodnight, Ermentrude. Sleep well.'

She was left to eat her supper, a delicious meal Beaker had devised with a good deal of thought. It was he who came to get the tray later, bringing with him fresh lemonade and a fragile china plate with mouth-watering biscuits.

'I make them myself, miss,' he told her, beaming at her praise of the supper. 'Mrs Burge will look in on you when she gets back, with a nice drop of hot milk.'

'Thank you, Beaker, you have been so kind and I'm giving you a lot of extra work.'

'A pleasure, miss.'

'I heard Charlie barking…'

'A spirited dog, miss, and a pleasure to have in the house. Humphrey and he are quite partial to each other. When you come downstairs tomorrow he will be delighted to see you.'

Emmy, left alone, ate some of the biscuits, drank some of the lemonade and thought about the professor. His household ran on oiled wheels, that was obvious. His Anneliese, when she married him, would have very little to do—a little tasteful flower-arranging perhaps, occasional shopping, although she thought that Beaker might not like that. And of course later there would be the children to look after.

Emmy frowned. She tried to imagine Anneliese nursing a baby, changing nappies or coping with a toddler and failed. She gave up thinking about it and thought about the professor instead, wishing he would come home again and come and see her. She liked him, she decided, even though he was difficult to get to know. Then, why should he wish her to know too much about him? She had no place in his life.

Much later she heard the front door close, and Charlie barking. He and Mrs Burge were home. She lay, watching the door. When it opened Mrs Burge came in, a suitcase in one hand, a glass of milk in the other.

'Still awake? I've brought everything you asked for, and Professor ter Mennolt went to see the estate agent at his home and fixed things up. No one's been to look at the house.' Mrs Burge's sniff implied that she wasn't surprised at that. 'We looked everywhere to make sure that things were just so. And there's some post. Would you like to read it now?'

She put the milk on the bedside table. 'Drink your milk first. It's time you were sleeping.'

Emmy asked hesitantly, 'Are you going home now, Mrs Burge?'

'No, ducks. I'll be here, just across the landing, if you want me. Now I'll just hang up your things…'

Emmy stifled disappointment. There was no reason why the professor should wish to see her. He must, in fact, be heartily sick of her by now, disrupting his life.

The professor was talking on the phone. Presently he got his coat, ushered Charlie into the back of the car and, with a word to Beaker, drove himself to St Luke's where one of his patients was giving rise to anxiety.

He got home an hour later, ate the dinner which Beaker served him with the air of someone who had long learned not to mind when his carefully prepared meals were eaten hours after they should have been, and went to his study to work at his desk with the faithful Charlie sprawled over his feet.

*　　*　　*

Waking the following morning, Emmy decided that she felt perfectly well again. She ate her breakfast in bed, since Mrs Burge told her sternly not to get up till later.

'Professor ter Mennolt went off an hour ago,' she told Emmy. 'What a life that man leads, never an hour to call his own.'

Which wasn't quite true, but Emmy knew what she meant. 'I suppose all doctors are at everyone's beck and call, but it must be a rewarding life.'

'Well, let's hope he gets his reward; he deserves it,' said Mrs Burge. 'Time that fiancée of his made up her mind to marry him.' She sniffed. 'Wants too much, if you ask me. Doesn't like this house—too small, she says...'

'Too small?' Emmy put down her cup. 'But it's a big house—I mean, big enough for a family.'

'Huh,' said Mrs Burge forcefully. 'Never mind a family, she likes to entertain—dinner parties and friends visiting. She doesn't much like Beaker, either.'

Emmy, aware that she shouldn't be gossiping, nonetheless asked, 'But why not? He's the nicest person...'

'True enough, love. Looks after the professor a treat.'

'So do you, Mrs Burge.'

'Me? I come in each day to give a hand, like. Been doing it for years, ever since the professor bought the house. A very nice home he's made of it, too. I have heard that he's got a tip-top place in Holland, too.

Well, it stands to reason, doesn't it? He's over there for the best part of the year—only comes here for a month or two, though he pops over if he's needed. Much in demand, he is.'

She picked up Emmy's tray. 'Now, you have a nice bath and get dressed and come downstairs when you're ready. I'll be around and just you call if you want me. We'd better pack your things later on; the professor's driving you home in the morning.'

So Emmy got herself out of bed, first taking a look at her lump before going to the bathroom. The swelling had almost gone and the cut was healing nicely. She stared at her reflection for several moments; she looked a fright, and she was going to wash her hair before anyone told her not to.

Bathed, and with her hair in a damp plait, she went downstairs to find Beaker hovering in the hall.

His, 'Good morning, miss,' was affable. 'There's a cup of coffee in the small sitting room; it's nice and cosy there.'

He led the way and opened a door onto a quite small room at the back of the house. It was furnished very comfortably, and there was a fire burning in the elegant fireplace. A small armchair had been drawn up to it, flanked by a table on which were newspapers and a magazine or two. Sitting in front of the fire, waving his tail, asking to be noticed, was Charlie.

Emmy, sitting down, could think of nothing more delightful than to be the owner of such a room and such a dog, with a faithful old friend like Beaker

smoothing out life's wrinkles. She said on a happy
sigh, 'This is such a lovely house, Beaker, and everything is so beautifully polished and cared for.'

Beaker allowed himself to smile. 'The master and
I, we're happy here, or so I hope, miss.' He went,
soft-footed, to the door. 'I'll leave you to drink your
coffee; lunch will be at one o'clock.'

He opened the door and she could hear Mrs Burge
Hoovering somewhere.

'I suppose the professor won't be home for lunch?'

'No, miss. Late afternoon. He has an evening engagement.'

She put on her coat and went into the garden with
Charlie after lunch. For one belonging to a town
house the garden was surprisingly large, and cleverly
planned to make the most of its space. She wandered
up and down while Charlie pottered, and presently
when they went indoors she sought out Beaker.

'Do you suppose I might take Charlie for a walk?'
she asked him.

Beaker looked disapproving. 'I don't think the professor would care for that, miss. Charlie has had a
long walk, early this morning with his master. He will
go out again when the professor comes home. There's
a nice fire burning in the drawing room. Mrs Burge
asked me to let you know that she'll be back this
evening if you should need any help with your packing. I understand that you are to make an early start.'

So Emmy retreated to the drawing room and curled
up by the fire with Charlie beside her and Humphrey

on her lap. She leafed through the newspapers and magazines on the table beside her, not reading them, her mind busy with her future. Christmas was too close for her to look for work; she would stay at home and help to get their new house to rights. There would be curtains to sew and hang, possessions to be stowed away in cupboards.

She wondered what the house was like. Her mother had written to tell her that it was delightful, but had had no time to describe it. There had been a slight hitch, she had written; the previous occupant's furniture was for the most part still in the house owing to some delay in its transport. 'But,' her mother had written, 'we shall be quite settled in by the time you come.'

Beaker brought tea presently; tiny sandwiches, fairy cakes and a chocolate cake which he assured her he had baked especially for her. 'Most young ladies enjoy them,' he told her.

Emmy was swallowing the last morsel when Charlie bounded to his feet, barking, and a moment later the professor came into the room.

His 'Hello,' was friendly and casual. He sat down, then enquired how she felt and cut himself a slice of cake.

'I'll run you home in the morning,' he told her. 'The day after tomorrow I shall be going to Holland.'

'There's no need,' said Emmy.

'Don't be silly,' said the professor at his most bracing. 'You can't go back to an empty house, and in a very short time you would be going home anyway.

There seems little chance of selling the house at the moment; I phoned the agent this morning. There's nothing of value left there, is there?'

She shook her head. 'No, only my bed and the bedclothes and a few bits of furniture.'

'There you are, then. We'll leave at eight o'clock.' He got up. 'Charlie and I are going for our walk—I shall be out tonight. Beaker's looking after you?'

'Oh, yes, thank you.'

'Mrs Burge will come again this evening. Ask for anything you want.'

His smile was remote as he went away.

She was still sitting there when he returned an hour later with Charlie, but he didn't come into the drawing room, and later still she heard him leave the house once more. Beaker, opening the door for Charlie to come in, said that Mrs Burge was in the kitchen if she needed her for anything. 'I'll be serving dinner in half an hour, Miss. May I pour you a glass of sherry?'

It might lift her unexpected gloom, thought Emmy, accepting. Why she should feel so downcast she had no idea; she should have been on the top of the world—leaving London and that pokey house and going to live miles away in Dorset. She wouldn't miss anything or anyone, she told herself, and the professor, for one, would be glad to see her go; she had caused enough disruption in his life.

Beaker had taken great pains with dinner—mushroom soup, sole *à la femme*, creamed potatoes and baby sprouts, and an apricot pavlova to follow these.

He poured her a glass of wine too, murmuring that the professor had told him to do so.

She drank her coffee in Humphrey's company and then, since she was heartily sick of her own company, went in search of Mrs Burge. There was still some packing to do, and that lady came willingly enough to give her help, even though it wasn't necessary. It passed an hour or so in comfortable chat and presently Emmy said that she would go to bed.

'We're to go early in the morning, so I'll say goodbye, Mrs Burge, and thank you for being so kind and helpful.'

'Bless you, ducks, it's been a pleasure, and I'll be up to see you off. Beaker will have breakfast on the table sharp at half past seven—I'll give you a call at seven, shall I?'

She turned on her way out. 'I must say you look a sight better than when you got here.'

Emmy, alone, went to the triple looking-glass on the dressing table and took a good look. If she was looking better now she must have looked a perfect fright before. No wonder the professor showed little interest in her company. Anyway, she reminded herself, his mind would be on Anneliese.

She woke in the morning to find her bedside lamp on and Mrs Burge standing there with a tray of tea.

'It's a nasty old day,' said Mrs Burge. 'Still dark, too. You've got half an hour. The professor's already up and out with Charlie.'

The thought of keeping him waiting spurred Emmy

on to dress with speed. She was downstairs with only moments to spare as he and Charlie came into the house.

His good morning was spoken warmly. He's glad I'm going, thought Emmy as she answered cheerfully.

'There's still time to put me on a train,' she told him as they sat down to breakfast. 'It would save you a miserable drive.'

He didn't bother to answer. 'The roads will be pretty empty for another hour or so,' he observed, just as though she hadn't spoken. 'We should get to Littleton Mangate by mid-morning. Ready to leave, are you?'

Emmy went to thank Beaker and Mrs Burge, and got into her coat while Beaker fetched her case down to the car. It was bitterly cold, and she took a few quick breaths before she got into the car, glad to see Charlie already sprawling on the back seat. It was almost like having a third person in the car, even though he obviously intended to go to sleep.

It was striking eight o'clock as they drove away, starting the tedious first part of their journey through London's streets and presently the suburbs.

CHAPTER SIX

IT WAS still quite dark, and the rain was turning to sleet. The professor didn't speak and Emmy made no attempt to talk. In any case she couldn't think of anything to say. The weather, that useful topic of conversation, was hardly conducive to small talk, and he had never struck her as a man who enjoyed talking for the sake of it. She stared out of the window and watched the city streets gradually give way to rows of semi-detached houses with neat front gardens, and these in turn recede to be replaced by larger houses set in their own gardens and then, at last, open country and the motorway.

Beyond asking her if she was warm enough and comfortable, the professor remained silent. Emmy sat back in her comfortable seat and thought about her future. She had thought about it rather a lot in the last few days, largely because she didn't want to think too much about the past few weeks.

She was going to miss the professor, she admitted to herself. She wouldn't see him again after today, but she hoped that he would be happy with Anneliese. He had annoyed her on several occasions, but he was a good man and kind—the sort of kindness which was practical, and if he sometimes spoke his mind rather too frankly she supposed he was entitled to do so.

As the motorway merged into the A303 he turned the car into the service station. 'Coffee? We've made good time. You go on in; I'll take Charlie for a quick trot. I'll see you in the café.'

The place was full, which made their lack of conversation easier to bear. Emmy, painstakingly making small talk and receiving nothing but brief, polite replies, presently gave up. On a wave of ill humour she said, 'Well, if you don't want to talk, we won't.' She added hastily, going red in the face, 'I'm sorry, that was rude. I expect you have a lot to think about.'

He looked at her thoughtfully. 'Yes, Ermentrude, I have. And, strangely, in your company I do not feel compelled to keep up a flow of chat.'

'That's all right, then.' She smiled at him, for it seemed to her that he had paid her a compliment.

They drove on presently through worsening weather. All the same her heart lifted at the sight of open fields and small villages. Nearing their journey's end, the professor turned off the A303 and took a narrow cross-country road, and Emmy said, 'You know the way? You've been here before?'

'No.' He turned to smile at her. 'I looked at the map. We're almost there.'

Shortly after that they went through a village and turned off into a lane overhung with bare winter trees. Round a corner, within their view, was Emmy's new house.

The professor brought the car to a halt, and after a moment's silence Emmy said, 'Oh, this can't be it,' although she knew that it was. The lodge itself was charming, even on a winter's day, but its charm was completely obliterated by the conglomeration of things around it, leaving it half-buried. Her father's car stood at the open gate, for the garage was overflowing with furniture. There was more furniture stacked and covered by tarpaulins in heaps in front of the house, a van parked on the small lawn to one side of the lodge and a stack of pipes under a hedge.

'Oh, whatever has happened?' asked Emmy. 'Surely Father hasn't...'

The professor put a large hand on hers. 'Supposing we go and have a look?'

He got out of the car and went to open her door and then let Charlie out, and together they went up the narrow path to the house.

It wasn't locked. Emmy opened it and called, 'Mother?'

They heard Mrs Foster's surprised voice from somewhere in the house and a moment later she came into the tiny hall.

'Darling—Emmy, how lovely to see you. We didn't expect you...' She looked at the professor. 'Is everything all right?'

He shook hands. 'I think it is we who should be asking you that, Mrs Foster.'

Mrs Foster had an arm round Emmy. 'Come into the kitchen; it's the only room that's comfortable. We hoped to be settled in by the time you came, Emmy. There's been a hitch...'

She led them to the kitchen with Charlie at their heels. 'Sit down; I'll make us some coffee.'

The kitchen wasn't quite warm enough, but it was furnished with a table and chairs, and there were two easy chairs at each side of the small Aga. China and crockery, knives and forks, spoons and mugs and glasses were arranged on a built-in dresser and there was a pretty latticed window over the sink.

Mrs Foster waved a hand. 'Of course all this is temporary; in a week or two we shall be settled in.'

'Mother, what has happened?' Emmy sat down at the table. Enoch and Snoodles had jumped onto her lap while George investigated Charlie.

The professor was still standing, leaning against the wall, silent. Only when Mrs Foster handed round the coffee mugs and sat down did he take a chair.

'So unfortunate,' said Mrs Foster. 'Mr Bennett, whom your father replaced, died suddenly the very day I moved down here. His furniture was to have been taken to his sister's house where he intended to live, but, of course, she didn't want it, and anyway he had willed it to a nephew who lives somewhere in the north of England. He intends to come and decide what to do with it, but he's put it off twice already and says there's no need for it to be put in store as he'll deal with it when he comes. Only he doesn't come and here we are, half in and half out as it were.'

She drank from her mug. 'Your father is extremely happy here, and since he's away for most of the day we manage very well. School breaks up tomorrow, so he will be free after that. We didn't tell you, Emmy, because we hoped—still do hope—that Mr Bennett's nephew will do something about the furniture.'

'Whose van is that outside?' asked Emmy.

'The plumber, dear. There's something wrong with the boiler—he says he'll have it right in a day or two.' Mrs Foster looked worried. 'I'm so sorry we weren't ready for you, but we'll manage. You may have to sleep on the sofa; it's in the sitting room.' She looked doubtful. 'There's furniture all over the place, I'm afraid, but we can clear a space...'

She looked at Emmy. 'I don't suppose the house is sold, Emmy?'

'No, Mother, but there have been several people to look at it. The agent's got the keys...'

'We didn't expect you just yet.' Her mother looked enquiring. 'Has something gone wrong?'

'I'll tell you later,' said Emmy. She turned to the professor, who still hadn't uttered a word. 'It was very kind of you to bring me here,' she said. 'I hope it hasn't upset your day too much.'

'Should I be told something?' asked her mother.

'Later, Mother,' said Emmy quickly. 'I'm sure Professor ter Mennolt wants to get back to London as quickly as possible.'

The professor allowed himself a small smile. He said quietly, 'There is a great deal you should be told, Mrs Foster, and if I may I'll tell it, for I can see that Ermentrude won't say a word until I'm out of the way.'

'Emmy's been ill,' said Mrs Foster in a motherly panic.

'Allow me to explain.' And, when Emmy opened

her mouth to speak, he said, 'No, Ermentrude, do not interrupt me.'

He explained. His account of Emmy's misfortunes was succinct, even dry. He sounded, thought Emmy, listening to his calm voice, as if he were dictating a diagnosis, explaining something to a sister on a ward round.

When he had finished, Mrs Foster said, 'We are deeply grateful to you—my husband and I. I don't know how we can thank you enough for taking such care of Emmy.'

'A pleasure,' said the professor in a noncommittal voice which made Emmy frown. Of course it hadn't been a pleasure; she had been a nuisance. She hoped that he would go now so that she need never see him again. The thought gave her such a pang of unhappiness that she went quite pale.

He had no intention of going. He accepted Mrs Foster's invitation to share the snack lunch she was preparing, and remarked that he would like to have a talk with Mr Foster.

'He comes home for lunch?' he enquired blandly.

'Well, no. He has it at school, but he's got a free hour at two o'clock; he told me this morning.'

'Splendid. If I may, I'll walk up to the school and have a chat.'

Emmy was on the point of asking what about when he caught her eye.

'No, Ermentrude, don't ask!' The animals had settled before the stove. The professor got up. 'I'll bring in your things, Ermentrude.'

He sounded impersonal and nonchalant, but something stopped her from asking the questions hovering on her tongue. Why should he want to talk to her father? she wondered.

They had their lunch presently—tinned soup and toasted cheese—sitting round the kitchen table, and Mrs Foster and the professor were never at a loss for conversation. Emmy thought of the silent journey they had just made and wondered what it was that kept him silent in her company. It was a relief when he got into his coat again and started on the five-minute walk to the school.

Mr Foster, if he was surprised to see the professor, didn't say so. He led the way to a small room near the classrooms, remarking that they would be undisturbed there.

'You want to see me, Professor?' He gave him a sharp glance. 'Is this to do with Emmy? She isn't ill? You say she is with her mother...'

'No, no. She has had a mild concussion and a nasty cut on the head, but, if you will allow me, I will explain...'

Which he did in the same dry manner which he had employed at the lodge. Only this time he added rather more detail.

'I am deeply indebted to you,' said Mr Foster. 'Emmy didn't say a word—if she had done so my wife would have returned to London immediately.'

'Of course. Ermentrude was determined that you should know nothing about it. It was unfortunate that she should have been made redundant with such short notice, although I believe she wasn't unduly put out about that. I had no idea that she was alone in the house until I returned to London.'

Mr Foster gave him a thoughtful look and wondered why the professor should sound concerned, but he said nothing. 'Well, once we have got this business of the furniture and the plumbing settled, we shall be able to settle down nicely. I'm sure that Emmy will find a job, and in the meantime there's plenty for her to do at home.'

'Unfortunate that Christmas is so close,' observed the professor. 'Is it likely that you will be settled in by then?'

Mr Foster frowned. 'Unfortunately, no. I had a phone message this morning—this nephew is unable to deal with the removal of Mr Bennett's furniture until after Christmas. He suggests that it stays where it is for the moment. I suppose we shall be able to manage…'

'Well, now, as to that, may I offer a suggestion? Bearing in mind that Ermentrude is still not completely recovered, and the discomforts you are living in, would you consider…?'

Emmy and her mother, left on their own, rummaged around, finding blankets and pillows. 'There's a mattress in the little bedroom upstairs, if you could manage on that for a few nights,' suggested Mrs Foster worriedly. 'If only they would take all this furniture away…'

Emmy, making up some sort of a bed, declared that

she would be quite all right. 'It won't be for long,' she said cheerfully. 'I'll be more comfortable here than I was in London. And Father's got his job— that's what matters.'

She went downstairs to feed the animals. 'The professor and Charlie are a long time,' she observed. 'I hope Charlie hasn't got lost. It's almost tea time, too, and I'm sure he wants to get back to London.'

The professor wasn't lost, nor was Charlie. Having concluded his talk with Mr Foster, the professor had whistled to his dog and set off for a walk, having agreed to return to the school when Mr Foster should be free to return home.

The unpleasant weather hadn't improved at all. Sleet and wet snow fell from time to time from a grey sky rapidly darkening, and the lanes he walked along were half-frozen mud. He was unaware of the weather, his thoughts miles away.

'I am, of course, mad,' he told Charlie. 'No man in his right senses would have conceived such a plan without due regard to the pitfalls and disadvantages. And what is Anneliese going to think?'

Upon reflection he thought that he didn't much mind what she felt. She had been sufficiently well brought up to treat his guests civilly, and if she and Ermentrude were to cross swords he felt reasonably sure that Ermentrude would give as good as she got. Besides, Anneliese wouldn't be staying at his home, although he expected to see a good deal of her.

He waited patiently while Charlie investigated a

tree. Surely Anneliese would understand that he couldn't leave Ermentrude and her parents to spend Christmas in a house brim-full of someone else's furniture and inadequate plumbing, especially as he had been the means of their move there in the first place. Perhaps he had rather over-emphasised Ermentrude's need to recuperate after concussion, but it had successfully decided her father to accept his offer.

He strode back to the school to meet Mr Foster and accompany him back to the lodge.

Emmy was making tea when they got there.

'You're wet,' she said unnecessarily. 'And you'll be very late back home. I've made toast, and there's a bowl of food for Charlie when you've dried him off. There's an old towel hanging on the back of the kitchen door. Give me that coat; I'll hang it on a chair by the Aga or you'll catch your death of cold.'

The professor, meekly doing as he was told, reflected that Ermentrude sounded just like a wife. He tried to imagine Anneliese talking like that and failed, but then she would never allow herself to be in a situation such as Emmy was now. She would have demanded to be taken to the nearest hotel. He laughed at the thought, and Emmy looked round at him in surprise. The professor didn't laugh often.

He helped her father out of his wet jacket, poured the tea and called her mother, who was hanging curtains in the small bedroom.

'They'll have to do,' she said, coming into the kitchen. 'I've pinned them up for the moment, and it does make the room look cosier.'

She smiled at the professor. 'Did you have a nice walk? Do sit down. Let Charlie lie by the stove; he must be tired. It's a wretched evening for you to travel.'

Emmy handed round toast and a pot of jam. The tea, in an assortment of cups and saucers, was hot and strong. She watched the professor spread jam on his toast and take a bite, and thought of Beaker's dainty teas with the fine china and little cakes. He looked up and caught her eye and smiled.

Mr Foster drank his tea and put down his cup. 'Professor ter Mennolt has made us a most generous offer. He considers that Emmy needs rest after her accident, and that as a medical man he cannot like the idea of her remaining here while the house is in such a state of confusion. He has most kindly offered to take us over to Holland for the Christmas period to stay in his house there. He will be going the day after tomorrow—'

'You said tomorrow...' interrupted Emmy.

'I find that I am unable to get away until the following day,' said the professor smoothly. 'But I shall be delighted to have you as my guests for a few days. Hopefully by the time you return the problems in this house will be resolved.' He added blandly, 'As a doctor, I would feel it very wrong of me to allow Ermentrude to stay here until she is quite fit.'

Emmy drew a deep breath. She didn't think he meant a word of it; he might look and sound like the learned man he undoubtedly was but his suggestion was preposterous. Besides, there was nothing wrong with her. She opened her mouth to say so and closed it again, swallowing her protest. She didn't stand a chance against that weighty professional manner.

She listened to her mother receiving his offer with delighted relief.

'Surely we shall upset your plans for Christmas? Your family and guests? How will you let them know? And all the extra work…'

The professor sounded reassuring. 'I'm sure you don't need to worry, Mrs Foster. If you can face the idea of Christmas in Holland, I can assure you that you will all be most welcome. Rather short notice, I'm afraid, but if you could manage to be ready by midday on the day after tomorrow?'

Mr and Mrs Foster exchanged glances. It was an offer they could hardly refuse. On their way they would have scrambled through the festive season somehow or other, always hopeful that Mr Bennett's furniture would have been moved by the time Emmy arrived. But now that seemed unlikely, and with Christmas in such a muddle, and Emmy not quite herself…

Mrs Foster said simply, 'Thank you for a most generous offer; we accept with pleasure. Only don't let us interfere with any of your family arrangements. I mean, we are happy just to have a bed and a roof over our heads…'

The professor smiled. 'It will be a pleasure to have you—I always think the more the merrier at Christmas, don't you?'

'Your family will be there?'

'I have two sisters with children and a younger brother. I'm sure they will be delighted to meet you.'

He got up. 'You will forgive me if I leave you now?'

He shook hands with Mr and Mrs Foster, but Ermentrude he patted on the shoulder in a casual manner and told her to take care.

When he had gone, Mrs Foster said, 'What a delightful man, and how kind he is. You know, Emmy, your father and I were at our wits' end wondering what to do about Christmas, and along comes Professor ter Mennolt and settles it all for us—just like that.'

Mr Foster was watching Emmy's face. 'A good man, and very well thought of in his profession, I believe. He tells me that he is engaged to be married. I dare say we shall meet his fiancée.'

Emmy said in a bright voice, 'Oh, I have met her— she came to St Luke's one day to see him—she'd been staying over here. She's beautiful, you know. Fair and slender, and has the most gorgeous clothes.'

'Did you like her?' asked her mother.

'No,' said Emmy. 'But I expect that was because she was the kind of person I would like to be and aren't.'

'Well,' said her mother briskly, 'let's get tidied up here and then think about what clothes to take with us. I've that long black skirt and that rather nice crêpe de Chine blouse; that'll do for the evening. What about you, Emmy?'

'Well, there's the brown velvet; that'll do.' It would have to; she had no other suitable dress for the evening. She thought for a moment. 'I could go in the jacket and skirt, and wear my coat over them. A blouse or two, and a sweater...I don't suppose we'll be there for more than a few days.'

'If we sell the house, you shall have some new clothes, and now your father's got this splendid post...'

'Oh, I've plenty of clothes,' said Emmy airily. 'And they don't matter. It's marvellous that Father's here, and this is a dear little house.'

She looked round her at the muddle—chairs stacked in corners, a wardrobe in the hall, Mr Bennett's piano still in the sitting room. They looked at each other and burst out laughing. 'When you're able to settle in,' said Emmy.

The professor, with Charlie beside him, drove back to Chelsea. 'I do not know what possessed me,' he told his companion. 'Anneliese is not going to like my unexpected guests, and yet what else could I do? Would you like to spend Christmas in such cold chaos? No, of course you wouldn't. Common humanity dictated that I should do something about it... Let me think...'

By the time he had reached his home his plans were made. Over the dinner which Beaker set before him he went through them carefully, and presently went to his study and picked up the phone.

Beaker, bringing his coffee later, coughed gently. 'Mrs Burge and I, sir, we miss Miss Foster.'

The professor looked at him over his spectacles. 'So do I, Beaker. By the way, she and her parents are going to Holland with me for Christmas. Due to unavoidable circumstances, the house they have moved to is unfit to live in for the moment and they have nowhere to go.'

Beaker's face remained impassive. 'A good idea, if I may say so, sir. The young lady isn't quite herself after that nasty attack.'

'Just so, Beaker. I shan't be leaving until the day after tomorrow—pack a few things for me, will you? Enough for a week.'

Beaker gone, the professor buried his commanding nose in a weighty tome and forgot everything else. It was only as he was going to bed that he remembered that he should have phoned Anneliese. It would be better to tell her when he got to Holland, perhaps. He felt sure that she would be as warmly welcoming to his unexpected guests as his sisters had promised to be.

Emmy slept badly; a mattress on the floor, surrounded by odds and ends of furniture which creaked and sighed during the night, was hardly conducive to a restful night. Nor were her thoughts—largely of the professor—none of which were of a sensible nature.

She got up heavy-eyed and her mother said, 'The professor is quite right, Emmy, you don't look at all yourself.' She eyed her much loved daughter worriedly. 'Was it very uncomfortable on the mattress? There's no room to put up a bed, and anyway we haven't got one until we can get yours from the house in London. Your father can sleep there tonight and you can come in with me...'

'I was very comfortable,' said Emmy. 'But there was such a lot to think about that I didn't sleep very well. I expect I'm excited.'

Mrs Foster put the eggs for breakfast on to boil. 'So am I. We'll pack presently—your father's going up to the school to find out where the nearest kennels are, then he can take these three later this evening.'

'I hope they'll be all right, but it's only for a few days. Wouldn't it be marvellous if we came back and found all Mr Bennett's furniture gone and the plumbing repaired?'

'We mustn't expect too much, but it would be nice. Directly after Christmas your father will go up to London and see the estate agent and arrange for your bed to be brought down here. You need never go back there unless you want to, Emmy.' Her mother turned round to smile at her. 'Oh, Emmy, isn't it all too good to be true?'

There was a good deal to do—cases to pack, hair to wash, hands to be attended to.

'I do hope the professor won't feel ashamed of us,' said Mrs Foster.

Emmy said quite passionately, 'No, Mother, he's not like that. He's kind and, and—' She paused. 'Well, he's nice.' And, when her mother gave her a surprised look, she added, 'He's quite tiresome at times too.'

Mrs Foster wisely said nothing.

They all went to bed early in a house strangely silent now that George and Snoodles and Enoch had been taken, protesting fiercely, to the kennels near Shaftesbury. Emmy had another wakeful night, worrying about her clothes and whether the professor might be regretting his generosity—and what would Anneliese think when she knew? She dropped off finally and had a nightmare, wherein his family, grotesquely hideous, shouted abuse at her. She was only too glad when it was time to get up.

They made the house as secure as they could, piling the furniture tidily under the tarpaulins and tying them down, parking her father's car as near the house as possible and covering it with more tarpaulins. There was just time to have a cup of coffee before the professor was due to arrive.

He came punctually, relaxed and pleasant, drank the coffee he was offered, stowed the luggage in the boot and invited everyone to get into the car.

Mr Foster was told to sit in front, for, as the professor pointed out, he might need directions. 'We're going from Dover—the hovercraft. It's quick, and there is quite a long journey on the other side.'

He got in and turned to look at Mrs Foster. 'Passports?' he asked. 'Keys and so forth? So easily forgotten at the last minute, and I have rushed you.'

'I think we've got everything, Professor...'

'Would you call me Ruerd?' His glance slid over

Emmy's rather pale face, but he didn't say anything to her.

It was another cold day but it wasn't raining, although the sky was dark. The professor drove steadily, going across country to pick up the motorway outside Southampton and turning inland at Chichester to pick up the A27 and then the A259. He stopped in Hawkshurst at a pub in the little town where they had soup and sandwiches.

'Are we in good time for the hovercraft,' asked Mrs Foster anxiously.

'Plenty of time,' he assured her. 'It takes longer this way, I believe, but the motorway up to London and down to Dover would have been packed with traffic.'

'You've been this way before?' asked Emmy's father.

'No, but it seemed a good route. On a fine day it must be very pleasant. I dislike motorways, but I have to use them frequently.'

They drove on presently, joining the A20 as they neared Dover. From the warmth of the car Emmy surveyed the wintry scene outside. How awful if she was to be seasick...

She forgot about it in the excitement of going on board, and, once there, since it was rather like sitting in a superior bus, she forgot about feeling sick and settled down beside her mother, sharing the tea they had been brought and eating the biscuits. Her father had gone to sleep and the professor, with a word of apology, had taken out some papers from a pocket, put on his spectacles and was absorbing their contents.

It was rough but not unbearably so. All the same it was nice to get back into the car.

'Not too tired?' asked the professor, and, once clear of the traffic around Calais, sent the car surging forward, out of France and into Belgium, where he took the road to Ghent and then on into Holland.

Emmy looked out of the window and thought the country looked rather flat and uninteresting. Instead she studied the back of the professor's head, and wished that she were sitting beside him. She caught the thought up short before it could go any further. All this excitement was going to her head, and any silly ideas must be squashed at once. Circumstances had thrown them together; circumstances would very shortly part them. That was an end of that.

She sighed, and then choked on a breath when the professor asked, 'What's the matter, Ermentrude?'

She had forgotten that he could see her in his mirror above the dashboard. 'Nothing, nothing,' she repeated. 'I'm fine. It's all very interesting.'

Which, considering it was now almost dark and the view held no interest whatsoever, was a silly answer.

It was completely dark by the time he turned in at his own gates and she saw the lights streaming from the house ahead of them. She hadn't expected anything like this. A substantial villa, perhaps, or a roomy townhouse, but not this large, square house, with its big windows and imposing front door.

As they got out of the car the door opened and

Solly and Tip dashed out, barking a welcome—a welcome offered in a more sedate fashion by Cokker, who greeted the guests as though three people arriving for Christmas without more than a few hours' warning was an everyday occurrence.

The hall was warm and splendidly lighted and there was a Christmas tree in one corner, not yet decorated. Cokker took coats and scarves, and the whole party crossed the hall and went into the drawing room.

'Oh, what a beautiful room!' said Mrs Foster.

'I'm glad you like it. Shall we have a drink before you go to your rooms? Would dinner in half an hour suit you?'

'Yes, please.' Mrs Foster beamed at him. 'I don't know about anyone else, but I'm famished.' She sat down by the fire and looked around her, frankly admiring. 'Ruerd, this is so beautiful and yet you choose to live a good part of your life in England?'

'I go where my work is,' he told her, smiling. 'I'm very happy in Chelsea, but this is my home.'

He crossed to the drinks table and went to sit by Mr Foster, talking about their journey, leaving Emmy to sit with her mother. Presently Cokker came, and with him a tall, stout woman, no longer young but very upright.

'Ah, Tiele,' said the professor. 'My housekeeper and Cokker's wife. She doesn't speak English but I'm sure you will manage very well.'

He said something to her in what Emmy supposed was Dutch.

'Tiele is from Friesland, so we speak Friese together…'

'You're not Dutch? You're Friesian?' asked Emmy.

'I had a Friesian grandmother,' he told her. 'Tiele will take you upstairs, and when you are ready will you come back here again? Don't hurry; you must be tired.'

On their way to the door Emmy stopped by him. 'Aren't you tired?' she asked him.

He smiled down at her. 'No. When I'm with people I like or doing something I enjoy I'm never tired.'

He smiled slowly and she turned away and followed her mother, father and Tiele up the wide, curving staircase. It was inevitable, I suppose, she thought, that sooner or later I should fall in love with him. Only it's a pity I couldn't have waited until we were back home and there would be no chance of seeing him again. I must, decided Emmy firmly, be very circumspect in my manner towards him.

There were a number of rooms leading from the gallery which encircled the stairs. Emmy watched her parents disappear into one at the front of the house before she was led by Tiele to a room on the opposite side. It was not a very large room, but it was furnished beautifully with a canopied bed, a William the Fourth dressing table in tulip wood, two Georgian *bergères* upholstered in the same pale pink of the curtains and bedspread, and a mahogany bedside table—an elegant Georgian trifle.

The one long window opened onto a small wrought-iron balcony; she peeped out onto the dark outside and turned back thankfully to the cheerful light of the rose-shaded lamps. There was a clothes cupboard too, built into one wall, and a small, quite perfect bathroom.

Emmy prowled around, picking things up and putting them down again. 'I wonder,' she said out loud, 'if Anneliese knows how lucky she is?'

She tidied herself then, brushed her hair, powdered her nose and went to fetch her parents.

'Darling,' said her mother worriedly. 'Should we have come? I mean, just look at everything...'

Her father said sensibly, 'This is Ruerd's home, my dear, and he has made us welcome. Never mind if it is a mansion or a cottage. I fancy that it is immaterial to him, and it should be to us.'

They went down to the drawing room and found the professor standing before his hearth, the dogs pressed up against him.

'You have all you want?' he asked Mrs Foster. 'Do say if you need anything, won't you? I rushed you here with very little time to decide what to pack.'

When Cokker came the professor said, 'I believe dinner is on the table. And if you aren't too tired later, sir, I'd like to show you some first editions I have. I recently found Robert Herrick's *Hesperides*—seventeenth century, but perhaps you would advise me as to the exact date?'

The dining room was as magnificent as the drawing room, with a pedestal table in mahogany ringed around by twelve chairs, those at the head and foot of the table being carvers upholstered in red leather.

It was a large room, with plenty of space for the massive side table along one wall and the small serving table facing it.

There were a number of paintings on the walls. Emmy, anxious not to appear nosy, determined to have a good look at them when there was no one about. At the moment she was delighted to keep her attention on the delicious food she was being offered. Smoked salmon with wafer-thin brown bread and butter, roast pheasant with game chips and an assortment of vegetables, and following these a *crème brûlée*.

They had coffee in the drawing room and presently the professor took Mr Foster away to his library, first of all wishing Mrs Foster and Emmy a good night. 'Breakfast is at half past eight, but if you would like to have it in bed you have only to say so. Sleep well.' His gaze dwelt on Emmy's face for a moment and she looked away quickly.

She was going to stay awake, she thought, lying in a scented bath. There were a great many problems to mull over—and the most important one was how to forget the professor as quickly as possible. If it's only infatuation, she thought, I can get over it once I've stopped seeing him.

She got into bed and lay admiring her surroundings before putting out the bedside light, prepared to lie awake and worry. She had reckoned without the comfort of the bed and the long day behind her. With a last dreamy thought of the professor, she slept.

CHAPTER SEVEN

EMMY was wakened in the morning by a sturdy young girl in a coloured pinafore, bearing a tray of tea. She beamed at Emmy, drew the curtains back, giggled cheerfully and went away.

Emmy drank her tea and hopped out of bed intent on looking out of the window. She opened it and stepped cautiously onto the balcony. The tiles were icy and her toes curled under with the cold, but the air was fresh and smelled of the sea.

She took great gulping breaths and peered down to the garden below. It was more than a garden; it stretched away towards what looked like rough grass, and beyond that she could glimpse the sea. She took her fill of the view and then looked down again. Directly under the balcony the professor was standing, looking up at her, the dogs beside him.

He wished her good morning. 'And go and put some clothes on, Ermentrude, and come outside.' He laughed then.

She said haughtily, 'Good morning, Professor. I think not, thank you. I'm cold.'

'Well, of course you are with only a nightie on. Get dressed and come on down. You need the exercise.'

Emmy felt light-headed at the sight of him, standing there, laughing at her.

She said, 'All right, ten minutes,' and whisked herself back into her room, leaving the professor wondering why the sight of her in a sensible nightdress with her hair hanging untidily in a cloud around her shoulders, should so disturb him in a way which Anneliese, even in the most exquisite gown, never had. He reminded himself that Anneliese would be coming to dinner that evening, and regretted the impulse to invite Emmy to join him.

She came through the side door to meet him, wrapped in her coat, a scarf over her hair, sensible shoes on her feet. Tip and Solly made much of her, and she said, 'Oh, what a pity that Charlie isn't here, too.'

'I think that Beaker might not like that. Charlie is his darling, as much loved as Humphrey.'

They had begun to walk down the length of the garden, and at its end he opened a wicket gate and led the way over rough grass until they reached the edge of the dunes with the sea beyond. There was a strong wind blowing, whipping the waves high, turning the water to a tumultuous steel-grey.

The professor put an arm round Emmy's shoulders to steady her. 'Like it?'

'Oh, yes, it's heavenly! And so quiet—I mean, no people, no cars...'

'Just us,' said the professor.

It wasn't full daylight, but she could see the wide sand stretching away on either side of them, disappearing into the early-morning gloom.

'You could walk for miles,' said Emmy. 'How far?'

'All the way to den Helder in the north and to the Hoek in the south.'

'You must think of this when you are in London…'

'Yes. I suppose that one day I'll come to live here permanently.'

'I expect you will want to do that when you're married and have a family,' said Emmy, and felt the pain which the words were giving her. Would Anneliese stand here with him, watching the stormy sea and blown by the wind? And his children? She pictured a whole clutch of them and dismissed the thought. Anneliese would have one child—two, perhaps—but no more than that.

She felt tears well under her eyelids. Ruerd would be a splendid father and his home was large enough to accommodate a whole bunch of children, but that would never happen.

'You're crying,' said the professor. 'Why?'

'It's the wind; it makes my eyes water. The air is like sucking ice cubes from the fridge, isn't it?'

He smiled then. 'An apt description. Let us go back and have breakfast before we decorate the tree—a morning's work. We will come again—whatever the weather, it is always a splendid view.

*   *   *

Breakfast was a cheerful meal; her parents had slept well and the talk was wholly of Christmas and the forthcoming gaiety.

'My sisters will come later today, my brother tomorrow. Anneliese—my fiancée—will be coming this evening to dinner.'

'We look forward to meeting her,' said Mrs Foster, politely untruthful. Maternal instinct warned her that Anneliese wasn't going to like finding them at Ruerd's house. Although from all accounts she had nothing to fear from Emmy, thought Mrs Foster sadly. A darling girl, but with no looks. A man as handsome as Ruerd would surely choose a beautiful woman for his wife.

They decorated the tree after breakfast, hanging it with glass baubles, tinsel, little china angels and a great many fairy lights. On top, of course, there was a fairy doll—given after Christmas to the youngest of his nieces, the professor told them.

'You have several nieces?' asked Mrs Foster.

'Three so far, and four nephews. I do hope you like children...'

'Indeed I do. Ruerd, we feel terrible at not having any presents to give.'

'Please don't worry about that. They have so many gifts that they lose count as to whom they are from.'

Emmy, making paper chains for the nursery, found him beside her.

'After lunch we'll go over the house, if you would like that, but, in the meantime, will you bring those upstairs and we'll hang them before the children get here?'

The nursery was at the back of the house behind a baize door. There was a night nursery, too, and a bedroom for nanny, a small kitchenette and a splendidly equipped bathroom.

'The children sleep here, but they go where they like in the house. Children should be with their parents as much as possible, don't you agree?'

'Well, of course. Otherwise they're not a family, are they?' She stood there, handing him the chains as he fastened them in festoons between the walls. 'Did you sleep here, too?'

'Oh, yes. Until I was eight years old. On our eighth birthdays we were given our own bedrooms.'

He hung the chains, and turned to stare at her. 'You like my home, Ermentrude?'

'Yes, indeed I do. I think you must be very happy here.'

She walked to the door, uneasy under his look. 'At what time do your sisters arrive?'

His voice was reassuringly casual again. 'Very shortly after lunch. It will be chaos for the rest of the afternoon, I expect. Several friends will be coming to dinner.'

She paused as they reached the stairs. 'You have been so kind to us, Professor, but that doesn't mean you have to include us in your family gatherings.' She saw his quick frown. 'I've put that badly, but you know quite well what I mean, don't you? Mother and Father and I would be quite happy if you would like us to dine alone. I mean, you weren't expecting us…'

She had made him angry. She started down the

staircase and wished that she had held her tongue, but she had had to say it. Perhaps if she hadn't fallen in love with him she wouldn't have felt the urge to make it clear to him that they were on sufferance, even if it was a kindly sufferance.

He put out a hand and stopped her, turned her round to face him, and when he spoke it was in a rigidly controlled voice which masked his anger.

'Never say such a thing to me again, Ermentrude. You and your parents are my guests, and welcome in my house. Be good enough to remember that.'

She stood quietly under his hand. 'All right, I won't,' she told him. 'Don't be so annoyed, there's no need.'

He smiled then. 'Should I beg your pardon? Did I startle you?'

'Oh, no. I think I've always known that you conceal your feelings.' She met his look and went pink. 'Now it's me who should say sorry. Goodness me, I wouldn't have dared talk to you like that at St Luke's. It must be because we're here.'

He studied her face, nodded and went on down the stairs, his hand still on her arm.

Lunch was a cheerful meal. The professor and Mr Foster seemed to have a great deal in common; neither was at a loss for a subject although they were careful to include Mrs Foster and Emmy.

Shortly afterwards the first of the guests arrived. The house seemed suddenly to be full of children, racing around, shouting and laughing, hugging the dogs, hanging onto their uncle, absorbing Emmy and her parents into their lives as though they had always been there.

There were only four of them but it seemed more—three boys and a girl, the eldest six years and the youngest two. A rather fierce Scottish nanny came with them, but she took one look at Emmy's unassuming person and allowed her to be taken over by her charges. So Emmy was coaxed to go to the nursery with the children and their mother, a tall young woman with the professor's good looks. She had shaken Emmy by the hand, and liked her.

'Joke,' she said with a smile. 'It sounds like part of an egg but it's spelt like a joke. I do hope you like children. Mine run wild at Christmas, and Ruerd spoils them. My sister Alemke will be here shortly; she's got a boy and two girls, and a baby on the way.' She grinned at Emmy. 'Are we all a bit overpowering?'

'No, no. I like children. Only, you see, the professor is so—well, remote at the hospital. It's hard to think of him with a family.'

'I know just what you mean.' Joke made a face. 'He loves children, but I don't think Anneliese, his fiancée, likes them very much. I sound critical, don't I? Well, I am. Why he has to marry someone like her I'll never know. Suitable, I suppose.'

She took Emmy's arm. 'I'm so glad you're here. Only I hope the children aren't going to plague you.'

'I shan't mind a bit. How old are your sister's children?'

'The boy is five, and the girls—twins—almost three. Let's go down and have tea.'

Her sister had arrived when they got down to the drawing room and there were more children, who, undeterred by language problems, took possession of Emmy.

Alemke was very like her sister, only younger. 'Isn't this fun?' she said in English as good as Emmy's own. 'I love a crowd. Our husbands will come later, and I suppose Aunt Beatrix will be here and Uncle Cor and Grandmother ter Mennolt. She's a bit fierce, but don't mind her. There'll be Ruerd's friends, too; it should be great fun. And Anneliese, of course.'

The sisters exchanged looks. 'We don't like her, though we try very hard to do so,' said Joke.

'She's very beautiful,' said Emmy, anxious to be fair.

'You've met her?'

'She came to St Luke's when I was working there, to see the professor.'

'Do you always call Ruerd "professor"?' asked Joke.

'Well, yes. He's—he's… Well, it's difficult to explain, but the hospital— He's a senior consultant and I was on the telephone exchange.'

Alemke took her arm. 'Come over here and sit with us while we have tea, and tell us about the hospital—wasn't there a bomb or something? Ruerd mentioned it vaguely. Anneliese was over there, wasn't she?'

Emmy accepted a delicate china cup of tea and a tiny biscuit.

'Yes, it must have been very difficult for the professor because, of course, he was busier than usual.'

Joke and Alemke exchanged a quick look. Here was the answer to their prayers. This small girl with the plain face and the beautiful eyes was exactly what they had in mind for their brother. They had seen with satisfaction that, beyond a few civil remarks, he had avoided Emmy and she had gone out of her way to stay at the other end of the room. A good sign, but it was unfortunate that Ruerd had given his promise to Anneliese. Who would be coming that evening, no doubt looking more beautiful than ever.

The children, excited but sleepy, were led away after tea to be bathed and given supper and be put to bed, and everyone else went away to dress for the evening. Emmy had seen with pleasure that her parents were enjoying themselves and were perfectly at ease in their grand surroundings. She reminded herself that before her father had been made redundant he and her mother had had a pleasant social life. It was only when they had gone to London and he had been out of work that they had had to change their ways.

Emmy took a long time dressing. The result looked very much as usual to her anxious eyes as she studied her person in the pier-glass. The brown dress was best described as useful, its colour mouse-like, guaranteed to turn the wearer into a nonentity, its modest style such that it could be worn year after year without even being noticed.

Emmy had bought it at a sale, searching for a dress to wear to the annual hospital ball at St Luke's two years previously, knowing that it would have to last for a number of years even if its outings were scanty. It hardly added to her looks, although it couldn't disguise her pretty figure.

She went slowly down the staircase, hoping that no one would notice her.

The professor noticed—and knew then why Emmy hadn't wanted to join his other guests. He crossed the hall to meet her at the foot of the staircase, and took her hand with a smile and a nod at her person. He said in exactly the right tone of casual approval, 'Very nice, Ermentrude. Come and meet the rest of my guests.'

His brothers-in-law were there now, but he took her first to an old lady sitting by the console table.

'Aunt Beatrix, this is Ermentrude Foster who is staying here over Christmas with her parents—you have already met them.'

The old lady looked her up and down and held out a hand. 'Ah, yes. You have an unusual name. Perhaps you are an unusual girl?'

Emmy shook the old hand. 'No, no. I'm very ordinary.'

Aunt Beatrix patted the stool at her feet. 'Sit down and tell me what you do.' She shot a glance at Emmy. 'You do do something?'

'Well, yes.' Emmy told her of the job at St Luke's.

'But, now Father has a post in Dorset, I can live there and find something to do while I train.'

'What for?'

'I want to embroider—really complicated embroidery, you know? Tapestry work and smocking on babies' dresses and drawn thread work. And when I know enough I'd like to open a small shop.'

'Not get married?'

'I expect if someone asked me, and I loved him, I'd like to get married,' said Emmy.

The professor had wandered back. 'Come and meet Rik and Hugo and the others.' He put a hand on her shoulder and led her from one to the other, and then paused by Anneliese, who was superb in red chiffon, delicately made-up, her hair an artless mass of loose curls.

'Remember Ermentrude?' asked the professor cheerfully.

'Of course I do.' Anneliese studied the brown dress slowly and smiled a nasty little smile. 'What a rush for you, coming here at a moment's notice. Ruerd told me all about it, of course. You must feel very grateful to him. Such a bore for you, having no time to buy some decent clothes. Still, I suppose you're only here for a couple of days.'

'Yes, I expect we are,' said Emmy in a carefully controlled voice. Just then the professor was called away. Anneliese turned round and spoke to a tall, stout woman chatting nearby. 'Mother, come and meet this girl Ruerd is helping yet again.'

Mevrouw van Moule ignored the hand Emmy put

out. She had cold eyes and a mean mouth, and Emmy thought, In twenty years' time Anneliese will look like that.

'I dare say you find all this rather awkward, do you not? You worked in a hospital, I understand.'

'Yes,' said Emmy pleasantly. 'An honest day's work, like the professor. He does an honest day's work, too.' She smiled sweetly at Anneliese. 'What kind of work do you do, Anneliese?'

'Anneliese is far too delicate and sensitive to work,' declared her mother. 'In any case she has no need to do so. She will marry Professor ter Mennolt very shortly.'

'Yes, I did know.' Emmy smiled at them both. It was a difficult thing to do; she wanted to slap them, and shake Anneliese until her teeth rattled in her head. 'So nice to see you again,' she told Anneliese, and crossed the room to join her mother and father, who were talking to an elderly couple, cousins of the professor.

The professor's two sisters, watching her from the other end of the room, saw her pink cheeks and lifted chin and wondered what Anneliese had said to her. When the professor joined them for a moment, Joke said, 'Ruerd, why did you leave Emmy with Anneliese and her mother? They've upset her. You know how nasty Anneliese can be.' She caught her brother's eye. 'All right, I shouldn't have said that. But her mother's there, too...'

She wandered away and presently fetched up beside Emmy.

'You crossed swords,' she said into Emmy's ear. 'Were they absolutely awful?'

'Yes.'

'I hope you gave them as good as you got,' said Joke.

'Well, no. I wanted to very badly, but I couldn't, could I? I'm a guest here, aren't I? And I couldn't answer back.'

'Why not?'

'Anneliese is going to marry Ruerd. He—he must love her, and it would hurt him if she were upset.'

Joke tucked her hand in her arm. 'Emmy, dear, would you mind if Ruerd was upset?'

'Yes, of course. He's—he's kind and patient and very generous, and he deserves to be happy.' Emmy looked at Joke, unaware of the feelings showing so plainly in her face.

'Yes, he does,' said Joke gravely. 'Come and meet some more of the family. We're endless, aren't we? Have you met my grandmother?'

Twenty people sat down to dinner presently. The table had been extended and more chairs arranged round it, but there was still plenty of room. Emmy, sitting between one of the brothers-in-law and a jovial man—an old friend of the family—could see her parents on the other side of the table, obviously enjoying themselves.

The professor sat at the head of the table, of course, with Anneliese beside him and his grandmother on his other hand. Emmy looked away and concentrated on something else. There was plenty to concentrate upon. The table for a start, with the lace table mats, sparkling glass and polished silver. There was an epergne at its centre, filled with holly, Christmas roses and trailing ivy, and candles in silver candelabra.

Dinner lived up to the splendour of the table: sorrel soup, mustard-grilled sole, raised game pie with braised celery, brussels sprouts with chestnuts, spinach purée and creamed potatoes, and to follow a selection of desserts.

Emmy, finding it difficult to choose between a mouth-watering trifle and a milanaise soufflé, remembered the bread and jam they had once eaten and blushed. She blushed again when the professor caught her eye and smiled. Perhaps he had remembered, too, although how he had thought of anything else but his beautiful Anneliese sitting beside him...

Emmy, savouring the trifle, saw that Anneliese was toying with a water ice. No wonder she was so slim. Not slim, thought Emmy—bony. And, however gorgeous her dress was, it didn't disguise Anneliese's lack of bosom. Listening politely to the old friend of the family talking about his garden, Emmy was thankfully aware that her own bosom left nothing to be desired. A pity about the brown dress, of course, but, since the professor had barely glanced at her, it hardly mattered—a potato sack would have done just as well.

Dinner over, the party repaired to the drawing room and Emmy went to sit by her mother.

Mrs Foster was enjoying herself. 'This is delightful, Emmy. When I think that we might still be at the lodge, surrounded by someone else's furniture... I do wish we had brought a present for Ruerd.'

'Well, there wasn't time, Mother. Perhaps we can send him something when we get back home. Has he said how long we're staying here?'

'No, but he told your father that he has to return to England on Boxing Day, so I expect we shall go back with him then.' Mrs Foster added, 'I don't like his fiancée; she'll not make him a good wife.'

They were joined by other guests then, and the rest of the evening passed pleasantly enough. Around midnight Anneliese and her mother went home. She went from one group to the other, laughing and talking, her hand on the professor's sleeve, barely pausing to wish Emmy and her mother goodnight.

'I'll be back tomorrow,' she told them. 'Ruerd has excellent servants but they need supervision. So fortunate that Ruerd offered you a roof over your heads for Christmas. Of course, it was the least anyone could do.'

She gave them a brittle smile and left them.

'I don't like her,' said Mrs Foster softly.

'She's beautiful,' said Emmy. 'She will be a most suitable wife for Ruerd.'

Alemke joined them then and they chattered together, presently joined by several other guests, until people began to drift home. All this while the professor had contrived to be at the other end of the room, going from one group to the other, pausing briefly to say something to Mrs Foster, hoping that Emmy was enjoying herself. The perfect host.

*   *   *

The next day was Christmas Eve, and Anneliese arrived for lunch wrapped in cashmere and a quilted silk jacket. At least she came alone this time, playing her part as the future mistress of Ruerd's house with a charm which set Emmy's teeth on edge.

Somehow she managed to make Emmy feel that she was receiving charity, even while she smiled and talked and ordered Cokker about as though she were already his mistress. He was called away to the phone, and she took the opportunity to alter the arrangements for lunch, reprimand Cokker for some trivial fault and point out to Emmy in a sugary voice that there would be guests for lunch and had she nothing more suitable to wear?

'No, I haven't,' said Emmy coldly. 'And if you don't wish to sit down to the table with me, please say so. I'm sure the professor won't mind if I and my mother and father have something on a tray in another room.' She added, 'I'll go and find him and tell him so...'

Anneliese said urgently, 'No, no, I didn't mean... It was only a suggestion. I'm sure you look quite nice, and everyone knows—'

'What does everyone know?' asked the professor from the door.

He looked from one to the other of them, and Emmy said in a wooden voice, 'Oh, you must ask Anneliese that,' and went past him out of the room.

The professor said quietly, 'The Fosters are my guests, Anneliese. I hope that you remember that— and that you are in my house!'

She leaned up to kiss his cheek. 'Dear Ruerd, of course I remember. But Emmy isn't happy, you know; this isn't her kind of life. She told me just now that she and her parents would be much happier having lunch by themselves. I told her that she looked quite nice—she's so sensitive about her clothes—and that everyone knew they had no time to pack sufficient clothes.'

She shrugged her shoulders. 'I've done my best, Ruerd.' She flashed him a smile. 'I'm going to talk to your sisters; I've hardly had time to speak to them.'

The professor stood for a moment after she had left him, deep in thought. Then he wandered off, away from the drawing room where everyone was having a drink before lunch, opening and closing doors quietly until he found Emmy in the garden room, standing by the great stone sink, doing nothing.

He closed the door behind him and stood leaning against it. 'You know, Emmy, it doesn't really matter in the least what clothes you are wearing. Anneliese tells me that you feel inadequately dressed and are shy of joining my guests. I do know that clothes matter to a woman, but the woman wearing them matters much more.

'Everyone likes you, Emmy, and you know me well enough by now to know that I don't say anything I don't mean. Indeed, they like you so much that Joke wants you to stay a few weeks and help her with the children while Nanny goes on holiday. Would you consider that? I shall be in England, Rik has to go to

Switzerland for ten days on business, and she would love to have your company and help.'

Emmy had had her back to him, but she turned round now. 'I wouldn't believe a word of that if it was someone else, but you wouldn't lie to me, would you?'

'No, Emmy.'

'Joke would really like me to stay and help with the children? I'd like that very much. But what about Mother and Father?'

'I'll take them back when I go in two days' time. Probably by then the problem of the furniture will have been settled.' He smiled. 'They will have everything as they want it by the time you get back.'

'I'll stay if Joke would like that,' said Emmy.

'She'll be delighted. Now come and eat your lunch—we will talk to your mother and father presently.'

She sat next to him at lunch, with Rik on her other side and Hugo across the table, and between them they had her laughing and talking, all thoughts of her clothes forgotten. That afternoon she went for a walk with Joke and Alemke and the children, down to the village and back again, walking fast in a cold wind and under a grey sky.

'There'll be snow later,' said Joke. 'Will you come to church tomorrow, Emmy? The family goes, and anyone else who'd like to. We have midday lunch and a gigantic feast in the evening. The children stay up for it and it's bedlam.'

There was tea round the fire when they got back,

with Anneliese acting as hostess, although, when Joke and Alemke joined the others, she said with a titter, 'Oh, dear, I shouldn't be doing this—Joke, do forgive me. I am so used to being here that sometimes I feel that I am already married.'

Several people gave her a surprised look, but no one said anything until Alemke started to talk about their walk.

The professor wasn't there and neither, Emmy saw, were her mother and father. She wondered if Anneliese knew that she had been asked to stay on after Christmas and decided that she didn't—for Anneliese was being gracious, talking to her in her rather loud voice, saying how glad she would be to be back in her own house, and did she know what kind of job she hoped to get?

Emmy ate Christmas cake and said placidly that she had no idea. Her heart ached with love for Ruerd but nothing of that showed in her serene face, nicely flushed by her walk.

She didn't have to suffer Anneliese's condescending conversation for long; she was called over to a group reminiscing about earlier Christmases, and presently Aunt Beatrix joined them, with Cokker close behind, bringing fresh tea. Everyone clustered around her, and Anneliese said bossily, 'I'll ring for sandwiches; Cokker should have brought them.'

Aunt Beatrix paused in her talk to say loudly, 'You'll do nothing of the kind. If I want sandwiches, Cokker will bring them. I dare say you mean well,' went on Aunt Beatrix tartly, 'but please remember that I am a member of the family and familiar with the household.' She added sharply, 'Why aren't you with Ruerd? You see little enough of each other.'

'He's doing something—he said he would have his tea in the study.' Anneliese added self-righteously, 'I never interfere with his work, *mevrouw*.'

Aunt Beatrix gave a well-bred snort. She said something in Dutch which, of course, Emmy didn't understand and which made Anneliese look uncomfortable.

Cokker returned then, set a covered dish before Aunt Beatrix, removed the lid to reveal hot buttered toast and then slid behind Emmy's chair. 'If you will come with me, miss, your mother requires you.'

Emmy got up. 'There's nothing wrong?' she asked him quietly, and he shook his head and smiled. 'You will excuse me, *mevrouw*,' said Emmy quietly. 'My mother is asking for me.'

She went unhurriedly from the room, following Cokker into the hall as Aunt Beatrix, reverting to her own tongue, said, 'There goes a girl with pretty manners. I approve of her.'

A remark tantamount, in the eyes of her family, to receiving a medal.

Cokker led the way across the hall and opened the study door, ushered Emmy into the room and closed the door gently behind her. The professor was there, sitting at his desk, and her mother and father were sitting comfortably in the two leather chairs on either side of the small fireplace, in which a brisk fire burned.

There was a tea tray beside her mother's chair and the professor, who had stood up as Emmy went in, asked, 'You have had your tea, Ermentrude? Would you like another cup, perhaps?'

Emmy sat down composedly, her insides in a turmoil. I must learn to control my feelings, she reflected, and said briskly, 'Cokker said that Mother wanted to see me.'

'Well, yes, dear—we all do. Ruerd was telling us that his sister would like you to stay for a while and help with her children. We think it's a splendid idea but, of course, you must do what you like. Though, as Ruerd says, you really need a holiday and a change of scene, and we can get the lodge put to rights before you come back home.'

Emmy could hear the relief in her mother's voice. The prospect of getting the lodge in order while cherishing her daughter—who, according to the professor, needed a quiet and comfortable life for a few weeks— was daunting. The lodge would be cold and damp, and there were tea-chests of things to be unpacked, not to mention getting meals and household chores. Having a semi-invalid around the place would be no help at all. Much as she loved her child, Mrs Foster could be forgiven for welcoming the solving of an awkward problem.

Wasn't too much concern being expressed about her health? wondered Emmy. After all, it had only been a bang on the head, and she felt perfectly all right.

'I'll be glad to stay for a little while and help Joke with the children,' she said composedly.

'Splendid,' said the professor. 'Ermentrude will be in good hands, Mrs Foster. Cokker and Tiele will look after my sister and the children and Ermentrude. Alemke will go home directly after Christmas, and so will Aunt Beatrix and the cousins. It will be nice for Cokker to have someone in the house. Joke will be here for a couple of weeks, I believe, and I'll see that Ermentrude will have a comfortable journey home.'

He's talking just as though I wasn't here, reflected Emmy. For two pins I'd say... He smiled at her then and she found herself smiling back, quite forgetting his high-handedness.

Dinner that evening was festive. Emmy wished that she had a dress to do justice to the occasion, but the brown velvet had to pass muster once again. Anneliese, in the splendour of gold tissue and chiffon, gave her a slight smile as she entered the drawing room—much more eloquent than words.

Despite that, Emmy enjoyed herself. Tonight it was mushrooms in garlic, roast pheasant and red cabbage and a mouth-watering selection of desserts. And a delicious red wine which Emmy found very uplifting to the spirits.

Anneliese's father came to drive her home later, and Emmy felt everyone relax. It was an hour or two later before the party broke up, everyone going to their beds, in a very convivial mood. She had hardly spoken to the professor, and his goodnight was friendly and casual.

'A delightful evening,' said Mrs Foster, bidding Emmy goodnight at her bedroom door. 'Ruerd is a delightful man and a splendid host. Although I cannot see how he could possibly be in love with Anneliese. A nasty, conceited woman, if you ask me.'

'She's beautiful,' said Emmy, and kissed her mother goodnight.

Christmas Day proved to be everything it should be. After breakfast everyone, children included, loaded themselves into cars and drove to the village church, where Emmy was delighted to hear carols just as she would have expected to hear in England—only they were sung in Dutch, of course. The tunes were the same; she sang the English words and the professor, standing beside her, smiled to himself.

Lunch was a buffet, with the children on their best behaviour because once lunch was over they would all go into the hall and the presents would be handed out from under the tree, now splendidly lighted. Everyone was there—Cokker and Tiele and the housemaids and the gardener—but no Anneliese.

'She'll come this evening,' whispered Joke. She added waspishly, 'When the children are all in bed and there is no danger of sticky fingers.'

Handing out the presents took a long time; there was a great deal of unwrapping of parcels and exclamations of delight at their contents, and the children went from one to the other, showing off their gifts.

There was a present for Mrs Foster, too—an evening handbag of great elegance—and for Mr Foster a box of cigars. For Emmy there was a blue cashmere scarf, the colour of a pale winter sky. It was soft and fine, and she stroked it gently. Every time she wore it, she promised herself, she would remember the professor.

Tea was noisy and cheerful but, very soon afterwards, the children—now tired and cross—were swept away to their beds. Nanny came to fetch them, looking harassed, and Emmy asked Joke if she might go with her. 'Just to help a bit,' she said diffidently.

'Oh, would you like to?' Joke beamed at her. 'Alemke has a headache, but I'll be up presently to say goodnight. You'd truly like to? I mean, don't feel that you must.'

Emmy smiled. 'I'd like to.'

She slipped away and spent the next hour under Nanny's stern eye, getting damp from splashed bathwater and warm from coaxing small, wriggling bodies into nightclothes. They were all settled at last and, with a nod of thanks from Nanny, Emmy went back downstairs. Everyone was dressing for dinner, she realised as she reached the hall.

Not quite everyone; she found the professor beside her.

She turned to go back upstairs again. 'I ought to be changing,' she said quickly. 'Thank you for my scarf. I've never had anything cashmere before.'

He didn't say anything, but wrapped his great arms round her and kissed her.

She was so taken by surprise that she didn't do

anything for a moment. She had no breath anyway. The kiss hadn't been a social peck; it had lingered far too long. And besides, she had the odd feeling that something was alight inside her, giving her the pleasant feeling that she could float in the air if she wished. If that was what a kiss did to one, she thought hazily, then one must avoid being kissed again.

She disentangled herself. 'You shouldn't...' she began. 'What I mean is, you mustn't kiss me. Anneliese wouldn't like it...'

He was staring down at her, an odd look on his face. 'But you did, Ermentrude?'

She nodded. 'It's not fair to her,' she said, and then, unable to help herself, asked, 'Why did you do it?'

He smiled. 'My dear Ermentrude, look up above our heads. Mistletoe—see? A mistletoe kiss, permissible even between the truest strangers. And really we aren't much more than that, are we?'

He gave her an avuncular pat on the shoulder. 'Run along and dress or you will be late for drinks.'

Emmy didn't say anything; her throat was crowded with tears and she could feel the hot colour creeping into her face. She flew up the staircase without a sound. Somewhere to hide, she thought unhappily. He was laughing at me.

But the professor wasn't laughing.

CHAPTER EIGHT

THERE was very little time left for Emmy to dress.
Which was perhaps just as well. She lay too long in
the bath and had to tear into her clothes, zipping up
the brown dress with furious fingers, brushing her hair
until her eyes watered.

She had made a fool of herself; the professor must
have been amused, he must have seen how his kiss
had affected her—like a silly schoolgirl, she told her
reflection. If only she didn't love him she would hate
him. She would be very cool for the entire evening,
let him see that she considered his kiss—his mistletoe
kiss, she reminded herself—was no consequence at
all.

Her mother and father had already gone downstairs; she hurried after them just in time to see
Anneliese making an entrance. Vivid peacock-blue
taffeta this evening. In a style slightly too girlish for
the wearer, decided Emmy waspishly, before going to
greet Grandmother ter Mennolt—who had spent most
of the day in her room but had now joined the family
party, wearing purple velvet and a cashmere shawl
fastened with the largest diamond brooch Emmy had
ever set eyes on.

Emmy wished her good evening and would have
moved away, but the old lady caught her arm. 'Stay,

child. I have seen very little of you. I enjoyed a talk
with your parents. They return tomorrow?'

'Yes, *mevrouw*. I'm staying for a little while to help
Joke while her nanny goes on holiday.'

'You will be here for the New Year? It is an important occasion to us in Holland.'

'I don't know; I shouldn't think so. Will it be a
family gathering again?'

'Yes, but just for the evening. You are enjoying
yourself?'

'Yes, thank you. Very much.'

'Excellent. Now run along and join the others.' The
old lady smiled. 'I must confess that I prefer the quiet
of my room, but it is Christmas and one must make
merry!'

Which described the evening very well—drinks before dinner sent everyone into the dining room full of
bonhomie, to sit down to a traditional Christmas dinner—turkey, Christmas pudding, mince pies, crack-
ers, port and walnuts…

The cousin sitting next to Emmy, whose name she
had forgotten, accepted a second mince pie. 'Of
course, not all Dutch families celebrate as we do here.
This is typically English, is it not? But you see we
have married into English families from time to time,
and this is one of the delightful customs we have
adopted. Will you be here for the New Year?'

'I don't know. I don't expect so. I'm only staying
for a few days while Nanny has a holiday.'

'We return home tomorrow—all of us. But we shall
be here again for New Year. But only for one night.

We are that rare thing—a happy family. We enjoy meeting each other quite frequently. You have brothers and sisters?'

'No, there is just me. But I have always been happy at home.'

'The children like you…'

'Well, I like them.' She smiled at him and turned to the elderly man on her other side. She wasn't sure who he was, and his English was heavily accented, but he was, like everyone else—except Anneliese and her parents—friendly towards her.

After dinner everyone went back to the drawing room, to talk and gossip, going from group to group, and Emmy found herself swept up by Joke, listening to the lively chatter, enjoying herself and quite forgetting the brown dress and the way in which the professor avoided her.

It was while Joke, her arm linked in Emmy's, was talking to friends of the professor's—a youngish couple and something, she gathered, to do with one of the hospitals—that Anneliese joined them.

She tapped Emmy on the arm. 'Ruerd tells me you are to stay here for a few weeks as nanny to Joke's children. How fortunate you are, Emmy, to find work so easily after your lovely holiday.' She gave a titter. 'Let us hope that it hasn't given you ideas above your station.'

Emmy reminded herself that this was the professor's fiancée and that after this evening she need not, with any luck, ever see her again. Which was just as well, for the temptation to slap her was very strong.

She said in a gentle voice, aware that her companions were bating their breath, 'I'm sure you will agree with me that work at any level is preferable to idling away one's life, wasting money on unsuitable clothes—' she cast an eloquent eye at Anneliese's flat chest '—and wasting one's days doing nothing.'

If I sound like a prig, that's too bad, thought Emmy, and smiled her sweetest smile.

Now what would happen?

Joke said instantly, 'You're quite right, Emmy—I'm sure you agree, Anneliese.' And she was backed up by murmurs from her companions.

Anneliese, red in the face, said sharply, 'Well, of course I do. Excuse me, I must speak to Aunt Beatrix…'

'You mean *our* aunt Beatrix,' said Joke in a voice of kindly reproval. Anneliese shot her a look of pure dislike and went away without another word.

'I simply must learn to hold my tongue,' said Joke, and giggled. 'I'm afraid I shall be a very nasty sister-in-law. Alemke is much more civil, although it plays havoc with her temper.'

She caught Emmy's sleeve. 'Come and talk to Grandmother. She will be going back to den Haag in the morning. Well, everyone will be going, won't they? Ruerd last of all, after lunch, and that leaves you and the children and me, Emmy.'

'I shall like that,' said Emmy. She was still shaking with rage. Anneliese would go to Ruerd and tell him how rude she had been, and he would never speak to her again…

She was talking to her mother when Anneliese went home with her parents. She gave them no more than a cool nod as she swept past them. The professor, as a good host should, saw them into their car and when he came back went to talk to his grandmother. It wasn't until everyone was dispersing much later to their beds that he came to wish the Fosters a good night and to hope that they had enjoyed their evening.

'I trust that you enjoyed yourself, too, Ermentrude,' he observed, looking down his splendid nose at her.

How nice if one could voice one's true thoughts and feelings, thought Emmy, assuring him in a polite voice that she had had a splendid evening.

He said, 'Good, good. I have to go to Leiden in the morning, but I shall see you before we go after lunch.'

For the last time, thought Emmy, and kissed her mother and father goodnight and went up the staircase to her bed.

Once breakfast was over in the morning people began to leave—stopping for a last-minute gossip, going back to find something they'd forgotten to pack, exchanging last-minute messages. They went at last, and within minutes the professor had got into his car and driven away too, leaving Emmy and her parents with Joke and the children.

Mrs Foster went away to finish her packing and Mr Foster retired to the library to read the *Daily Telegraph*, which Cokker had conjured up from somewhere. Since Joke wanted to talk to Tiele about the running of the house once the professor had gone, Emmy dressed the children in their outdoor things, wrapped herself in her coat, tied a scarf over her head and took them off to the village, with Solly and Tip for company.

They bought sweets in the small village shop and the dogs crunched the biscuits old Mevrouw Kamp offered them while she took a good look at Emmy, nodding and smiling while the children talked. Emmy had no doubt that it was about her, but the old lady looked friendly enough and, when she offered the children a sweetie from the jar on the counter, she offered Emmy one too. It tasted horrid, but she chewed it with apparent pleasure and wondered what it was.

'*Zoute* drop,' she was told. 'And weren't they delicious?'

For anyone partial to a sweet made of salt probably they were, thought Emmy, and swallowed the last morsel thankfully.

They lunched early as the professor wanted to leave by one o'clock. He joined in the talk—teasing the children, making last-minute arrangements with his sister, discussing the latest news with Mr Foster. But, although he was careful to see that Emmy had all that she wanted and was included in the talk, he had little to say to her.

I shan't see him again, thought Emmy, and I can't bear it. She brightened, though, when she remembered that she would be going back to England later and there was a chance that he might take her if he was on one of his flying visits to one or other of the hospitals. The thought cheered her so much that she was able to bid him goodbye with brisk friendliness and thank him suitably for her visit. 'It was a lovely Christmas,' she told him, and offered a hand, to have it engulfed in his.

His brief, too cheerful, 'Yes, it was, wasn't it?' made it only too plain that behind his good manners he didn't care tuppence...

She bade her mother and father goodbye, pleased to see what a lot of good these few days had done them. A little luxury never harmed anyone, she reflected, and hoped that the lodge would be quickly restored to normal.

'When you get home everything will be sorted out,' her mother assured her. 'Your father and I feel so rested we can tackle anything. Take care of yourself, love, won't you? Ruerd says you could do with a few more days before you go job-hunting.'

If it hadn't been for the children the house would have seemed very quiet once its master had driven away, but the rest of the day was taken up with the pleasurable task of re-examining the presents which they had had at Christmas, and a visit to the village shop once more to buy paper and envelopes for the less pleasurable task of writing the thank-you letters.

On the following day they all got into Joke's car and drove along the coast as far as Alkmaar. The cheese museum was closed for the winter, but there was the clock, with its mechanical figures circling round it on each hour, and the lovely cathedral church, as well as the picturesque old houses and shops. They lunched in a small café, off *erwtensoep*— a pea soup so thick that a spoon could stand upright in it—and *roggebrood*. The children made Emmy repeat the names after them, rolling around with laughter at her efforts.

It was a surprisingly happy day, and Emmy was kept too busy to think about the professor. Only that night as she got into bed did she spare him a thought. He would be back in Chelsea by now, with Beaker looking after him. He would have phoned Anneliese, of course. He would miss her, thought Emmy sleepily, although how a man could miss anyone as disagreeable as she was a bit of a puzzle.

There was a phone call from her mother in the morning. They had had a splendid trip back; Ruerd had taken them right to their door, and there had been a letter waiting for them, telling them that the furniture would be removed in a day's time.

'So now we can get things straight,' said her mother happily. 'And Ruerd is so splendid—he unloaded a box of the most delicious food for us, and a bottle of champagne. One meets such a person so seldom in life, and when one does it is so often for a brief period. We shall miss him. He sent his kind regards, by the way, love.'

An empty, meaningless phrase, reflected Emmy.

She was to have the children all day as Joke was going to den Haag to the hairdresser's and to do some

shopping. It was a bright, cold day, so, with everyone
well wrapped-up, she led them down to the sea,
tramping along the sand with Tip and Solly gavotting
around them. They all threw sticks, racing up and
down, shouting and laughing to each other, playing
tag, daring each other to run to the water's edge and
back.

Emmy shouted with them; there was no one else
to hear or see them, and the air was exhilarating. They
trooped back presently, tired and hungry, to eat the
lunch Cokker had waiting for them and then go to the
nursery, where they sat around the table playing
cards—the littlest one on Emmy's lap, her head
tucked into Emmy's shoulder, half asleep.

They had tea there presently and, since Joke wasn't
back yet, Emmy set about getting them ready for bed.
Bathed and clad in dressing gowns they were eating
their suppers when their mother returned.

'Emmy, you must be worn out. I never meant to
be so long, but I met some friends and had lunch with
them and then I had the shopping to do. Have you
hated it?'

'I've enjoyed every minute,' said Emmy quite
truthfully. 'I had a lovely day; I only hope the children did, too.'

'Well, tomorrow we're all going to den Haag to
have lunch with my mother and father. They were
away for Christmas—in Denmark with a widowed
aunt. They'll be here for New Year, though. You did
know that we had parents living?'

'The professor mentioned it.'

'Christmas wasn't quite the same without them, but we'll all be here in a few days.'

'You want me to come with you tomorrow?' asked Emmy. 'I'm quite happy to stay here—I mean, it's family...'

Joke smiled. 'I want you to come if you will, Emmy.' She wondered if she should tell her that her parents had been told all about her by Ruerd, and decided not to. It was his business. They had never been a family to interfere with each other's lives, although she and Alemke very much wished to dissuade him from marrying Anneliese.

There was undoubtedly something Ruerd was keeping to himself, and neither of them had seen any sign of love or even affection in his manner towards Anneliese, although he was attentive to her needs and always concerned for her comfort. Good manners wouldn't allow him to be otherwise. And he had been careful to avoid being alone with Emmy at Christmas. Always polite towards her, his friendliness also aloof. Knowing her brother, Joke knew that he wouldn't break his word to Anneliese, although she strongly suspected that he had more than a casual interest in Emmy.

They drove to den Haag in good spirits in the morning. The children spoke a little English and Emmy taught them some of the old-fashioned nursery rhymes, which they sang for most of the way. Only as they reached a long, stately avenue with large houses on each side of it did Emmy suggest that they should stop. Joke drove up the short drive of one of these houses and stopped before its ponderous door. 'Well, here we are,' she declared. 'Oma and Opa will be waiting.'

The door opened as they reached it and a stout, elderly woman welcomed them.

'This is Nynke,' said Joke, and Emmy shook hands and waited while the children hugged and kissed her. 'The housekeeper. She has been with us since I was a little girl.' It was her turn to be hugged and kissed before they all went into the hall to take off coats and scarves and gloves, and go through the arched double doors Nynke was holding open for them.

The elderly couple waiting for them at the end of the long, narrow room made an imposing pair. The professor's parents were tall—his father with the massive frame he had passed on to his son, and his mother an imposing, rather stout figure. They both had grey hair, and his father was still a handsome man, but his mother, despite her elegant bearing, had a homely face, spared from downright plainness by a pair of very blue eyes.

No wonder he has fallen in love with Anneliese, reflected Emmy, with that lovely face and golden hair.

The children swarmed over their grandparents, although they were careful to mind their manners, and presently stood quietly while Joke greeted her parents.

'And this is Emmy,' she said, and put a hand on Emmy's arm. 'I am so glad to have her with me for a few days—she's been staying with her parents over Christmas at Huis ter Mennolt. Rik's away, and it's lovely to have company.'

Emmy shook hands, warmed by friendly smiles and greetings in almost accentless English. Presently Mevrouw ter Mennolt drew her to one side and, over coffee and tiny almond biscuits, begged her to tell her something of herself.

'Ruerd mentioned that he had guests from England when he phoned us. You know him well?'

The nice, plain face smiled, the blue eyes twinkled. Emmy embarked on a brief résumé of her acquaintance with the professor, happily unaware that her companion had already had a detailed account from her son. It was what he *hadn't* said which had convinced his mother that he was more than a little interested in Emmy.

Watching Emmy's face, almost as plain as her own, she wished heartily for a miracle before Anneliese managed to get her son to the altar. Mevrouw ter Mennolt had tried hard to like her, since her son was to marry the girl, but she had had no success, and Anneliese, confident in her beauty and charm, had never made an effort to gain her future mother-in-law's affection.

Emmy would, however, do very nicely. Joke had told her that she was right for Ruerd, and she found herself agreeing. The children liked her and that, for a doting grandmother, was an important point. She hadn't forgotten Anneliese once flying into a rage during a visit because Joke's youngest had accidentally put a grubby little paw on Anneliese's white skirt. It was a pity that Ruerd hadn't been there, for her lovely face had grown ugly with temper. Besides, this quiet, rather shabbily dressed girl might be the one woman in the world who understood Ruerd, a man whose feelings ran deep and hidden from all but those who loved him.

Emmy was handed over to her host presently, and although she was at first wary of this older edition of the professor he put her at her ease in minutes, talking about gardening, dogs and cats, and presently he bade her fetch her coat.

'We have a garden here,' he told her. 'Not as splendid as that at Huis ter Mennolt, but sufficient for us and Max. Let us take the dogs for a quick run before lunch.'

They went through the house, into a conservatory, out of doors onto a terrace and down some steps to the garden below. Max, the black Labrador, Solly and Tip went with them, going off the path to search for imaginary rabbits, while Emmy and Ruerd's father walked briskly down its considerable length to the shrubbery at the end.

All the while they talked. At least, the old man talked, and a great deal of what he said concerned his son. Emmy learned more about Ruerd in fifteen minutes than she had in all the weeks she had known him. She listened avidly; soon she would never see him again, so every small scrap of information about him was precious, to be stored away, to be mulled over in a future empty of him.

Back at the house she led the children away to have their hands washed and their hair combed before lunch. They went up the stairs and into one of the bathrooms—old-fashioned like the rest of the house, but lacking nothing in comfort. She liked the house. It wasn't like Huis ter Mennolt; it had been built at a later date—mid-nineteenth century, she guessed—and the furniture was solid and beautifully cared for. Beidermeier? she thought, not knowing much about it. Its walls were hung with family portraits and she longed to study them as she urged the children downstairs once again, all talking at once and laughing at her attempts to understand them.

She was offered dry sherry in the drawing room while the children drank something pink and fizzy—a special drink they always had at their grandmother's, they told her, before they all went into the dining room for lunch.

It was a pleasant meal, with the children on their best behaviour and conversation which went well with eating the lamb chops which followed the celery soup—nothing deep which required long pauses while something was debated and explained—and nothing personal. No one, thought Emmy, had mentioned Anneliese once, which, since she was so soon to be a member of the family, seemed strange.

Christmas was discussed, and plans for the New Year.

'We shall all meet again at Huis ter Mennolt,' explained Joke. 'Just for dinner in the evening, and to wish each other a happy New Year. Ruerd will come back just for a day or two; he never misses.'

They sat around after lunch, and presently, when the children became restive, Emmy sat them round a table at the other end of the drawing room and suggested cards. 'Snap', 'beggar your neighbour' and 'beat your neighbour out of doors' she had already taught them, and they settled down to play. Presently she was making as much noise as they were.

It was a large room; the three persons at the other end of it were able to talk without hindrance, and, even if Emmy could have heard them, she couldn't have understood a word. Good manners required them to talk in English while she was with them, but now they embarked on the subject nearest to their hearts—Ruerd.

They would have been much cheered if they had known that he was in his office at St Luke's, sitting at his desk piled with patients' notes, charts and department reports, none of which he was reading. He was thinking about Emmy.

When he returned to Holland in a few days' time, he would ask Anneliese to release him from their engagement. It was a step he was reluctant to take for, although he had no feeling for her any more, he had no wish to humiliate her with her friends. But to marry her when he loved Ermentrude was out of the question. Supposing Ermentrude wouldn't have him? He smiled a little; then he would have to remain a bachelor for the rest of his days.

He would have his lovely home in Holland, his pleasant house in Chelsea, his dogs, his work…but a bleak prospect without her.

*   *   *

Joke, Emmy and the children drove back to Huis ter Mennolt after tea. With the coming of evening it was much colder. 'We shall probably have some snow before much longer,' said Joke. 'Do you skate, Emmy?'

'No, only roller-skating when I was a little girl. We don't get much snow at home.'

'Well, we can teach you while you are here.' Joke added quickly, 'Nanny isn't coming back for another couple of days. Her mother has the flu, and she doesn't want to give it to the children. You won't mind staying for a few days longer?'

Emmy didn't mind. She didn't mind where she was if the professor wasn't going to be there too.

'You've heard from your mother?' asked Joke.

'Yes; everything is going very well at last. The furniture will be gone today and the plumber has almost finished whatever it was he had to do. By the time the term starts they should be well settled in. I ought to have been there to help...'

'Well, Ruerd advised against it, didn't he? And I dare say your mother would have worried over you if you had worked too hard or got wet.'

'Well, yes, I suppose so.'

Emmy eased the smallest child onto her lap so that Solly could lean against her shoulder. Tip was in front with the eldest boy. It was a bit of a squash in the big car, but it was warm and comfortable, smelling of damp dog and the peppermints the children were eating.

The next morning Joke went back to den Haag. 'Cokker will look after you all,' she told Emmy.

'Take the children out if you like. They're getting excited about New Year. Everyone will be coming tomorrow in time for lunch, but Ruerd phoned to say he won't get here until the evening. I hope he'll stay for a few days this time. He'll take you back with him when he does go. If that suits you?' Joke studied Emmy's face. 'You do feel better for the change? I haven't asked you to do too much?'

'I've loved every minute,' said Emmy truthfully. 'I like the children and I love this house and the sea-shore, and you've all been so kind to me and Mother and Father.'

'You must come and see us again,' said Joke, and looked at Emmy to see how she felt about that.

'I expect I shall have a job, but it's kind of you to invite me.'

'Ruerd could always bring you over when he comes,' persisted Joke.

'Well, I don't suppose we shall see each other. I mean, he's in London and I'll be in Dorset.'

'Will you mind that?' said Joke.

Emmy bent over the French knitting she was fixing for one of the girls.

'Yes. The professor has helped me so often—you know, when things have happened. He—he always seemed to be there, if you see what I mean. I shall always be grateful to him.'

Joke said airily, 'Yes, coincidence is a strange thing, isn't it? Some people call it fate. Well, I'm off. Ask Cokker or Tiele for anything you want. I'll try and be back in time for tea, but if the traffic's heavy I may be a bit late.'

The day was much as other days—going down to the seashore, running races on the sand, with Emmy carrying the youngest, joining in the shouting and laughing and then going back to piping hot soup and *crokettes*, and, since it was almost New Year, *poffertjes*—tiny pancakes sprinkled with sugar.

The two smallest children were led upstairs to rest then, and the other two went to the billiard room where they were allowed to play snooker on the small table at one end of the room.

Which left Emmy with an hour or so to herself. She went back to the drawing room and began a slow round of the portraits and then a careful study of the contents of the two great display cabinets on either side of the fireplace. She was admiring a group of figurines—Meissen, she thought—when Cokker came into the room.

'Juffrouw van Moule has called,' he told her. 'I have said that *mevrouw* is out, but she wishes to see you, miss.'

'Me? Whatever for?' asked Emmy. 'I expect I'd better see her, hadn't I, Cokker? I don't expect she'll stay, do you? But if the children want anything, could you please ask Tiele to go to them?'

'Yes, miss, and you will ring if you want me?'

'Thank you, Cokker.'

Anneliese came into the room with the self-assurance of someone who knew that she looked perfection itself. Indeed she was beautiful, wrapped in a soft blue wool coat, with a high-crowned Melusine hat perched on her fair hair. She took the coat off and tossed it onto a chair, sent gloves and handbag after it and sat down in one of the small easy chairs.

'Still here, Ermentrude.' It wasn't a question but a statement. 'Hanging on until the last minute. Not that it will do you any good. Ruerd must be heartily tired of you, but that is what happens when one does a good deed—one is condemned to repeat it unendingly. Still, you have had a splendid holiday, have you not? He intends that you should return to England directly after New Year. He will be staying on here for a time; we have the wedding arrangements to complete. You did know that we are to marry in January?'

She looked at Emmy's face. 'No, I see that you did not know. I expect he knew that I would tell you. So much easier for me to do it, is it not? It is embarrassing for him, knowing that you are in love with him, although heaven knows he has never given you the least encouragement. I suppose someone like you, living such a dull life, has to make do with daydreams.'

Anneliese smiled and sat back in her chair.

'It seems to me,' said Emmy, in a voice she willed to keep steady, 'that you are talking a great deal of nonsense. Is that why you came? And you haven't told me anything new. I know that you and the professor are to be married, and I know that I am going back to England as soon as Nanny is back, and I know that you have been very rude and rather spiteful.'

She watched with satisfaction as Anneliese flushed brightly. 'I believe in being outspoken too. We dislike each other; I have no use for girls like you. Go back to England and find some clerk or shopkeeper to marry you. It is a pity that you ever had a taste of our kind of life.' She eyed Emmy shrewdly. 'You do believe me, don't you, about our marriage?'

And when Emmy didn't answer she said, 'I'll prove it.'

She got up and went to the phone on one of the side-tables. 'Ruerd's house number,' she said over her shoulder. 'If he isn't there I will ring the hospital.' She began to dial. 'And you know what I shall say? I shall tell him that you don't believe me, that you hope in your heart that he loves you and that you will continue to pester him and try and spoil his happiness.'

'You don't need to phone,' said Emmy quietly. 'I didn't believe you, but perhaps there is truth in what you say. I shall go back to England as soon as I can and I shan't see him again.'

Anneliese came back to her chair. 'And you'll say nothing when he comes here tomorrow? A pity you have to be here, but it can't be helped. Luckily there will be a number of people here; he won't have time to talk to you.'

'He never has talked to me,' said Emmy. 'Only as a guest.' Emmy got up. 'I expect you would like to go now. I don't know why you have thought of me as a—well, a rival, I suppose. You're beautiful, and

I'm sure you will make the professor a most suitable wife. I hope you will both be happy.'

The words had almost choked her, but she had said them. Anneliese looked surprised, but she got into her coat, picked up her gloves and bag and went out of the room without another word. Cokker appeared a minute later.

'I have prepared a pot of tea, miss; I am sure you would enjoy it.'

Emmy managed a smile. 'Oh, Cokker, thank you. I'd love it.'

He came with the tray and set it down beside her chair. 'The English, I understand, drink tea at any time, but especially at moments of great joy or despair.'

'Yes, Cokker, you are quite right; they do.'

She wasn't going to cry, she told herself, drinking the hot tea, forcing it down over the lump of tears in her throat.

She tried not to think about the things Anneliese had said. They had been spiteful, but they had had the ring of truth. Had she been so transparent in her feelings towards Ruerd? She had thought—and how silly and stupid she had been—that his kiss under the mistletoe had meant something. She didn't know what, but it had been like a spark between them. Perhaps Anneliese was right and she had been allowing herself to daydream.

Emmy went pale at the thought of meeting him, but she had the rest of the day and most of tomorrow in which to pull herself together, and the first chance she got she would go back to England.

The children had their tea and she began on the leisurely task of getting them to bed after a rousing game of ludo. They were in their dressing gowns and eating their suppers when Joke got back, and it wasn't until she and Emmy had dined that Emmy asked her when Nanny would be coming back.

'You are not happy. I have given you too much to do—the children all day long...'

'No, no. I love it here and I like being with the children, only I think that I should go home as soon as Nanny comes back. I don't mean to sound ungrateful—it's been like a lovely holiday—but I must start looking for a job.'

Emmy spoke briskly but her face was sad, and Joke wondered why. She had her answer as Emmy went on in a determinedly cheerful voice, 'Anneliese called this afternoon. I should have told you sooner, but there were so many other things to talk about with the children. She only stayed for a few minutes.'

'Why did she come here? What did she say?'

'Nothing, really; she just sort of popped in. She didn't leave any messages for you. Perhaps she wanted to know something to do with tomorrow. She will be coming, of course.'

'Oh, yes, she will be here. Was she civil? She doesn't like you much, does she?'

'No; I don't know why. She was quite polite.'

I could tell you why, thought Joke—you've stolen

Ruerd's heart, something Anneliese knows she can
never do.

She said aloud, 'Nanny phoned this evening while
you were getting the children into bed. She will be
back the day after tomorrow. I hate to see you go,
Emmy.'

'I shan't forget any of you, or this house and the
people in it,' said Emmy.

She had no time to think about her own plans. The
house was in a bustle, getting ready for the guests.
Tiele was in the kitchen making piles of *oliebolljes*—
a kind of doughnut which everyone ate at New
Year—and the maids were hurrying here and there,
laying the table for a buffet lunch and getting a guest
room ready in case Grandmother ter Mennolt should
need to rest.

'She never misses,' said Joke. 'She and Aunt
Beatrix live together at Wassenaar—that's a suburb
of den Haag. They have a housekeeper and Jon, the
chauffeur, who sees to the garden and stokes the
boiler and so on. The aunts and uncles and cousins
you met at Christmas will come—oh, and Anneliese,
of course.'

Almost everyone came for lunch, although guests
were still arriving during the afternoon. Anneliese had
arrived for lunch, behaving, as Joke said sourly, as
though she were already the mistress of the house.
Her parents were with her, and a youngish man whom
she introduced as an old friend who had recently returned to Holland.

'We lost touch,' she explained. 'We were quite close...' She smiled charmingly and he put an arm round her waist and smiled down at her. She had spoken in Dutch, and Alemke had whispered a translation in Emmy's ear.

'How dare she bring that man here?' she added. 'And Ruerd won't be here until quite late this evening... Oh, how I wish something would happen...'

Sometimes a wish is granted. The professor, by dint of working twice as hard as usual, was ready to leave Chelsea by the late morning. Seen off by Beaker and Charlie, he drove to Dover, crossed over the channel and made good time to his house. It was dark when he arrived, and the windows were ablaze. He let himself in through a side door, pleased to be home, and even more pleased at the thought of seeing Emmy again. He walked along the curved passage behind the hall and then paused at a half-open door of a small sitting room, seldom used. Whoever was there sounded like Anneliese. He opened the door and went in.

CHAPTER NINE

IT WAS indeed Anneliese, in the arms of a man the professor didn't know, being kissed and kissing with unmistakable ardour.

With such ardour that they didn't see him. He stood in the doorway, watching them, until the man caught sight of him, pushed Anneliese away and then caught her hand in his.

The professor strolled into the room. 'I don't think I have had the pleasure of meeting you,' he said pleasantly. 'Anneliese, please introduce me to your friend.'

Anneliese was for once at a loss for words. The man held out a hand. 'Hubold Koppelar, an old friend of Anneliese.'

The professor ignored the hand. He looked down his splendid nose at Koppelar. 'How old?' he asked. 'Before Anneliese became engaged to me?'

Anneliese had found her tongue. 'Of course it was. Hubold went away to Canada; I thought he would never come back…'

The professor took out his spectacles, put them on and looked at her carefully. 'So you made do with me?'

Anneliese tossed her head. 'Well, what else was

there to do? I want a home and money, like any other woman.'

'I am now no longer necessary to your plans for the future, though?' asked the professor gently. 'Consider yourself free, Anneliese, if that is what you want.'

Hubold drew her hand through his arm. 'She wants it, all right. Of course, we hadn't meant it to be like this—we would have let you down lightly...'

The professor's eyes were like flint, but he smiled. 'Very good of you. And now the matter is settled there is no need for us to meet again, is there? I regret that I cannot show you the door at this moment, but the New Year is an occasion in this house and I won't have it spoilt. I must ask you both to remain and behave normally until after midnight. Now, let us go together and meet my guests...'

So Emmy, about to go upstairs to get into the despised brown dress, was one of the first to see him come into the hall, with Anneliese on one side of him and the man she had brought with her on the other. It was easy to escape for everyone else surged forward to meet him.

'Ruerd, how lovely,' cried Joke. 'We didn't expect you until much later...'

'An unexpected surprise,' said the professor, and watched Emmy's small person disappear up the staircase. Nothing of his feelings showed on his face.

He made some laughing remark to Anneliese and went to talk to his grandmother and father and mother, then presently to mingle with his guests before everyone went away to change for the evening.

Emmy didn't waste much time on dressing. She took a uninterested look at her person in the looking-glass, put a few extra pins into the coil of hair in the nape of her neck and went along to the nursery to make sure that the children were ready for bed. As a great treat, they were to be roused just before midnight and brought downstairs to greet the New Year, on the understanding that they went to their beds punctually and went to sleep.

It seemed unlikely that they would, thought Emmy, tucking them in while she wondered how best to arrange her departure just as soon as possible.

To travel on New Year's Day would be impossible, but if she could see the professor in the morning and ask him to arrange for her to travel on the following day she would only need to stay one more day. And with so many people in the house it would be easy enough to keep out of the way. Anyway, he would surely be wrapped up in Anneliese. Emmy would get up early and pack, just in case there was some way of leaving sooner.

Fortune smiled on her for once. Sitting in a quiet corner of the drawing room was Oom Domus, middle-aged and a widower. He told her that he was going to the Hook of Holland to catch the ferry to England late on New Year's Day. 'It sails at midnight, as you may know. There will be almost no trains and buses or ferries tomorrow. It is very much a national holiday here.'

'Do you drive there?' asked Emmy.

'Yes; I'm going to stay with friends in Warwickshire.'

Emmy took a quick breath. 'Would you mind very much giving me a lift as far as Dover? I'm going back to England now that Nanny will be back tomorrow.'

If Oom Domus was surprised he didn't show it. 'My dear young lady, I shall be delighted. You live in Dorset, do you not? Far better if I drive you on to London and drop you off at whichever station you want.'

'You're very kind. I—I haven't seen the professor to tell him yet, but I'm sure he won't mind.'

Oom Domus had watched Ruerd not looking at Emmy, just as she was careful not to look at him. He thought it likely that both of them would mind, but he wasn't going to say so. He said easily, 'I shall leave around seven o'clock tomorrow evening, my dear. That will give you plenty of time to enjoy your day.'

As far as Emmy was concerned the day was going to be far too long. She wanted to get away as quickly as she could, away from Ruerd and his lovely home, and away from Anneliese.

Aunt Beatrix joined them then, and Emmy looked around her at the laughing and talking people near her. There was no sign of the professor for the moment, but Anneliese was there, as beautiful as ever, in yards of trailing chiffon. She was laughing a great deal, and looked flushed. Excitement at seeing Ruerd again? Or drinking too much?

Emmy took a second glass of sherry when Cokker offered it; perhaps if she drank everything she was offered during the evening it would be over more quickly. She caught sight of the professor's handsome features as he came across the room; she tossed back the sherry and beat a retreat into a group of cousins, who smilingly welcomed her and switched to English as easily as changing hats.

If the professor had noticed this, he gave no sign, merely passed the time of day with his uncle and went to talk to Joke.

'You look like a cat who's swallowed the cream,' she told him. 'What's going on behind that bland face of yours?'

When he only smiled she said, 'Nanny's back tomorrow. Have you arranged to take Emmy home?'

'No, not yet.'

'For some reason she's keen to go as soon as possible—said she has to find a job.'

'I'll talk to her when there's a quiet moment. Here's Cokker to tell us that dinner is served.'

Twenty persons sat down to the table which had been extended for the occasion, and Emmy found herself between two of the professor's friends—pleasant, middle-aged men who knew England well and kept up a lively conversation throughout the meal.

Emmy, very slightly muzzy from her tossed-back sherry, ate her mushrooms in garlic and cream, drank a glass of white wine with the lobster Thermidor and a glass of red wine with the kidneys in a calvados and cream sauce. And another glass of sweet white wine with the trifle and mince pies...

The meal was leisurely and the talk lively. The professor's father, sitting at the head of the table, listened gravely to Anneliese, who was so animated that Emmy decided that she really had drunk too much. Like me, reflected Emmy uneasily. He had Grandmother ter Mennolt on his other side, who, excepting when good manners demanded, ignored Anneliese. The professor was at the other end of the table, sitting beside his mother with Aunt Beatrix on his other side. Emmy wondered why he and Anneliese weren't sitting together. Perhaps there was a precedent about these occasions...

They had coffee at the table so that it was well after eleven o'clock before everyone went back to the drawing room. Anneliese was with Ruerd now, her friend at the other end of the room talking to Joke's husband. Emmy wondered if the professor would make some sort of announcement about his forthcoming marriage; Anneliese had told her that it was to be within the next few weeks, and presumably everyone there would be invited.

Nothing was said, and just before twelve o'clock she slipped away to rouse the children and bring them down to the drawing room. The older ones were awake—she suspected that they hadn't been to sleep yet—but the smaller ones needed a good deal of rousing. She was joined by Joke and Alemke presently, and they led the children downstairs, where they stood, owl-eyed and excited, each with a small glass of lemonade with which to greet the New Year.

Someone had tuned into the BBC, and Cokker was going round filling glasses with champagne. The maids and the gardener had joined them by now, and there was a ripple of excitement as Big Ben struck the first stroke. There were cries of *Gelukkige Niewe Jaar!* and the children screamed with delight as the first of the fireworks outside the drawing-room windows were set off.

Everyone was darting to and fro, kissing and shaking hands and wishing each other good luck and happiness. Emmy was kissed and greeted too, standing a little to one side with the smallest child—already half-asleep again despite the fireworks—tucked against her shoulder. Even Anneliese paused by her, but not to wish her well. All she said was, 'Tomorrow you will be back in England.'

Hubold Koppelar, circling the group, paused by her, looked her over and went past her without a word. He wasn't sure who she was; one of the maids, he supposed, detailed to look after the children. Anneliese would tell him later. For the moment they were keeping prudently apart, mindful of the professor's words, uttered so quietly but not to be ignored.

Emmy had been edging round the room, avoiding the professor as he went from one group to the other, exchanging greetings, but he finally caught up with her. She held out a hand and said stiffly, looking no higher than his tie, 'A happy New Year, Professor.'

He took the hand and held it fast. 'Don't worry,

Ermentrude. I'm not going to kiss you; not here and now.'

He smiled down at her and her heart turned over.

'We shall have a chance to talk tomorrow morning,' he told her. 'Or perhaps presently, when the children are back in bed.'

Emmy gazed at him, quite unable to think of anything to say, looking so sad that he started to ask her what was the matter—to be interrupted by Aunt Beatrix, asking him briskly if he would have a word with his grandmother.

He let Emmy's hand go at last. 'Later,' he said, and smiled with such tenderness that she swallowed tears.

She watched his massive back disappear amongst his guests. He was letting her down lightly, letting her see that he was going to ignore a situation embarrassing to them both. She felt hot all over at the thought.

It was a relief to escape with the children and put them back into their beds. She wouldn't be missed, and although there was a buffet supper she couldn't have swallowed a morsel. She went to her room, undressed and got into bed, lying awake until long after the house was quiet.

There was no one at breakfast when she went downstairs in the morning. Cokker brought her coffee and toast, which she didn't want. Later, she promised herself, when the professor had a few minutes to spare, she would explain about going back to England with

Oom Domus. He would be pleased; it made a neat
end to an awkward situation. Anneliese would have
got her way, too... She hadn't seen Anneliese after
those few words; she supposed that she was spending
the night here and would probably stay on now the
professor was home.

Emmy got up and went to look out of the window.
Ruerd was coming towards the house with Tip and
Solly, coming from the direction of the shore. If she
had the chance she would go once more just to watch
the wintry North Sea and then walk back over the
dunes along the path which would afford her a
glimpse of the house beyond the garden. It was something she wanted to remember for always.

She went back upstairs before he reached the
house; the children must be wakened and urged to
dress and clean their teeth. Joke had said that they
would be leaving that afternoon at the same time as
Alemke and her husband and children.

'Everyone else will go before lunch,' she had told
Emmy. 'My mother and father will stay for lunch, of
course, but Grandmother and Aunt Beatrix will go at
the same time as the others.'

Cousins and aunts and uncles and family and
friends began to take their leave soon after breakfast,
and, once they had gone, Emmy suggested that she
should take the children down for a last scamper on
the sands.

'Oh, would you?' asked Joke. 'Just for an hour, so
they can let off steam? Nanny will be waiting for us

when we get home. They're going to miss you, Emmy.'

The professor was in his study with his father. Emmy bundled the children into their coats, wrapped herself up against the winter weather outside and hurried them away before he should return. She still had to tell him that she was leaving, but perhaps a brisk run out of doors would give her the courage to do so.

At the end of an hour, she marshalled her charges into some sort of order and went back to the house, and, since their boots and shoes were covered in damp sand and frost, they went in through the side door. It wasn't until it was too late to retreat that she saw the professor standing there, holding the door open.

The children milled around him, chattering like magpies, but presently he said something to them and they trooped away, leaving Emmy without a backward glance. She did her best to slide past the professor's bulk.

'I'll just go and help the children,' she began. And then went on ashamed of her cowardice, 'I wanted to see you, Professor. I'd like to go back to England today, if you don't mind. Oom Domus said he would give me a lift this evening.' When he said nothing she added, 'I've had a lovely time here, and you've been so kind. I'm very grateful, but it's time I went back to England.'

He glanced at her and looked away. 'Stay a few more days, Ermentrude. I'll take you back when I go.'

'I'd like to go today—and it's so convenient, isn't

it? I mean, Oom Domus is going over to England this evening.'

'You have no wish to stay?' he asked, in what she thought was a very casual voice. 'We must talk…'

'No—no. I'd like to go as soon as possible.'

'By all means go with Oom Domus.' He stood aside. 'Don't let me keep you; I expect that you have things to do. Lunch will be in half an hour or so.'

She slipped past him, and then stopped as he said, without turning round, 'You have avoided me, Ermentrude. You have a reason?'

'Yes, but I don't want to talk about it. It's—personal.' She paused. 'It's something I'd rather not talk about,' she repeated.

When he didn't answer, she went away. It hadn't been at all satisfactory; she had expected him to be relieved, even if he expressed polite regret at her sudden departure. He had sounded withdrawn, as though it didn't matter whether she came or went. Probably it *didn't* matter, she told herself firmly. He must surely be relieved to bring to an end what could only have been an embarrassing episode. As for the kiss, what to her had been a glorious moment in her life had surely been a mere passing incident in his.

She went to her room and sat down to think about it. She could, of course, write to him, but what would be the point? He would think that she was wishful of continuing their friendship—had it been friendship? She no longer knew—and that would be the last thing he would want with his marriage to Anneliese imminent. Best leave things as they were, she decided, and tidied her hair, looked rather despairingly at her pale face and went down to lunch.

She had been dreading that, but there was no need. The professor offered her sherry with easy friendliness and during lunch kept the conversation to light-hearted topics, never once touching on her departure. It seemed to her that he was no longer interested in it.

She made the excuse that she still had some last-minute packing to do after lunch. If she remained in the drawing room it would mean that everyone would have to speak in English, and it was quite likely they wanted to discuss family matters in their own language. It had surprised her that Anneliese hadn't come to lunch—perhaps Ruerd was going to her home later that day. Everyone would be gone by the late afternoon and he would be able to do as he pleased.

Of course, she had no packing to do. She went and sat by the window and stared out at the garden and the dunes and the sea beyond. It would be dark in a few hours, but the sun had struggled through the clouds now, and the pale sunlight warmed the bare trees and turned the dull-grey sea into silver. It wouldn't last long; there were clouds banking up on the horizon, and a bitter wind.

She was turning away from the window when she saw the professor with his dogs, striding down the garden and across the dunes. He was bare-headed, but wearing his sheepskin jacket so that he looked even larger than he was.

She watched him for a moment, and then on an impulse put on her own coat, tied a scarf over her head and went quietly downstairs and out of the side door. The wind took her breath as she started down the long garden, intent on reaching Ruerd while she still had the courage. She was going away, but she had given him no reason and he was entitled to that, and out here in the bleakness of the seashore it would be easier to tell him.

The wind was coming off the sea and she found it slow going; the dunes were narrow here, but they were slippery—full of hollows and unexpected hillocks. By the time she reached the sands the professor was standing by the water, watching the waves tumbling towards him.

The sun had gone again. She walked towards him, soundless on the sand, and when she reached him put out a hand and touched his sleeve.

He turned and looked at her then, and she saw how grim he looked and how tired. She forgot her speech for a moment.

'You ought not to be out in this weather without a hat,' she told him. And then, 'I can't go away without telling you why I'm going, Ruerd. I wasn't going to—Anneliese asked me not to say anything—but perhaps she won't mind if you explain to her... I'm going because I'm in love with you. You know that, don't you? She told me so. I'm sorry you found out; I didn't think it showed. It must have been awkward for you.'

She looked away from him. 'You do see that I had to tell you? But now that I have you can forget all about it. You've been kind. More than kind.' She gulped. 'I'm sure you will be very happy with Anneliese…'

If she had intended to say anything more she was given no opportunity to do so. Wrapped so tightly in his arms that she could hardly breathe she heard his voice roaring above the noise of the wind and waves.

'Kind? Kind? My darling girl, I have not been kind. I have been in love with you since the moment I first saw you, spending hours thinking up ways of seeing more of you and knowing that I had given Anneliese my promise to marry her. It has been something unbearable I never wish to live through again.'

He bent his head and kissed her. It was even better than the kiss under the mistletoe, and highly satisfactory. All the same, Emmy muttered, 'Anneliese…?'

'Anneliese no longer wishes to marry me. Forget her, my darling, and listen to me. We shall marry, you and I, and live happily ever after. You do believe that?'

Emmy peeped up into his face, no longer grim and tired but full of tenderness and love. She nodded. 'Yes, Ruerd. Oh, yes. But what about Anneliese?'

He kissed her soundly. 'We will talk later; I'm going to kiss you again.'

'Very well,' said Emmy. 'I don't mind if you do.'

They stood, the pair of them, just for a while in their own world, oblivious of the wind and the waves and the dogs running to and fro.

Heaven, thought Emmy happily, isn't necessarily

sunshine and blue skies—and she reached up to put her arms round her professor's neck.

At the end of the garden, Oom Domus, coming to look for her, adjusted his binoculars, took a good look and hurried back to the house. He would have a lonely trip to England, but what did that matter? He was bursting with good news.

ROSES FOR CHRISTMAS

CHAPTER ONE

THE LOFT WAS warm, dusty and redolent of apples; the autumn sunshine peeping through its one dusty window tinted the odds and ends hanging on the walls with golden light, so that the strings of onions, cast-off skates, old raincoats, lengths of rope, worn-out leather straps and an old hat or two had acquired a gilded patina. Most of the bare floor was taken up with orderly rows of apples, arranged according to their kind, but there was still space enough left for the girl sitting in the centre, a half-eaten apple in one hand, the other buried in the old hat box beside her. She was a pretty girl, with light brown hair and large hazel eyes, extravagantly lashed and heavily browed, and with a straight nose above a generous, nicely curved mouth. She was wearing slacks and a thick, shabby sweater, and her hair, tied back none too tidily, hung down her back almost to her waist.

She bit into her apple and then bent over the box, and its occupant, a cat of plebeian appearance, paused in her round-the-clock washing of four kittens to lick the hand instead. The girl smiled and took another bite of apple, then turned to look behind her, to where a ladder led down to the disused stable below. She knew the footsteps climbing it and sighed to herself; holidays were lovely after the bustle and orderly precision of the ward in the big Edinburgh hospital where she was a Sister; the cosy homeliness of the manse where her parents and five brothers and sisters lived in the tiny village on the northernmost coast of Scotland, was bliss, it was only a pity that on this particular week's holiday, both her elder brothers, James and Donald, should be away from home, leaving Henry, the youngest and only eight years old, recovering from chickenpox, with no one to amuse him but herself. She doted on him, but they had been fishing all the morning, and after lunch had been cleared away she had gone to the loft for an hour's peace before getting the tea, and now here he was again, no doubt with some boyish scheme or other which would probably entail climbing trees or walking miles looking for seashells.

His untidy head appeared at the top of the ladder. 'I knew you'd be here, Eleanor,' he said in a satisfied voice. 'There's something I must tell you—it's most exciting.'

'Margaret's home early from school?'

He gave her a scornful look, still standing some way down the ladder so that only his head was visible. 'That's not exciting—she comes home from school every day—besides, she's only my sister.'

Eleanor trimmed the core of her apple with her nice white teeth. 'I'm your sister, Henry.'

'But you're old...'

She nodded cheerfully. 'Indeed I am, getting on for twenty-five, my dear. Tell me the exciting news.'

'Someone's come—Mother's invited him to tea.'

Eleanor's eyebrows rose protestingly. 'Old Mr MacKenzie? Not again?'

Her small brother drew a deep breath. 'You'll never guess.'

She reached over for another apple. 'Not in a thousand years—you'd better tell me before I die of curiosity.'

'It's Fulk van Hensum.'

'Fulk? Him? What's he here for? It's twenty years…' She turned her back on her brother, took a bite of apple and said with her mouth full: 'Tell Mother that I can't possibly come—I don't want to waste time talking to him; he was a horrid boy and I daresay he's grown into a horrid man. He pulled my hair…nasty arrogant type, I've never forgotten him.'

'I've never forgotten you, either, Eleanor.' The voice made her spin round. In place of Henry's head was the top half of a very large man; the rest of him came into view as she stared, so tall and broad that he was forced to bend his elegantly clad person to avoid bumping his head. He was very dark, with almost black hair and brown eyes under splendid eyebrows; his nose was long and beaky with winged nostrils, and his mouth was very firm.

Eleanor swallowed her apple. 'Well, I never!' she declared. 'Haven't you grown?'

He sat down on a convenient sack of potatoes and surveyed her lazily. 'One does, you know, and you, if I might say so, have become quite a big girl, Eleanor.'

He somehow managed to convey the impression

that she was outsized, and she flushed a little; her father always described her as a fine figure of a woman, an old-fashioned phrase which she had accepted as a compliment, but to be called quite a big girl in that nasty drawling voice was decidedly annoying. She frowned at him and he remarked lightly: 'Otherwise you haven't changed, dear girl—still the heavy frown, I see—and the biting comment. Should I be flattered that you still remember me?'

'No.'

'Could we let bygones be bygones after—let me see, twenty years?'

She didn't answer that, but: 'You've been a great success, haven't you? We hear about you, you know; Father holds you up as a shining example to Donald.'

'Donald? Ah, the medical student. I'm flattered. What's in the box?'

'Mrs Trot and her four kittens.'

He got up and came to sit beside her with the box between them, and when he offered a large, gentle hand, the little cat licked it too.

'Nice little beast. Don't you want to know why I'm here?' He chose an apple with care and began to eat it. 'How peaceful it is,' he observed. 'What are you doing now, Eleanor? Still a nurse?'

She nodded. 'In Edinburgh, but I'm on a week's holiday.'

'Not married yet?' And when she shook her head: 'Engaged?'

'No—are you?'

'Married? No. Engaged, yes.'

For some reason she felt upset, which was ridiculous, because for all these years she had remembered him as someone she didn't like—true, she had been barely five years old at their first meeting and tastes as well as people change; all the same, there was no need for her to feel so put out at his news. She asked the inevitable female question: 'Is she pretty?'

The dark eyes looked at her thoughtfully. 'Yes, ethereal—very small, slim, fair hair, blue eyes—she dresses with exquisite taste.'

Eleanor didn't look at him. She tucked Mrs Trot up in her old blanket and got to her feet, feeling, for some reason, a much bigger girl than she actually was and most regrettably shabby and untidy. Not that it mattered, she told herself crossly; if people came calling without warning they could take her as they found her. She said haughtily: 'Tea will be ready, I expect,' and went down the ladder with the expertise of long practice. She waited politely for him at the bottom and then walked beside him out of the stable and across the cobbled yard towards the house. She walked well, her head well up and with a complete lack of self-consciousness, for she was a graceful girl despite her splendid proportions and tall, although now her head barely reached her companion's shoulder.

'It hasn't changed,' her companion observed, looking around him. 'I'm glad my father came just once again before he died; he loved this place. It was a kind of annual pilgrimage with him, wasn't it?'

Eleanor glanced up briefly. 'Yes—we were all

sorry when he died, we all knew him so well, and coming every year as he did...' She paused and then went on: 'You never came, and now after all these years you have. Why?'

They had stopped in the open back porch and he answered her casually: 'Oh, one reason and another, you know.' He was eyeing her in a leisurely fashion which she found annoying. 'Do you always dress like this?'

She tossed back her mane of hair. 'You haven't changed at all,' she told him tartly. 'You're just as hateful as you were as a boy.'

He smiled. 'You have a long memory.' His dark eyes snapped with amusement. 'But then so have I, Eleanor.'

She led the way down the flagstoned passage and opened a door, while vivid memory came flooding back—all those years ago, when he had picked her up and held her gently while she howled and sobbed into his shoulder and even while she had hated him then, just for those few minutes she had felt secure and content and very happy despite the fact that moments earlier she had been kicking his shins—she had lost her balance and fallen over and he had laughed, but gently, and picked her up...it was silly to remember such a trivial episode from her childhood.

The sitting room they entered wasn't large, but its heterogeneous mixture of unassuming antiques and comfortable, shabby armchairs, handmade rugs and bookshelves rendered it pleasant enough. It had two occupants: Eleanor's mother, a small, pretty woman, very neatly dressed, and her father, a good deal older than his wife, with thick white hair and bright blue eyes in a rugged face. He was in elderly grey tweeds and only his dog collar proclaimed his profession.

'There you are,' exclaimed Mrs MacFarlane. 'So you found each other.' She beamed at them both. 'Isn't it nice to meet again after all these years? Fulk, come and sit here by me and tell me all your news,' and when he had done so: 'Did you recognise Eleanor? She was such a little girl when you last saw her.'

Eleanor was handing plates and teacups and saucers. 'Of course he didn't recognise me, Mother,' she explained in a brisk no-nonsense voice. 'I was only five then, and that's twenty years ago.'

'A nice plump little thing you were, too,' said her father fondly, and smiled at their guest, who remarked blandly: 'Little girls so often are,' and Eleanor, although she wasn't looking at him, knew that he was secretly laughing. It was perhaps fortunate that at that moment Henry joined them, to sit himself down as close to him as possible.

'Are you going to stay here?' he enquired eagerly. 'I mean, for a day or two? And must I call you Doctor van Hensum, and will you...?'

'Call me Fulk, Henry, and yes, your mother has very kindly asked me to stay for a short visit.'

'Oh, good—you can come fishing with us, Eleanor and me, you know, and there's an apple tree she climbs, I daresay she'll let you climb it too if you like.'

'Eat your bread and butter, Henry,' said Eleanor in the same brisk voice. 'I'm sure Doctor van Hensum doesn't climb trees at his age, and probably he's not in the least interested in fishing.' She cast the doctor a smouldering glance. 'He may want to rest...'

She caught the quick gleam in his eyes although his voice was meek enough. 'As to that, I'm only thirty-six, you know, and reasonably active.'

'Of course you are,' declared Mrs MacFarlane comfortably, and passed him the cake. 'I can remember you fishing, too—and climbing trees—Eleanor used to shriek at you because you wouldn't let her climb trees too.' She laughed at the memory and her daughter ground her splendid teeth. 'So long ago,' sighed her mother, 'and I remember it all so vividly.'

And that was the trouble, Eleanor told herself, although why the memory was so vivid was a mystery beyond her.

'And now,' interpolated her father, 'you are a famous physician; of course your dear father was a brilliant man—you were bound to follow in his footsteps, and your mother was a clever woman too, and an uncommonly pretty one. I'm afraid that we none of us can hold a candle to your splendid career, although Eleanor has done very well for herself, you know; in her own small sphere she has specialized in medicine and is very highly thought of at her hospital, so I'm told.' He added with a touch of pride: 'She's a Ward Sister—one of the youngest there.'

'I can hardly believe it,' observed Fulk, and only she realized that he was referring to her careless appearance; no one, seeing her at that moment would have believed that she was one and the same person as the immaculately uniformed, highly professional young woman who ruled her ward so precisely. A pity he can't see me on duty, she thought peevishly, and said aloud: 'Donald—he's younger than I—is at Aberdeen and doing very well. He's going in for surgery.'

She encountered the doctor's gaze again and fidgeted under it. 'He was in his pram when you were here.'

He said smoothly: 'Ah, yes, I remember. Father always kept me up to date with any news about you; there's Mary—she's married, isn't she?—and Margaret?'

'Here she is now,' said Mrs MacFarlane, 'back from school—and don't forget James, he's still at boarding school.' She cast a fond look at her last-born, gobbling cake. 'Henry's only home because he's had chickenpox.'

There was a small stir as Margaret came in. She was already pretty and at twelve years old bade fair to outshine Eleanor later on. She embraced her mother, declaring she was famished, assured Eleanor that she would need help with her homework and went to kiss her father. She saw the doctor then and said instantly: 'Is that your car in the lane? It's absolutely wizard!'

Her father's voice was mildly rebuking. 'This is Fulk van Hensum, Margaret, he used to come and stay with us a long time ago—you remember his father? He is to stay with us for a day or so.'

She shook hands, smiling widely. 'Oh, yes—I remember your father and I know about you too.' She eyed him with some curiosity. 'You're very large, aren't you?'

He smiled slowly. 'I suppose I am. Yes, that's my car outside—it's a Panther de Ville.'

It was Henry who answered him. 'I say, is it really? May I look at it after tea? There are only a few built, aren't there—it's rather like an XJ12, isn't it? With a Jag engine...'

The big man gave him a kindly look. 'A motorcar enthusiast?' he wanted to know, and when Henry nodded, 'We'll go over it presently if you would like that—it has some rather nice points...' He smiled at the little boy and then addressed Eleanor with unexpected suddenness. 'When do you go back to Edinburgh?'

She looked up from filling second cups. 'In a few days, Friday.'

'Good, I'll drive you down, I've an appointment in that part of the world on Saturday.'

She said stiffly: 'That's kind of you, but I can go very easily by train.'

Her mother looked at her in some astonishment. 'Darling, you've said a dozen times how tedious it is going to Edinburgh by train, and then there's the bus to Lairg first...'

'I drive tolerably well,' murmured the doctor. 'We could go to Lairg and on to Inverness. It would save you a good deal of time, but of course, if you are nervous…'

'I am not nervous,' said Eleanor coldly. 'I merely do not want to interfere with your holiday.'

'Oh, but you're not,' he told her cheerfully. 'I have to go to Edinburgh—I've just said so. I came here first because I had some books my father wanted your father to have.'

Which led the conversation into quite different channels.

It was a crisp, bright October morning when Eleanor woke the next day—too good to stay in bed, she decided. She got up, moving quietly round her pretty little bedroom, pulling on slacks and a sweater again, brushing and plaiting her hair. She went down to the kitchen without making a sound and put on the kettle; a cup of tea, she decided, then a quick peep at Mrs Trot and the kittens before taking tea up to her parents; and there would still be time to take Punch, the dog, for a short walk before helping to get breakfast.

She was warming the pot when Fulk said from the door: 'Good morning, Eleanor—coming out for a walk? It's a marvellous morning.'

She spooned tea carefully. 'Hullo, have you been out already?'

'Yes, but I'm more than willing to go again. Who's the tea for?'

'Me—and you, now you're here.'

He said softly: 'I wonder why you don't like me, Eleanor?'

She poured tea into two mugs and handed him one, and said seriously: 'I think it's because you arrived unexpectedly—quite out of the blue—you see, I never thought I'd see you again and I didn't like you when I was a little girl. It's funny how one remembers...'

He smiled. 'You were such a little girl, but I daresay you were right, I was a horrid boy—most boys are from time to time and you were bad for me; you made me feel like the lord of creation, following me around on those fat legs of yours, staring at me with those eyes, listening to every word I said—your eyes haven't changed at all, Eleanor.'

Her voice was cool. 'How very complimentary you are all of a sudden. You weren't so polite yesterday.'

He strolled over and held out his mug for more tea. 'One sometimes says the wrong thing when one is taken by surprise.'

She didn't bother to think about that; she was pursuing her own train of thought. 'I know I'm big,' she said crossly, 'but I don't need to be reminded of it.'

He looked momentarily surprised and there was a small spark of laughter in his eyes, but all he said was: 'I won't remind you again, I promise. Shall we cry truce and take the dog for a walk? After all, we shall probably not meet again for another twenty years or even longer than that.'

She was aware of disappointment at the very thought. 'All right, but I must just go up to Mother and Father with this tray.'

He was waiting at the kitchen door when she got

down again, and Punch was beside him. 'I must take Mrs Trot's breakfast over first,' she warned him.

They crossed the back yard together and rather to her surprise he took the bowl of milk she was carrying from her and mounted the ladder behind her while Punch, wary of Mrs Trot's maternal claws, stayed prudently in the stable. The little cat received them with pleasure, accepted the milk and fish and allowed them to admire her kittens before they left, going down the short lane which separated the manse and the small church from the village. The huddle of houses and cottages was built precariously between the mountains at their back and the sea, tucked almost apologetically into a corner of the rock-encircled sandy bay. As they reached the beach they were met by a chilly wind from the north, dispelling any illusion that the blue sky and sunshine were an aftertaste of summer, so that they were forced to step out briskly, with Punch tearing down to the edge of the sea and then retreating from the cold waves.

Eleanor was surprised to find that she was enjoying Fulk's company; it was obvious, she told herself, that he had grown into an arrogant man, very sure of himself, probably selfish too, even though she had to admit to his charm. All the same, he was proving himself a delightful companion now, talking about everything under the sun in a friendly manner which held no arrogance at all, and when they got back to the house he surprised her still further by laying the breakfast table while she cooked for Margaret before she left for school. Half way through their activities,

Henry came down, rather indignant that he had missed the treat of an early morning walk, but more than reconciled to his loss when Fulk offered to take him for a drive in the Panther. The pair of them went away directly after breakfast and weren't seen again until a few minutes before lunch, when they appeared in the kitchen, on excellent terms with each other, and burdened with a large quantity of flowers for Mrs MacFarlane, whisky for the pastor and chocolates for Margaret. And for Eleanor there was a little pink quartz cat, a few inches high and most beautifully carved, sitting very straight and reserved, reminding her very much of Mrs Trot.

'We had the greatest fun,' Henry informed his waiting family, 'and I had an ice cream. We went to the hotel in Tongue—one of those with nuts on top, and the Panther is just super. When I'm grown up I shall have one, too.'

Eleanor, the little cat cradled in her hand, smiled at him lovingly. 'And so you shall, my dear, but now you're going straight up to the bathroom to wash your hands—dinner's ready.'

The rest of the day passed pleasantly enough, and if she had subconsciously hoped that Fulk would suggest another walk, she had no intention of admitting it to herself. As it was, he spent most of the afternoon with his host and after supper they all played cards until the children's bedtime.

She wakened at first light the next morning, to hear her brother's excited whispering under her window, and when she got out of bed to have a look, it was to see him trotting along beside the doctor, laden with fishing paraphernalia—Punch was with them, too; all three of them looked very happy, even from the back.

They came in late for breakfast with a splendid catch of fish, which provided the main topic of conversation throughout the meal, and when they had finished Mrs MacFarlane said brightly: 'Well, my dears, fish for dinner, provided of course someone will clean it.' A task which Fulk undertook without fuss before driving Mr MacFarlane into Durness to browse over an interesting collection of books an old friend had offered to sell him.

So that Eleanor saw little of their guest until the late afternoon and even then Henry made a cheerful talkative third when they went over to visit Mrs Trot. It was while they were there, sitting on the floor eating apples, that Fulk asked her: 'What time do you leave tomorrow, Eleanor?'

'Well, I don't want to leave at all,' she replied promptly. 'The very thought of hospital nauseates me—I'd like to stay here for ever and ever...' She sighed and went on briskly: 'Well, any time after lunch, I suppose. Would two o'clock suit you?'

'Admirably. It's roughly two hundred and fifty miles, isn't it? We should arrive in Edinburgh in good time for dinner—you don't have to be in at any special time, do you?'

'No—no, of course not, but there's no need...really I didn't expect...that is...'

'There's no need to get worked up,' he assured her kindly. 'I shouldn't have asked you if I hadn't wanted to.' He sounded almost brotherly, which made her pleasure at this remark all the more remarkable, although it was quickly squashed when he went on to say blandly: 'I've had no chance to talk to you about Imogen.'

'Oh, well—yes, of course I shall be delighted to hear about her.'

'Who's Imogen?' Henry enquired.

'The lady Fulk is going to marry,' his big sister told him woodenly.

He looked at her with round eyes. 'Then why didn't she come too?'

Fulk answered him good-naturedly, 'She's in the south of France.'

'Why aren't you with her?'

The doctor smiled. 'We seem to have started something, don't we? You see, Henry, Imogen doesn't like this part of Scotland.'

'Why not?' Eleanor beat her brother by a short head with the question.

'She considers it rather remote.'

Eleanor nodded understandingly. 'Well, it is—no shops for sixty miles, no theatres, almost no cinemas and they're miles away too, and high tea instead of dinner in the hotels.'

Fulk turned his head to look at her. 'Exactly so,' he agreed. 'And do you feel like that about it, too, Eleanor?'

She said with instant indignation: 'No, I do not— I love it; I like peace and quiet and nothing in sight but the mountains and the sea and a cottage or two—

anyone who feels differently must be very stupid...'
She opened her eyes wide and put a hand to her
mouth. 'Oh, I do beg your pardon—I didn't mean
your Imogen.'

'Still the same hasty tongue,' Fulk said mockingly,
'and she isn't my Imogen yet.'

It was fortunate that Henry created a welcome di-
version at that moment; wanting to climb a tree or
two before teatime, so that the rest of the afternoon
was spent doing just that. Fulk, Eleanor discovered,
climbed trees very well.

They played cards again until supper time and after
their meal, when the two gentlemen retired to the pastor's study, Eleanor declared that she was tired and
would go to bed, but once in her room she made no
effort to undress but sat on her bed making up her
mind what she would wear the next day—Fulk had
only seen her in slacks and a sweater with her hair
hanging anyhow. She would surprise him.

It was a pity, but he didn't seem in the least surprised. She went down to breakfast looking much as
usual, but before lunchtime she changed into a well
cut tweed suit of a pleasing russet colour, put on her
brogue shoes, made up her pretty face with care, did
her hair in a neat, smooth coil on the top of her head,
and joined the family at the table. And he didn't say
a word, glancing up at her as she entered the room
and then looking away again with the careless speed
of someone who had seen the same thing a dozen
times before. Her excellent appetite was completely
destroyed.

It served her right, she told herself severely, for allowing herself to think about him too much; she had no reason to do so, he was of no importance in her life and after today she wasn't likely to see him again. She made light conversation all the way to Tomintoul, a village high in the Highlands, where they stopped for tea. It was a small place, but the hotel overlooked the square and there was plenty to comment upon, something for which she was thankful, for she was becoming somewhat weary of providing almost all the conversation. Indeed, when they were on their way once more and after another hour of commenting upon the scenery, she observed tartly: 'I'm sure you will understand if I don't talk any more; I can't think of anything else to say, and even if I could, I feel I should save it for this evening, otherwise we shall sit at dinner like an old married couple.'

His shoulders shook. 'My dear girl, I had no idea... I was enjoying just sitting here and listening to you rambling on—you have a pretty voice, you know.' He paused. 'Imogen doesn't talk much when we drive together; it makes a nice change. But I promise you we won't sit like an old married couple; however old we become, we shall never take each other for granted.'

She allowed this remark to pass without comment, for she wasn't sure what he meant. 'You were going to tell me about Imogen,' she prompted, and was disappointed when he said abruptly: 'I've changed my mind—tell me about Henry instead. What a delightful child he is, but not, I fancy, over-strong.'

The subject of Henry lasted until they reached Edinburgh, where he drove her to the North British Hotel in Princes Street, and after Eleanor had tidied herself, gave her a memorable dinner, managing to convey, without actually saying so, that she was not only a pleasant companion but someone whom he had wanted to take out to dinner all his life. It made her glow very nicely, and the glow was kept at its best by the hock which he offered her. They sat for a long time over their meal and when he at last took her to the hospital it was almost midnight.

She got out of the car at the Nurses' Home entrance and he got out with her and walked to the door to open it. She wished him goodbye quietly, thanked him for a delightful evening and was quite taken by surprise when he pulled her to him, kissed her hard and then, without another word, popped her through the door and closed it behind her. She stood in the dimly lit hall, trying to sort out her feelings. She supposed that they were outraged, but this was tempered by the thought that she wasn't going to see him again. She told herself firmly that it didn't matter in the least, trying to drown the persistent little voice in the back of her head telling her that even if she didn't like him—and she had told herself enough times that she didn't—it mattered quite a bit. She went slowly up to her room, warning herself that just because he had given her a good dinner and been an amusing companion there was no reason to allow her thoughts to dwell upon him.

CHAPTER TWO

THE MORNING WAS dark and dreary and suited Eleanor's mood very well as she got into her uniform and, looking the very epitome of neatness and calm efficiency, went down to breakfast, a meal eaten in a hurry by reason of the amount of conversation crammed in by herself and friends while they drank tea and bolted toast and marmalade.

She climbed the stairs to Women's Medical, trying to get used to being back on the ward once more, while her pretty nose registered the fact that the patients had had fish for breakfast and that someone had been too lavish with the floor polish—the two smells didn't go well together. Someone, too, would have to repair the window ledge outside the ward door, and it was obvious that no one had bothered to water the dreadful potted plant which lived on it. Eleanor pushed the swing doors open and went straight to her little office, where Staff Nurse Jill Pitts would be waiting with the two night nurses.

The report took longer than usual; it always did on her first day back, even if she had been away for a short time; new patients, new treatments, Path Lab reports, news of old patients—it was all of fifteen minutes before she sent the night nurses to their breakfast, left Jill to see that the nurses were starting on their various jobs, and set off on her round. She spent some time with her first three patients, for they were elderly and ill, and for some weeks now they had all been battling to keep them alive; she assured herself that they were holding their own and passed on to the fourth bed; Mrs McFinn, a large, comfortable lady with a beaming smile and a regrettable shortness of breath due to asthma, a condition which didn't prevent her wheezing out a little chat with Eleanor, and her neighbour, puffing and panting her way through emphysema with unending courage and good humour, wanted to chat too. She indulged them both; they were such dears, but so for that matter were almost all the patients in the ward.

She spent a few minutes with each of them in turn, summing up their condition while she lent a friendly ear and a smile; only as she reached the top of the ward did she allow a small sigh to escape her. Miss Tremble, next in line, was a cross the entire staff, medical and nursing, bore with fortitude, even if a good deal of grumbling went on about her in private. She was a thin, acidulated woman in her sixties, a diabetic which it seemed impossible to stabilize however the doctors tried. Painstakingly dieted and injected until the required balance had been reached, she would be sent home, only to be borne back in again sooner or later in yet another diabetic coma, a condition which she never ceased to blame upon the hospital staff. She had been in again for two weeks now, and on the one occasion during that period when it had been considered safe to send her home again to her downtrodden sister, she had gone into a coma again as she was actually on the point of departure, and it was all very well for Sir Arthur Minch, the consultant physician in charge of her case, to carry on about it; as Eleanor had pointed out to him in a reasonable manner, one simply didn't turn one's back on hyperglycaemia, even when it was about to leave the ward; she had put the patient back to bed again and allowed the great man to natter on about wanting the bed for an urgent case. He had frowned and tutted and in the end had agreed with her; she had known that he would, anyway.

She took up her position now at the side of Miss Tremble's bed and prepared to listen to its occupant's long list of complaints; she had heard them many times before, and would most likely hear them many more times in the future. She put on her listening face and thought about Fulk, wondering where he was and why he had come to Edinburgh. She would have liked to have asked him, only she had hesitated; he had a nasty caustic tongue, she remembered it vividly when he had stayed with them all those years ago, and she had no doubt that he still possessed it. She could only guess—he could of course be visiting friends, or perhaps he had come over to consult with a colleague; he might even have a patient... She frowned and Miss Tremble said irritably: 'I'm glad to see that you are annoyed, Sister—it is disgraceful that I had to have Bovril on two successive evenings when my appetite needs tempting.'

Eleanor made a soothing reply, extolled the virtues

of the despised beverage, assured Miss Tremble that
something different would be offered her for her supper that evening, and moved on to the next bed, but
even when she had completed her round and was back
in her office, immersed in forms, charts and the answering of the constantly ringing telephone she was
still wondering about Fulk.

But presently she gave herself a mental shake; she
would never know anyway. Thinking about him was
a complete waste of time, especially with Sir Arthur
due to do his round at ten o'clock. She pushed the
papers to one side with a touch of impatience; they
would have to wait until she had checked the ward
and made sure that everything was exactly as it
should be for one of the major events in the ward's
week.

She ran the ward well; the patients were ready with
five minutes to spare and the nurses were going, two
by two, to their coffee break. Eleanor, longing for a
cup herself, but having to wait for it until Sir Arthur
should be finished, was in the ward, with the faithful
Jill beside her and Mrs MacDonnell, the part-time
staff nurse, hovering discreetly with a student nurse
close by to fetch and carry. She knew Sir Arthur's
ways well by now; he would walk into the ward at
ten o'clock precisely with his registrar, his house doctor and such students as had the honour of accom-
panying him that morning. Eleanor, with brothers of
her own, felt a sisterly concern for the shy ones,
whose wits invariably deserted them the moment they
entered the ward, and she had formed the habit of

stationing herself where she might prompt those rendered dumb by apprehension when their chief chose to fire a question at them. She had become something of an expert at mouthing clues helpful enough to start the hapless recipient of Sir Arthur's attention on the path of a right answer. Perhaps one day she would be caught red-handed, but in the meantime she continued to pass on vital snippets to any number of grateful young gentlemen.

The clock across the square had begun its sonorous rendering of the hour when the ward doors swung open just as usual and the senior Medical Consultant, his posse of attendants hard on his heels, came in—only it wasn't quite as usual; Fulk van Hensum was walking beside him, not the Fulk of the last day or so, going fishing with Henry in an outsize sweater and rubber boots, or playing Canasta with the family after supper or goodnaturedly helping Margaret with her decimals. This was a side of him which she hadn't seen before; he looked older for a start, and if anything, handsomer in a distinguished way, and his face wore the expression she had seen so often on a doctor's face; calm and kind and totally unflappable—and a little remote. He was also impeccably turned out, his grey suit tailored to perfection, his tie an elegant understatement. She advanced to meet them, very composed, acknowledging Sir Arthur's stately greeting with just the right degree of warmth and turning a frosty eye on Fulk, who met it blandly with the faintest of smiles and an equally bland: 'Good morning, Eleanor, how nice to be able to surprise you twice in only a few days.'

She looked down her nose at him. 'Good morning, Doctor van Hensum,' she greeted him repressively, and didn't smile. He might have told her; there had been no reason at all why he shouldn't have done so. She almost choked when he went on coolly: 'Yes, I could have told you, couldn't I? But you never asked me.'

Sir Arthur glanced at Eleanor. 'Know each other, do you?' he wanted to know genially.

Before she could answer, Fulk observed pleasantly: 'Oh, yes—for many years. Eleanor was almost five when we first met.' He had the gall to smile at her in what she considered to be a patronising manner.

'Five, eh?' chuckled Sir Arthur. 'Well, you've grown since then, Sister.' The chuckle became a laugh at his little joke and she managed to smile too, but with an effort for Fulk said: 'She had a quantity of long hair and she was very plump.' He stared at her and she frowned fiercely. 'Little girls are rather sweet,' his voice was silky, 'but they tend to change as they grow up.'

She all but ground her teeth at him; it was a relief when Sir Arthur said cheerfully: 'Well, well, I suppose we should get started, Sister. Doctor van Hensum is particularly interested in that case of agranulocytosis—Mrs Lee, isn't it? She experienced the first symptoms while she was on holiday in Holland and came under his care. Most fortunately for her, he diagnosed it at once—a difficult thing to do.' His eye

swept round the little group of students, who looked
suitably impressed.

'Not so very difficult in this case, if I might say
so,' interpolated Fulk quietly. 'There was the typical
sore throat and oedema, and the patient answered my
questions with great intelligence...'

'But no doubt the questions were intelligent,' remarked Sir Arthur dryly, and the students murmured
their admiration, half of them not having the least idea
what their superiors were talking about, anyway.

They were moving towards the first bed now, and
Eleanor, casting a quick look at Fulk, saw that he had
become the consultant again; indeed, as the round
progressed, his manner towards her was faultless; politely friendly, faintly impersonal—they could have
just met for the first time. It vexed her to find that
this annoyed her more than his half-teasing attitude
towards her when he had entered the ward. He was a
tiresome man, she decided, leading the way to Mrs
Lee's bed.

That lady was making good progress now that she
was responding to the massive doses of penicillin, and
although her temperature was still high and she remained lethargic, she was certainly on the mend. Sir
Arthur held forth at some length, occasionally pausing
to verify some point with the Dutch doctor and then
firing questions at random at whichever unfortunate
student happened to catch his eye. Most of them did
very well, but one or two of them were tongue-tied
by the occasion. Eleanor, unobtrusively helping out
one such, and standing slightly behind Sir Arthur, had

just finished miming the bare bones of the required information when she realized that Fulk had moved and was standing where he could watch her. She threw him a frowning glance which he appeared not to see, for the smile he gave her was so charming that she only just prevented herself from smiling back at him.

Perhaps he wasn't so bad after all, she conceded, only to have this opinion reversed when, the round over, she was bidding Sir Arthur and his party goodbye at the ward door, for when she bade Fulk goodbye too, he said at once: 'You'll lunch with me, Eleanor,' and it wasn't even a question, let alone a request, delivered in a silky voice loud enough for everyone to hear.

'I'm afraid that's impossible,' she began coldly, and Sir Arthur, quite mistaking her hesitation, interrupted her to say heartily: 'Nonsense, of course you can go, Sister—I've seen you dozens of times at the Blue Bird Café'—an establishment much favoured by the hospital staff because it was only just down the road and they were allowed to go there in uniform—'Why, only a couple of weeks ago you were having a meal there with young Maddox, although how he managed that when he was on call for the Accident Room I cannot imagine.'

He turned his attention to Fulk. 'The Blue Bird isn't exactly Cordon Bleu, but they do a nice plate of fish and chips, and there is the great advantage of being served quickly.' He looked at Eleanor once

more. 'You intended going to your dinner, I suppose?
When do you go?'

She didn't want to answer, but she had to say
something. 'One o'clock,' she told him woodenly and
heard his pleased: 'Excellent—what could be better?
Van Hensum, we shall have time to talk over that case
we were discussing.' He beamed in a fatherly fashion
at Eleanor, fuming silently, and led the way down the
corridor with all the appearance of a man who had
done someone a good turn and felt pleased about it.
Fulk went with him, without saying another word.

Eleanor snorted, muttered rudely under her breath
and went to serve the patients' dinners, and as she
dished out boiled fish, nourishing stew, fat-free diets,
high-calorie diets and diabetic diets, she pondered
how she could get out of having lunch with Fulk. She
wasn't quite sure why it was so important that she
should escape going with him, because actually she
liked the idea very much, and even when, as usual,
she was battling with Miss Tremble about the amount
of ham on her plate, a small part of her brain was still
hard at work trying to discover the reason. All the
same, she told herself that her determination not to
go was strong enough to enable her to make some
excuse.

She was trying to think of one as she went back to
her office with Jill, to give her a brief run-down of
jobs to be done during the next hour—a waste of
time, as it turned out, for Fulk was there, standing
idly looking out of the window. He had assumed his
consultant's manner once more, too, so that Eleanor

found it difficult to utter the refusal she had determined upon. Besides, Jill was there, taking it for granted that she was going, even at that very moment urging her not to hurry back. 'There's nothing much on this afternoon,' she pointed out, 'not until three o'clock at any rate, and you never get your full hour for dinner, Sister.' She made a face. 'It's braised heart, too.'

Fulk's handsome features expressed extreme distaste. 'How revolting,' he observed strongly. 'Eleanor, put on your bonnet at once and we will investigate the fish and chips. They sound infinitely more appetizing.'

Eleanor dabbed with unusually clumsy fingers at the muslin trifle perched on her great knot of shining hair. 'Thanks, Jill, I'll see.' She sounded so reluctant that her right hand looked at her in amazement while Fulk's eyes gleamed with amusement, although all he said was: 'Shall we go?'

The café was almost full, a number of hospital staff, either on the point of going on duty or just off, were treating themselves to egg and chips, spaghetti on toast or the fish and chips for which the café was justly famous. Fulk led the way to a table in the centre of the little place, and Eleanor, casting off her cloak and looking around, nodded and smiled at two physiotherapists, an X-ray technician, and the senior Accident Room Sister with the Casualty Officer. There were two of the students who had been in Sir Arthur's round that morning sitting at the next table and they smiled widely at her, glanced at Fulk and gave her the thumbs-up sign, which she pointedly ignored, hoping that her companion hadn't seen it too. He had; he said: 'Lord, sometimes I feel middle-aged.'

'Well,' her voice was astringent, 'you're not—you're not even married yet.'

His mouth twitched. 'You imply that being married induces middle age, and that's nonsense.' He added slowly: 'I imagine that any man who married you would tend to regain his youth, not lose it.'

She gaped at him across the little table. 'For heaven's sake, whatever makes you say that?' But she wasn't to know, for the proprietor of the Blue Bird had made his way towards them and was offering a menu card. He was a short, fat man and rather surprisingly, a Cockney; the soul of kindness and not above allowing second helpings for free to anyone who was a bit short until pay day. He stood looking at them both now and then said: "'Ullo, Sister, 'aven't met yer friend before, 'ave I?"

'No, Steve—he's a Dutch consultant, a friend of Sir Arthur Minch. Doctor van Hensum, this is Steve who runs the café.'

The doctor held out a hand and Steve shook it with faint surprise. 'Pleased ter meet yer,' he pronounced in gratified tones. 'I got a nice bit of 'ake out the back. 'Ow'd yer like it, the pair of yer? Chips and peas and a good cuppa while yer waiting.'

A cheerful girl brought the tea almost at once and Eleanor poured the rich brew into the thick cups and handed one to Fulk. 'Aren't you sorry you asked me out now?' she wanted to know. 'I don't suppose you've ever had your lunch in a place like this before.'

He gave her a thoughtful look. 'You're determined to make me out a very unpleasant fellow, aren't you? I wonder why?' He passed her the sugar bowl and then helped himself. 'No, I've never been in a place quite like this one before, but I've been in far worse, and let me tell you, my girl, that your low opinion of me is completely mistaken.'

'I never…' began Eleanor, and was interrupted by the arrival of the hake, mouthwatering in its thick rich batter coat and surrounded by chips and peas; by the time they had assured Steve that it looked delicious, passed each other the salt, refused the vinegar and refilled their cups, there seemed no point in arguing. They fell to and what conversation there was was casual and good-humoured. Presently, nicely mellowed by the food, Eleanor remarked: 'You were going to tell me about Imogen.'

He selected a chip with deliberation and ate it slowly. 'Not here,' he told her.

'You keep saying that—you said it in the car yesterday. Do you have to have soft music and stained glass windows or something before she can be talked about?'

He put his head on one side and studied her face. 'You're a very rude girl—I suppose that's what comes of being a bossy elder sister. No, perhaps that's too sweeping a statement,' he continued blandly, 'for Henry assured me that you were the grooviest—I'm a little vague as to the exact meaning of the word, but presumably it is a compliment of the highest order.'

'Bless the boy, it is.' She hesitated. 'I'd like to thank you for being so kind to him—he's a poppet, at least we all think so, and far too clever for his age, though he's a great one for adventure; he's for ever falling out of trees and going on long solitary walks with Punch and tumbling off rocks into the sea when he goes fishing. We all long to tell him not to do these things, but he's a boy…having you for a companion was bliss for him.' .

'And would it have been bliss for you, Eleanor?' Fulk asked in an interested voice, and then: 'No, don't answer, I can see the words blistering your lips. We'll go on talking about Henry—he's not quite as strong as you would like, your father tells me.'

She had decided to overlook the first part of his remark. 'He's tough, it's just that he catches everything that's going; measles, whooping cough, mumps, chickenpox—you name it, he's had it.'

He passed his cup for more tea, eyed its rich brown strength, sugared it lavishly and took a sip with an expressionless face. 'I shudder to think what this tea is doing to our insides,' he remarked lightly. 'Have you a good doctor?'

'Doctor MacClew. He's quite old now, but he's been our doctor all our lives. He's a dear and so kind, although I daresay he's old-fashioned by your standards.'

'My standards?' He looked quite shocked. 'My dear Eleanor, you're at it again, turning me into someone I'm not. Why should you suppose that I would set myself up above another doctor, probably twice my age and with at least twice my experience, and who has had to improvise, make decisions, take risks, diagnose without X-rays and be his own Path Lab in an emergency? I, remember, have the whole range of modern equipment and science behind me—I need not open my mouth until all the answers have been given me.'

She said indignantly: 'Don't exaggerate. That's not true; a good physician doesn't need any of those things—they only confirm his opinion. You know as well as I do that you could manage very well without them.'

He lifted his thick brows in mock surprise. 'Why, Eleanor, those are the first kind words you have uttered since we met.' He grinned so disarmingly that she smiled back at him. 'Well, you know it's true.'

He said slowly, watching her: 'Do you know I believe that's the first time you've smiled at me? Oh, you've gone through the motions, but they didn't register. You should smile more often.' He heaved a sigh. 'How delightful it is not to be quarrelling with you.'

She eyed him with disfavour. 'What a beastly thing to say! I've not quarrelled with you, I've been very polite.'

'I know, I'd rather quarrel, but not now—let's call a truce.'

She seized her opportunity. 'Tell me about Imogen.'

He leaned back on the hard wooden chair. 'What do you want to know?'

Eleanor was so surprised at his meek acceptance of her question that she didn't speak for a moment. 'Well, what does she do and where does she live and where will you live when you're married, and is she very pretty?' She added wistfully: 'You said she was small…'

'Half your size and very, very pretty—you forgot to ask how old she is, by the way. Twenty-six, and she doesn't do anything—at least, she doesn't have a job. She doesn't need to work, you see. But she fills her days very nicely with tennis and swimming and riding and driving—and she dances beautifully. She lives in den Haag and I live near Groningen, about a hundred and fifty miles apart—an easy run on the motorway.'

'But that's an awful long way to go each weekend,' observed Eleanor.

'Every weekend? Oh, not as often as that, my dear. Besides, Imogen stays with friends a good deal—I did tell you that she's in the south of France now and later on she will be going to Switzerland for the winter sports.' His voice was very level. 'We decided when we became engaged that we would make no claims on each other's time and leisure.'

'Oh,' said Eleanor blankly, 'how very strange. I don't think I'd like that at all.'

'If you were engaged to me? But you're not.' He smiled thinly. 'A fine state of affairs that would be!

You would probably expect me to sit in your pocket and we should quarrel without pause.'

'Probably.' Her voice was colourless. 'I think I'd better go back to the ward, if you don't mind…' She was interrupted by the cheerful booming voice of Doctor Blake, Sir Arthur's right-hand man, who clapped a hand on her shoulder, greeted her with the easy friendliness of a long-standing acquaintance and asked: 'May I sit down? It's Doctor van Hensum, isn't it? I've just been with Sir Arthur and he mentioned that you might be here still—I'm not interrupting anything, am I?'

'I'm just on my way back to the ward,' said Eleanor, and wished she wasn't. 'I'm a bit late already.' She smiled a general sort of smile and got to her feet. 'Thanks for the lunch,' she said quickly and hardly looking at Fulk. He had got to his feet too, and his 'Goodbye, Eleanor,' was very quiet.

She had no time to think about him after that, for Miss Tremble had seen fit to go into a coma and it took most of the afternoon to get her out of it again. Eleanor missed her tea and the pleasant half hour of gossip she usually enjoyed with the other Sisters and went off duty a little late, to change rapidly and catch a bus to the other side of the city where an aunt, elderly, crotchety but nevertheless one of the family, would be waiting to give her supper. It had become a custom for Eleanor to visit her on her return from any holidays so that she might supply her with any titbits of news, and although it was sometimes a little tiresome, the old lady had got to depend upon her visits. She spent a dull evening, answering questions and listening to her companion's various ailments, and when she at last escaped and returned to the hospital, she was too tired to do more than climb into bed as quickly as possible.

It was two more days before she discovered, quite by chance, that Fulk had gone back to Holland only a few hours after they had shared their meal together in the Blue Bird Café, and for some reason the news annoyed her; she had been wondering about him, it was true, but somehow she had taken it for granted that he would come and say goodbye before he left, although there was no reason why he should have done so, but one would have thought, she told herself peevishly, that after making such a thing about taking her to lunch, he could at least have mentioned that he was on the point of leaving; he hadn't even said goodbye. She paused in her reflections: he had, even though he hadn't told her he was leaving; probably thinking it was none of her business, anyway—nor was it.

She glared at her nice face in the silly little mirror on the office wall and went back to her work once more, and while she chatted with her patients and listened to their complaints and worries, she decided that Fulk wasn't worth thinking about, quite forgetting that she had told herself that already. She would most probably not see him again; she could forget him, and the beautiful Imogen with him. She finished her round and went back down the ward, the very picture of calm efficiency, and went into her office, where she sat at her desk, staring at the papers she was supposed to be dealing with while she speculated about Imogen; it was strange that although she had never met the girl and was never likely to, she should have such strong feelings of dislike for her.

CHAPTER THREE

THE DAYS SLID BY, October became November and
the bright weather showed no sign of giving way to
the sleet and gales of early winter. The ward filled
up; acute bronchitis, pneumonia, flu in a variety of
forms, followed each other with an almost monoto-
nous regularity. Eleanor, brimming over with good
health and vitality herself, had her kind heart wrung
by every fresh case. They got well again, of course,
at least the vast majority did, what with antibiotics
and skilled nursing and Sir Arthur and his assistants
keeping a constant eye upon them all, but Eleanor,
wrapping some elderly lady in a shabby winter coat,
preparatory to her going home, wished with all her
heart that they might stay in the ward, eating the plain
wholesome food they never cooked for themselves,
enjoying the warmth and the company of other elderly
ladies; instead of which, going home so often meant
nothing more than a chilly, lonely bed-sitter.

They weren't all elderly, though. There was the
teenager, who should have been pretty and lively and
nicely curved, but who had succumbed to the craze
for slimming and had been so unwise about it that
now she was a victim of anorexia nervosa; the very
sight of food had become repugnant to her, and although she was nothing but skin and bone, she still

wanted to become even slimmer. Eleanor had a hard time with her, but it was rewarding after a week or two to know that she had won and once again her patient could be persuaded to eat. And the diabetics, of course, nothing as dramatic as Miss Tremble, but short-stay patients who came in to be stabilized, and lastly, the heart patients; the dramatic coronaries who came in with such urgency and needed so much care, and the less spectacular forms of heart disease, who nonetheless received just as much attention. Eleanor didn't grudge her time or her energy on her patients; off-duty didn't matter, and when Jill remonstrated with her she said carelessly that she could give herself a few extra days later on, when the ward was slack.

And towards the end of November things did calm down a bit, and Eleanor, a little tired despite her denials, decided that she might have a long weekend at home. She left the hospital after lunch on Friday and took the long train journey to Lairg and then the bus to Tongue, warmly wrapped against the weather in her tweed coat and little fur hat her mother had given her for the previous Christmas, and armed with a good book, and because it was a long journey, she took a thermos of tea and some sandwiches as well. All the same, despite these precautions, she was tired and hungry by the time she reached the manse, but her welcome was warm and the supper her mother had waiting was warm and filling as well. She ate and talked at the same time and then went up to bed. It was heavenly to be home again; the peace and quiet of it were a delight after the busy hospital life. She curled up in her narrow little bed and went instantly to sleep.

She was up early, though, ready to help with the breakfast and see Margaret and Henry off to school, and then go and visit Mrs Trot and her fast-growing family. 'We'll have to find homes for them,' she declared as she helped with the washing up.

'Yes, dear.' Mrs MacFarlane emptied her bowl and dried her hands. 'We have—for two of them, and we thought we'd keep one—company for Mrs Trot, she's such a good mother—that leaves one.'

'Oh, good.' Eleanor was stacking plates on the old-fashioned wooden dresser. 'What's all this about Henry going climbing?'

'His class is going this afternoon, up to that cairn—you know the one? It's about two miles away, isn't it? Mr MacDow is going with them, of course, and it's splendid weather with a good forecast. He's promised that they'll explore those caves nearby.'

'The whole class? That'll be a dozen or more, I don't envy him.'

Mrs MacFarlane laughed. 'He's very competent, you know, and a first-class climber—the boys adore him.' She looked a little anxious. 'Do you suppose that Henry shouldn't have gone?'

'Oh, Mother, no. Can you imagine how he would feel if he were left behind? Besides, he's pretty good on his own, remember, and he knows the country almost as well as I do.'

Her mother looked relieved. 'Yes, that's true,' she smiled. 'I've always said that if I got lost on the mountains I wouldn't be at all frightened if I knew you were searching for me.'

Eleanor gave her mother a daughterly hug. 'Let's get on with the dinner, then at least Henry can start out on a full stomach. Are they to be back for tea? It gets dark early…'

'Five o'clock at the latest, Mr MacDow said—they'll have torches with them…I thought we'd have treacle scones and I baked a cake yesterday—he'll be hungry.'

Henry, well fed, suitably clothed, and admonished by his three elder relations to mind what the teacher said and not to go off by himself, was seen off just after one o'clock. The afternoon was fine, with the sky still blue and the cold sunshine lighting up the mountains he was so eager to climb. Not that there was anything hazardous about the expedition; they would follow the road, a narrow one full of hairpin bends, until they reached the cairn in the dip between the mountains encircling it, and then, if there was time, they would explore the caves.

'I shall probably find something very exciting,' said Henry importantly as he set off on his short walk back to the village school where they were to foregather.

Eleanor stood at the door and watched them set out, waving cheerfully to Mr MacDow, striding behind the boys like a competent shepherd with a flock of sheep. She said out loud: 'I'd better make some chocolate buns as well,' and sniffed the air as she turned to go indoors again; it had become a good deal colder.

She didn't notice at first that it was becoming dark

far too early; her mother was having a nap in the
sitting room, her father would be writing his sermon
in his study and she had been fully occupied in the
kitchen, but now she went to the window and looked
out. The blue sky had become grey, and looking towards the sea she saw that it had become a menacing
grey, lighted by a pale yellowish veil hanging above
it. 'Snow,' she said, and her voice sounded urgent in
the quiet kitchen and even as she spoke the window
rattled with violence of a sudden gust of wind. It was
coming fast too; the sea, grey and turbulent, was already partly blotted out. She hurried out of the kitchen
and into the sitting room and found her mother still
sleeping, and when she went into the study it was to
find her father dozing too. She took another look out
of the window and saw the first slow snowflakes falling; a blizzard was on the way, coming at them without warning. She prayed that Mr MacDow had seen
it too and was already on the way down the mountain
with the boys. She remembered then that if they had
already reached the cairn, there would be no view of
the sea from it, the mountains around them would cut
off everything but the sky above them. She went back
to her father and roused him gently. 'There's a blizzard on the way,' she told him urgently. 'What ought
we to do? The boys...'

The pastor was instantly alert. 'The time,' he said
at once. 'What is the time, my dear?'

She glanced at the clock on the old-fashioned mantelpiece. 'Just after three o'clock.'

'MacDow gave me some sort of timetable—he usually does, you know, so that we have some idea...if I remember rightly, they were to have reached the cairn by half past two. He intended to give them a short talk there; interesting geographical features and so on, and between a quarter to three and the hour they would enter the caves and remain there until half past three. They're simple caves, nothing dangerous, and it's possible they're still inside them, unaware of the weather conditions. He's sensible enough to remain in them until the weather clears—it's probably only a brief storm.'

He got up and went to look from the window in his turn. The snow was coming down in good earnest now and the wind had risen, howling eerily round the little house. 'I'm afraid,' said the pastor, 'that this is no brief storm. With this wind there'll be drifts and the road will be blocked and there's no visibility... We'd better get a search party organised.' He looked worried. 'It's a pity that almost all the men are at work...'

'I'll wake Mother,' Eleanor told him, 'while you ring Mr Wallace.' She sped back into the sitting room, roused her mother, and went back into the hall to get her boots and anorak; she would be going with Mr Wallace, the owner of the only garage within miles, and any other man available, she hadn't been boasting when she had said that she knew the surrounding country like the back of her hand, even in the worst weather she had a natural instinct for direction. She was tugging on her boots when someone rang the front door bell and she called: 'Come in, the door's open.' It would be someone from the village come to consult the pastor about the dangers of the weather.

It wasn't anyone from the village; it was Fulk, standing there, shaking the snow from his shoulders. 'Hullo, everyone,' he said cheerfully, just as though he had seen them only an hour or so previously, 'what filthy weather,' and then: 'What's wrong?'

They were all in the hall now and it was Mrs MacFarlane who explained: 'The children—Henry's class at school—they went up the mountain for a geographical climb—more than a dozen of them with Mr MacDow, their teacher. They're all properly clothed and equipped, but this weather—there was no warning—it's a freak blizzard; it could last for hours and it's not very safe up there in bad weather.' Her voice faltered a little.

His voice was very calm. 'A dozen or more boys—is Henry with them?'

The pastor nodded. 'We were just deciding what's the best thing to do—there are very few men in the village at this time of day…'

He paused and Mrs MacFarlane said suddenly: 'It's wonderful to see you, Fulk.'

Eleanor hadn't said a word. Relief at the sight of Fulk had given way to the certainty that now everything would be all right; he looked dependable, sure of himself and quite unworried, whatever his hidden feelings might be; probably it was his very bulk which engendered such a strong feeling of confidence in him, but it was a pleasant sensation, like handing someone else a heavy parcel to carry.

'How far up?' he asked, and looked at her.

'There's a cleft in the mountains about two miles up—it's on the right of the road and there's a cairn...it's sheltered on all sides and there are caves quite close by. They were going to explore them.'

She looked out of the window again. The howling gale and the snow were, if anything, rather worse.

'The road?'

'Narrow—about one in six, perhaps more in some places, and there are three hairpin bends.'

He said nothing for a moment and then grinned suddenly, reminding her very much of Henry when he was plotting something. 'Is there a bus in the village?'

She understood at once. 'Yes, Mr Wallace has one, a fourteen-seater, old but reliable—he's got chains too.'

'Good. We'll want rope, torches, blankets—you know all that better than I do—whisky too, shovels and some sacks.'

'How many men will you take?' asked the pastor. 'There aren't many to choose from, I'm afraid: old MacNab and Mr Wallace, and myself, of course.'

'One with me—if we make a mess of it, a search party can start out on foot. Give us an hour.'

'I'm coming with you,' Eleanor said quietly.

Fulk didn't seem surprised. 'I thought you might. I'm going to see about borrowing that bus—could you get some tea in flasks to take with us?'

Eleanor was already on the way to the kitchen. 'I'll see to it. How did you come?'

'With the Panther. I drove straight into the stable—I hope that's all right?' He nodded cheerfully to all three of them as he opened the door, letting in a flurry of snow and a powerful gust of wind before shutting it behind him.

He was back in a surprisingly short time, the lights of the bus lightening the snowy gloom as he came to a slithering halt before the door. He got out, leaving the engine running, and came indoors bringing Mr Wallace with him.

'Ye'll need a man who kens the road,' remarked that gentleman once they were inside. They stamped the snow off their boots and shook their shoulders, making havoc in Mrs MacFarlane's neat hall.

'Well,' said Fulk, 'Eleanor said she would come—she knows the way.' He smiled at Mr Wallace with great charm. 'I should value your advice on this—it seems a fairly sensible idea, for if we make a mess of things you would be here to organize a search party on foot, something I wouldn't know a thing about. I understand the men are away from home until the evening.'

Mr Wallace nodded. 'Building an extension on the hotel in Tongue, though they'll not get far in this, neither will they get home all that easy.' He gave a not unfriendly grunt. 'Ye're a good driver? My bus isn't any of your fancy cars, ye ken.'

'I've taken part in a number of rallies,' murmured Fulk, and left it at that, and Mr Wallace grunted again. 'We'll need to clear the school house—aye, and get blankets too.'

Fulk nodded. 'Are there enough men to mount a search if necessary?'

'Aye,' said Mr Wallace again, 'we'll manage. Ye'd best be off.'

Fulk turned to look at Eleanor standing patiently, muffled in her hooded anorak, slacks stuffed into boots, a woollen scarf tugged tight round her throat and a pair of woollen mitts on her hands. 'OK?' he asked, and didn't wait for her answer. 'We'll be back as soon as possible,' he assured her parents. 'Give us a couple of hours, won't you?'

He bent to kiss Mrs MacFarlane on the cheek, swept Eleanor before him out of the house and opened the bus door for her. 'Thank God you're a great strapping girl,' he observed as he climbed into the driver's seat beside her, 'for I fancy we shall have to do a good deal of shovelling on the way.'

Eleanor said 'Probably,' in a cold voice; until that moment she had been more than glad to see him, now she wasn't so sure. Even in the most awkward of situations no girl likes to be described as strapping.

They didn't speak again for a little while; Fulk was occupied in keeping the bus on the road down to the village and then out on the other side, away from the sea towards the mountains. The snow was falling fast now, tossed in all directions by the violence of the wind. The road had disappeared too, although the telegraph wires were a guide until they reached the side road which would take them up between the mountains.

Fulk braked gently. 'Up here?' and Eleanor, staring

ahead at the little she could see, said: 'Yes—we must be mad.'

Her companion laughed. 'Though this be madness, yet there is method in't—and that's your Shakespeare, and a very sensible remark too.' He changed gear and started up the narrow road.

They were soon in trouble; the first bend came after a hundred yards or so, and although it wasn't a sharp one and it was still possible to see its curve, the bus skidded on the bank of snow which had already built up along its edge. Fulk prepared to get out. 'Keep the engine going, whatever you do,' he cautioned her, and disappeared into the swirling snow, armed with sacks and shovel. It seemed an age before he climbed in again, the snow thick on him. Eleanor slid back into her own seat and brushed him down as best she could, then sat tensely while he hauled the bus round the bend. It went with reluctance, sliding and slipping, but the sacks held the back wheels and they were round at last.

'I don't dare to stop now,' said Fulk. 'The sacks will have to stay—is it straight ahead?'

'Yes—there's a spiky rock on the left before the next bend, it's a sharp one and there's bound to be a drift—I should think we'll both have to dig.'

He spared a brief, smiling glance. 'OK, if you say so—it'll mean leaving the bus, though.' He began to whistle, and she realized that he was enjoying himself, and upon reflection she was bound to admit that so was she, in a scary kind of way.

It took them ten minutes' hard digging to clear the

angle of the road when they reached it. Eleanor had got out when she saw the rock, and floundered ahead in the appalling weather, looking for landmarks—a stunted tree, the vague outline of the railing which guarded the angle of the road. Once she was sure of them she waved to Fulk, who joined her with the shovels, leaving the bus reluctantly ticking over. They worked together until they had made some sort of track, so that Fulk, with a great deal of skill and muttered bad language, was able to go on again, toiling up the road, narrower and steeper now but happily sheltered a little on one side from the gale, so that although there were great drifts piling up on the opposite bank, their side of the road was still fairly clear.

Eleanor blew on her cold fingers. 'We're nearly half way—there's a left-hand bend in about fifty yards—very exposed, I'm afraid.'

Fulk chuckled. 'Eleanor, if ever I should need to go to the North Pole, remind me to take you with me; you seem to have an instinctive sense of direction.' He had raised his voice to a shout, for the wind, now that they were higher, was howling round the bus, beating on its windows, driving the snow in thick, crazily spiralling flurries.

Eleanor wiped the windscreen uselessly. 'It's somewhere here,' she cried, and as the windscreen wipers cleared the view for a few seconds: 'You can just see the beginning of the curve—there's a stone…it's blocked further on,' she added rather unnecessarily.

'Work to do, girl,' said Fulk cheerfully, 'and for

heaven's sake don't go wandering off; I'd never find you again. Out you get, I'll fetch the shovels.'

It was hard work, even clearing a rough path just wide enough for the bus was an agonisingly laborious business. Eleanor, shovelling away with her young strong arms, found herself wondering how her companion's Imogen would have fared. Would she have shovelled? Would she have come on the crazy trip in the first place? Decidedly not; she would have stayed behind by the fire, and when Fulk returned she would have greeted him with girlish charm, deliciously scented and gowned, and with not a hair out of place, and he would have called her his precious darling, or something equally silly. Eleanor, her spleen nicely stirred, shovelled even harder.

It was heaven to get back into the bus at last. She sat, huffing and puffing in its warm haven, looking like a snowman. Fulk, getting in beside her, looked her over carefully. 'Cold but cuddly,' he pronounced, and leaned over to kiss her surprised mouth. Heaven knew what she might have said to that, but he gave her no chance to speak, starting at once on the slow business of coaxing the bus along the road once more, an operation fraught with such difficulties that she was kept fully occupied peering ahead, ready to warn him should he get too near to the low stone wall, just visible, guarding the outer edge of the road. The other side was shut in now by towering rocks, which, while forbidding, at least served as a guide.

'The cairn's on the right,' declared Eleanor, 'where the rock stops, and for heaven's sake be careful, there's a kind of canyon, fairly level once you get into it. If they're sheltering anywhere near, they must surely see our lights.'

Fulk didn't answer. He was fully occupied in keeping the bus steady; it took several attempts to get round the rocks and into the canyon, for the bus danced and skidded as though its wheels were legs, but once they were between the walls of rock, it was comparatively peaceful—true, the wind howled like a banshee and the snow was as thick as ever, but there was a semblance of shelter. Fulk skidded to a slow halt, leaving the engine running. 'Journey's end,' he declared. 'Now to find everyone and stow them away before we die of exposure.'

They got out and stood, holding hands for safety's sake, striving to pierce the gloom around them. 'Someone's shouting,' cried Eleanor, 'and there's a torch—look, over there, to our right,' and when she would have started off, found herself held firmly against Fulk.

'No, wait—stay just where you are while I get the rope.'

She hadn't thought of that in the excitement and relief of knowing that the boys were safe and found; she waited patiently while he secured the rope to the bus and paid out a length of it, slinging the coils over one arm. 'Now we can all get back,' he pointed out, and took her by the arm. 'Switch on your torch, the more light the better.'

The boys were all together, close against an overhanging rock which afforded them some shelter, and when they would have plunged forward to meet them, Fulk shouted: 'Stay where you are—where's Mr MacDow?'

It was Henry who shouted back. 'He's here, behind us, Fulk—he's hurt his leg. He fell down outside the cave and now he doesn't answer us any more.'

Eleanor heard Fulk mutter something, then shout: 'Is there anyone in the caves still?'

There was a chorus of 'No's' and a babble of voices explaining that when they had wanted to leave the caves the entrance had been almost completely blocked with snow. 'We had to dig with our hands,' explained Henry, and then: 'Can we go home now—it's cold.'

Fulk was tying the rope round himself. 'This minute,' he bellowed hearteningly. 'Eleanor, I'll stay here and have a look at MacDow, get this lot collected up and hustle them into the bus and make sure that every one of them has a hand on the rope— Understood?'

She heard herself say in a meek voice, 'Yes, Fulk,' and blundered away, going to and fro through the knee-deep snow, organising the little group of boys, making sure that they understood that they were to use the rope as a guide and never let go. She had them lined up and ready to start when Fulk loomed up beside her. 'Could you manage to bring back a couple of splints—luckily Mr Wallace put a couple in the bus. MacDow has a fractured tib and fib.'

She nodded and urged the boys to get started. It wasn't far, but the snow was deep and the rope awkward to hold, but they made it at last and she opened

the bus door in almost tearful relief and helped the
boys on board. They were cold and frightened too and
she would have liked to have given them the hot tea,
but she must get the splints to Fulk first; she set them
rubbing their arms and legs and taking off wet boots,
dragged out the splints, and as an afterthought, the
folded stretcher she found beside them, and made her
unwieldy way back to where Fulk was waiting.

He hailed her with a 'Splendid girl!' when he saw
the stretcher, and proceeded to splint the broken leg,
using Mr MacDow's scarf as well as his own to tie
it on, and when Eleanor would have helped get the
schoolmaster on to the stretcher, he waved her on one
side, lifting the man gently himself. When he was
ready he shouted: 'I hate to ask you, but can you
manage the foot end? He's a small man, thank the
Lord; I'll have to wind the rope as we go—do you
think you can do it?'

She nodded sturdily and they set off slowly because
of winding the rope, which somehow he managed to
do without putting the stretcher down, a mercy, actually, for she was quite sure that if she had had to
put her end down she would never have been able to
pick it up again. She was speechless with exhaustion
when they arrived at the bus, and when she would
have helped Fulk drag the stretcher on board and into
the aisle between the boys, he shook his head and
told her in a no-nonsense voice to get in first. She
scrambled through the door, leaving it open and sub-
siding on to the nearest seat, feeling peculiar, vaguely
aware that two of the boys were hauling on one end

of the stretcher, helping Fulk, and that she was going to faint unless she did something about it. But it was Fulk who did that; she felt a great arm steady her while he held a brandy flask to her lips and poured the stuff relentlessly down her throat. She choked, said 'Ugh!' and felt almost at once much better.

'How silly of me,' she declared stoutly, and met his dark concerned gaze firmly. 'I'm fine,' she told him, feeling dreadful. 'I'll get some hot tea into these boys before we start back.'

Just for a moment she thought that he was going to kiss her again, but he only smiled briefly, took the brandy from her and said: 'I'll follow behind with this, but MacDow first, I think, though I daresay he will prefer whisky.'

She managed a smile at that and fetched the tea, doling it out into the plastic beakers her mother had thoughtfully provided. The boys were being very good, even laughing a little as they struggled out of their wet coats and boots. She went up and down the bus, pouring the drinks down their willing throats, handing out biscuits, climbing carefully over poor Mr MacDow, lying on the floor in everyone's way; he was feeling easier now; he had come to nicely and the whisky had put fresh heart into him so that he took the biscuit she offered him and nibbled at it.

The bus seemed quite crowded, what with a dozen small boys, recovering their spirits fast, the stretcher, herself and Fulk; there was a lot of melting snow too, and Eleanor, feeling an icy trickle in her neck, wondered which was worse, to be numb with cold or hor-

ribly damp. She forgot the unpleasantness of both
these sensations in the sheer fright of the return journey. The boys more or less settled and Mr MacDow
as comfortable as he could be made, she took her seat
by Fulk once more, sitting speechless while he ma-
noeuvred the bus backwards on to the road again, an
undertaking which took some considerable time, and
on their way at length, staring out at the white waste
around her through the curtain of snow, she felt a
strong urge to beg him not to go another inch, to stop
just where he was and let someone come and rescue
them; an absurd idea, bred from cowardice, she
chided herself silently, and closed her eyes to shut out
the awful possibilities waiting in store for them on
the way down. She opened them almost immediately;
if he could sit there driving so calmly, then she could
at least do her part. 'You need to keep a bit to the
left,' she warned him. 'I'll tell you when we reach
the corner—shall we have to get out and dig again?'

'Probably, but not you this time—I'll take a couple
of the bigger boys with me.'

Which he did, and after that the journey became
rather less of a nightmare; true, they skidded and
bumped around and once shot across the road in an
alarming manner, but the road was easier to make out
as they descended it, so that she was able to leave her
seat from time to time to see how the boys were far-
ing, wrapping them more closely in blankets and taking round more biscuits. It was a relief to find that
Mr MacDow had gone to sleep.

She could hardly believe it when the bus rocked to

an uneasy halt and Fulk shouted: 'Everybody out—one at a time and no shoving!'

Every house in the village had its lights on and the school house doors were standing wide; willing helpers helped the children out of the bus and hustled them inside where anxious mothers claimed their offspring and began the task of getting them into dry clothes, feeding them hot milk and massaging cold arms and legs. There were no men back yet, Mr Wallace told them, but he had done them proud, with a roaring stove and hot drinks and offers of help to get the children to their homes. They lifted Mr MacDow out last of all and carried him to the warmth of the stove and Eleanor, getting awkwardly out of her anorak and kicking off her boots, paused only long enough to call a brief 'Hullo,' to her father before going to help Fulk. The leg was set as well as it could be done with what they had at their disposal, and Mr MacDow, very white, was given another generous dose of whisky before Fulk asked: 'Is there a telephone working?'

Mr MacFarlane shook his head. 'I'm afraid not. The most I can promise is that the moment it's possible they'll get it mended—they're very quick about it. Should MacDow be in hospital?'

'It would be better for him, though it's possible to manage as we are. Shall I just take a quick look at the boys? Those who live near enough could go home, the rest will have to be given a bed for the night. I've my case in the car, I'll give MacDow something to ease the pain and get him home too. Is there someone to look after him?'

'His wife—she's expecting a baby, though.' Eleanor sounded doubtful.

'In that case, if she would be so kind as to put me up for the night I could keep an eye on him.' He glanced round. 'If I could have a hand, we could get him home—but we had better check the boys first.'

A job which was quickly done. The boys seemed little the worse for their adventure, in fact, now that it was all over, they were beginning to enjoy themselves. They went, one by one, escorted by mothers, grannies and big sisters, until there was only Henry left.

Fulk collected Mr Wallace and old Mr MacNab, who had stayed to help with the schoolmaster. 'We'll go now. Eleanor, stay here with your father and Henry, I'll be back in ten minutes.'

'Why?' She was a little impatient; she wanted to get home and eat a huge meal and then go to bed and sleep the clock round.

He didn't answer her directly, only said: 'Ten minutes,' and went away, leaving the three of them by the stove. Eleanor fell asleep at once and only roused when Fulk's voice wakened her with: 'Come on, home.'

She looked at him owl-eyed, said 'Oh,' in a lost voice and got herself to her feet, dragging on her anorak and boots once more and hunting for her torch, and then following the others out into the cold night. The snow had slowed its mad pace and the wind, although strong, was no longer a gale. It was dark too, for the electricity had failed while she slept. It was a miracle that it had survived so long, but they had their torches and with Fulk leading the way, battled their way in single file until the dim light from the oil lamp in the manse hall told them that they were home.

Mrs MacFarlane had the door open before they could reach it, and whatever worry she had felt she effectively concealed now. 'Into the sitting room,' she greeted them. 'There's hot coffee ready and while you're drinking it I'll get Henry into a hot bath—he can have his supper in bed.' She smiled at them all, although her eyes anxiously sought Fulk's face. 'He's all right, Fulk?'

He smiled reassuringly. 'Cold and hungry, that's all. Bed and bath are just the thing. He behaved splendidly—they all did.'

Henry puffed out his chest. 'I wasn't really frightened,' he declared, 'though it was very cold.'

His mother put a hand on his shoulder. 'You shall tell me all about it, dear, but we mustn't be too long; Eleanor will want a bath too—and Fulk.' She glanced round as they were leaving the room. 'You'll spend the night, Fulk?'

He explained about spending the night at Mr MacDow's house. 'But I would love a bath, if I may…'

Mrs MacFarlane nodded briskly. 'Of course, and you'll stay for supper too—they won't expect you back for a little while, will they? I'm on edge to hear all about it, but first things first.' With which words she led Henry upstairs.

They had their supper round the fire. Eleanor, warm at last from her bath, her hair plaited tidily and wrapped in a thick dressing gown, could have slept sitting there. She spooned her soup slowly, content to be back home and safe with Fulk sitting unconcernedly opposite her. She frowned a little, her tired mind grappling with the fact that it was possible to like someone very much even when one didn't like him at all. It didn't make sense, and she gave up presently, thinking that it was absurd to suppose that she had ever not liked him. After all, she had been a very little girl when she had vowed to hate him for ever—and a girl had a right to change her mind. She smiled sleepily at him and was strangely disturbed at his intent, unsmiling look. He said good night very shortly afterwards, and Eleanor went upstairs to bed, to wake in the night and wonder about that look. She turned over and curled herself into a ball under the bedclothes; probably they would bicker just as they always did when next they met. It would be nice if they didn't, she thought sleepily as she closed her eyes again.

CHAPTER FOUR

THE BRIGHT SUNSHINE and complete lack of wind just didn't seem true the next morning. Eleanor took an astonished look out of the window, dressed quickly in an elderly kilt and thick jersey, and went downstairs to breakfast. Her mother looked up as she went into the kitchen. 'There you are, darling,' she said happily. 'How lovely to have yesterday over and done with. Breakfast's ready—don't forget it's church at ten o'clock.'

Eleanor nodded. 'I hadn't forgotten, Mother, but there'll be time to clear the path before I need to dress.' She carried the plates to the table and went to call Henry. 'When's Margaret coming back?' she asked as they sat down at the table.

'As soon as the snow plough clears the road, and I imagine they will be out already—that was a freak blizzard, it didn't get far. The men were telling me that the telephone was still working between Durness and the west coast, although the lines were down to the south of us, and beyond Lairg the roads are pretty clear. I wonder how Fulk got on at the MacDows'.' He glanced at his son. 'Henry, are you not hungry?'

Three pairs of eyes stared at the youngest member of the family. Usually he ate as much as the three of them together, but now, this morning he was pecking at his food in a manner totally unlike him.

'Do you feel ill, darling?' his mother asked anxiously.

'I'm just not hungry—I expect I'll eat an enormous dinner to make up for it.'

Eleanor studied him unobtrusively; he looked all right, a little pale perhaps, and certainly listless; could be that he hadn't got over his chickenpox as well as they thought he had. Doctor MacClew might go over him again—she hoped worriedly that the boy hadn't caught a chill; it would be a miracle if they all escaped with nothing at all.

She had intended asking Henry to help her with the snow on the path between the manse and the little church, but instead she helped her mother wash up, made the beds and went outside on her own. There was still an hour before church and the exercise would do her good. She was almost ready when a large hand came down on hers, so that she was forced to stop shovelling.

'Good morning,' said Fulk. 'None the worse for our little adventure, I see. Here, give me that and go and make yourself decent for church.'

'No, I won't,' said Eleanor immediately. 'For one thing, I'm dressed for it and you're not.'

He still had her hand fast. 'And for the other thing?' he prompted her softly.

'Well, I don't much like being told what to do.' She looked up at him and the question tripped off her tongue before she could stop it. 'Does Imogen do exactly as you say?'

He didn't look in the least put out, only a little surprised. 'It's hard to say; I don't remember any occasion when it was necessary for me to ask her to do anything.'

She blinked. 'How funny!'

The dark eyes became cold, he said silkily: 'Funny? Perhaps you would explain...'

She said hastily: 'I didn't mean funny funny—just strange. Don't you see much of each other?' She went on staring at him, asking for trouble and not much caring.

'I hardly feel that it is any of your business, Eleanor, and if you're trying to cast doubts into my head, I can assure you that it's a waste of time.' His voice was as cold as his eyes; he wasn't bothering to conceal his anger. But she was angry too now, with him and with herself for starting the whole miserable conversation in the first place.

'You're awful,' she said, making it even worse, 'just as bad as you used to be; I might have known...I thought just once or twice that I'd been mistaken, that you'd changed, but you haven't.' She tossed her head. 'Here, take the beastly shovel!' Her glance swept over his undoubtedly expensive tweeds and well-tailored camel hair topcoat. 'You'll look very silly shovelling snow in Savile Row suiting, but that's your affair!'

She flounced back indoors, muttering at his roar of laughter.

When she came downstairs twenty minutes later,

in her tweed coat and little fur hat, it was to find him
in the sitting room, talking to the rest of the family,
and he looked as though he had never seen a snow
shovel in his life. He got to his feet as she went in
and said gravely: 'I like that hat,' and added to the
room at large: 'It's surprising what clothes do for a
woman.'

Her father turned round to look at her. 'Indeed, yes.
Fulk is quite right, my dear, that is a pretty hat,
though I thought you looked very nice yesterday in
that hooded thing.'

'Father, my oldest anorak!'

'Your father's got something there—you did look
nice. You looked sensible and trustworthy too, exactly the kind of companion a man wants when he's
on a ticklish job.'

She gasped. 'Well, I never…after all the things you
said!'

He grinned. 'Coals of fire, Eleanor.'

'A whole scuttle of them—what's come over you?'

He answered lightly, 'Oh, a change of heart,' and
got to his feet again. 'Ought we to be on our way?'

The church was very full. Even those who usually
attended only upon special occasions had turned up,
deeming yesterday's occurrence well worth a few
prayers of thanks. The small building, bursting at the
seams, rocked to the thankful voices, and Eleanor,
who sang quite well in an amateurish way, sang too,
a little off-key on the top notes but making up for
that by her enthusiasm. Fulk, standing beside her,
glanced at her several times, and Mrs MacFarlane,

watching him, wondered if her daughter's slightly off-key rendering of the hymns nettled him at all, then changed her mind when she saw the little smile tugging the corners of his mouth.

Fulk went back to the MacDows' house after church, casually taking Eleanor with him. 'And before you fly into a temper because you don't want to come,' he informed her as soon as they were out of earshot of the rest of the family, 'I want to ask you something. Does Henry strike you as being his usual self?'

'Oh, you've noticed it, too,' she exclaimed, quite forgetting that she had intended to be coolly polite and nothing more. 'You don't think he's sickening for something?'

'I can't tell, but I had an idea in church. Would your mother and father allow him to come and stay with me for a few weeks?' He saw her sudden look of alarm. 'No, don't instantly suspect that he's dying of some obscure disease—he's a tough little boy and healthy enough, but he has a good brain, much above average, I should imagine, and he tends to work it too hard. A holiday wouldn't do him any harm, away from lessons and even the remote chance of going to school. I'll keep a fatherly eye on him and he'll be free to roam where he likes. I live in the country, you know, and there's plenty for him to do. I'll see that if he must read, it will be nothing to tease that brain of his...'

They were almost at the MacDow croft. 'Why are you doing it?' asked Eleanor, then wished she hadn't spoken, for it sounded rude and for the moment at any rate, they were friends. But Fulk only answered placidly: 'I like the boy.'

'It's a marvellous idea,' she ruminated, half aloud, and then choosing her words carefully: 'Will there be anyone else? I mean, does anyone else live in your house?'

His smile held a tinge of mockery. 'Still determined to think the worst of me, Eleanor?' And when she said sharply: 'No, of course not,' he went on smoothly: 'I've a housekeeper, a good sort who will feed Henry like a fighting cock—there are a couple of other people around too, but Imogen won't be there; that's what you really wanted to know, wasn't it? And if you credit me with entertaining young women while she's away then I must disappoint you—my household would do credit to a monk.'

'I can't think why you should suppose me to be interested in your private life,' declared Eleanor haughtily. She tossed her head rather grandly, tripped up on a hidden lump of snow and fell flat on her face. Fulk scooped her up, stood her on her feet, brushed her down, kissed her swiftly and said gently: 'There's no need to get uppity.' A remark she didn't have time to answer because they were on the doorstep and Mrs MacDow was opening the door.

The schoolmaster was sitting in a chair drawn up to the fire, a pair of very out-of-date crutches by his side. He greeted them cheerfully and when Eleanor expressed surprise at seeing him there in his dressing gown, smoking his pipe and looking almost normal, he laughed and assured her that it was all the doctor's doing.

'Not ideal,' murmured Fulk. 'The crutches are heirlooms from some bygone age, but they'll do until we can get you into Durness. They'll do an X-ray and put the leg in plaster and a walking iron—all you'll need then is a good stout stick.'

They stayed talking for a few minutes, lighthearted argument as to the ill-fated climbing expedition. 'We should have been in a pretty bad way if you hadn't come along,' said Mr MacDow. 'We knew a search party would come out after us sooner or later, but if they'd waited until there were enough men, the boys would have been in poor shape to tackle the scramble down. That was a brilliant idea bringing the bus, though how you managed to get it up there beats me.'

'We had our difficult moments,' Fulk acknowledged. 'Luckily Eleanor proved to be a sort of pocket compass.'

They looked at her and she went a faint pink, so that she looked quite eye-catching, what with flushed cheeks and the fur hat crowning her brown hair. 'I couldn't have driven the bus,' she pointed out, 'and if the men had been here they would have found the way just as well—better, perhaps.'

'They wouldn't have fancied taking that bus,' declared the schoolmaster. 'We'll be indebted to you, Doctor—I doubt if we'll ever be able to do the same for you, but you've made a great many friends in the village.'

'Thank you—and that reminds me, I wanted a word

with you about young Henry. I've spoken to Eleanor already, but I should appreciate your advice before I say anything to Mr MacFarlane.'

Eleanor had to admit that he put his case very well; Mr MacDow agreed wholeheartedly that Henry was far too clever for his age. 'A real boy, make no mistake about that,' he observed, 'but the laddie tires himself out, reading beyond his years; working away at problems, wanting to know this, that and the other. He could miss a few weeks at school and never know the difference. If you say it would do the boy some good then I'll not say nay, Doctor, provided his father hasn't any objection.'

The pastor had no objection at all and his wife was openly delighted. 'What a dear man you are, Fulk,' she exclaimed. 'It's just what will do him the most good; his head is stuffed with algebra and science and learning to play chess, and there's no stopping him.' She looked so happy and relieved that Eleanor bent to kiss her swiftly in understanding. 'He's over in the loft,' said Mrs MacFarlane, 'feeding Mrs Trot and the kittens, do go and tell him yourself.' She added in an offhand way, 'Go with Fulk, will you, Eleanor? Henry forgot to take the milk with him, and Mrs Trot will need it before the evening.'

Henry was sitting where his big sister usually sat, on the floor with the kittens playing round him, while Mrs Trot ate her dinner. He had heard them on the ladder and turned his head to watch them. 'I thought it was you,' he remarked. 'It isn't our dinnertime yet, is it?'

'Almost.' Eleanor chose an apple and offered it to Fulk before taking one for herself; they shared the sack of potatoes and munched contentedly for a minute or two until Fulk asked: 'Henry, how do you feel about spending a week or two with me in Holland?'

The little boy's face became one large grin. 'Me? Honour bright? Just me? Oh, Fulk, how absolutely smashing!' The grin faded. 'I have to have a passport. I was reading about that the other day—I haven't got one.'

'That's OK, that can be arranged, but we'll need to go to Glasgow for it. I tell you what, if I take Eleanor back tomorrow, you could come with us and we could see about it on the way—that's provided the roads are clear. We can get your photo taken and go to the Passport Office and see what they can do for us. If it's OK, we'll come back here and pack your bags.'

'Oh, golly!' Henry was on his feet, capering round the bare boards, only to stop abruptly. 'I'll have to leave the kittens.' His face fell as he picked up the smallest and ugliest of them, the one no one wanted. 'No one's offered for Moggy.'

Eleanor felt a glow of warmth as Fulk exclaimed instantly: 'I will—I've a dog and my housekeeper has a cat of her own, but we could do with a kitten. We'll take him with us.'

'I say—really? You mean that, Fulk?'

'I mean it—I'm partial to kittens around the house.'

Eleanor's tongue was too quick for her once more. 'Supposing your Imogen doesn't like him?'

Fulk turned a bland face to hers. 'My dear girl,

don't you know that people in love are prepared to do anything for the loved one's sake?'

An observation which depressed her very much; quite possibly Imogen was a very nice girl, prepared to sacrifice her own likes and dislikes just to please Fulk; which was a pity, because it was hard to dislike a nice girl, and she had made up her mind to dislike Imogen. She contented herself by saying: 'Well, I wouldn't know about that. I say, there's really no need to take me back tomorrow—Edinburgh will be right out of your way, and the roads…'

'Nervous? Surely not after yesterday's little trip. We can go via Glasgow and if there's any hitch or waiting about to be done, we can take you to the hospital and then go back there.'

He made it all sound so easy—convenient, almost. She found herself agreeing with him as Henry tidied the kittens back into their box, planted Mrs Trot beside them and announced that he was quite ready for his dinner.

The meal was an animated one, with everyone talking at once, and Eleanor was the only one, so she thought, to notice that Henry ate hardly anything at all. But she wasn't; she looked up and caught Fulk's eyes upon her and knew that he had seen it too and wasn't going to say anything. Obedient to that dark glance, she didn't say anything either.

The snow ploughs and the weather had done their work by morning; the roads were clear, the telephone and the electricity were once more functioning and although there was a good deal of snow still lying around it wasn't likely to hinder them much. Fulk was at the manse by half past ten, having got up early and driven Mr MacDow, wedged on to the back seat, into Durness, where they had X-rayed the limb, clapped it in plaster and a walking iron and handed him back to Fulk, who had in turn handed him over to his own doctor's care. He brought the news that the road to Lairg was more or less clear and beyond that there should be no difficulties, and they left at once, stopping to lunch in Inverness at the Station Hotel, where even the magnificence of the restaurant and the remarkable choice of food did little to increase Henry's appetite. Of course, he was excited, thought Eleanor worriedly as she joined in the cheerful talk of her companions. Whatever was wrong with the boy's appetite hadn't affected his spirits.

The Panther made light work of the hundred and seventy miles remaining of their journey, so that they reached the Passport Office with half an hour to spare before it closed for the day and they would have been there sooner, only they had stopped on the way for some instant passport photos of Henry. Eleanor stayed in the little outer office while Fulk and Henry went to see what could be done. It was a dull little room, with nothing to read but pamphlets about emigrating and a stern warning of the dire punishment awaiting anyone who tampered with their passport. She read these interesting titbits of information several times, and then for lack of anything else to do, found paper and pen in her handbag and amused herself making a list of things she would like to buy; it was a long list and imaginative and she headed it boldly 'Things I would like to have,' and underlined it twice. She was on the point of crossing out the more frivolous items when Fulk and Henry came back, looking pleased with themselves; obviously they had been successful. She stood up, dropped her handbag, her gloves and the paper and asked: 'Is it OK?' to the two bent forms scrabbling round on the floor picking up her possessions.

Henry lifted his head. 'Rather. Fulk talked—they were super. We're to call and fetch it when we go.'

'And when's that?'

'The day after tomorrow.' Fulk spoke absentmindedly, Eleanor's piece of paper in one hand. 'What's this—don't tell me I shouldn't read it for it's not a letter. Besides, you shouldn't drop things all over the place so carelessly.'

'I was surprised,' she excused herself. 'It's only a list.'

She put out a hand which he instantly took hold of and held. 'Sable coat,' he read in an interested voice, 'Gina Fratini dress, Givenchy scarf, Marks and Spencer sweater, toothpaste,' he chuckled and went on slowly, 'surgical scissors, every paperback I want, roses for Christmas. Seems a pretty sensible list to me, but why roses for Christmas, Eleanor?'

She tugged at her hand to no good purpose. 'Oh, it's just something silly, you know...I mean, if anyone bothered to give me roses, masses of them, I mean, not just six in cellophane—when everyone else was having potted hyacinths and chrysanthemums, I'd know that I meant something to—to someone...' She paused because he was looking at her rather strangely. 'Like the sables,' she went on chattily, 'and the Givenchy scarf...'

'But not the toothpaste,' he suggested, half laughing.

'No.' She took the odds and ends Henry was holding out to her and stuffed them away and said brightly: 'How nice that everything went off without a hitch. Aren't you wildly excited, Henry?'

Henry said that yes, he was, and began to explain exactly how a passport was issued and the conditions imposed. 'And wasn't it clever of Fulk to know that he had to have a letter from Father to show them?' he demanded. 'I shall be glad when I'm grown up and can do those sort of things.' He cast a disparaging look at his surroundings. 'May we go soon?'

Fulk took them to tea; to the Central Hotel, large and impressive with its draperies and its mirrors and chandeliers. Henry looked round, his eyes wide. He had never been in such a place before for his tea, and it was an experience which he was enjoying. Eleanor blessed Fulk for his understanding of a small boy's idea of a treat, and tried not to worry at the small meal her brother was making.

They took her back to Edinburgh when they had finished, going with her to the Nurses' Home door, after a protracted walk across the forecourt because Henry wanted to know exactly where everything was and how many people worked in the hospital for how many hours and how much money. 'I shall be a fa-

mous doctor,' he told them, 'a physician, like Fulk.
Perhaps I might be your partner—you'll probably be
needing one by the time I'm grown up, Fulk.'

'Very probably,' Fulk agreed gravely. 'Now let us
say goodbye to Eleanor and make for home, shall we?
It's a long drive; you can sit in the back and go to
sleep, if you wish.'

'Go to sleep? Of course I shall sit with you in front
and watch the dashboard and you can explain…'

'You're sure you want him?' asked Eleanor, giving
her brother a hug and looking anxiously at Fulk over
his small shoulder.

'Quite sure.' He smiled and held out his hand.
'Don't work too hard,' he advised her, and didn't say
goodbye, only put her case inside the door for her and
then cast an arm round Henry's bony frame and
turned away. She was tempted to delay them with
some question or other; she didn't want to be left, but
she remembered that he had a journey of many hours
before him. She went through the door and closed it
quietly without looking back.

She felt bad-tempered in the morning, due, she told
herself, to the long car journey the day before and all
the excitement during the blizzard. That it might also
be due to the fact that Fulk hadn't bothered to say
goodbye to her was something she had no intention
of admitting, not even to herself. Despite her best efforts, she was snappy with the nurses and found the
patients tiresome too, and making the excuse that she
had to wash her hair and make a telephone call home,
she didn't go, as she usually did, to the Sisters' sitting

room when she got off duty, but retired to her room, where she sat on her bed and brooded.

Hunger drove her down to supper, and in the babble of talk round the table, her unusual quietness was hardly noticed, although several of her closer friends wondered if she were starting a cold or merely feeling unsettled after her weekend. Probably the latter, they decided, and bore her off to drink tea with them, carefully not asking questions. Someone had asked her at breakfast that morning if she had found the blizzard very awful and she had answered so briefly that they had concluded that for some reason or other she didn't want to talk about it.

She felt a little better the next morning, though; she was a girl with plenty of common sense, to let herself be put out by something which wasn't important to her was plain foolish; she went on duty determined to be nice to everyone and succeeded very well, plunging into the daily problems of the ward with zest, listening to Miss Tremble's everlasting grumbles and conducting a round with Sir Arthur and his retinue with her usual good humour and efficiency. It was at the end of this time-consuming exercise that he, sipping coffee in her office, remarked: 'You look washed out, Sister. Shovelling snow evidently doesn't agree with you.'

'Shovel...how did you know that, sir?' She put down her cup and eyed him in some surprise.

'Van Hensum told me—he must have worked you too hard.'

She rushed to Fulk's defence. 'No—indeed no, Sir

Arthur, I did very little, he was the one who did everything.'

'H'm, well—he didn't mention his own activities.'

She told her companion at some length, sparing no details. 'So you see,' she concluded, 'he was pretty super.' She frowned; the whole family had got into the habit of using Henry's favourite word. 'He...' she began; there was no other word— 'He was super.'

Sir Arthur studied his nails and hid a smile. 'I have always found Doctor van Hensum—er—pretty super myself, purely from a professional point of view, of course.' He got up. 'Many thanks for the coffee, Sister.' He glanced at his watch. 'Dear me, is that the time?' He wandered to the door and she accompanied him down the short corridor which led to the swing doors, where he nodded affably, muttered something about being late as usual and hurried away.

Eleanor went back into the ward and plunged into her work once more. The temptation to sit down somewhere quiet and think about Fulk was tempting but pointless. Her mind edged away from the idea that it would be nice if he were to call with Henry on their way to Holland, but Fulk didn't do things to oblige people, only to please himself. This glaring untruth caused her to frown so heavily that Bob Wise, the Medical Officer on duty, walking down the ward to meet her, asked: 'I say, are you angry with me about something?'

She hastened to deny it with such friendliness that he was emboldened to ask her to go out with him that evening. A film, he suggested diffidently, and brightened visibly when she agreed. He was a pleasant young man, very English; he had paid her what she realized was a rare compliment when he had first come to the hospital, telling her that she spoke like an English girl, a remark which she rightly guessed had been born from homesickness and the girl he had left behind him. They had become casual friends since then and from time to time spent an evening together.

So she went to the cinema with him and afterwards sat over a cup of coffee with him in a nearby café, while he told her the latest news of his Maureen. They had known each other since childhood; he had told her that the first time they had met, and their plans had been settled long ago. Eleanor, listening to him discussing the wedding which was at least two years away, wondered what it would be like to have your future cut and dried; to know that you would never be tempted to fall in love with anyone else—it would be wonderful to be as sure as that. She had fancied herself in love on several occasions, of course, but never so deeply that she had felt that life would stop for her when she fell out of it again. Her mother had declared on more than one occasion that she was hard to please; perhaps she was. She sighed a little and begged Bob to describe, just once more, the engagement ring he had bestowed upon Maureen.

She was so busy the next morning that she had no time to think of anything at all but her work. She heaved a sigh when she had dished the dinners, sent most of the nurses to their own meal, and started on her second round of the day, this time accompanied by the most junior nurse on her staff. They tidied beds as they went, made the patients comfortable for their short afternoon nap, and under Eleanor's experienced eye the little nurse took temperatures, had a go at the blood pressures, and charted the diabetics. They had reached Miss Tremble's bed and were, as usual, arguing with that lady, this time about the freshness of the lettuce she had had on her dinner plate, when she broke off her diatribe to say: 'Here's that nice doctor again, Sister.'

Eleanor managed not to turn round and take a look, but the little nurse did. 'Ooh, isn't he groovy—I think he's in a hurry, Sister.'

She couldn't go on pretending that he wasn't there. She turned round and started to walk down the ward towards him with Miss Tremble's urgent: 'And don't forget that we haven't finished our discussion, Sister,' and the little nurse, uncertain as to what she should do, dogging her footsteps.

Fulk was businesslike. 'Forgive me for coming into the ward without asking you first, Sister,' he said, all politeness. 'I did mention it to Sir Arthur, but it seemed best not to telephone you.' He smiled: 'We are rather short of time.'

'We?'

'Henry is here too and dying to see you. I hope you won't mind, I left him in your office.' He glanced at the little nurse and gave her a nice smile. 'Could Nurse keep an eye on the ward for a couple of minutes while you say goodbye to him?'

'Yes, of course. Nurse Angus, you could take Miss Robertson's temp, and have a go at her BP too—I'll only be a moment.'

She walked down the ward beside Fulk without speaking, partly because he was behaving like a consultant again and partly because she couldn't think of anything to say, but once through the door and in the office with Henry prancing round her, Fulk became Fulk once more, his dark face alight with amusement. 'Well, Henry,' he asked, 'I'm right, aren't I? She doesn't look like Eleanor at all, does she?'

She stood while they looked her over slowly. 'No,' said her brother at last, 'she doesn't. I like you better with your hair hanging down your back, Eleanor, and up an apple tree or fishing, though you look very important in that funny cap.' He looked at Fulk. 'Don't you like her better when she's home?' he appealed.

'Oh, rather. She terrifies me like this, all no-nonsense and starch.' Fulk grinned at her. 'Looking at you now,' he declared thoughtfully, 'I can see that you have changed quite a bit since you were five—for the better. I am not of course discussing your character.'

He gave her no time to answer this, but: 'We have to go, we're on our way to Hull. Henry wants to know when he can telephone you once we get home.'

'I'm off until one o'clock tomorrow—will you have got there by then?'

'Lord, yes. Say goodbye, boy, or we shall miss the ferry.'

She bent to Henry's hug, slipped some money into

his hand and begged him to send her a postcard or two, then gave him a sisterly pat on the back, for Fulk was already at the door. 'Have fun,' she said, and added a casual goodbye to Fulk who, although he had said nothing, she felt sure was impatient to be gone, but he came back from the door.

'Don't I get a kiss too?' he asked at his silkiest, and not waiting for her to speak her mind, bent his head.

When they had gone she stood looking at the closed door; Henry had kissed her with childish enthusiasm, but Fulk's technique had been perfect; moreover the enthusiasm hadn't been lacking, either.

CHAPTER FIVE

HENRY TELEPHONED the next day, his breathless voice gabbling excitedly over the wire into her interested ear. The journey had been super, so had the Panther, so was Fulk's house, and Moggy hadn't minded the dog at all and had settled down very well and wasn't that super too?

Eleanor agreed that everything was just as super as it could be; she wasn't going to get any interesting details from him, that was apparent, and she was disappointed when he rang off without any mention of Fulk other than a highly detailed account of his driving.

A series of postcards followed, inscribed in her brother's childish hand, and from the sparse information they conveyed, she concluded that life for him was just about as perfect as a small boy could wish for, although exactly what made it so wasn't clear, and when she telephoned her mother it was to hear that his letters home were almost as brief as the cards he sent and exasperatingly devoid of detail.

It was almost a week after Henry had gone that he mentioned, on a particularly colourful postcard, that his throat was a bit sore; the information had been sandwiched between the statement that he had been to a museum at Leeuwarden, and had eaten something

298

called *poffertjes* for his supper, so that she had scarcely noted it. Mrs MacFarlane had written to say that Fulk had telephoned several times to say that Henry appeared to be enjoying himself, so much so that on the last occasion he had suggested that the boy might like to spend another week or so with him so that he could be in Holland for the feast of Sint Nikolaas. 'And of course your father and I said yes at once,' wrote her mother. 'How kind Fulk is.'

Very kind, Eleanor had to agree, feeling somehow deflated as she finished the letter and hurried off to change out of uniform. Perry Maddon, the Casualty Officer, was taking her to the theatre that evening and she was quite looking forward to it; he was another nice lad, she thought as she slid swiftly into a plain wool dress, but she would have to take care not to encourage him. At the moment they were good friends and that, as far as she was concerned, was how it was going to stay. He wasn't the man she could marry—she didn't give herself time to consider the matter further, but caught up her coat and made for the hospital entrance.

The evening was a success, the play had been amusing and afterwards they had coffee and sandwiches at the Blue Bird and walked down the road to the hospital, talking lightly about nothing in particular. It had been a pleasant evening, Eleanor decided as she tumbled into bed, so why had she this sudden feeling of impending disaster? So strong that it was keeping her awake. It couldn't be the ward; Miss Tremble, usually the root of any trouble, had been

perfectly all right all day, and although there were
several ill patients she didn't think that they would
take a dramatic turn for the worse. She did a mental
round of the ward in her sleepy head, trying to pin-
point the probable cause of her disquiet. 'My silly
fancy,' she chided herself out loud, and went at last
to sleep.

Only it wasn't fancy; Fulk van Hensum came the
next day, walking into the ward as she served the
patients' dinners from the heated trolley in the middle
of the ward. She was facing away from the door so
she didn't see him come in, but the little nurse, her
hand outstretched to take the plate of steamed fish
Eleanor was handing her, said happily: 'He's here
again, Sister.'

'And who is here?' queried Eleanor, busy with the
next plate. 'Sir Arthur? One of the porters? The Pro-
vost himself?'

The little nurse giggled. 'It's that great big man
who came last time, Sister.' She smiled widely over
Eleanor's shoulder, and Eleanor put down the plate
and turned her head to have a look.

It was Fulk all right, standing very still just inside
the ward door. He said at once: 'Good day to you all.
Sister, might I have a word with you?'

His voice was calm, as was his face, but she went
to him at once. 'Something's wrong,' she said, low-
voiced. 'Will you tell me, please?' She lifted her
lovely eyes to meet his dark steady gaze.

'It's Henry, isn't it?' she added, and took comfort
from his reassuring little smile. When he spoke his

voice held the considered, measured tones of a doctor and he took her hands in his and held them fast; their grip was very comforting. 'Yes, it's Henry. He has rheumatic fever.'

Her mouth felt dry. 'I remember now, he had a sore throat—he wrote that on one of those postcards... Is he—is he very ill?'

'You mean, is he going to die, don't you, my dear? No, he's not. He's very ill but not, I think, dangerously so.' His smile became very gentle. 'If that had been the case I shouldn't have left him, you know.'

'No, of course not. How silly of me, I'm sorry. Is he in hospital?'

Fulk's brows rose a little. 'Certainly not. He's at my home with two excellent nurses to look after him. The only thing is, he wants you, Eleanor.'

'Then I must go to him—may I come back with you?' She raced on, thinking out loud without giving him a chance to answer her. 'No, that won't do—I expect you're over here on business of your own, but I could go tonight. They probably won't give me leave, but I shall go just the same. I must telephone Mother first, though, and you'll have to tell me where you live—you wouldn't mind, would you?'

He had her hands still in his. 'Dear girl, how you do run on, and there's no need. I'm here to take you to Henry; I've already telephoned your parents and I've been to see your Principal Nursing Officer. You're free to go just as soon as you can hand over to your staff nurse. I'm on my way to Tongue now to fetch Margaret; she's coming too, for when Henry feels better he'll want to be up and about, and he mustn't do too much too soon, you know that as well as I—I thought she might help to amuse him during his enforced idleness. She will be ready and waiting for me; we'll be back to pick you up within a few hours.'

She looked at him in bewilderment. 'Fulk, Tongue's three hundred miles from here, even in that car of yours it would take you hours...'

'Of course it would, but I've a plane to fly me up to Wick, and as good luck would have it, James is at the manse and will drive Margaret to the airport to meet me; we should both arrive there at about the same time and be back here without much time lost.'

She smiled rather shakily at him. 'You've thought of everything. Thank you, Fulk. Tell me what time I'm to be ready and where I'm to meet you.'

'Good girl!' He looked at his watch. 'There'll be a taxi to take you to the airport—can you be ready by five o'clock? You may have to wait for a little while, for I'm not sure just how long we shall be. Bring enough luggage for a couple of weeks—and don't forget your passport, and when you get to the airport go to the booking hall and wait until we come. OK?'

Eleanor nodded. 'Yes. Oh, Fulk, how kind you are—I feel so mean...'

He didn't ask her why she felt mean, only smiled faintly and gave her back her hands. 'Go and finish those dinners,' he advised her. *'Tot ziens.'*

A little over four hours later, sitting quietly in the airport, her one piece of luggage at her feet, Eleanor had the leisure to look back over the afternoon. It had been all rush and bustle, of course, but there had been no difficulties; Fulk must have seen to those. She had merely done exactly as he had told her to do, trying not to think too much about Henry, keeping her mind on prosaic things, like what to wear and what to pack. She had taken the minimum of everything in the end, and worn her warm tweed coat over a green jersey dress, and because it was a cold evening and it might be even colder in Holland, she had put on the little fur hat and the fur-lined gloves she had bought herself only that week. She looked very nice, and several men turned to give her a second look, although she was quite unaware of this—indeed, she was unaware of Fulk standing a little way off, looking at her too, until she had a feeling that she was being watched, and when she saw who it was she stood up quickly, relief sending a faint colour into her pale face as he walked over to her and picked up her baggage.

'You haven't been waiting too long?' he asked. 'Margaret's waiting in the plane—if you're ready?'

Perhaps he was tired, she thought as she walked beside him; his voice had sounded austere and formal, as though her being there annoyed him. Perhaps it did, but it was no time to split hairs as to who liked whom or didn't. Henry was the only one who mattered. She followed him through the formalities, taken aback to find that he had chartered a plane to take them over to Holland; she had supposed that they were going on a normal flight, but perhaps there wasn't a direct flight to Groningen. It must be costing him the earth, she worried silently, but there wasn't time to think about that now; Margaret, waiting eagerly for them, was full of messages from her mother and father and questions about Henry, all jumbled up with excited talk about her journey. 'And wasn't it lucky that I had my passport for that school trip last summer,' she wanted to know, 'and that James was home. There's a letter from Mother in my pocket. She's very worried, but she says she knows Henry's going to be all right with you and Fulk there— Oh, look, we're moving!'

It was only when they were airborne and Margaret had become silent enough for Eleanor to gather her wits together that she realized what the journey had entailed for Fulk. He had been very efficient and it must have taken his precious time—consultants hadn't all that time to spare from their work—and the cost...her mind boggled at that. She turned round to where he was sitting behind them, wanting to tell him how grateful she was, and found him asleep. He looked different now, the faint arrogance which she detected from time to time in his face had gone. He bore the look of a tired man enjoying an untroubled nap, and for some reason it put her in mind of that time, so long ago, when he had picked her up and comforted her. He had been safe then, he was safe now; nothing could happen to her... Her face softened and she smiled faintly, then composed her face quickly, but not quickly enough.

'Now, why do you look at me like that?' demanded

Fulk softly. 'I could almost delude myself into believing that you had changed your opinion of me.'

'You have been very kind,' she began primly, and he grinned.

'Ah, back to normal and that disapproving tone of yours.'

'That's unfair!' she cried. 'I was just going to thank you for being so absolutely marvellous, and now you mock at me and it's impossible for me to say it...'

'So don't, dear girl; my motives have been purely selfish, you know. If you're with Henry I shall feel free to come and go as I please.'

'That's not true—of all the silly tales! You know as well as I do...' She stopped and looked away for a moment and then back again at his smiling face. 'I'm truly grateful.'

He said, gently mocking: 'That I should live to see the day when Eleanor MacFarlane is grateful to me,' and then, before she could protest at that: 'What is in that cardboard box?'

'Crowdie—Henry loves it. I thought, when he gets better and begins to eat, he might like it on his bread and butter. There's a little Orkney cheese too. They'll keep in the fridge—you've got one, haven't you?'

There was a gleam at the back of his eyes. 'I believe so—if not, I'll get one the moment we arrive.'

She looked at him in astonishment. 'But surely you must know what you've got in your own house?'

'Well, I'm a busy man, you know—I tend to leave such things to my housekeeper.'

'The sooner you have a wife, the better,' declared

Eleanor matter-of-factly. 'She'll see to your household. I expect your housekeeper will be glad to have someone to consult about such things.'

'Well, I shall have a wife soon, shan't I?' His voice was meek. 'Though I have a strong feeling that Imogen won't wish to be bothered with such things as fridges—she isn't very interested in the kitchen.'

'Oh, I'm sure she will be once you're married,' said Eleanor hearteningly.

'And you? Do you like the kitchen, Eleanor?'

She drew Margaret's sleeping head on to her shoulder. 'Yes, of course, but it wouldn't do if I didn't, living where we do—you've seen for yourself how far away it is; we have to be independent of shops, you know.'

'You don't hanker after the bright lights?' He asked the question half seriously.

'No—at least I don't think so; I don't know much about them.'

'So if some man living at the back of beyond wanted to marry you, you wouldn't hesitate to say yes?'

'If I loved him I wouldn't hesitate, but then it wouldn't matter where he lived.'

He gave a little nod, much in the manner of one who had solved himself a problem. 'Is Margaret asleep?' and when she said yes: 'You had better close your own eyes—it may be well past your bedtime by the time you get your sleep tonight.' His voice was cold and formal again, he closed his eyes as he spoke and she looked at him indignantly; he had a nasty way of making her feel, when it suited him, of no account.

Hours later, sitting by Henry's bed, holding his hot hand in hers, she had all the time in the world to concede that Fulk's advice had been good. She had dozed off, still indignant, and had only wakened as they came in to land at Eelde airport, a little to the south of Groningen, where she and Margaret had been bustled out with ruthless efficiency by Fulk, guided through Customs and told to get into the back seat of the waiting Panther, and when Margaret had declared with sleepy peevishness that she was hungry and wanted to go to bed, he had told her with bracing kindness that she would be given her supper in no time at all and be tucked up in bed before she knew where she was; he gave Eleanor no such assurance, though, and she bit back the yawn she longed to give and tried to appear alert and wide awake. Not that that had mattered at all, for he didn't look back at her once, which didn't stop her asking the back of his head: 'Do you live in Groningen? Is the city far from here?'

He answered her over a shoulder as he took the car away from the airport approach roads and turned into a country road which seemed to her to be very dark. His voice was a little impatient. 'Ten kilometres to the north, but we only go through the outskirts. I live another eight kilometres further on.' He turned away again, under the impression, she decided crossly, that he had told her all she needed to know of the geographical details. She sat in silence then, Margaret

once more asleep beside her, and looked out of the
window—not that she had been able to see much,
only the road ahead, spotlighted by the car's powerful
headlights, but presently the road had woven itself
into the city's edge and she gazed out upon the lighted
windows of the houses and stared up at the rooftops.
It was a pity that it was such a dark night, for she
could see so little, and very soon they had left the
streets behind them once more and were back in the
country. She tried again, being a dogged girl. 'What
is the name of the village you live in?'

'I don't live in a village. The nearest one is called
Ezingum.' He had sounded impatient still and she had
lapsed into silence once more, straining her eyes to
see what was outside the window. She was rewarded
by a glimpse of water presently—a river, a canal perhaps, never the sea? She wanted to ask the silent man
in front of her, but he would only grunt or at best
answer her with that same impatience.

She sighed, much louder than she knew, and had
been surprised when Fulk said quietly: 'We're almost
home,' and turned the car into a narrow lane—but it
wasn't a lane; she had caught a glimpse of towering
gateposts on either side of the car. It was a drive,
running between grass banks with the wintry outlines
of larch trees above them. They rounded a bend and
Eleanor saw Fulk's house for the first time. Henry had
described it as a nice house and she had conjured up
a rather vague picture in her mind of a pleasant villa
in the residential part of Groningen, but from the
number of lighted windows and the impressive porch

before which they were stopping, it wasn't in the least like that. This house, even in the semi-dark, was large and solid—the manse would probably fit very nicely into its hall. She had wakened Margaret then, hushed her fretful voice demanding to know where they were, and got out of the car because Fulk had opened the door for her. As she stood beside him on the smooth gravel sweep, he had said briefly: 'Welcome to Huys Hensum, both of you,' then swept them up the steps to the front door, open now and with a little round dumpling of a woman waiting for them.

'Juffrouw Witsma,' he had introduced her, shaking her hand and saying something to her in his own language, and they had all gone into the house...

Eleanor looked at the clock, took Henry's pulse, slipped the thermometer under his thin arm, and checked his breathing. His temperature was up a little since she had taken it last. She charted it and looked anxiously at his small white face. He was sleeping now, but he was restless too, although Fulk had expressed satisfaction at his condition. She settled back into her chair and allowed her thoughts to wander once more.

Her first glimpse of the house had taken her off balance; obviously her previous conception of Fulk as being a successful doctor, comfortably off, but no more than that, would have to be scrapped. His home, even at the first glance, had been revealed as old, magnificent and splendidly furnished. He had led them across the lofty square hall, with its polished floor strewn with rugs, its panelled walls and enormous chandelier hanging from an elaborate ceiling, into what she had supposed to be the sitting room, a room large enough to accommodate ten times their number, but somehow homelike with its enormous armchairs and sofas flanking the hooded fireplace, handsomely framed portraits on the walls and a variety of charming table lamps set on fragile tables. He had invited them to sit down, saying that he would go at once to Henry to see how he did. He was back within a short while, reassuring them at once that the boy was holding his own nicely. 'He wants to see you, Eleanor,' he had told her. 'I haven't told him that Margaret is here, time for that when he feels more himself. Juffrouw Witsma has supper ready for us— I suggest that we have it at once so that Margaret can go to bed.'

She had agreed at once, only begging that she might see Henry first, and he had raised no objection, merely remarking that if she didn't mind, he and Margaret would start their meal. 'And then if you are not back, I'll take Margaret up to her room and see her settled in,' he promised, 'but first I will show you where Henry is.'

The stairs were oak and uncarpeted, with a massive banister, and at their top she followed him across a wide landing and down two steps into a little passage, thickly carpeted. With his hand on one of the three doors in it, he turned to her. 'The day nurse is still here, I shall be taking her back to Groningen in the morning, but I arranged with the hospital that unless I telephoned, there would be no need for the night nurse.' He stared down at her, his eyes half hidden by their lids. 'Your room is next door and communicates with his, and he will be quite safe to leave while he is sleeping, but you will do just as you wish—you have only to ask for anything you require and if you would prefer the night nurse to come, I will see to it at once.'

She had thanked him sincerely. 'You are being so very kind and you have done so much already...there's no need of a nurse; if you don't mind, I'd like to be with Henry, just in case he wakes up during the night.'

He had nodded without comment and opened the door for her. She remembered how the beauty of the room had struck her and the feeling of gratitude towards Fulk for not dismissing Henry as just another little boy, prone to clumsiness and a little careless, but had considered him worthy of such handsome surroundings. But she had barely glanced at the blue and white tiled chimneypiece, the massive pillow cupboard, the tallboy and the little games table with the half-finished jigsaw puzzle on it, her eyes had flown to the narrow bed with its carved headboard and blue counterpane. Henry had looked very small and white lying there. She could hardly remember speaking to the nurse, who smiled and shook hands; she had gone at once to the chair drawn up to the bedside and sat down in it and taken her brother's hot little paw in her own hands. He had opened his eyes and said in a thread of a voice: 'Eleanor—Fulk said he'd fetch you. I'll go to sleep now.'

She had stayed quietly there while Fulk took the nurse down to her supper with Margaret and himself, promising that he would be back very shortly. 'I'm quite all right,' she had assured him, longing for a cup of tea.

He had smiled then. 'At least let me take your coat,' he suggested, 'and do be a sensible girl; you will be in and out of this room all night unless I am much mistaken, and if you don't eat you will be fit for nothing.'

He had been right, of course. He had come back surprisingly quickly and taken her place by the sleeping boy, urging her not to hurry: 'And if Henry wakes,' he had promised, 'I'll tell him you're at supper. Margaret is in her room—the second door facing the stairs—one of the maids is unpacking for her. I expect you would like to say goodnight to her.' He sat down and picked up a book and Eleanor, feeling herself dismissed, went out of the room.

Margaret, much refreshed by her supper, was disposed to be excited. 'Only imagine, a maid to unpack,' she told Eleanor, 'and there's a bathroom, all for me, and look at this room, isn't it sweet?'

It was indeed charming, pink and white and flowery with its white-painted furniture and chintz roses scattered over the curtains. Eleanor had admired it, kissed her sister goodnight and gone downstairs, where she found the housekeeper hovering in the hall, ready to lead her to her supper, a meal taken in another vast room, furnished with graceful mahogany pieces which could have been Sheraton. She had eaten her way through soup, ham soufflé, light as air, and baked apples smothered in cream and had been happily surprised when Juffrouw Witsma, looking a little puzzled, brought in a tea tray and set it before her. She went back upstairs presently, feeling a good deal better both in self and in temper, and Fulk must have seen it, for he said at once: 'That's better. Did you get your tea?'

Eleanor had beamed widely at him. 'Oh, yes, thank you. Do you drink tea in the evening here—with your supper, I mean?'

His mouth had twitched, but she hadn't seen it. 'Well, no, but I thought that you might like it.'

She had told him that he was most thoughtful and he had said smoothly: 'Oh, there's a streak of good in every villain, you know,' and gone on to speak of Henry and his treatment. 'He's very slightly better, I fancy. It's a question of nursing and keeping him at rest while the antibiotics get to work.' He walked to the door. 'There's a bell by the bed, you have only to ring.' He had gone before she could utter a word.

Eleanor shook her head free of her thoughts and glanced at the clock again, a splendid cartel model in bronze. It was well after midnight and Fulk hadn't returned, although he had said that he would. She considered unpacking and getting ready for bed and then returning to her chair; she could doze well enough in it—she would give Fulk another half hour, she decided, just as he opened the door and came quietly towards her.

He studied the chart she offered him, cast an eye

over the child and said reassuringly: 'Never mind the
temperature, it should settle in a day or two. I've telephoned the manse to let them know we've arrived
safely—they send you their love. Now go and have
your bath and get ready for bed, I'll sit here in the
meantime—I've some writing to do.'

There seemed no point in arguing; she went to her
room and looked around her. Someone had unpacked
her things; her nightie and dressing gown had been
carefully arranged on a chair, her slippers beside it.
The bed, a delicate rosewood affair canopied in pale
pink silk, had been turned down and the pink-shaded
lights on the bedside tables switched on. It was a
lovely room, its dressing table and tallboy matching
the rosewood of the bed, its gilded mirrors and chintz-
covered chairs giving it an air of luxury. Eleanor
kicked off her shoes and, her tired feet inches deep
in carpet, went to investigate the various doors. A
cupboard, a vast one, handsomely equipped with
lights and drawers and shelves so that her own few
bits and pieces looked quite lost in it; and then a
bathroom, small and pink and gleaming, with an ex-
travagant supply of towels and soaps and bath luxu-
ries to make her eyes sparkle. She ran a bath, dithered
blissfully between Christian Dior and Elizabeth Arden
and rushed out of her clothes; she would allow herself
ten minutes.

It was a little longer than that before she went back
to Henry's room, swathed in her blue quilted dressing
gown, her hair plaited carelessly. Fulk stood up as

she went in, casting her the briefest of glances as he busied himself collecting his papers.

'My room is at the front of the house, in the centre of the gallery,' he told her. 'If you want help, don't hesitate to call me—in any case I shall look in early in the morning, and we can discuss things then. He still has two more days on antibiotics, it's a question of patience.'

Eleanor nodded, fighting down an urge to cast herself on to his shoulder and burst into tears, something she felt he would dislike very much. When she had been a little girl, he had frequently called her a watering pot and she had no intention of giving him the chance to do so again. So she wished him a calm goodnight and took up her position by Henry's bed once more.

He wakened several times during the next few hours, staring at her with round hollow eyes, obediently swallowing his medicine, taking the drink she offered, but about three o'clock he fell into a more natural sleep, and presently, despite her efforts not to do so, Eleanor fell asleep too. She wakened two hours later; Henry was still sleeping and Fulk, in a dressing gown of great magnificence, was standing on the other side of the bed, looking at her. She struggled to get rid of the sleep fogging her head and mumbled apologetically: 'I must have dropped off—it was three o'clock…'

'Go to bed,' Fulk urged her with an impersonal kindness which nonetheless brooked no refusal. 'I'll stay here for an hour or so.'

She yawned widely. Bed would be heaven and with Fulk here to look after Henry, she knew that she would sleep, but she said at once: 'No, I can't do that; you have to go to Groningen in the morning—you said so.'

'I can go later.' He dismissed the matter. 'Do as I say, Eleanor—you'll be of no use to anyone as you are.'

Not perhaps the kindest way of putting it, but true, nevertheless. She got to her feet and said uncertainly: 'Very well, but you will call me? If I could just sleep for a couple of hours...'

He hadn't moved from the bed, he didn't look at her either, only said softly: 'Of course you will be called,' and bent over Henry.

She trailed off into the bedroom, her anxious mind full of the possibility of Henry's heart being damaged by his illness, so tired that she couldn't think about it properly any more. Her thoughts became a jumble of ward jobs she might have left undone before she left, her mother's worried letter, the fact that she had forgotten to bring any handkerchiefs with her, Miss Tremble's diet, which really didn't matter anyway, Henry's small white face and Fulk, popping up over and over again. She was wondering about that when she fell asleep.

CHAPTER SIX

ELEANOR WAKENED to find a fresh-faced young girl by her bed, holding a tray. She smiled when Eleanor sat up, put the tray on her knees, went to open the long brocade curtains, saying something friendly in a soft voice as she did so, and went away.

Eleanor shook the last wisps of sleep from her head, registered that it was light and morning, even if a grey one, and saw that the little Sèvres clock on the table beside her showed the hour to be half past eight.

She bounced out of bed and, dressing gown askew, no slippers on her feet, tore silently into the next room. Fulk was exactly as she had left him, the sheets of closely written paper scattered round his chair bearing testimony to his industry. There was a tray of coffee on the small table drawn up beside him; fragrant steam rose from the cup he was about to pick up. Henry was asleep.

Fulk raised his head and looked at her; at any other time she would have been furious at the mocking tilt of his eyebrows, but now she had other things on her mind. 'Why didn't you call me?' she demanded in a whispered hiss.

The eyebrows expressed surprise as well as mockery. 'Did Tekla not bring you your breakfast? I asked her to do so.'

'Yes, she did.' She added a belated thank you. 'But it's half past eight.' She paused to survey him; he looked tired, but perhaps that was due to his unshaven chin and all the writing he had done. 'You have to go to Groningen,' she reminded him.

'How tedious that remark is becoming, Eleanor.' His voice was tolerant but his eyes still mocked her. 'I'm quite capable of organising my own day without your help, you know, and in any case at the moment you are being nothing but a hindrance. Go and eat your breakfast and put some clothes on.' The glance he gave her left her in no doubt as to what he thought of her appearance. 'You can have half an hour.'

He began to write once more, pausing only to add: 'Henry has slept soundly. We will discuss his treatment before I leave the house.'

She looked at him blankly, realizing dimly at that moment that her childish opinion of him had undergone a change, which considering his arrogant manner towards her was a little bewildering. She bit her lip and drew in her breath like a hurt child, murmured incoherently and turned on her heel. Fulk reached the door a second or so before she did and caught her by the shoulders. 'Why do you have to look like that?' he asked her harshly, and when she asked: 'Like what?', he went on: 'Like you used to when I wouldn't let you climb trees.' He gave her a little shake. 'I never thought...' he began, then went on in quite a different voice: 'I'm sorry, Eleanor—I had no right to speak to you like that. You've been wonderful—I whisked you away with no warning and then allowed you to sit here all night.' He bent and kissed her cheek gently. 'Now go and dress and eat your breakfast—please, Eleanor.'

She smiled then. 'You must be tired too, and you've a day's work before you. You've been so kind, Fulk—I keep saying that, don't I?—but I can never thank you enough.' She added shyly: 'You've changed.'

'We have both changed—no, that's not right, you've not changed at all.'

Refreshed by a hasty breakfast, she bathed and dressed in a russet skirt and sweater, piled her hair neatly, and went back to Henry's room. Fulk was waiting for her. 'I'll be back within half an hour,' he told her from the door, and then: 'You haven't made up your face, it looks nice like that.'

She was left staring at the closing door, but only for a moment, for Henry opened his eyes at that moment and said in a wispy voice: 'Gosh, I'm thirsty.'

She gave him a drink, persuaded him to take his medicine, took his temperature and pulse, and washed his face and hands. 'And later on,' she told him firmly, 'after Fulk has been to see you, I shall give you a bedbath and change the sheets, and then you'll have another nice nap before lunch. Do you ache, my dear?'

Henry nodded. 'A bit, but I feel better, I think. When is Fulk coming?'

'Very soon—he's been sitting here for these last

few hours while I had a sleep. He has to go to the hospital this morning.'

Henry closed his eyes, 'He's super,' he mumbled, 'I shall certainly be a doctor when I'm a man, I'm quite certain of that now—I shall be like Fulk; very clever and kind.'

'Yes, dear.' She smiled at him. 'Now stick out your tongue and I'll clean it for you. No, you can't do it; I'm sure Fulk has told you that you will get well much more quickly if you just lie still. I know it's a dead bore, but in a few days you'll be able to sit up. Shall I tell you a secret? Margaret came with us, she's coming to see you presently, and when you're better she'll be able to play cards with you.'

Henry smiled. 'Smashing—and will you read to me, too?'

'Certainly. Are there any English books here?'

'Dozens and dozens, they're in the library downstairs. Fulk lets me go there whenever I want, just so long as I put the books back again. He bought some in Groningen for me, too.'

'Splendid, we'll go through them together later. Now you're going to drink your milk, my dear.'

Fulk came back a few minutes later. Immaculately dressed, freshly shaved, he showed no sign of tiredness. His manner was friendly as he checked his small patient's pulse, gently examined him and pronounced himself satisfied. 'Two more days of antibiotics,' he stated, 'and by then you will be feeling much better, but that won't mean that you can get up, because you can't—it's important that you rest even if you think it a waste of time, so you will do exactly what Eleanor tells you—you understand that, old chap?'

He glanced at Eleanor, who murmured agreement; antibiotics might bring about a wonderful improvement in rheumatic fever; they also caused the patient to feel so well that there was a danger of him getting up too soon and doing far too much, and that would do his heart no good at all.

'Why?' asked Henry.

The big man eyed the small boy thoughtfully. 'Since you are going to be a doctor one day, you are quite entitled to know the reasons for lying still and having everything done for you. I will explain them to you, but not now, for it would take quite a long time and I haven't even five minutes—I'm due at the hospital.' He grinned cheerfully at the white face on the pillow, barely glancing at Eleanor as he wished them *tot ziens*. She supposed that she had been included in his farewell, even if with such unflattering casualness, and her own 'goodbye' was cool. She took care not to watch him as he left the room too, so that it was all the more vexing when he popped his handsome head round the door again and found her gaze fixed upon it.

'You'll need some time off,' he reminded her. 'If you agree, Margaret could sit with Henry for an hour and certainly while you have your meals—she's a sensible child, isn't she?' He smiled at her suddenly. 'Why were you looking like that?' he asked.

'Like what?'

'Disappointed—bewildered—wistful, I'm not sure

which. Never mind, I'll find out some time.' He had
gone, and this time he didn't come back.

The day passed slowly. There wasn't a great deal
for Eleanor to do, but Henry, normally the best-
tempered child in the world, was rendered querulous
by his illness, so that she was constantly occupied
with him. It was only after he had fallen into an uneasy sleep in the early afternoon that she felt free to
ring the bell and ask for Margaret to take her place
while she ate her lunch; there would be no question
of her taking time off; it wouldn't be fair on Margaret
to leave her for more than a short time with her
brother. Eleanor whispered instructions to her young
sister and slipped from the room, to make her way
downstairs to where her belated lunch was to be
served in a small room behind the dining room in
which she had had her supper on the previous evening. It was a cheerful apartment, with an open fire,
a circular table accommodating six chairs, a mahogany side-table, beautifully inlaid, and a bow-fronted
cabinet with a fluted canopy, its panels delicately
painted. There was a tapestry carpet on the polished
floor and the white damask cloth and shining silver
and glass made the table very inviting. She sat down,
apologising in English for her lateness, an apology
which Juffrouw Witsma waved aside with nods and
smiles and a gentle flow of soothing words which,
while making no sense at all to Eleanor, nevertheless
conveyed the assurance that coming down late to
lunch was a trifling matter which wasn't of the least
consequence.

The fresh-faced girl, Tekla, served her with a thick, delicious soup and then bore the plate away to return with a tray laden with a covered dish, a nicely arranged assortment of breads, cheeses and cold meats and a pot of coffee. The covered dish, upon investigation, contained an omelette which Eleanor devoured with a healthy appetite before pouring her coffee from the beautiful old silver coffee pot, and while she sipped the delicious brew from a delicate porcelain cup, she couldn't help but reflect upon the splendid style in which Fulk lived. Imogen was a lucky girl—that was, Eleanor reminded herself hastily, if she could put up with his occasional arrogance and his nasty habit of ignoring other people's remarks when he wished, although it wasn't likely that he would ignore Imogen. She switched her thoughts rather hastily, because for some reason or other she found that she didn't want to think about her.

She finished her meal quickly, not wanting to be away too long from Henry, and besides, she still had to go to the library and find a book so that when the invalid wakened presently she could read aloud to him.

There were a number of doors and several passages leading from the hall. She ignored the sitting room and the archway beside the staircase because it obviously led to the kitchen, and tried the door across the hall—Fulk's study; she cast an interested eye over the heavy masculine furniture, the enormous desk with its high-backed chair, the equally large wing chair drawn up to the old-fashioned stove, and the one or two rather sombre portraits on the panelled walls, and then shut the door again, wishing very much to stay and examine the room inch by inch.

She tried the big arched double doors next, facing the sitting room. This, then, was the library; she sighed with pleasure at the sight of so many books ranged on the shelves, the gallery running round the upper walls, and the little spiral staircase leading to it. There were two solid tables too with well upholstered leather chairs drawn up to them and reading lamps conveniently placed. She wandered round, wanting to pull out a handful of books and sit there and browse through them, but that wouldn't do at all; she glanced at her watch and quickened her steps, examining the shelves as she went. Henry had been right, there were quite a few children's books; she selected two or three and hurried back upstairs.

Henry was still asleep. Eleanor went over to where Margaret was perched anxiously by the bed and thanked her warmly. 'Darling, what are you going to do now?' she asked. 'You're not bored?'

Her sister shook her head. 'My goodness, no! Fulk telephoned someone he knew who has a daughter as old as I am, and she's coming over to spend the afternoon. Her name's Hermina and she speaks a little English.' She added seriously: 'Will you be all right if we go into the gardens for a walk?'

Eleanor glanced outside. It was a grey afternoon, but dry. 'Yes, love, but let me know when you come back, won't you? Is Hermina staying for tea?'

'Yes. Fulk said he'd be home for tea, too—but he's got to go out this evening.'

Evidently he preferred to share his plans with Margaret, thought Eleanor huffily, and then felt ashamed of the thought because he had been so kind to them all. She kissed her sister gently and took her place by the bed, and when she had gone, whiled away the time until he woke up, hot and cross and in a good deal of pain, by leafing through the books she had brought from the library: *Moonfleet, Treasure Island* and *The Wind in the Willows*. On the front page of each Fulk had written his name in a neat, childish hand, very much at variance with the fearful scrawl in which he had written Henry's notes.

She bathed Henry's hot face and hands, gave him a cooling drink and coaxed him to take his medicine. His temperature was still far too high, she noted worriedly, but took comfort from the fact that the antibiotics still had two days to go. She sat down again, picked up *The Wind in the Willows* and began to read aloud, stopping after half an hour to turn on the lamp and glance at the clock. Henry was lying quietly, listening to her placid reading, feeling for the moment a little better. She read on, with short intervals for him to have a drink, aware of a longing for a cup of tea herself. She embarked on chapter three, telling herself that Margaret would be along at any moment now.

But when the door eventually opened it was Fulk, not Margaret, who came in. He said hullo in a quiet voice and went at once to Henry, and only when he had satisfied himself that the boy was no worse he said: 'There is tea for you in the sitting room, Eleanor. The little girls are just finishing theirs, but Juffrouw Witsma will make you a fresh pot.'

'What about you?'

'I? I shall sit here with Henry.'

'Your tea?'

His voice held faint impatience. 'I had tea at the hospital.' He went to the door and held it open for her, and she found herself going across the wide gallery and down the staircase without having said a single word.

Margaret jumped up as she went into the sitting room. 'I was just coming to you when Fulk came home,' she explained, 'and he said he was going to sit with Henry while you came down to tea—you don't mind, Eleanor?'

'Not a bit.' Eleanor glanced at the girl standing beside her sister and smiled. 'Is this Hermina?' she wanted to know as she shook hands. The girl was pretty, with pale hair and blue eyes and a wide smile; excellent company for Margaret, and how thoughtful of Fulk... She frowned, remembering how impatient he had been with her only a few minutes ago.

She poured herself a cup of tea from the little silver pot Juffrouw Witsma had set beside her and bit into a finger of toast. The two girls had wandered off to start a game of cards at the other end of the room, and she was left alone with her thoughts. But they were small comfort to her, what with Henry so poorly and Fulk treating her as though she were an evil necessity in his house—and yet upon occasion he had been rather nice… She poured herself another cup of tea, ate a piece of cake and went back upstairs.

'There wasn't all that hurry,' observed Fulk from his chair. He closed a folder full of notes as he spoke and got to his feet. 'Go and get your coat and take a brisk walk outside—the gardens are quite large.'

'I don't want…' began Eleanor, and caught his eye. 'Very well, but can you spare the time? Margaret could come…'

He sighed. 'I have the time,' he told her in a patient voice which made her grit her teeth. 'I wouldn't have suggested it otherwise. I have asked Juffrouw Witsma to sit here while you have dinner this evening, otherwise arrange things to suit yourself, but you must have exercise.' He picked up a book and sat down again. 'I shall be out.'

'Where?' asked Henry unexpectedly.

'That's rude, Henry,' Eleanor pointed out. 'You mustn't ask those sort of questions.'

Fulk cast down his book and strolled over to the bed. 'Hullo, boy—you're better—not well, but better. All the same, you will go on lying here doing nothing until I say otherwise.' He glanced quickly at Eleanor and addressed the boy. 'I'm going out to dine.'

'Who with?'

'Henry!' said Eleanor, mildly admonishing.

'Imogen's parents.'

'The lady you're going to marry?'

Fulk only smiled and the boy went on: 'Are they nice? As nice as Mummy and Daddy?'

Fulk thought for a moment. 'They're charming; their home is well ordered and they know all the right people.'

'Is it a big house? As big as this one?'

'Not quite as big.'

'I like your house,' his patient informed him seriously, 'but I like my home too, though I expect you find it rather small. Does the lady you're going to visit cook the dinner?'

The big man's mouth twitched as though he were enjoying a private joke. 'No, never. Now, your mother is a splendid cook, and even though your home is small it's one of the nicest houses I've been in.'

Henry beamed at him rather tiredly. 'Yes, isn't it—though I expect you'd rather live here.'

'Well, it is my home, isn't it?' He turned to Eleanor. 'Supposing you telephone your mother and father before you settle down for the evening? Tell them that this young man is picking up nicely and if he's as good tomorrow as he's been today, we'll bring the telephone up here and he can speak to them himself.'

'Oh, you really are super!' Henry declared, and fell instantly asleep.

Fulk went back to his chair. 'Well, run along, Eleanor.' He glanced at the slim gold watch on his wrist and smiled in casual, friendly dismissal, so that she went to her room without saying anything, put on her coat, snatched up her headscarf and mitts and went crossly downstairs. As soon as Henry was fit to be moved, she promised herself rashly, she would take him home, not bothering to go into the difficulties of such an undertaking. Not for the first time, she wondered why Fulk had bothered to bring her over to his home; Henry's persuasive powers, most likely, certainly not from his own wish.

It was cold and almost dark outside, with a starry, frosty sky and a cold moon which lighted her path for her. She walked briskly right round the house along the gravel drive which surrounded it and then down to the gates and back again. The house, now that she had the time to look at it properly in the moonlight, was even bigger than she had at first thought; she stood still, trying to imagine what it would be like to live in it and have it for a home, and while she stood there she heard a dog barking and remembered that she hadn't yet seen the dog Henry had mentioned, nor for that matter had she seen Moggy. She went indoors and poked her head round the sitting room door, where the girls were still playing cards.

'Have you seen Fulk's dog?' she asked her sister.

'Oh, yes—he's an Irish wolfhound, his name's Patrick O'Flanelly, but Fulk calls him Flan. Henry's kitten is here too—he's over here in the corner.'

She led the way to the other end of the room where Moggy lay sleeping in an old shopping basket lined with a blanket. 'Flan goes everywhere with Fulk, you know, he's in the kitchen now, having his supper, do you want to see him?'

'Yes, I'd love to, but not now, I'm going back to sit with Henry.'

Margaret slid a hand into hers. 'Fulk says Henry's better and that in a few days he'll be able to sit up and play some games with me. Are you going to telephone home? The place you have to call is here by the telephone—Fulk left it for you.'

He might get impatient with her, but he wasn't to be faulted when it came to making things easy for her. She dialled the overseas exchange and a few minutes later heard her mother's voice.

'Henry's better,' she said at once because she knew that that was what her mother wanted to hear, and went on to reassure her before handing the telephone over to Margaret and hurrying back upstairs; it would never do for Fulk to be late for his dinner engagement.

It seemed very quiet after he had told her what to do for Henry, said a brief goodnight and gone away without a backward glance, indeed, she had the impression that he was glad to be going. Her brother was drowsing and she sat tiredly, hardly thinking, waiting for him to wake up so that she could do the variety of chores necessary for his quiet night, and if his temperature was down, she promised herself, and he seemed really better, she would get ready for bed and then sit with him until he fell asleep and then go to bed herself. She yawned widely at the very thought, then got up to study her brother's sleeping face; he did look better, and Fulk had said that he was, and she was quite sure that he would never have gone out for the evening unless he had felt easy in his mind about the boy.

It struck her all at once that she had no idea where Fulk had gone; she would have to go downstairs and find out, she was actually on her way to the door when her eye lighted on a fold of paper tucked into *The Wind in the Willows*. It was a note, brief and to the point, telling her that should she need Fulk, he could be reached at a Groningen number. 'The Atlanta Hotel,' he had scrawled. 'Don't hesitate to let me know if you are worried. If I have left the hotel, try this number.' He had printed it very clearly so that she could make no mistake. She read the businesslike missive through once more, wondering whose the second number was; not the hospital, she knew that already. She told herself sharply not to be nosey.

It was past midnight before Henry finally fell into a quiet sleep. Margaret had tiptoed in to say goodnight hours before; Eleanor decided to have her bath and get ready for bed, something which she did speedily, with the door open so that she might hear the slightest sound, but Henry slept on, with none of the restless mutterings and tossing and turning of the previous night. She glanced at the small enamel clock on the dressing table, decided that she would read until one o'clock and went back to her chair once more; she should have chosen a book for herself while she had been in the library; now she would have to content herself with *The Wind in the Willows*, a book she had read many times already. She settled down to enjoy Toad's activities.

The clock's silvery chimes recalled her to the time. She looked once more at Henry, sleeping peacefully, yawned widely and then gave a choking gasp as Fulk said from the door: 'Still up? There's no need tonight, you know—he's better.'

She peeped at him through the curtain of hair she hadn't bothered to plait. He was leaning against the door jamb, his hands in the pockets of his exquisitely tailored dinner jacket; elegant and self-assured and not over-friendly. She wondered why. Perhaps dining with Imogen's parents had filled his mind with thoughts of her, and coming back to herself, sitting untidily wrapped in a dressing gown and her hair any-how, could be irritating to him. She said apologeti-cally: 'I know—I'm going to bed now; I've been reading and I forgot the time.'

He came across the room and took the book from her knee. 'Well, well,' his eyebrows rose an inch, 'bedtime stories. A little old for Toad, aren't you, Eleanor?'

'I've been reading it to Henry,' she snapped, 'and I don't see what age has to do with it, anyway,' she said pointedly: 'It's your book.'

He was leafing through it. 'Yes, but I fancy I've outgrown it.'

'And that's a pity, though from what I remember of you, you probably didn't enjoy it when you were a little boy.'

He grinned at her. 'Meaning that even at an early age I had already formed my regrettable character?'

She remembered the trouble he had taken over Henry, and how he had gone to the rescue of the children on that snowy afternoon, and was filled with contrition. 'Oh, Fulk, I didn't mean that, really I didn't. I suppose I'm tired and my tongue's too sharp—and how could we possibly agree about anything?'

He put the book down. 'Now, why not?'

'Well, we don't lead the same kind of life, do we? All this...?' She waved a hand at the luxurious room. 'And me—I like sitting in the loft at home with Mrs Trot...' It sounded very silly when she had said it, and she wasn't looking at him, so she didn't see his smile.

'One can have the best of both worlds,' he observed blandly.

'Now what on earth do you mean by that?' she demanded in a whisper.

'Never mind now. Has Henry slept all the evening?'

'Yes, and so restfully too. Do you suppose he'll wake before morning?'

'Unlikely—the antibiotics have taken effect; he'll feel fighting fit in the morning and it will take our united efforts to keep him quiet in bed.'

She fetched a small sigh. 'It's such a load off my mind—we all love him very much, you see. I'll never be able to thank you enough for all you've done.'

'I may take you up on that one day.' He bent and

kissed her cheek lightly. 'Now let us examine these charts.'

He studied her carefully kept records, took Henry's pulse, used his stethoscope on the small sleeping chest, expressed satisfaction at his findings, and went to the door. 'With care he'll do, and no after-effects, either.'

His smile was so kind that she found herself saying: 'What a dear you are! I do hope you had a pleasant evening; I don't suppose you get out much.'

'Er—no—not when Imogen is away. The evening was pleasant enough. Imogen's mother was interested to hear about Henry and sends her good wishes for his speedy recovery.'

'How very kind of her.' She was laying the charts tidily on the table. 'You must miss Imogen very much.'

He didn't answer her, merely wished her goodnight and closed the door soundlessly. If she hadn't been so tired she might have wondered at that. As it was she took a final look at her small brother and went thankfully to her bed.

CHAPTER SEVEN

FULK HAD BEEN quite right; Henry wakened in the morning feeling so much more himself that he wanted to get up; Eleanor was arguing gently with him about it when Fulk walked in and said at once: 'Ah, good— I see that you are on the road to recovery, boy. Eleanor, go and have your breakfast while I explain to Henry just why he has to stay quietly in bed for a little longer.' He glanced at her. 'You slept? Good. I've had breakfast and I don't need to leave the house for an hour, so don't hurry back.' His smile dismissed her.

Margaret caught her up on the staircase and tucked a hand into hers. 'It's all so grand,' she confided, 'but Fulk doesn't seem to notice it, does he?'

'Well, I suppose when you've lived in a place like this all your life, it's as much home to him as the manse is to us, dear.'

'Fulk says Henry's better, he says that if I ask you nicely you might let me come and talk to Henry later on. May I?'

They had reached the small room where they had their breakfast and sat down at the table, essayed a *'Goeden morgen,'* to Tekla and made much of Flan who had joined them silently. Margaret offered him a piece of toast and said: 'I went to see Moggy just

335

now, he's in the kitchen with Juffrouw Witsma—he likes her cat, you know, but he had his breakfast here with Fulk, he always does.'

Eleanor was conscious of surprise; Fulk was a busy man and yet he hadn't just consigned Moggy to the care of his housekeeper, he had offered him companionship as well. She hadn't expected it. 'Does he?' she commented, 'how nice.' Fulk had qualities she hadn't suspected. 'He doesn't have much time...'

Margaret slipped Flan some more toast. 'No, he doesn't, does he? But when he comes home in the evening he always fetches Moggy to sit with him. Flan sits with him too, of course.'

They ate their breakfast without haste while they discussed various ways of amusing Henry during his convalescence. 'Cards,' declared Margaret emphatically, 'he loves playing cards.'

'As long as he doesn't get too excited. Draughts, too, and what about Ludo?'

Margaret curled her lip. 'Eleanor, that's a child's game!'

'But Henry's a child, dear.'

'Oh, I know that, but he's so bright for his age— why, he's been playing chess with Daddy ever since last winter.'

'Heavens! What about Monopoly? That's a good game, but he might get too excited. Anyway, I'll ask Fulk.'

But there was no opportunity to do that when she went back upstairs. Fulk had resumed his role of doctor again, and beyond giving her his precise instruc-

tions about her brother, he had nothing more to say,
indeed, his very manner discouraged her from anything but a meek: 'Yes, Fulk, no, Fulk,' in answer.

The day passed without incident, and Henry was
so much improved by the afternoon that Eleanor felt
justified in allowing Margaret to sit with him for a
brief while, so that she might take a brisk walk in the
gardens. They were larger than she had thought and
in excellent order. She poked around, exploring paths
and examining the variety of shrubs and trees bor-
dering them, and it was quite half an hour before she
returned to the house, to find a Mercedes outside the
front door; it was a 450SE, and a new model, all
gleaming coachwork and chromium. It looked a little
vulgar. Perhaps it belonged to Hermina's father, although Eleanor couldn't remember Margaret saying
that her new friend would be coming that afternoon.
She mounted the steps, pausing in the vestibule to
take off her boots, for she had got them muddy at the
edge of the pond she had discovered behind the
house, and it would never do to sully the shining
floors. She tugged off her headscarf, pulling her hair
askew as she did so, and with the boots dangling from
one hand, opened the inner door and started for the
stairs. She had a stockinged foot on the lowest tread
when the drawing room door opened and a woman
came out and stood looking at her.

She was of middle age, handsome in a large way
and dressed with taste and, Eleanor guessed, great expense. Her voice, when she spoke, was commanding

and her English, although fluent, was heavily accented.

'You are the nurse?' She sounded surprised too, which wasn't to be wondered at, thought Eleanor reasonably; the word hardly conjured up a windswept hairdo, stockinged feet and muddy boots dangling...

She said: 'Yes, I am. Did you want me?'

The lady advanced a foot or two. 'Do you know who I am?' she enquired.

'I'm afraid I don't—ought I to?' Eleanor hoped her voice didn't betray her growing dislike of her interrogator.

'Did the professor not tell you?'

'The professor? Who's he?...oh, you mean Fulk.' Eleanor smiled and met a stony stare.

'I,' said the lady weightily, 'am the professor's future mother-in-law.'

Eleanor stopped herself just in time from saying 'Poor Fulk', and murmured a polite how do you do instead. Surely Imogen wasn't like this dreadful woman—Fulk must love her very much to be able to put up with her mother. She said, still polite: 'It was kind of you to enquire about my brother—he's better today; we're all very relieved.'

Imogen's mother inclined her severely coiffured head graciously. 'I am glad to hear it. I must say that you are hardly what I imagined you to be.' Her cold eyes swept over Eleanor's somewhat tatty person, so that she felt constrained to say: 'Oh, I look better in uniform—and now if you will excuse me I must go back to my brother. I expect you're waiting for Fulk?'

'No, Nurse, I came to see you. As Imogen is not here, I felt it to be my duty...'

'To look me over and make sure that I wasn't getting my claws into Fulk?' asked Eleanor, quite forgetting her manners. 'Well, I daresay you feel better about it now—I'm not the glamorous type, you see—I just work for a living. Goodbye, Mevrouw...I don't know your name, I'm afraid.'

She started up the stairs and was brought to a halt by the commanding voice. 'Oss van Oss, Nurse, Baroness Oss van Oss—and you are quite correct. I can quite see now why Fulk is not in the least attracted to you—I am greatly reassured. I told him last night that I considered it a little irregular for you to be in his house, and I advised him to obtain one of the older nurses from his hospital in your place now that the little boy is no longer dangerously ill. I would not wish to influence him unduly, but I have dear Imogen's feelings to consider.'

Eleanor had swung round to face the Baroness. 'Can't she look after her own feelings?' she enquired pertly, and then: 'What a horrid conversation this is, isn't it? You might as well know that your daughter's feelings are of no importance to me, but my brother's health is. I shall stay here until he is better, and since, as you have just told me, Fulk isn't in the least attracted to me, I can't see what all the fuss is about. Goodbye, Baroness Oss—no, Oss van Oss, isn't it?'

She went on her way unhurriedly, aware that she was being stared at, and despite her deliberate step, she seethed with rage. How dared the woman come to look her over, and how dared Fulk allow it? She was just beginning to like him despite his offhand manner, now she found herself disliking him more than ever. She would have something to say when she saw him!

Which wasn't until much later, although he came in the early evening to see Henry; but he brought someone with him, an elderly man, who called Henry little man and herself dear lady, and muttered a good deal to himself. Fulk introduced him as Professor van Esbink, explaining that he had thought a second opinion of Henry's condition might reassure them all. Eleanor hadn't answered him and had given him a stony stare when he smiled at her, so that the smile turned into a mocking one before he turned away to answer his learned colleague's questions. Any other man might have been disconcerted, but Fulk wasn't like other men. She became very professional in her manner and when she saw the two gentlemen to the door, her manner was not only professional, it was glacial, at least towards Fulk.

'You've taken umbrage,' said Henry from his bed, and when, an hour later, Fulk came back he pointed this interesting fact out to the doctor. 'Eleanor is in a temper,' he said, 'and I don't know why.'

Fulk glanced across the room to where Eleanor was standing, measuring medicine into a glass. 'She's plain ratty,' he declared cheerfully, 'and I think I know why.'

'Why?' asked Henry with interest.

'Since I have no intention of telling you, I

shouldn't waste time asking, boy. Let us concentrate instead on what Professor van Esbink had to say about you. He agrees with me that you are doing very nicely, but just as I explained to you, you still have to remain quietly in bed, though I think that Margaret might come and play some quiet game with you for a couple of hours each day, and I daresay Moggy would be glad to visit you.'

'Oh. I say—may he really come? On to my bed?'

'Why not? And certainly he may stay here as long as he likes. I daresay that once he has been shown the way, he'll pop in and out as the fancy takes him.' He smiled down at the boy. 'I'll go and find Margaret and ask her to bring him up here for a little while, shall I?'

He was back very soon with Margaret, clutching Moggy. The kitten was settled under Henry's hand, and his sister ensconced in a chair by the bed. 'And no sitting up, Henry,' said Fulk firmly. 'Margaret, ring the bell if you should need us, I'm going to take Eleanor down to dinner.'

Eleanor cast him a look to freeze a man's bones. 'I am not hungry, thank you.'

He said nothing at all, merely crossed the room, took her by the arm and led her away, hurrying her down the staircase so fast that she had much ado not to trip up.

In the drawing room he shut the door behind them and invited her to sit down by the fire. 'And what would you like to drink?' he enquired solicitously. 'Not spirits, I think; they might only serve to inflame your temper even more. How about Madeira? Pleasantly alcoholic without clouding the mind.'

She accepted the glass he offered her, for there was really nothing else she could do about it. Besides, it gave her a few minutes in which to gather her thoughts; she had no wish to lose her temper; calm, cool, reasoning, with a slight hint of hurt feelings would fill the bill very well.

'I'm waiting for the outburst,' he prompted blandly, so that she was instantly possessed of a great desire to speak her mind. But she made a strong effort to keep her cool; her voice was mild as she said slowly: 'Your future mother-in-law came this afternoon, but I expect you know that already.'

'Juffrouw Witsma told me when I came in. I wondered if she would.'

Eleanor put her glass carefully down on the charming little lamp table at her elbow. 'You knew she was coming? To look me over? I cannot quite understand why you could not have reassured her sufficiently; it would have saved her a journey.' Her voice, despite her best efforts, became a little shrill. 'She was good enough to explain to me that as you were not in the least attracted to me she felt quite at ease about me, although she considered that I should be—removed...' She choked on rage. 'How dared you allow her...she's a detestable woman, and I have no intention of apologizing to you for saying so; it's to be hoped that your Imogen doesn't take after her.' Her wrathful voice petered out before the expression on Fulk's face, but it served to fan her temper at the same time. 'If I go, I shall take Henry too,' she told him flatly. 'I'll get an ambulance if it takes every penny I've got—and I hope I never, never see you again!'

She picked up her glass and was annoyed to find that her hand was trembling so that it was hard to hold it steady. Fulk must have seen it too, for he came over to her, took the glass from her and put it down again. 'A family heirloom,' he explained mildly. 'You know, Eleanor, it is a remarkable thing that you can stir up my deepest feelings with such ease; at one moment I am so angry with you that I could cheerfully wring your neck, and at the next I find abject apologies for my shocking behaviour tripping off my tongue. Of course I discussed you with Baroness Oss van Oss, but hardly in the manner which she implied—indeed, I imagined that she was joking when she said that she would like to meet you and see what you were like for herself, and when she persisted, I told her that I could see no reason why she shouldn't if she wished—I imagined that it would be a friendly visit, no more; I had no idea that she was going to upset you and I am deeply sorry for that. And as for all that nonsense about replacing you with another nurse, I have no intention of doing any such thing; you will remain until you are perfectly satisfied that Henry is well again.' He smiled wryly. 'You know, I have the strongest feeling that we should be laughing about the whole thing, enjoying the joke together. And here we are, quarrelling again.'

'People who don't like each other always quarrel,' said Eleanor, not bothering to look at him.

'Ah, yes—I was forgetting that you have a long-standing dislike of me; not even the common denominator of Henry's illness has altered that, has it?' He put her glass back into her hand. 'Drink up and we will go in to dinner. I'm hungry.'

It was disconcerting that, just when she was striving to reduce her rage to reasonable argument, he should dampen it down by wanting his dinner. She wasn't sure if she wanted to laugh about it or have a good cry.

She found herself in the dining room, facing him across the broad expanse of linen set with heavy old silver and delicate glass, and rather to her surprise she found that she was hungry too, and after a little while, enjoying herself. The food was delicious and Fulk's gentle flow of small talk was undemanding and mildly amusing. She studied his face as he bent to pull gently on one of Flan's ears—the dog was sitting like a statue beside his chair, watching him with adoring eyes. Fulk was smiling a little and she wondered if she had been mistaken at the expression on his face when she had mentioned Imogen. She still wasn't quite sure what it had been, only it had made her uncertain; perhaps she had been mistaken about him, too—perhaps all her ideas about him had been wrong. It was an ever-recurring thought which refused to be dispelled, and the memory of her strongly voiced wish never to see him again struck her so forcibly that she put down her spoon and stared at the contents of her plate, wondering what she should do about it.

'Don't you like caramel custard?' asked Fulk. 'I'll

ring and get Juffrouw Witsma to bring something else.'

Eleanor transferred her gaze from her plate to his face. 'I like it very much, thank you.' She went on quite humbly: 'Fulk, I'm sorry I was so rude just now—about Baroness Oss van Oss, I mean. I had no right to speak like that and I'm sure your Imogen is the nicest and most beautiful girl in the world, and if you want to discuss me with anyone, I—I really don't mind; I'm only the nurse, after all, and I don't care about anything except getting Henry well again so that he'll grow up strong and healthy.'

He got up and came round the table to sit carelessly on it beside her so that he could look down into her face. 'My dear Eleanor,' he begged, 'for heaven's sake don't talk like that, it just isn't you—so meek and penitent. And you're not 'only the nurse,' he paused, his dark eyes looking over her head, 'you are a great many things...' His sombre expression was gone, he grinned at her. 'Shall we telephone your people before we go upstairs?'

Henry had a relapse the next day; not a severe one but sufficient to delay his convalescence. Eleanor, looking back on those few days when they were happily past, wondered how she would have got through them without Fulk's help. Henry had been querulous and difficult and the very mention of another nurse coming to relieve Eleanor caused him to toss and turn in such a frenzy of unrest that the idea was given up and Fulk took turns with Eleanor in nursing him, something which he did with no fuss at all, apparently being quite able to work at his consulting rooms and the hospital by day, and sit up for a good part of each night without any ill effects.

Happily the relapse had been a brief one; on the fourth day Henry had woken up with a temperature which was almost normal again, demanding tea and toast and Margaret to talk to. Eleanor, hearing voices in her brother's room at five o'clock in the morning, had gone at once to see what the matter was, and discovered Fulk sitting back in his chair, sharing a pot of tea with his patient. He had taken one look at her distraught countenance and said comfortably: 'Fetch a tooth mug, Eleanor, and join us in our early tea; Henry is debating the important question as to what he would like for his breakfast. I fancy that we are out of the wood.'

She had gone back into the bathroom and picked up the mug and then sat down on the edge of the bath. She had been wanting to have a good cry for some time now, but somehow the opportunity had never occurred, but now, opportunity or not, the tears poured down her cheeks, willy-nilly. She hardly noticed when Fulk took the mug from her, wiped her face with a towel and sat down beside her. 'Watering pot,' he said kindly, 'you weep as copiously as you used to when you were a little girl.'

She sniffed into the towel. 'So would you if you were me,' she declared in a muffled voice. 'I've been so afraid that Henry...do you suppose there will be any lasting damage?'

'Unlikely.' Fulk had put an arm round her and it

felt very comforting. 'This setback only means that he has to take a little longer to get on to his feet again.'

Eleanor sniffed. 'You're sure?' And then because of the look of surprise on his face: 'Oh, I do beg your pardon, just for a moment I forgot who you were—of course you're sure. How happy Mother and Father will be...' She sat up and felt his arm slacken. 'I'll get dressed and get some breakfast for Henry—shall I get some for you too? You've been sitting there since twelve o'clock, you must be hungry. If you're very quick, you could get at least three hours' sleep before you need to leave.'

'So I could, but I won't, I'll have breakfast with Henry and you. Scrambled eggs for him and weak tea, and I'll have eggs and bacon—three eggs, and toast and marmalade and coffee—you have whatever you like for yourself. Don't dress; if Henry has a light meal now he will probably sleep again for several hours and that will do him good as well as keep him quiet.' He studied her face. 'You don't look too bad,' he remarked. 'Off with you and I'll come down and carry the tray up for you—fifteen minutes, OK?'

'OK,' she smiled rather mistily, and went down to the kitchen, a vast room with a vaulted ceiling, cupboards which would have housed a family, an imposing dresser which took up the whole of one wall, and enough labour-saving gadgets to gladden the heart of the most pernickety woman—no wonder Juffrouw Witsma always looked so contented! Eleanor peered around her with envy and opened the nearest cupboard door.

Fulk had been right again; Henry ate every morsel of his frugal breakfast, murmured 'Super,' and went at once to sleep, not to wake again until the morning was far advanced, demanding something else to eat. And that evening when Fulk came home they all played a sedate game of Ludo, careful not to get too excited about it, and when finally Henry had been tucked down for the night they went down to dinner, leaving Tekla on guard, because, as Fulk pointed out, she was a sensible girl with a string of small brothers and sisters of her own and knew how to handle children. Their meal was a cheerful one, for Margaret and Fulk were on excellent terms with each other and between them soon had Eleanor laughing with them.

The week passed quickly after that, with Henry improving rapidly—too rapidly, for he wanted to do everything at once. It was easier when at the end of the week, Fulk said that he might sit out for an hour or two each day, so that he and Margaret could amuse themselves at the small card table, and Eleanor seized these brief periods in which to take brisk walks, enjoying the wintry weather and the cold wind after so many days indoors. She ventured out of the grounds after the first day, exploring the narrow lanes running between the flat, frost-covered water meadows. There wasn't a great deal to see, but it was peaceful as well as invigorating. She told herself that she felt much better for these outings, while at the same time aware that there was a hard core of sadness somewhere deep inside her, which for some reason or other she was loath to probe.

She saw little of Fulk; he left early each morning and sometimes he wasn't back until after they had had their dinner in the evening. He saw Henry twice a day, of course, but his remarks were mostly limited to the boy's condition, and recommendations as to his further treatment. Walking briskly back to the house on the Friday afternoon, Eleanor found herself looking forward to the weekend; Fulk would be home.

He arrived after tea, driving the Daimler Sovereign he used for the short journey to and from the hospital and his consulting rooms. Eleanor, who happened to be in the hall when he came in, thought that he looked tired and bad-tempered with it; he must have had a tiresome day. She said 'Hullo,' in a conciliatory voice and asked: 'Shall I ask someone to bring you some tea?'

He had shrugged himself out of his topcoat and started across the hall towards his study, his briefcase in his hand. 'No time,' he told her briefly, and went inside, closing the door firmly behind him. Eleanor went upstairs to make sure that Henry wasn't getting above himself, cautioned him in a sisterly fashion, bade Margaret keep a sharp eye on her brother and went downstairs again to look for Moggy. She was returning from the kitchen, the kitten tucked under one arm, when she encountered Fulk once more, and urged on by a wish to see his tired face smile, asked: 'Did you have a bad day?'

He checked his stride to look at her. He was in a

bad temper all right, his dark face frowning, his mouth a straight line; it surprised her very much when he said: 'No,' but she waited a moment, thinking that he might want to say something else. When he did speak, she was even more surprised.

'I'm going away for the weekend,' he said in a bland, cold voice she didn't much care for. 'Henry's quite safe to leave; in any case, I've asked Professor van Esbink to keep an eye on him. I'm leaving in half an hour and when I return on Tuesday I shall go straight to my rooms, so if you wish to say anything, you had better say it now.'

Eleanor stood, her mouth a little open, quite unable to think of a single word to say. When he said, still in that hateful voice: 'You're not usually so short of words,' she snapped her mouth shut and then said: 'What am I supposed to say? I'll wish you a pleasant weekend if that's what you want, though in your present nasty temper I should be sorry for your companions, but perhaps you'll feel better by the time you get to wherever you're going.'

'Fishing!' he declared. 'You want to know where I'm going, don't you? Cannes—to see Imogen.'

Eleanor was conscious of a peculiar sensation which she didn't have time to ponder. She said with false cheerfulness: 'How nice for you both,' and then more urgently: 'You're never going to drive all that way and then back again by Tuesday?'

He raised his brows. 'Why ever not?'

'It's miles—you're tired already...'

His voice was silky now. 'Eleanor, I brought you

here to look after your brother. And now, if you will excuse me.'

'It's too far,' declared Eleanor wildly.

'Roughly seven hundred and fifty miles—fifteen hours' driving on excellent roads.' He smiled thinly. 'If it makes you feel better, I shall only drive six or seven hours before I rack up for the night. I should be in Cannes some time during tomorrow afternoon.'

'But coming back?' she persisted, and then drew a sharp breath as he said blandly: 'I haven't been so fussed over since I had a nanny.'

She stood just where she was, watching him go, listening to the high-powered whine of the Panther. It sounded very loud in the quiet house.

'Fuss over him!' said Eleanor to no one in particular. 'Of course I fuss over him, and how fantastic it is that I've only just this minute discovered that I'm in love with the wretch.' The sad feeling could be explained now, as well as the eager looking forward to the weekend; perhaps she had known all the time without realizing it.

She kissed the top of Moggy's furry little head and started slowly up the staircase; the less she thought about it the better; by the time she saw Fulk again on Tuesday she would have forced herself to accept the idea and turn her back on it—because that was what she was going to have to do. She allowed herself a few moments of pure envy of Imogen, wondering what it would be like to know that a man loved you so much that he would make a round trip of fifteen hundred miles just to be with you for a day. She sighed so deeply that Moggy became dislodged and stuck a needlelike claw into her arm; she didn't feel it, her thoughts were with Fulk, driving through the dark winter evening and on into an even darker night, intent on reaching his Imogen as quickly as possible.

Eleanor paused at the top of the stairs; if she had been Imogen she would have gone half way—no, the whole way, to meet Fulk. After all, the girl did nothing, while he was wearing himself to a shadow, what with his work at the hospital, his own practice, and staying up half the night with Henry. That there was something absurd in describing a large man of fifteen stone or thereabouts as being worn to a shadow didn't cross her mind. She could only imagine him going to sleep at the wheel of his powerful car and crashing somewhere remote and dying before anyone could reach him. She opened Henry's door, offered Moggy to her brother and allowed herself to be persuaded to enjoy a game of three-handed whist. She played very badly; understandable enough, considering that her head was full of Fulk and nothing else.

The weekend dragged by on leaden feet for Eleanor. Somehow she got through it, thankful that Henry was indeed well again and that Margaret was perfectly content to stay where she was. She telephoned her parents each evening because Fulk had told her to do so, giving them a racy account of Henry's progress and even venturing to speak of his return in the not too distant future. 'Perhaps for Christmas,' she essayed. 'I've not given a thought to presents yet, we're miles from the shops, you know, and I haven't been able to get out much—I'll have to rush round and buy them when we get back.' The thought of the ward and of Miss Tremble, who would certainly be there, and all the rush and bustle of Christmas in hospital gave her no joy at all, and her feelings must have sounded in her voice, for her mother asked: 'You're all right, dear? You sound…perhaps you're tired.'

Eleanor agreed that she was and handed the receiver to Margaret.

It was late on Tuesday evening before she saw Fulk. It had been a cold day with a hint of snow. Probably it was this inclement weather as well as his long drive which had so lined and sharpened his handsome features. Henry had been asleep for some time and Margaret was flitting around in her dressing gown, putting off her own bedtime for as long as possible while Eleanor carried up the lemonade which Henry might want in the night before going downstairs once again to fetch Moggy to sleep on the end of the invalid's bed. She was on her way upstairs once more, the little beast under her arm, when the door behind her opened and shut, and when she turned round: 'How's Henry?' asked Fulk.

She saw his tired face. 'He's splendid. Professor van Esbink telephoned twice, but there was no need for him to come.'

Fulk threw his coat and gloves into a chair and crossed the hall to stand at the foot of the stairs. 'I know, he telephoned me this morning. He has a high opinion of you, Eleanor, did you know that? He would like you to work for him.'

She digested this flattering information in silence and jumped when he said sharply: 'Well, aren't you going to ask me if I had a pleasant weekend?'

'Well, I did want to,' she told him spiritedly, 'but I didn't feel like being snubbed.'

He moved very fast; he was beside her almost before she had finished speaking. She hadn't bargained for it and he was far too near for her peace of mind, and that peace was wholly shattered when he kissed her quite fiercely on her mouth, all without saying a word. He was back in the hall again while she was still blinking over it.

'I'm going to have something to eat,' he told her in a perfectly ordinary voice. 'I'll be up to see Henry later.'

CHAPTER EIGHT

FULK DIDN'T COME for almost an hour, which gave Eleanor time to find a number of good reasons for his behaviour. It had been a kind of reaction, she told herself; he had been with Imogen and probably he was missing her terribly, and because Eleanor had been the only girl around he had probably kissed her to relieve his unhappy feelings. It was a silly argument, but she couldn't think of a better one. The obvious thing to do was to ignore the whole incident, which wasn't very easy, but by the time he did appear, she had succeeded in acquiring a calm manner and a placid face, although beneath this exemplary façade her feelings were churning around inside her in a most disturbing manner.

But it had all been rather a waste of time, for he had barely looked at her and his manner, when he spoke, was very much that of the family doctor—affable, impersonal and just a little out of reach. He stayed only long enough to assure himself that all was well with Henry before wishing her a casual good night and going away again, and she went to bed shortly afterwards, quite bewildered and very unhappy.

Henry was allowed up the next day; dressed, he looked small and thin and far too pale, but his appetite was excellent and although his exercise was very lim-

ited, he was at least on his feet once more. The
weather was still wintry, but Fulk, after the first couple of days, took him for short drives each day, fitting
them in, Eleanor suspected, during his lunch hour, but
when she had remonstrated about this, he had told her
quite sharply that he had plenty of free time during
the middle of the day and that he enjoyed the drives
as much as his passenger did.

It would be Sint Nikolaas in a few days; Eleanor,
who had heard all about it from Margaret, who had
in her turn got it from Hermina, wondered if Fulk
intended to do anything about it. She didn't like to
bring the subject up in case he felt that she was expecting him to celebrate the occasion in some way,
but on the other hand Margaret had told Henry about
it and she had heard them speculating together as to
whether they would be getting any presents; she
would have to do something about it after all. Until
this moment she hadn't needed any money; she had
a little English money with her, but no Dutch, and it
looked as though she would need some; she didn't
like the idea, but she would have to talk to Fulk about
it.

But there was no need; at breakfast the next morning, a meal at which she arrived a little late because
of Henry's small demands, Margaret was already
broaching the matter. Fulk, immersed in his mail, as
he almost always was, got to his feet as she joined
them, wished her good morning and went back to his
letters. Eleanor didn't think that he looked over-
friendly, but Margaret hadn't noticed his withdrawn

expression, or if she had, she had decided to ignore it.

'Fulk,' she said cheerfully, 'I want to go to some shops and I expect Eleanor does too, only I don't know how to set about it. I haven't any money, though Eleanor has, but it's pounds. Could we leave Henry for just a little while, do you suppose?'

He put down the letter he was reading and gave her his full attention. 'My dear child, that can easily be arranged—how stupid of me not to have thought of it before.' He glanced at Eleanor, his eyebrows raised. 'Why did you not ask me sooner?'

'Well—I hadn't thought about it, not until yesterday, and I had no idea that Margaret was going to say anything to you—I'd made up my mind to ask you myself.'

'You should have asked sooner. I'm afraid that I can't spare the time to stay with Henry, but I will arrange for a nurse to come for the day and keep him company—would tomorrow suit you?'

He smiled nicely at her, although she had the impression that his mind was occupied by some other matter. She said diffidently: 'Well, if it's not being too much of a bother...'

He was reading his letter again. 'None whatever,' he assured her. He got up to go very shortly afterwards, pausing only to say: 'Let me have what money you wish to change, Eleanor, and I will give you guldens for it.'

When he had gone Eleanor turned to her sister. 'Darling,' she cried, 'whatever made you ask Fulk? I mean, he was so preoccupied. I'd thought about it too, but really this morning of all times, when you could see that he had all those letters.'

'Pooh,' said Margaret forcefully, 'he'd read them all ages ago. He wasn't busy at all, just staring at that letter he was holding—he'd read it at least six times— I watched him. Besides, I want to buy Henry something for Sint Nikolaas, he'll be frightfully disappointed if he doesn't get a present. How shall we go? I suppose Groningen is the nearest place?'

'I should think so—perhaps there's a bus. I wonder if a taxi would cost a lot?' Eleanor frowned. 'And when are we to go? In the morning or after lunch, and do you suppose there will be someone in the shops who'll speak English?'

She worried about it on and off during the rest of the day, which turned out to be a waste of time, for when Fulk came home he told them that he would return during the midday break and drive them into Groningen and pick them up again when he had finished his work in the afternoon. 'Better still,' he suggested, 'I'll show you where my consulting rooms are and you can come there. Eleanor, if you will come with me, I'll give you the money you require.'

She fetched her purse and followed him across the hall to his study. 'I'm not sure how much we need to spend,' she told him. 'It's just a present for Henry, and I want to buy something for Margaret, too...'

He had gone to his desk and opened a drawer. 'How much money can you spare?' he asked her bluntly.

'Well, would ten pounds be enough?' It sounded a lot of money and they hadn't much to buy.

He had his head bent so that she couldn't see his
face, he said gently: 'I daresay—all the same, supposing I let you have more than that; you can repay
me later. I should perhaps have warned you that it is
customary to give everyone a small gift on Sint Nikolaas Eve; perhaps you should buy some small trifle
for Juffrouw Witsma and Tekla and Bep—oh, and old
Mevrouw Brom, too.'

'Oh, yes, of course, if that's the thing to do. I
thought it was just for children.'

She watched him counting out the notes, loving
every dark hair on his head and every line on his
good-looking face, and there were lines, she could see
that; perhaps he was working too hard, that long journey to Cannes must have tired him out. She cried
soundlessly: 'Oh, Fulk, why did you have to fall in
love with the wrong girl?' and because he was holding the money out to her with thinly veiled impatience, took it from him, thanked him quietly and left
him alone.

He had gone in the morning when she got down to
breakfast. The nurse, a cheerful young girl, arrived
just after ten o'clock, and Henry, happy enough now
that he knew the shopping expedition was largely for
his benefit, seemed content to stay with her. Eleanor
and Margaret had an early lunch and when Fulk got
back they were ready and waiting for him.

He had Margaret beside him on their short journey,
apparently enjoying her cheerful chatter, but his manner was remote, although kind enough, when he had
occasion to address Eleanor. 'We'll go to my rooms
now and from there you can walk to the shops—

they're close by and you can't possibly get lost. I shall be ready about four o'clock, so don't bother with tea, we'll have it together before we go home.'

They were in the city now, driving along a street with a wide canal running beside it, but presently Fulk turned into a narrow road which led to a square lined with old red brick houses, before one of which he stopped. 'I'm on the ground floor,' he explained. 'Ring and walk in when you come back.' He got out and opened the doors for them to get out too. 'Go straight across the square and down that passage you can see in that corner, it will bring you out into one of the shopping streets.' He nodded briefly. 'Enjoy yourselves. Forgive me, I'm late,' he told them, and went up the stone steps and in through the front door. As they walked away, Eleanor wondered if he had had any time for lunch; she thought it unlikely.

They had a lovely afternoon, first window-shopping, to gaze at the tempting displays of jewellery, leatherwork, scarves and party clothes suitable for the festive season, but presently, aware that they were quite unable to buy the pink velvet dress Margaret coveted, or the crocodile handbag Eleanor had set her heart upon, they made their modest purchases, handkerchiefs and scarves for the staff at Huys Hensum, a game of Scrabble for Henry as well as a sketchbook and coloured pencils—over Fulk's present they pondered for some time; everything had cost a good deal more than Eleanor had anticipated and many of the things which they might have chosen were far too expensive, but finally they decided on a book. It was *The Ascent of Man* which, Margaret pointed out, he would read with pleasure. 'He's very clever,' she urged, 'and clever people read that kind of book.'

It was while Eleanor was paying for it—and a lot of money it was too—that she noticed her small sister's downcast face. 'What is it, love?' she asked. 'Have you changed your mind—we can easily find something else…'

Margaret shook her head. 'No—the book's fine, it's just that I wanted some money to buy something, but we haven't any left, have we?'

Eleanor peered into her purse. She had used up the ten pounds and almost all of the extra money Fulk had advanced her. 'Well, no,' she admitted, 'only a few of those little silver things—*dubbeltjes*, but I tell you what we'll do, we'll go back to Fulk's rooms—it's almost time, anyway, and I'll borrow some more money from him and we can come back quickly and get what you want before we meet him for tea. Will that do?'

They found their way back easily enough to the square, rang the old-fashioned brass bell, and walked in, just as Fulk had told them to do. There was a door on the left of the narrow hall with his name on it and they went in: the waiting room, richly carpeted, nicely furnished, too, with flowers and plenty of magazines—none of your upright chairs and last year's *Woman's Own* laid out like fish on a slab with a gas fire burning economically low. Here the chairs were comfortable, dignified, and upholstered in a pleasing damask in various shades of blue. There were plenty of tables to accommodate handbags, gloves and parcels, too. Eleanor thoroughly approved of it; she approved too of the nice, cosy-looking nurse sitting at her desk; a woman to inspire confidence in the most timid of patients and probably very competent as well. She smiled at them now and spoke in excellent English.

'Professor van Hensum is occupied with his last patient—if you would seat yourselves?'

But there was no need, for as she spoke the door at the other end of the room opened and a military-looking gentleman marched out with Fulk just behind him. He went across to the nurse and said something to her, exchanged some laughing remark with his departing patient and went to Eleanor and Margaret.

'Have you had a good shop?' he wanted to know. 'I'll be two minutes.' He turned away, but Margaret slid a hand into his to stop him. 'Fulk, please will you lend us some more money? Eleanor hasn't any left and there's something I want to buy.'

His hand was already in his pocket. 'How much do you need? Fifty gulden, a hundred?'

'For heaven's sake!' exclaimed Eleanor. 'That's far too much. Margaret, could you manage with ten gulden, or perhaps fifteen?'

'I tell you what we'll do,' said Fulk easily, 'we'll go along to the shops now and you can decide how much you want to spend when we get there. Eleanor, do you want to borrow any more for yourself?'

She was grateful to him for being so matter-of-fact about it. There was still some small thing to choose for Margaret. She did some hasty mental arithmetic; she had some more money at Huys Hensum, but not

much, and she had no intention of being in his debt.
'Ten gulden would be nice if you could spare it,' she
told him, and wondered why he smiled.

She was grateful when they reached the shops, too,
for he suggested that she might like to go off on her
own while he stayed with Margaret. It left her free to
buy the headscarf Margaret had admired before re-
joining them outside Vroom and Dreesman's main
entrance. Eleanor had to wait a few minutes for them
and whiled away the time watching the passers-by
thronging the pavements, the women warmly clad
with scarves pulled tight against the wind, the children encased in bright woollen outfits, their chubby
faces, blue-eyed and pink-cheeked, peering out from
under knitted caps, the men, large and solid in thick,
short topcoats and a sprinkling of fur caps—and all
of them laden with parcels.

Eleanor felt all at once lonely and far from home
and her thoughts must have been reflected in her face,
for Fulk said at her elbow: 'You're sad, and I wonder
why?' He didn't wait for an answer, however, but
took them to a nearby café; a cheerful, colourful
place, warm and faintly Edwardian with its dark red
carpet and panelled walls and little round tables. They
drank their tea and ate rich cream cakes to the accom-
paniment of Margaret's happy chatter, lingering over
the meal so that it was quite dark when they left the
café at length and went back to Fulk's consulting
rooms. During their drive home it was Margaret who
did most of the talking, and although Fulk laughed
and joked with her readily enough he was absent-

minded, and as for Eleanor, she could think of nothing to say at all, for her head was full of Fulk.

At the house she went straight to Henry's room so that the nurse could be freed to return to Groningen with Fulk. Her brother greeted her happily, thanked the nurse nicely, expressed the opinion that he would like to meet her again, and watched silently while Eleanor added her own thanks to his together with a box of chocolates, gaily wrapped. When the nurse had gone, he asked: 'Why did you give her a present?'

'Well, it was kind of her to come at such short notice to keep you company.'

Henry thought this over. 'Yes. She was nice to Moggy and Flan too. Her name's Wabke and it's her day off, she told me, but Fulk asked her to come and sit with me and she did because she likes him very much, and he gave her fifty gulden...'

'Fifty? Good gracious, I wonder...' She had no chance to worry about whether she should pay him back fifty gulden or not, because Henry asked urgently: 'Did you have tea?'

'Yes, dear.' She had tossed off her hat and coat and gone to sit on the side of his bed.

'So did we. We had a very short walk, just round the house, and then Tekla brought our tea to the sitting room; sandwiches and cake and little biscuits with nuts on them and hot buttered toast. We ate quite a great deal. Wabke says this is a very grand house. Is it, Eleanor?'

'Well, yes, it is rather.' She was still doing sums, wondering if she had enough money to pay Fulk the fifty gulden as well as the money she had borrowed.

Henry cut into her calculations with: 'What did you have for tea?'

'Oh, gorgeous cakes,' she brought her mind back with difficulty to their conversation, 'though I think your tea sounded lovely. My cake was chocolate and pineapple and whipped cream arranged on a piece of pastry.'

'What did Margaret have?'

Eleanor was saved from the details by Fulk's entrance. His 'Hullo, old chap, how's the day been?' was uttered in his usual kindly tones, but he didn't look at her at all.

Henry grinned tiredly. 'Super! I like Wabke. Gosh, it's smashing to feel like me again. We went for a walk, you know, ever such a short one, and then we played Ludo and cards, only Wabke isn't very good at games, but she laughs a lot and she liked Moggy and Flan. I hope I shall see her again before I go home.'

'I'll make a note of it,' Fulk assured him gravely, and took his pulse. 'You've done enough for today, though—supper in bed and go to sleep early—remember what I told you? I'll come and see you before I go in the morning.' He glanced at last at Eleanor. 'I shall be out this evening.'

She stopped him at the door. 'Oh—then could you spare a minute…?'

'Unless it's urgent, no. I'm late already.' He smiled faintly. 'Good night, Eleanor.'

Which left her feeling snubbed and still fretting about the fifty gulden. And where was he going? It was none of her business, of course, but she did want to know. Being in love, she decided as she got ready for bed some hours later, was no fun at all, and why couldn't she have fallen for someone like Perry Maddon, who liked her for a start, instead of Fulk, who didn't like her at all half the time, and he had far too much money too and led the kind of life she wouldn't enjoy. That wasn't true; she would enjoy it very much, living in this large, magnificently appointed house, with Juffrouw Witsma and Tekla and Bep to run it. Wearing beautiful clothes too, going out with Fulk to balls and parties, secure in the knowledge that he would come racing home each evening because he couldn't bear to be parted from her...the sad feeling inside her which she had managed until now to ignore, dissolved into silent tears.

She didn't go down to breakfast the next morning until she was sure that Fulk had gone, making the excuse to Margaret that Henry had slept late. Her sister gave her a disconcerting stare. 'You've been crying,' she stated. 'You never cry—what's the matter, Eleanor?'

'Nothing, love—I think I'm just a little tired, and I've been so worried about Henry.' Eleanor managed to smile. 'I'll have a cup of coffee and feel fine again. I thought we might write the labels for the presents—Henry could do Fulk's.'

It was a small task, quickly done. She helped Henry, now becoming very independent and inclined to do more than he ought, and then with Margaret, walked in the gardens. There was a nice little wild corner almost out of sight of the house, where there were squirrels and any number of birds. They stopped to feed them and then went on to the pond to feed the ducks. 'What a pity,' Eleanor observed, 'that Fulk has so little time to enjoy his own garden.'

'Oh, but he does,' protested Henry. 'Before I was ill, we used to come here every day after lunch before Fulk went back to his work. Flan came too; we went around looking at things. He must have a lot more patients now, for he doesn't come for lunch any more, does he? He's not often home for tea, either, is he?'

A remark which set Eleanor's unhappy thoughts on an even more unhappy course. It really seemed as though Fulk didn't want to see more of her than he absolutely had to. Perhaps, despite what he had said, Imogen's mother had impressed him with the unwisdom of having her in the house and risking Imogen's feelings being hurt, but in that case, why didn't the girl come back and keep an eye on the situation herself? Not that there was a situation. Eleanor frowned, wondering how much longer it would be before Henry would be fit to travel home; Christmas wasn't far off now and that was a good arguing point. She had already made up her mind to talk to Fulk that evening; she would broach the subject at the same time.

She had no chance until after tea. She had sat on tenterhooks, playing cards with the children while she listened for the car, and when she had at last heard it, she threw in her hand in a manner to bring a flood of remonstrances from her companions, and heedless of their annoyed cries, ran downstairs. She reached the hall as he opened the house door and barely giving him time to get inside, said: 'Fulk, I'd like to speak to you, could it be now?'

He raised his eyebrows. 'If it's as urgent as all that, and presumably it is. You look ready to burst with your feelings, Eleanor. Come into the study.'

He shut the door behind her and waved her to a chair. 'Talk up, dear girl,' he begged her. 'I'll listen, but I've things to do at the same time, if you have no objection.'

It was awkward addressing his broad back while he bent over his desk opening and shutting drawers, taking things out and putting other things away. He looked at the clock too, which hardly encouraged her. Eleanor drew a deep breath. 'It's three things really,' she began ungrammatically. 'I want to know how much money I owe you, and that includes what you paid the nurse who came to look after Henry yesterday, and then I want to know how soon he can go home...' She saw him stiffen and hurried on: 'We can never thank you enough for all you've done, but we must be a perfect nuisance to you.' And when he didn't say anything: 'And if he isn't well enough to travel, I'll go if you want me to. I've been thinking, Baroness Oss van Oss was quite right—I mean, about me being here and Imogen not liking it. I wouldn't have liked it either, I'd have come...' She paused just in time and changed what she had nearly said to: 'I wouldn't want to—that is, I don't want to upset her even though there's no reason for it, but if I go home you could let her know and she wouldn't mind Henry being here, would she?' She was quite unaware of the pleading in her voice.

She thought she heard Fulk laugh, but of course she must have been mistaken; what was there to laugh about? She sighed a little and waited for him to answer.

He shut a final drawer and leaned against the corner of the desk, jingling his keys gently up and down in one large, well-kept hand.

'You were a tiresome little girl,' he remarked in a gentle voice, 'always wanting to know things, and now that you're grown up you are still tiresome, though perhaps not quite in the same way. I haven't the least idea how much you owe me; when I have the time I will see about it and let you know, since you will only nag me until I do. And no, Henry is not well enough to go home, and no, I do not wish you to leave my house, and may I add in passing that Baroness Oss van Oss never has and never will influence me in any way. There is only one person who can do that, but she hasn't yet realized that. And now you really must excuse me—I've a date.'

Eleanor stood up too quickly. 'Oh, I didn't know,' she said blankly, and was rendered speechless by his bland: 'How should you? I didn't mention it before.'

She had had no intention of asking, but she heard herself enquiring: 'Are you going away again?'

'Yes. I'll go and see Henry before I leave and if there is anything I think you should know, I'll leave a note on the mantelpiece.'

She said fiercely: 'I don't understand you; you tell me I'm not to go home and yet you make a point of keeping out of my way—I suppose it's for Henry's sake.'

His face was in the shadows. 'Suppose what you like, Eleanor,' he offered calmly, and she turned on her heel and snatched at the door handle.

'I hope you have a nice weekend,' she answered, still fierce, 'although I couldn't care less!' She went through the door and shut it rather violently behind her.

She spent a good deal of the evening trying to cheer up a glum Henry and a disappointed Margaret. 'But he won't be here for Sint Nikolaas,' Henry argued for the tenth time, 'and we've got him a present.'

'He can have it when he gets back,' Eleanor assured him in a cheerful voice which sounded overloud in her own ears. 'We can give the others their presents and watch the TV, there'll be a special programme and you know you love the colours.'

'But we can't understand what they're saying,' Margaret pointed out in a discouraged voice. 'Do you suppose Fulk forgot?'

'No, of course not, but we have all forgotten that he's engaged to Imogen, and I expect he wants to be with her so that he can give her a present...'

'She could have come here,' grumbled Henry. 'I wonder what he'll give her?'

'Rubies and diamonds and emeralds,' stated Margaret positively. 'He's very rich, Hermina told me so. If I were just a little older and he were just a little younger, I should cut Imogen out and marry him myself.' She looked at Eleanor. 'I don't know why you don't, darling Eleanor; you're just a nice age for him and though I've never seen a photograph of her, I'm sure you're a hundred times prettier—besides, wouldn't it be lovely for all of us? We could come and stay with you, and mind the babies while you and Fulk go away on marvellous holidays together. I...'

Eleanor knew her voice was sharp. 'Margaret, what nonsense you do talk!' She was helped by Henry's, 'Anyway, you don't like him, do you, Eleanor, you said so in the loft—you said he was a horrid boy.'

'Pooh,' cried Margaret, 'that's a load of hooey, that was years ago; of course you like him, don't you, Eleanor?'

'He's grown into a very kind and—and nice man,' said Eleanor cautiously.

'I wouldn't call him nice, exactly, I mean you don't notice nice people very much, do you? And you do notice Fulk. But he's smashing, all right, his eyes twinkle and he laughs—I mean a real laugh, and when he's cross he goes all quiet instead of shouting.'

Eleanor eyed her sister in some astonishment, agreeing with every word, but all she said was: 'Darling, how observant you are.'

She devised several activities to keep them busy the next morning, and in the afternoon, as it was a fine if cold day, they went for their usual walk before tea, which they had round a splendid fire in the sitting room while they watched the various festivities in honour of the saint. Eleanor switched it off presently, however, because Henry was beginning to look a little tired, and they all went upstairs to his room where she settled him before the fire in a comfortable chair, fetched the games table and suggested that he and Margaret might like to have a game of draughts while she went to the kitchen to see what was for his supper.

She had turned the angle of the staircase and had paused to admire the prospect of the hall below her when the front door opened and her mother and father walked in, followed by Fulk.

Her joyous cry of 'Fulk!' she drowned very quickly by her breathless exclamation of: 'Mother, Father!' as she raced down the staircase to fling herself at her smiling parents. 'Oh, what a glorious surprise!' she babbled. 'Won't Henry and Margaret be thrilled— they're up in his room.' She looked at Fulk then. 'I thought you'd gone to spend Sint Nikolaas with Imogen.'

He said nothing, although he smiled and his dark eyes held a gleam which might have been anger, or possibly amusement as he suggested to Mrs Mac-Farlane that they might like to see Henry before they did anything else.

After that the evening went like a bomb. Henry, so excited that he could hardly speak, consented to lie down on his bed and rest on the understanding that he should join the rest of the party for dinner later on, and Margaret undertook to unpack for her mother, never ceasing to talk as she did so. Fulk had taken Mr MacFarlane down to the sitting room for a drink, suggesting that the ladies might like a cup of tea upstairs, 'For you'll want to gossip,' he declared, 'and there's plenty of time before dinner.'

Eleanor was left to coax Henry to rest, to tidy away the children's game and then to follow her mother and sister to the big bedroom in the front of the house, where she sat on the bed, joining in the conversation and pouring the tea when it came. It wasn't until the evening was over, with Henry safely tucked up in bed and the rest of them saying their good nights, that she had a moment alone with Fulk. The other three had gone across the hall to look at a particular portrait in the dining-room which they had been talking about, leaving Fulk lounging by the french window in the drawing room, waiting for Flan to come in, and Eleanor, standing, very erect, by the door. She plunged into speech at once, for there was no knowing how long they might be left alone, and although she had thought over what she was going to say, she realized now that she had forgotten every word; better get it over with. She relaxed a little and said soberly: 'Fulk, I must thank you for all the trouble you've taken to bring Mother and Father here, and the expense and the time—I only wish you were as happy as we all feel.'

He had turned his head to watch her. Now he said blandly: 'It merely required a telephone call or two, a couple of free days which I had owing to me, anyway, and as to the expense, I'm sure that by now someone must have told you that I am a wealthy man.'

'Well—yes, Hermina told Margaret and she told me, but you could have had all the money in the world and still not done it.' She gulped, 'Oh, I feel so mean—you see, I thought you'd gone to Cannes again, to your Imogen, and I was beastly enough to mind about it, and that's where you should be really, not here with us. You could have gone out dancing and dining and having fun.' She went on feverishly, seeing it all in her mind's eye. 'There would be sunshine, wouldn't there, and you could have gone riding too and given each other presents, and...'

His short laugh stopped her, his voice was all silk. 'Hardly that. Imogen considers the feast of Sint Niko-laas old-fashioned.' He smiled with a trace of mock-ery while she tried to find something to say and then went on, still silkily: 'When we came in this evening, you cried my name—oh, you remembered to cover it up quickly, but not quite quickly enough. Why, El-eanor?'

She had hoped that he hadn't heard. She said lamely: 'I was surprised; I thought you were miles away...'

He came and stood in front of her, but she didn't look at him. 'It's nice to think that I'm on your mind, even when I'm not here.' He laughed again, quite cheerfully this time. 'Although perhaps it was those few guldens you owe me which were on your mind—was that it?'

She seized on that, thankful for an excuse, and then, anxious to get away from him, embarked on a disjointed speech which became more and more mud-dled as she went along, happily unaware of the unholy delight in his eyes. She was brought to a sudden stop by his kiss. 'Your thoughts show very plainly on your pretty face, my dear,' he told her gently, and opened the door and ushered her out.

CHAPTER NINE

SINT NIKOLAAS WOULD BE coming in the evening after tea, which meant that the day was spent, by Henry and Margaret at least, in a state of anticipation. With the exception of Eleanor and her brother, the whole party went to church in the morning, and for the benefit of Mr MacFarlane, Fulk drove them to Groningen to the Martinikerk, so that during lunch the conversation largely concerned this magnificent edifice with its sixteenth-century wall paintings in the choir and its five-storied spire. 'A pity that you were unable to see it for yourself, my dear,' remarked Eleanor's father. 'Should you go to Groningen before you return to Scotland, you must make a point of visiting it.' He turned to Fulk. 'I was much struck by the architecture of the village church we passed on our way home— in the Roman-Gothic style, I fancy.'

Eleanor, eating her delicious ragout of game, wondered if Fulk was bored; he didn't appear to be, indeed, he seemed to know as much about the building of churches as her father did. She listened to him telling her father that that particular style of building was only to be found in the most northerly provinces of the country, and entering into a discussion concerning the differences between the early and late Gothic style of architecture, but he was too well-mannered to allow their talk to monopolize the conversation and switched easily enough to other matters, and soon everyone was talking in a more lighthearted fashion, especially Henry, who, having been a very good boy all the morning, was now inclined to get excited; something which Eleanor saw quickly enough; so did Fulk, for as soon as lunch was finished and before they all went into the drawing room for their coffee, he suggested in the mildest of voices that Henry should have his afternoon rest a little earlier than usual. 'You don't want to miss Sint Nikolaas' arrival,' he pointed out, 'and if you take a nap now, you will be downstairs again in plenty of time for tea.'

Henry agreed cheerfully enough and Eleanor bore her small brother away, tucked him up, admonished him in sisterly tones to be good, and went back to the drawing room, where she spent the rest of the afternoon listening to her mother's quiet voice talking about the various small happenings at home, and answering suitably when she was expected to. But she left most of the talking to Margaret, who had a great deal to say and had them all laughing over her various experiences, for unlike Eleanor, she had been to the village on various occasions, had tea at Hermina's home, and spent a good deal of time with Juffrouw Witsma in the kitchen, watching her cook and learning Dutch at the same time. It was Fulk who remarked: 'I'm afraid that Eleanor hasn't had the same opportunities as Margaret, for she has been tied hand and foot to Henry. I don't know what I should have done without her help, for I have been able to go about my daily work knowing that he was safe with her.'

They all looked at her, and she looked at her shoes, feeling foolish, and her mother said thoughtfully: 'Well, we shall have to make it up to her in some way,' and smiled across at Fulk as she spoke, and he agreed with a smile before enquiring about Mrs Trot. 'Moggy fits very well into our household,' he observed, 'and Flan adores him.' The big dog lifted his head and thumped his tail, drawing attention to himself, and the talk, naturally enough, turned to dogs.

Tea was over and everyone was sitting round talking in a desultory fashion when there was a thunderous knock on the door, and Henry, who had been sitting silently with his ears cocked for the slightest sound, got out of his chair. Fulk got up too, observing that Sint Nikolaas was punctual as usual and they had better see what he had left at the door, and with Henry beside him, went out of the room, to return very shortly with a large, bulging sack. He set it down in the centre of the room, saying: 'Margaret, go to the kitchen and fetch everyone here, will you? And then you and Henry shall hand round the presents.'

There were gifts for everyone there, even for Mr and Mrs MacFarlane, a thoughtful act on Fulk's part which engendered Eleanor's instant gratitude, and when the sack was at last empty, Henry, being the youngest person present, was allowed to open his parcels first.

He opened each gift carefully, and there were quite a number, for besides the presents Eleanor and Margaret had bought, there were a variety of things to please a small boy, and the last package of all, an air gun, complete with pellets and a target board, caused him to shout with delight.

'We'll fix the target up tomorrow,' Fulk promised, and Henry, for all his clever little brain still uncertain about the good saint who handed out presents so lavishly, asked: 'How could Sint Nikolaas possibly know that I wanted a gun?'

Fulk shrugged his broad shoulders. 'It's something most boys want. When you've got the hang of it we'll do some clay pigeon shooting, if you like. Now it's Margaret's turn.'

The pink velvet dress she had so much admired was at the bottom of the pile. She shook it free from its folds of tissue paper and all she could say was: 'Oh, Fulk—it's the dress I showed you when we were shopping in Groningen!' She ran across the room and flung her arms round his neck and kissed him soundly. 'Oh, you really are groovy,' she told him fervently, and raced away to try it on.

By the time it came to Eleanor's turn, everyone was in high spirits; somehow Fulk had managed to create the right atmosphere of excitement and pleasure and the traditional wine they were drinking certainly helped him. She began on the little pile before her, feeling like a child again; the crocodile handbag was in the third box she opened; the very one she had admired with Margaret, and her sister, a charming picture in her new pink dress and perched on the side of Fulk's chair, called out: 'I pointed it out to Fulk, Eleanor, but I never knew—honestly I didn't.'

It was a beautiful thing; Eleanor had never had anything like it before, probably she never would again. She laid it down carefully and looked at Fulk, watching her. 'Thank you,' she said in a voice which quavered a little, 'it's marvellous—you shouldn't have done it, but it's quite—quite…' Words failed her when he asked, laughing: 'Don't I get the same treatment as Margaret gave me?'

There was a little wave of laughter and there was really no way out. She crossed the room and kissed him, aware of the eyes watching her. The kiss was light and brief and she managed some sort of laughing remark before she sat down again and opened the rest of the presents she had been given; it was a relief when she got to the last one and everyone turned their attention to Juffrouw Witsma, whose turn it was.

Being the master of the house, Fulk opened his gifts last of all. His devoted staff had given him handkerchiefs and a rather dreadful tie which he declared was exactly to his taste; Eleanor had no doubt that he would wear it just because they had given it to him, although the blinding paisley pattern was hardly his style. He opened the book last of all, declaring that it was just what he had intended getting for himself, and then went round thanking everyone; when he reached Eleanor his thanks were brief. 'I've kissed all the other women,' he told her in a soft voice, 'but I'm not going to kiss you, Eleanor—and you're welcome to make what you like of that.'

He grinned suddenly at her before going to open the champagne without which he declared Sint Nikolaas Avond was incomplete.

Everything was back to normal in the morning; Eleanor got down to breakfast to find Fulk already behind his paper, and although he wished her good morning, his detached manner gave her the impression that for him at least life was real, life was earnest. There was no one else there and he seemed to feel no need for conversation, but continued to read *De Haagsche Post* while he finished his coffee. Presently he folded it carefully, gathered up his letters, said goodbye to her in the tones of a man who was simply upholding the conventions, mentioned that he would see Henry before he left for the hospital, and went from the room, leaving her feeling strangely hollow. Not that she allowed her feelings to overcome her; when her family joined her a few minutes later, she was the life and soul of the breakfast table.

Mr and Mrs MacFarlane were to stay a week, and it had already been decided that Henry should remain where he was until a few days before Christmas. He was doing well now, but as Fulk had pointed out, he was living in a strict routine now, with long rest periods, early bedtime and a kind but firm refusal to indulge any ambitious whims he might think up. The longer he kept to this routine, the better chance he had of permanent recovery, and when his parents protested that the boy was giving Fulk a great deal of trouble he shrugged it off with: 'Not in the least. I have already told you that Eleanor takes the brunt of caring for him, and heaven knows the house is large enough for us all.'

A remark, which, when relayed to Eleanor, did nothing to improve her spirits. She and her mother were walking in the garden and Mrs MacFarlane, having delivered this facer, went on: 'Such a good, kind man; he will make a splendid husband. I wonder what this Imogen of his is like? I would have thought that she would have wanted to spend more time with him...'

'Fulk went to see her,' Eleanor explained in a calm little voice, 'just for the weekend—he must love her very much to go all that way just for a weekend...'

'There are other reasons for taking long journeys,' remarked her parent, and before Eleanor could ask her what she meant, she asked: 'What about you, darling? Will you have to go straight back to the hospital, or will you be able to come home for Christmas?'

'I hadn't thought about it.' And it was true, she hadn't. 'I'd better write and find out, hadn't I? Though I'm sure they'll expect me, you know what Christmas is like on the wards, and I wouldn't dare be away.' She fell silent, contemplating Christmas without Fulk, and not only Christmas; the rest of the year, and all the years after that.

It was during dinner that evening that Fulk remarked to the table in general that he thought that Eleanor deserved a day out. 'And now that you are here,' he suggested pleasantly, 'she could quite safely have one, could she not?' He addressed Mr Mac-Farlane. 'She would have the chance to see the Martinikerk for herself, and there are one or two splendid museums. I have arranged to take a day so that I may go with her.'

He smiled round the table and everyone, with the exception of Eleanor, smiled back, agreeing with him in a pleased chorus, not realizing that the subject of this treat hadn't been given a chance to accept or refuse it.

During the animated discussion which followed as to the best way of cramming as much as possible into a day's outing, Eleanor remained silent; not that anyone noticed; they were all too busy putting forward their own views as to what constituted the highlights of sightseeing. Her father, naturally enough, had a good deal to say about churches, and the Martinikerk in particular, but he was drowned by Margaret's insistent voice raised on behalf of old castles, and her mother, a poor third, voiced the view that perhaps a nice look at the shops would be the thing. Fulk, sitting back in his chair, listened courteously to their arguments, saying little, while he watched Eleanor, but presently he gathered the threads of the conversation skilfully together in such a way that each felt that he or she had contributed a valuable piece of advice and suggested that they should go into the drawing room for coffee. It was a chance that Eleanor took. Mumbling that she would see if Henry was comfortable, she flew upstairs, where she spent quite an unnecessary amount of time shaking up her brother's pillows while she tried to decide what to do. A day out with Fulk would be heaven, there could be no argument about that; on the other hand, he hadn't asked her, had he? Not in so many words. He was making a gesture, rewarding her for her long hours in the sickroom. Well, she didn't want a reward! She gave the surprised Henry's pillow still another shake and went downstairs. The drawing room door was shut and she could hear voices and laughter from behind it; she suddenly didn't want to go in and half turned on the staircase to go to her room when Fulk's study door opened and he put his head out.

'Ah, I thought so—I could practically smell the paintwork blistering under your bad temper.'

'I am not in a bad temper!'

'Come in, then—we'll have a cosy chat.'

She stayed exactly where she was. 'What about?'

'Our day out tomorrow, of course.'

She looked down her nose at him. 'I wasn't aware that I had been invited to go anywhere with anyone,' she informed him coldly.

'Quite right, dear Eleanor, you haven't. You would have refused point blank, wouldn't you, but now that everyone has gone to such trouble to suggest where we should go, and your mother is here to look after Henry, you can't very well refuse, can you?'

'I can't think why you should want to spend a day with me.'

His eyes narrowed. 'Coming from any other girl, I wouldn't believe a word of that,' he told her blandly, 'but from you...' His voice became friendly and warm. 'I haven't had a day out myself for a long time. I need a break.'

She said instantly: 'You went to Cannes to see Imogen.'

He agreed affably, and then: 'You're a little old-fashioned, Eleanor.'

'I'm very old-fashioned, if you want to know. We don't move very fast with the times where I come from.'

'So I realized. It may astonish you to know that the people around these parts don't either—very behind the times, we are. Now, having settled that to our mutual satisfaction, will you spend the day with me tomorrow, Eleanor?'

She knew then that she had never intended doing anything else but that; let the absent Imogen look after herself; she had no one else to blame and she must be a very conceited girl if she didn't imagine that Fulk might need a little female society from time to time. She said frankly: 'I'd like to very much, thank you, Fulk.'

It was pouring with rain when she got up the next morning; cold heavy rain rattling down like a steel curtain from a uniformly grey sky. Eleanor stood looking at it from her bedroom window, resigned to the fact that there would be no day out. It didn't look any better from Henry's room either; she was finishing off a few small chores for him when Fulk walked in. His good morning was cheerful. 'I hope you like rain,' he observed cheerfully, 'for we're going to get plenty of it today—the wind's cold too, so wear a thick coat, you can keep dry under my umbrella.'

She found herself smiling. 'I didn't think we'd be going...'

He looked surprised. 'Why not? You don't strike me as being one of those girls who fuss at getting a bit wet.'

She assured him happily that indeed she wasn't fussy, and went down to breakfast in the best of spirits.

Looking back at the end of the day, she wasn't sure

which part of it she had enjoyed most; the great
church had been wonderful—all that space and lofti-
ness, so had the Municipal Museum, where she had
spent a long time gazing at the regional costumes.
They had had coffee afterwards in the Grand Hotel
Frigge and then gone on to look at the university,
which she found too modern for her taste, although
the variety of coloured caps worn by the students in-
trigued her.

They had left Fulk's car outside his rooms and
walked through the rain, arm-in-arm under Fulk's umbrella, for that was the only way in which to see the
city properly, he told her. They went through the narrow streets between the two main squares, pausing to
admire the variety of old houses lining the canals,
peering down centuries-old alleys, looking down into
the cold grey water from the small bridges as they
crossed them. It was on one of these that Fulk had
quite suddenly kissed her, one arm sweeping her
close, the other still holding the umbrella and even in
this rather awkward situation, he contrived to carry
out the exercise with an expertise which took her
breath. She had looked up at him, rain dripping down
her pretty face, a little flushed now, uneasily aware
that she had kissed him back, if not expertly, at least
with enthusiasm.

'You're very pretty in the rain,' Fulk had said, and
taken her by the arm and walked her on through the
almost empty little streets, pointing out anything of
interest with an ease of manner which made her wonder if he made a habit of kissing girls on bridges
whenever he felt like it. She wondered if she should

make some lighthearted remark to that effect, but she had been unable to think of one; silence was probably the best thing, with of course, suitable observations about the house he was telling her about.

They went back to the car after a little while and drove up to the coast to Warffrum, where there was a castle converted into a hotel. They had lunched there, beginning with *Erwten* soup to warm them up and going on to sole Murat and Charlotte Russe, sitting over their coffee until the afternoon sky began to darken from grey to black and Fulk suggested that for the last hour or two she might like to look round the shops in Groningen, something she was very willing to do, although she had been very careful not to express admiration for any article which caught her fancy; she wasn't sure, but if he could buy a crocodile handbag just because she had admired it, he could just as likely purchase any of the trifles which caught her eye, so she confined her admiration to the fabulously expensive jewellery, taking care to remark a cool 'How nice,' to anything she judged to be within his pocket.

She was quite unaware that her painstaking efforts were affording her companion a good deal of amusement, but she found it a relief when he suggested that they might have tea before they went back home, and she agreed readily enough when he had asked her if it would be a good idea to buy Henry a book about air pistols and guns. At the same time he had bought a box of chocolates for Margaret, pointing out gravely that children should be treated equally, an opinion which she shared and which occupied them pleasantly as they drove back.

They had rounded off the day with a hilarious game of Monopoly after dinner, and Henry, for a treat, had been allowed to stay up until nine o'clock. The rest of them had stayed up much longer than that and the great Friese wall clock in the hall was chiming midnight when they went to their beds. Eleanor, lingering to thank Fulk for her day, had been a little chilled by the cool courtesy of his reply, so that she had gone up to bed wondering if his apparent enjoyment of it had been nothing but good manners. But surely mere good manners didn't necessitate kissing her in the middle of a bridge?

The week went very quickly after that; it was Friday evening again in no time at all, with her parents packed and ready to leave and Fulk, whom she had hardly seen during the last few days, wishing her goodbye with the unwelcome information that he wouldn't be coming straight back this time. 'There's a seminar in Edinburgh on Monday,' he told her, 'and I hope to attend it; I shan't be back until the middle of the week. You know what to do for Henry and if you are in the least worried you can telephone me. Have you any messages?'

She couldn't think of one. She kissed her parents goodbye and wished them all a safe journey, wanting with all her heart to be free to go with them. The house was very quiet when they had gone; the children went to bed and she was left to roam round on her own, a prey to her thoughts, picturing Fulk at her home, driving down to Edinburgh, meeting people she didn't know, living a life in which she had no share. She went to bed at last, feeling lost.

He came back on Wednesday evening and almost as soon as he had entered his front door the telephone rang, and Eleanor, who had heard the car arriving and had come into the hall, paused.

'Yes, answer it, there's a good girl,' he begged her, 'while I get out of this coat.'

She went into the study and lifted the receiver gingerly, hoping that whoever was on the other end wouldn't break into a torrent of Dutch. She said: 'Hullo?' which could do no harm anyway and a girl's voice answered, a sharp voice asking a sharp question.

'Wait a minute,' said Eleanor in English. 'Professor van Hensum is just back, I'll call him.'

The voice spoke English now. 'You are Eleanor? You are still there…' There was a tinkling laugh. 'Fetch Fulk, tell him it is Imogen.'

He was strolling across the hall to take the receiver from her. 'Who is it?' he asked, 'or is it someone speaking double dutch?'

'It's Imogen.' She didn't wait, but went out of the room, closing the door carefully behind her and going back to Henry and Margaret. She had often imagined Imogen's voice, and now she had heard it; it merely served to confirm her opinion of the girl. She embarked on a game of spillikins with the children and when presently Fulk joined them, Imogen wasn't mentioned.

She met him at breakfast the next morning; Henry still had his breakfast in bed and Margaret had taken

Flan for a walk and beyond an exchange of good mornings they had nothing to say to each other, only as Fulk went from the room he told her: 'I have no idea when I shall be home, if you want me urgently, telephone the hospital.' His smile was brief, although she heard him whistling cheerfully as he went out of the house.

It was almost tea time when Eleanor, leaving Margaret to entertain Henry, went down to the kitchen to fetch the tea tray; if Fulk wasn't coming home there seemed no point in making a lot of extra work. She was crossing the hall when the front door bell rang and she went to see who it was. Juffrouw Witsma was in her room and Tekla would be busy in the kitchen. A girl stood outside and before Eleanor could utter a word had pushed past her into the hall. A quite beautiful girl, wrapped in a fur coat, her guinea-gold hair tucked up under a little fur cap, her legs encased in the kind of boots Eleanor had always wanted and never been able to afford. She walked into the centre of the hall before she said in English: 'Where is Fulk?'

'You're Imogen,' declared Eleanor, not answering. She got a cold look for her pains.

'Naturally.' She frowned. 'This filthy weather, how I hate it, and this frightful barn of a house...'

'It's a very beautiful house,' said Eleanor sharply, 'and it can't be summer all the year round.'

'Oh, yes, it can.' Imogen walked back to where Eleanor was standing and stared at her, rather as though she were a piece of furniture or something at a fair. 'I came to see you. Mama said that you were pretty, and I suppose you are in a large way, but not in the least chic—I wonder what Fulk sees in you?'

'Nothing,' said Eleanor quickly, 'nothing at all—he's in love with you.'

Imogen smiled, her lovely mouth curling in a sneer. 'Rubbish! You are—how do you say?—dim. Well, I have seen you for myself; I shall go.' She walked to the door and actually had her hand on its handle when Eleanor cried: 'But you can't—Fulk won't be long, at least I don't think so; he usually comes home after tea. Couldn't you telephone his rooms or the hospital and tell him you're here?'

Imogen was pulling her coat collar close. 'Why should I wish to see him?'

'But you're going to marry him—you love him,' declared Eleanor, persevering.

'No, I'm not, and I don't.' Imogen disappeared in a whirl of fur, only her expensive perfume lingering after her as she crashed the heavy door shut.

'Well,' said Eleanor on a long-drawn breath, 'now what?'

It was at that precise moment that she turned her head and saw Fulk standing in the doorway of his study, his shoulders wedged comfortably against the door jamb, his hands in his pockets.

'There you are!' she exclaimed. 'Just in time—for heaven's sake go after her. It's Imogen—if you run…'

'My dear Eleanor,' said Fulk calmly, 'I never run, and even if I went after her, what would I say?'

'Why, that you love her, of course.'

'But I don't.'

Her brows drew together in a quite fierce frown. 'But you're going to marry her.'

He smiled a little. 'I heard Imogen tell you in no uncertain terms that she wasn't going to marry me.'

She gave him a scornful look. 'Women always say things like that. I expect she's walking down the road crying her eyes out.'

'Not Imogen; she'll have a taxi waiting.'

'Don't quibble—what does it matter, taxi or walking…'

'It doesn't matter at all,' he agreed placidly. 'I can't think why you're making such a business of the whole thing.'

She was bewildered, but she wasn't going to give up. Later on, when she was alone again, she could nurse her broken heart. 'But you're…!' she began again.

'If you are going to tell me once more—erroneously—that I love Imogen, I shall do you a mischief.' His voice was still unworried. 'I haven't been in love with her for quite some time—since, in fact, I climbed the ladder to the loft and saw you sitting there in your old clothes and your hair streaming… You looked— well, never mind that for the moment. And Imogen— she has never loved me, you know, I imagine that she was flattered at the idea of being mistress of this house and having all the money she wanted, but love—no, my dear. All the same, I had to be certain, didn't I? That's why I went to see her; I don't think I was surprised and certainly not in the least upset to find that she was—er—consoling herself with an American millionaire—short and fat and going bald, but still a millionaire.' He added almost apologetically: 'An American millionaire is so much richer than a Dutch one, you know.'

'You're not a millionaire?' Eleanor wanted to know.

'Well, yes—at least, in Holland, I am.' He strolled across the hall towards her. 'I suppose if I were to offer you this house and my millions you would kick them right back at me, Eleanor?'

'Yes.' She had seen the look on his face, and although her heart begged her to stay just where she was, she took a prudent step backwards.

But he had seen that. 'No, don't move, my darling; it would not be of the least use, you know, I should only come after you.' He smiled at her and her unhappy heart became whole once more.

'If I offered you my heart and my love would you throw them back at me too?' he asked.

'No.' Her voice was a whisper. There was no mistaking the look upon his face now. She took another step back and felt the stairs against her heel. She had reached the second tread when she was halted by his: 'Come down off the staircase, dear Eleanor.'

She supposed she would always do what he wanted her to do from now on. She reached the floor once more and he took her hands in his.

'Oh, my dear darling,' he said, 'come into the little sitting room,' and he opened the door and drew her gently inside. The whole charming place smelled delicious; there was an enormous bunch of red roses lying on the table and Eleanor cried: 'Oh, how glorious!' and wrinkled her charming nose in delight.

'Roses for Christmas,' said Fulk, 'just to prove that you do mean something to someone, my dear love.' He pulled a tatty piece of paper from his pocket. 'The last thing on your list, though I promise you they will be the first of many.'

He pulled her close. 'It's been you all the time, my darling. How strange it is that one can love someone and not know it.' He bent to kiss her, not once, but several times and slowly. 'Of course, boys of sixteen don't always know these things.'

She looked at him enquiringly and he kissed her again. 'You were almost five, sweetheart; I pulled your hair and you kicked my shins and fell over, do you remember? And when I picked you up you were warm and grubby and soft and you cried all over me; I lost my heart then, but never knew it.'

His arm tightened around her. 'Will you marry me, Eleanor? And you had better say yes, for I shan't let you go until you do.'

Eleanor heaved a sigh. 'Oh, Fulk, of course I will—and don't ever let me go.' She leaned up to kiss him and sighed again; she had never been so happy. 'I wonder...' she began dreamily, and was interrupted by the opening of the door.

'Juffrouw Witsma has made a cake,' Henry informed them, 'and I'm rather hungry. Do you suppose I might have a slice?'

Fulk still had tight hold of Eleanor. 'Certainly you may—two slices if you wish, and give Margaret some too—and don't hurry too much over eating it.'

'Thank you.' Henry looked at them with interest. 'Are you kissing Eleanor, Fulk?'

'Indeed I am.'

'Are you going to marry her?'

'We were discussing that when you came in.'

'I can take a hint,' said Henry in a tolerant voice. 'I suppose you won't mind if I just mention it to Margaret?'

'By all means do so.' Fulk's voice gave no sign of impatience, but perhaps Henry saw something in his eye, for he turned to go. 'There's a bowl of fruit on the sideboard,' he informed them. 'Might we have an apple too? If we have to wait while you talk, we may get hungry.'

'Eat any of the fruit you fancy,' Fulk told him, and when the door had shut: 'Now, where had I got to? I think perhaps, if you agree, my darling, I'll begin again from the beginning; I rather enjoyed hearing you say that you would marry me.'

Eleanor lifted her head from his shoulder. There was really no need to say anything to that. She smiled and kissed him instead.